THE ZENITH LORD

DAMEON COX

Lezen Publishing

The Zenith Lord

Lezen Publishing

Original Cover Concept: Kästle Olson
Map Illustrations: Kästle Olson

Manufactured in the United States of America
ISBN 978-0-9960063-2-3

Dedicated to

John R. Cox
Simply, the best brother ever...

&

In memory of

Raul R. Whyte
Simply, the best friend ever...

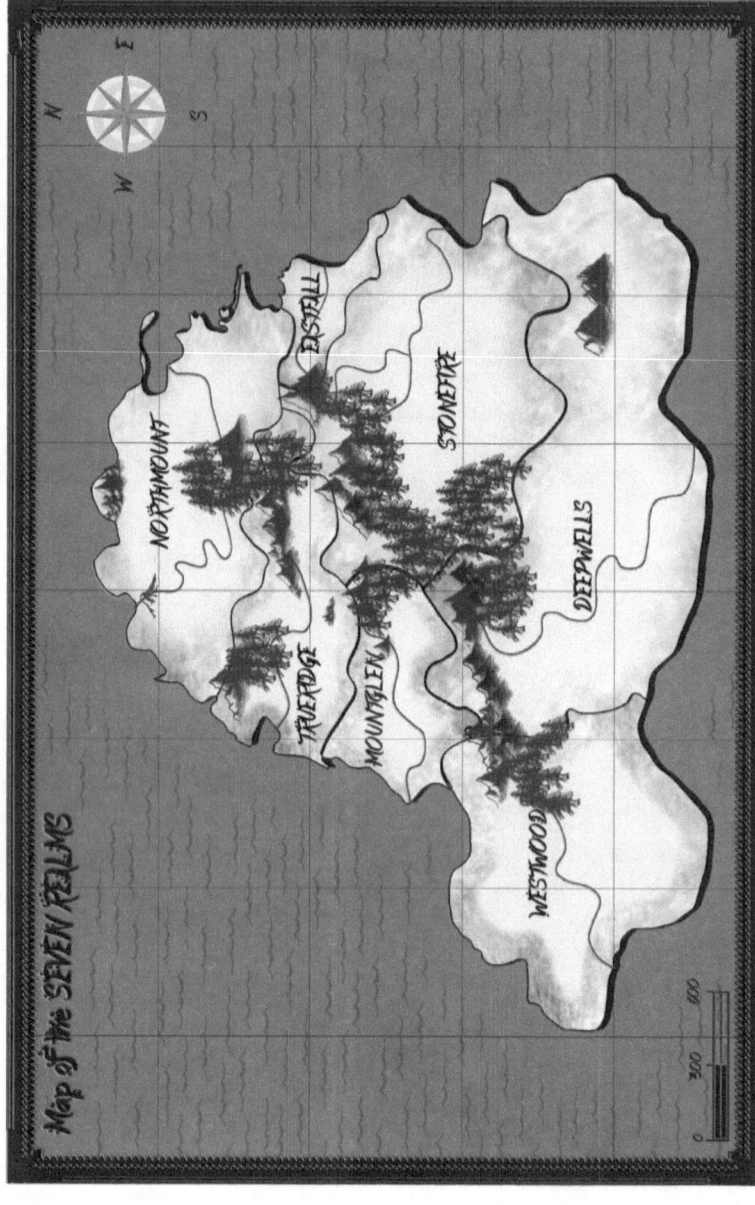

Map of the SEVEN REALMS

Map of The Western Kingdoms

OELSEN

OZID

HAMPTOR

1

THE presence floated near the ceiling of the opulent room, watching the lone occupant of an immense bed encased by canopy and drapes tied back at the four bedposts inlaid with gold. He had surveyed the space earlier, a large bedchamber in the grandest of keeps, with side rooms for both clothes and refreshment. A suite made for exhibition by the vain and pretentious, yet rarely seen by more than his son, the staff, and a woman brought in from time to time. Richly appointed furniture with gold inlay—the pattern matching the bed, a walk-in fireplace, built-in bookcases filled to overflowing, overstuffed plush chairs, and a large, marble-topped table formed a study area and more than fulfilled its arrogant purpose. The few candles that burned increased its illusion of size.

The giant bed swallowed Eric, High Lord Mountglen's towering, thin frame except for his overly long feet that made peaks in the bedcloths. His sharp, angular face, black eyes, thin hooknose and large ears looked freakish with the covers pulled up to his neck.

* * *

AS he settled into large pillows waiting for sleep, his musings drifted to the coach ride earlier that day. He remembered the children waving from a field. The children always waved. He wondered why; he never waved back. *The innocence of children, was I ever that innocent?*

No, his memory did not journey that far back. *My spirit belongs to Dark's Source, with all the pain and horror that entails,*

1

if indeed it exists. He wished no Dark One or his Source existed. His long, slender fingers automatically grasped the Dark Stone hanging from his neck by a gold chain. Its power flowed, relaxing him, and a wave of pleasure seeped through him until it became ecstasy, and then ecstasy approached pain in the degree of its manifestation, pulling him into sleep and dreams of pleasure.

The dream started normally enough, except for his awareness that it was a dream. That sent fear through his mind; he had never experienced that phenomenon before. He floated in a void of dark shadows that churned in roiling currents around him. A single idea surged through his consciousness. *You belong to the Dark One and to me!*

Mountglen sat straight up in bed, awake and shaking with a burning sensation on his chest.

He pulled the Dark Stone from his sleepcloth, made barely visible by the dim candlelight and clutched it for comfort. His hand burned with its unusual heat, but he did not let it go.

Darkness returned to his senses as a disembodied voice filled his mind. *"Your use of the Dark Stone called me. You have utilized it to pleasure yourself and to provide your success in many things."*

Mountglen's words, a barely audible, ragged whisper, came slowly. "I am Eric, High Lord Mountglen. I have not summoned anyone!" Fear surged through him.

The swirling shadows and currents coalesced into a tall, dark figure; the head, shrouded under a cowl, pulled in the little surrounding light and dissolved it in the blackness within. The presence gave the room the same feeling of Mountglen's dream, a void.

The presence's deep, rumbling voice hissed with disdain *"High Lord? You are nothing without the Dark Stone! The Stone's influence has given you capabilities, and you have prospered by them."*

Mountglen's reply projected equal disdain; "I am ruler

of Mountglen, descendent of the Heroes of the Seven Realms, and I know you not!"

The dark robe's long sleeve barely stirred, but a searing pain gripped Mountglen's arm, traveling slowly through his chest to the rest of his limbs, and then exploded in his head. His back arched in spasm. He fought to scream, his mouth gaping open, but no sound came, and he had never felt such agony.

As quickly as it has come, the pain vanished, leaving him gasping for breath. He slumped back against the pillows, his body trembling and his strength gone.

Mountglen cringed and pushed himself farther back into the mountain of pillows. Words came to his mind and ears at the same time, creating a disturbing feeling of deep power. *"You hold the Dark Stone. You used its power to sow pain and ruin on your adversaries, and gained great benefit for yourself as well. You murmured your desires to the Dark Stone, and it heard you, and your avarice and lust for power became fulfilled.*

"I, too, heard your pathetic pleadings. I control many forces in the void and have considerable power in your world. Through your dreams and desires, I know you for the true man you are. Your heart is as black as the Dark Stone you wear. You have murdered, raped, thieved, and borne false witness to achieve your own ends, and still that is not enough. You want what is not yours: the lands, titles, power, and wealth of your nephew, the Zenith Lord." The twin voices of mind and hearing became softer but even more menacing. *"You summoned me through the Dark Stone's use as if you had called out my name! Did you think your deeds went without consequence? Your spirit belongs to Dark's Source, and to me!"*

Mountglen's mind raced. *How can this thing cause pain so great? Pain and ruin...* Agony spread through his body again, jerking him upright. He threw his arms up in a useless attempt to defend against the indefensible and pleaded, "Please...no more! Just tell me what you desire." The pain left him with a soreness that racked his body.

Mountglen's color faded from its normal whiteness into pallor.

"Desire? I desire your service to the Dark One and to me. I already have your spirit for all time. What else is there?" Mountglen whimpered as the eerie voice continued. *"What more can you offer except service? Your hate and loathing reached me through the Dark Stone, and I have felt it for a long time. The Dark Stone's power is increasing, and now I am able to come to you and make myself known."*

Mountglen's priorities fell into order—the upmost, staying alive. With the pain he had suffered in the last few minutes, he dare not call his guards. His voice became soft, calculating. "You wish to…make yourself known to me?"

"Do you acknowledge that your spirit belongs to the Dark One and me?"

Mountglen yielded a low moan of finality from the apparition's words. His mind shook off the voice generated in his head, and a single revelation took hold. *This is a negotiation; perhaps I'll live after all!* Mountglen's reply was flat. "Yes."

"What do you know about the Dark Stone you wear?"

Mountglen forced confidence into his voice that he did not feel. "My father gave it to me. It has brought me pleasure."

"It has brought you much more than pleasure!" The presence roared. *"It has given you the intuitive feelings that have made you successful in all your dealings!"*

Mountglen rebelled at the thought that his successes were not truly his own, but dared not interrupt.

"Now, through the Dark Stone and through me, you may earn even greater rewards. It will require much service to the Dark One and to me. Success and failure will provide appropriate rewards beyond your petty thinking. You will be the Zenith Lord in your world, and hold even more power in the void when you journey to me. It is your choice. But, you will not have the Dark Stone for your comfort if you make the wrong choice. Do you remember when you

last gave up the Stone?"

Mountglen knew he was defeated. He could no longer live without the Dark Stone's pleasures. He had tried, once. His abject sigh accompanied his cluttered thoughts. *How can this Stone do so much?* He opened his hand and looked at his object of ruin. "It is the same since coming into my keeping."

"No!" The simulacrum shimmered beside Mountglen's bed. *"Fool, do you think the Stone physically changes while its power grows? The Dark Stone you wear is now strong enough for me to come into your world that I may help you obtain your dreams."*

Mountglen's voice grew incredulous. "What is your price? What is it you want in return?"

"I already have your spirit—it belongs to Dark's Source and will be mine to use in the void as I see fit." Mountglen struggled to keep from shouting obscenities. *"I can see into your world through the Dark Stone until that time. I will feed on the power of those you dispatch whom do not belong to Light's Source. That and your spirit are payments enough. I require nothing if you refuse my offer; the joy of your eternal pain will be mine soon enough. Your refusal means nothing to you if a future without the Dark Stone and your coming torment contents you. Believe me, the pain you felt is nothing more than a pinprick in the void."*

The presence's voice changed to hold all the womanly enchantments in Mountglen's licentious dreams. *"But you need not feel any pain at all. You may feel great pleasure instead. It is your choice."*

Mountglen gained some bravado. "When will I receive what you promise?" He might have seen a smile form within the cowl, if he only knew how to channel the Dark Stone's power.

"You must be patient. There are few with the power I have obtained under my Master. My supremacy will increase over time as yours will through me." The black shape floated to the end of the bed, expanding to fill the space from the top of the mattress to the canopy, ten feet high. *"First, you must freely*

*give me your oath. Your afterlife belongs to the Dark One. Service
to the Dark One through me is your only chance of a reward in the
void. Fail, and you will know torment you never imagined in both
worlds. Your only hope now is through me."*

The phantasm reduced itself to Mountglen's dimen-
sions and floated over him at an angle: mere feet away
from his head and the hem of his cloak no more than an
inch from the bedcloths over his feet. His tone changed
to a soft purring; his words now flowed like oily scum
across a fetid pond. *"You may call me Shadure. Let my name
fill your mind, think only of me. I will hear and come to you. I will
only offer this once. You must decide quickly."*

"You expect me to decide…" The Stone vanished
from its gold frame. Dull aches came from Mountglen's
joints; his vision blurred, and his head throbbed.
Loneliness, despair, and grief filled him while his mind
sunk into a black pool of horror. His breaths became
short and shallow and stabs of fire shot lanced through
his chest. *Is this to be my life without the Dark Stone?*
Mountglen's mind settled on one imperative.
Rationalizations no longer matter! I must have it back!

With his first contracted murder, Mountglen had
resigned himself long ago that, if there truly was an
afterlife, he belonged to the Dark One. Payment for his
deeds was irreversible if the Dark One existed, or so he
had believed. Now…perhaps not. "You have my oath."

Shadure's black form shimmered with satisfaction.
*"And you have mine. I will aid you in your desires. I am pleased
that you have joined with me in this effort to insure our mutual
goals."*

Now his voice exuded command. *"There is something you
must do quickly."* Enmity bathed both the tones of
Shadure's words in Mountglen's mind and the sound that
eerily floated to his ears. *"Soon, there will be another
Greatstone born. You must stop this birth for both our interests.
This child will be the undisputed heir to the Dais. You must do as I
order if you ever wish to have the Seven Realms for yourself. You*

have agents in Stonefire. Use them for this. There must be no link back to you.

"It may do great harm if my existence is known before we are ready. Remember the price of my displeasure. Remember also the sensual pleasure I bring you through the Dark Stone, and the great riches and power you have and will gain from fulfilling service to the Dark One and to me."

The voice slid to a low, throaty purr. *"You are a man of action—do not call me for unimportant reasons. Grasp the Stone when you need me and call the void with your mind. I will come."*

Mountglen started from the sudden emptiness he felt as Shadure relinquished his mind. The Dark Stone's mild heat again warmed his hand, and the maladies of age receded to nothing again.

He sat up in bed, wide-eyed and sweating. His sleepcloth clung to his damp, bony chest. He remembered the dream vividly and wondered *could it be other than a dream?* Terrible aches coursed throughout his muscles, the event's only evidence.

* * *

SHADURE smiled, hidden from Mountglen's view by his lack of understanding regarding the forces around him. Forces wrapped into the Dark Stone that Shadure had not disclosed.

* * *

MOUNTGLEN whispered, "Shadure is right. It will complicate the fulfillment of my desires if that fool Jarod Greatstone whelps a brat." He leaned back against his pillows. "I'd much rather be the tormentor than the tormented in the afterlife."

His only remaining question came from a lifetime of deceit. *Could it have been only a dream?* Sharp pain soared through his arm before the query completely formed, not as severe as before, but enough for him to cry out and gasp for air. Blackness swirled around him. He felt its presence in front of his face, and cringed in involuntary obeisance. The pain drained from his arm while he heard a sinister laugh echo in his mind.

The light knock at his door caused a frown. "...Enter."

A guard ventured cautiously into the room. "High Lord, I passed by and heard a cry. Is something wrong?"

Mountglen's gelid stare froze the guard in place. He strained to force words out. "...No trouble. Send Thord to me at once." The guard bowed himself from the room, closing the door; he looked relieved.

Within minutes, the bedchamber door opened. Mountglen watched his man slither across the room. *How can someone so large* glide *with such stealth and grace?* Thord's scars over heavily muscled arms, face, and many more hidden beneath his leathers added to his already fierce countenance. The cruelest scar began at the corner of his mouth and ended at his right ear. His eyes held the promise of pain to anyone foolish enough to challenge him. His deep, grating voice reverberated around the room. "High Lord?"

Mountglen's throat suffered from his unuttered screams as if they had burst forth. His vocal cords felt like they might break with tension, and his first few words came out sounding like a cock's spur against slate. "Thord, I have an important task for you to fulfill."

He rose from the bed and walked past the table to the bookshelves behind. "Light candles for the table." Thord did his master's bidding without a change of expression or comment. Mountglen walked slower than usual, feeling a hint of pain in every step. He selected a book and returned to the table where Thord lounged to the right of his chair.

Mountglen sat and carefully opened the book to reveal a hidden compartment. He removed its contents, a small, brown bottle with a cork sealed in wax. Thord's face grimaced in recognition. His eyes stared with interest, and the left side of his mouth curled in a gruesome smile; he leaned forward with new alertness.

"Here is what you are to do…"

2

SHEER draperies fell in soft folds around the bed. Candles and a blazing fireplace cast flickering lights that lit the interior. Golden flecks in radiant emerald eyes caught the light as well. Dark auburn hair spread over the pillows behind the woman, and sweat glistened on her nude body. "You are wonderful." Her voice softened to a moan.

Jarod Greatstone, Zenith Lord of the Seven Realms, cupped his wife's chin and then slowly let his hand flow downward. She loved his strong fingers as they danced lightly over her abdomen and around to the small of her back, leaving a shiver of delight where they passed. He kissed her gently while disentangling himself to lay on his back beside her. Their vigorous lovemaking over, the afterglow enveloped them in languorous pleasure. She watched him relax completely. His strong, handsome face smiled with enticing, full lips. His shoulder length, sandy colored hair spread across the pillow.

His deep voice reflected a sound of wonderment, "How long have you known?"

Maress rolled on her side to face him. "You might have known a few weeks earlier. I could have sent a message, but telling you in person, seeing the joy in your face is something that I will always remember and treasure."

She assured him that Mother Mavis had given her a thorough examination, and that everything had been fine. He asked her all the questions the Mother said he would, and she took great delight in answering them. "I sent a message to Mother and Father. The babe will be born in the spring, and I'm sure they'll want to be here."

Jarod's expression grew pensive. "I can hurry the inspections only so much. I can be here for a time before the birth and then continue them, or I may be able to get them completed and return in time."

Maress cut him off with a look. "My darling, I have considered long on this. I prefer that you complete your travels and be here for the birth and afterward, for a few months, if it can be arranged. The Mother tells me that it's more important to be here afterwards than before." Her playful smile was rewarded with a loving tease of his lips at her nipples. "Can the realms do without you for a few months?"

He chuckled. "The realms will have to be content with my absence for the next few years. When I complete these inspections, I will be through with travel for some time. The High Lords can come to me, as it should be." Jarod said the last with a smile and a glint in his eye. They both knew that certain trips would always be required in the future.

"Can we have a banquet to announce our news?"

He smiled slyly. "We can—if you don't embarrass me!"

"Embarrass you!" Maress sputtered. "When have I *ever* embarrassed you?"

"Oh, I seem to remember a banquet with soft music and light conversation. A soft, caressing hand lay gently on my thigh, and then did what you usually do when you want to see me melt and stiffen at the same time."

Maress gasped in a mock indignation while he continued. "You timed it to the exact moment that father came into the room. Then, as we rose, you took my napkin! Even with the water pitcher hiding my— condition, I saw several faces flush crimson, and after sitting back down, the bard sang of nothing but racing stallions for an hour!"

Maress giggled. "Now, perhaps I will see you appear a little pink when I announce that you will deliver several babes in a few months!"

"You...you wouldn't...would you?" The look she gave him accomplished what she intended and he pulled her to him. The gentle kiss bathed her in bliss.

"No, my dear, I suppose I won't."

He rose and pulled the sheer drapes open before walking to extinguish the candles. Maress watched the light play against rippling muscles while he strode across the room. *Oh, my dear Jarod, I don't think I could ever tell you the depth of my love for you. I could never find the words to express it. You are my life; you give my spirit breath to live. My ladies-in-waiting tell me I light up the room at the sound of your voice, and I suppose I do. I never dreamt that I could be this happy.*

Jarod walked toward the bed with only the light from the fireplace. Maress pulled the feather comforter over her and held its corner up for him to slide in beside her. She marveled again at the muscles that felt like warm, yielding marble, next to her. Curling up next to her husband, she listened as his breathing slowed to the regular cadence of sleep before drifting off beside him.

3

ZENITH Lady Maress Greatstone felt the child inside her kick a third time in as many minutes. The activity brought a smile to her face; the signs promised a son, if the babe's strength gave any indication, and her salubrious habits would ensure a good birth, at least as much as possible.

She paused in her needlework to check her progress on a bell pull for the nursery. It showed a snowy mountain peak at the top, followed by the face of a golden deathcat against a crimson samite background. The creature's long fangs glistened with rare silver threads as her hand worked its way down the fabric.

Maress had never seen a deathcat; few people had in populated areas. *Could they possibly be the size the stories portray?* In contrast to the deathcat's beauty, additional animal heads came from myths of creatures believed to be common before the Great War. *They can't be real,* she decided. *Nothing so terrible could exist, except as descriptions placed in the heads of children to make them behave.* In the illustrated books, the heads did not look particularly menacing; it was the actions contributed to them that fostered terror. They still made excellent children's tales on dark, rainy nights, not that any adult believed such tales. She remembered hearing them as a young girl and afterwards, how hard and long it took to go to sleep, and decided not to include them.

Lady Suzan's soft knock, follow by her entrance, signaled a respite for the Zenith Lady. Most admired Lady Suzan's beauty like the rest of Maress' ladies-in-waiting, yet none of them approached Maress' exquisiteness, not to mention the glow she had acquired with her pregnancy. Full waves of dark auburn hair cradled her face. Lustrous skin rivaled the finest china with the texture of fine wormcloth. The warmth and brightness of her personality matched her emerald-green eyes, as rare as the jewels that defined them. In contrast, her low, smoky voice produced enchantment in practically all who heard her.

"My Zenith Lady, your water is quite cool this morning. The fruit looks good, and for some reason, they sent sweets on your morning tray. May I help you to table?"

Maress' chuckle became a throaty purr. "No, lately it's the only exercise I get. Come again in an hour, and perhaps you can help me do something with my hair that approaches social acceptance."

Lady Suzan's smile and voice warmed, "My Zenith Lady." She bowed her head and closed the door quietly when she left.

The water, cool as promised, tasted slightly bitter. Maress finished her firstmeal and returned to her bed and needlework.

She put the bell pull aside after many stitches and lifted herself upward to find comfort, only to feel a sharp pain in her lower abdomen. She sucked in air from the jolt of the second pain a few seconds later. *Don't panic! I have a month to go—it cannot be time yet.*

The next pain brought a scream, and she fell partially from the bed, her head swimming. She saw the stylized face of a deathcat floating in darkness before she slowly lost consciousness.

4

MOTHER Mavis Grant directed all hospice concerns for the Seven Realms. The Zenith and his father before him supported her efforts working with the real world, without the power to channel a graystone. Her knowledge and practice of physical medicine was unequalled, and brought her high regard throughout the Seven Realms.

Healers worked through the small power contained in their graystones, increasing her medicine's potency. The results hastened healing ten-fold, although it could cause an unfavorable reaction in extremely rare cases. Little friction grew between the groups of herbalists and healers, and when it did, resolution came quickly. They agreed that the patient's health came first.

The Mother's short statue and tendency toward a plump figure belied the fire and energy packed into her every fiber. Her past beauty now presented her with grace. Her hair, the whitest, with the look, body, and fullness of fine wool, formed a flowing crown atop her head. Light gray eyes searched each person they fell upon deeply, and she gave her undivided attention to those that beheld them.

She came to the Spires fifteen days ago to prepare for the upcoming birth. Mother Mavis had been mid-wife to the current Zenith Lord, his father, and his father before him. She had brought each of them into the world with care and skill. Her heart swelled with pride from taking part in the birth of four Zeniths.

The Spires, the seat of power for Zenith Lords, was a huge complex that towered over the city of Stonefire and its population of just over four million people. Stonefire, the name of the Zenith's realm and his capital city, referred to throughout the Seven Realms as "The City," wore colors of blue and white in celebration for the upcoming birth of a new part of the Zenith.

Mother Mavis did not like the Spires; it felt oppressive and overbearing to her, and she cared little for the constant activity. It did not help that the largest building in the Seven Realms, probably the whole world—and certainly her world—housed five thousand troops inside the inner walls. *Only the Blessed One knows how many more between the outer and inner walls,* she thought.

The Spires stood from the time of the Great War, two millennia ago; some say it predated it. It got its name from three spires of solid rock, positioned equilaterally a mile apart in a perfect triangle, each spire rising to a point seven hundred feet in the air. No one had ever climbed them; the rock gave little to grab on to, and their near-vertical faces cowed the best mountain climbers. The ground between them lay flat from time, man, and nature. Several levels below ground, corridors had been hewn from solid rock down to an underground river that brought fresh water, took away waste, and provided power to the various lifts and miscellaneous machinery throughout the complex. Bright red dye used centuries ago to test the river's route, revealed nothing. The rivers of Stonefire ran clear of dye, the water pure and sweet. The assumption had been made that the waste emptied into the sea.

Mother Mavis did not know how the pulleys and lifts worked for people, food, and supplies; she only knew that they did. The Zenith Lord's residence occupied the top floor, twelve levels aboveground, built between two of the three monoliths. She had set up a birthing room next to the Zenith Lord and Lady's suite.

She felt pride for her Zenith Lord and all he had accomplished in his short time on the Dais, expanding the quality of life of his subjects. She raised him from birth until his Age-of-Man time. She had substituted as surrogate mother after the Zenith Lady Danora went to Light's Source during Jarod's birth.

Sunlight of a crisp new day shone on her through an open window when she heard a muffled cry, long and terrible. Hurrying to the Zenith Lady's rooms, she pulled the heavy door open in time to see the Zenith Lady, Maress, slip from the bed in her effort to rise, a scream dying on her lips. The shriek—heard through the open door—brought guardsmen running from their post at the entrance to the Chambers. Mother Mavis stood erect when the guardsmen entered.

"Find the Zenith Lord and bring him here. Bring my supplies from the birthing room. Send for the ladies-in-waiting to assist me, and have the kitchen send up boiling water. Send for a master healer." She pointed to one of the guardsmen, "Help me lift the Zenith Lady onto the bed." The guardsman froze for a moment, looking stunned at the order to lay hands on the Zenith Lady; with a start, he came out of it and stumbled toward the bed. Mavis had not noticed Apex Lord Kyle Byrne, the Captain of the Zenith's Guard enter the room.

"Do what she commands!" he boomed across the room. "Pikeman Lawrence, coordinate the Mother's tasks. I will assist the Mother myself. On the run, GO!"

"Thank you, my son," Mavis and the captain went to the Zenith Lady's aid.

Lady Suzan and Lady Gayle came a few minutes later. They could not see anything different at first. The girls were shocked when Zenith Lady's color became discernible, pale and drawn. Lady Suzan's comment was awed, "She was fine a few minutes ago!"

The Mother recognized Lady Gayle. "Is your mother in the Spires, child?" The girl nodded. "Send a guardsman for her to come at once." The girl left briefly; the sound of running boots broke off when she closed the door, returning to the foot of the bed.

The Mother saw the girls' fear and unfamiliarity with crisis. They had neither the experience nor force of will for what lay ahead. "When Lady Deanna arrives, you ladies may retire, but stay available." The girls showed some relief and tried to smile. The Mother put them to work situating the room the way she desired while she kept a watchful eye on her patient.

Shortly, Lady Deanna entered the room. She advanced halfway to the bed. Her face froze when she saw the condition of her Zenith Lady.

Mother Mavis looked to the girls and spoke before Lady Deanna could begin. "You ladies may go to your rooms now. Remain available, and say nothing about what you have seen, or your mothers won't have much hide to further remove when you are returned to them."

The force and choice of the Mother's words startled the girls. They bowed their heads and hurried from the room after one look from Lady Deanna's stern face echoing the Mother's remark.

Lady Deanna looked into the Mother's clear gray eyes. "Are you sure?"

"No. Nevertheless, I'm deeply afraid. All the signs are there; we will know soon enough. I needed someone with experience. I'm glad you are here."

"I will pray to Light's Source while we work." She took the cooling cloth from the Mother and began to apply it to Maress' head, face, and arms.

Kyle motioned the Mother aside. "I have never seen anyone so red and marked. What is it you fear will happen? Mother, I have known you most of my life. I'm Jarod's best friend. You must—"

The Mother cut him off with an upraised hand, then took his arm and led him away from Maress' hearing. She spoke softly, trying to sound unafraid. "Lady Deanna helped me before Jarod's birth. An assassin murdered a visiting Lord from Northmount. The assassin talked after his capture. He used a poison from across the East Sea and said no more. He managed to take—what must have been—an overdose from a hollowed ring he wore, and died almost at once. He said one more word before he died, 'Darkstone!' I have never seen those symptoms again, until now. I can only hope it's something else. Send for High Healer Tobias Sternwood."

*   *   *

KYLE'S stunned expression grew hard. Jarod, his best friend, and they loved one another as much as any two brothers could. Kyle, six years older than him, arrived at the Spires at age ten. The two boys had bonded together from the start. The Mother believed he still looked to Kyle as an older brother. She knew Kyle felt a need to protect him beyond the scope of his position. Someone declared war by doing this deed." Kyle's anger boiled under a calm pose. *I won't rest until I find the perpetrator, and I hope to kill him with my bare hands!* He stepped to the door leading to the corridor and motioned for a guardsman. After whispering in his ear, he went to a chair near the bed to keep vigil. Shortly, a soft knock came at the door. Kyle rushed to answer it and whispered to the short, wiry man in dark clothes, "We suspect poison, start your investigation!"

Kyle motioned to his officer posted in the hall and whispered, "I want a hundred men posted around the entrances to the Chambers. Search each room except this one and the one adjoining. Pray you miss nothing! Place an additional hundred men at the entrances to the two floors below. Distribute the men half on guard and half patrolling the area. Seal the Spires. Now!"

*   *   *

THE last order made Damish's jaw drop. He had never heard of an incident when the Spires had been sealed. He recovered quickly, brought his right fist up to his heart in salute and seconds later, his running footfalls diminished as he sped away to carry out the Apex Lord's orders.

5

SOME priests commanded the ability to imprint messages on a bird's mind through the weak power of a graystone. The priest assigned to Jarod Greatstone's party had fallen ill several days ago, and remained behind at a hospice. Jarod did not wait for a replacement. He refused any delay that impeded his return to the Spires and Maress.

The sun arched toward the west as night came, while each minute felt as if an hour passed. Fast riders raced to the Zenith Lord, who traveled with an inspection team seven to eight hours hard ride to the southeast. Messages for fresh horses flew ahead of them.

* * *

MARESS drifted in and out of consciousness without ever becoming completely lucid. Her raging fever was the highest Mother Mavis had ever encountered. Perspiration poured from her body, soaking the bed linens. Lady Deanna labored to keep Maress and the bed dry and clean. Pustulous sores devastated her body, producing a dark, putrid fluid. The stench gagged her attendants. Mother Mavis forced liquids on Maress to keep her hydrated during the increasingly rare times she neared consciousness.

Mavis examined the position of the babe, listening with her body-horn used to find the fetus' heart sounds. The babe sounded strong, with good movement, but his position needed changing along the birth canal. Mother Mavis began the slow process of arranging the babe properly. The entire procedure took nearly an hour. Maress seemed unaware of the events happening to her, deepening Mother Mavis' concern and anxiety for both mother and child.

Maress began to moan, quietly at first, then gradually louder, until her screams filled the room. She became nearly aware; but soon lapsed into a deeper stupor, and the sporadic moans continued. Mother Mavis found it increasingly difficult to focus on her charge, feeling the strain of many hours of time and effort.

The faint sound of a trumpet floated up on the wind. Mother Mavis breathed a sigh of relief. The Zenith Lord's fanfare cheered her. She wondered at the speed he must have traveled to cover that distance in so short a time. The riders must have carried mounts to leave at intervals for his return trip, insuring a fresh mount at the ready when needed. Shouts penetrated the heavy door.

* * *

THE huge door swung outward. Jarod saw Mother Mavis look up while he ran the last few yards to his bedchamber. His shirt and tunic lay plastered to his skin, drenched with perspiration and covered with dirt and mud from his long ride. *Great Light's Source, I've never seen her look so worried, not even when father died!*

He slowed to a crawl when he entered the room, afraid of what he might find. *Damn, the stench! What or who has done this? Why didn't they inform me sooner?* Jarod stood in shock, and then let out a long, low moan. His heart crumbled as the realization of his wife's condition crushed his spirit.

Already near exhaustion, his shoulders sagged as the full measure of Maress' condition bore into him. He hesitantly turned away; pain flooded his countenance while he searched for an answer from Mother Mavis.

"Everything we know to do is being done, my dear one. We are all doing the best we know how. She's unconscious, and you can do no good for her now. You must be near exhaustion. Go with Kyle next door and refresh yourself. I'm sure Rolo has food and wine for you, and I think I heard them pour a bath after the first trumpet sounded. You will want her to see you looking well. I will call you at once if she shows any sign of progress."

Kyle came to his side and lightly took his arm.

Jarod looked down, still searching Mavis' face. He loved the old woman. She and Travis raised him until his Age-of-Man time. She smiled at him, but the look he knew so well told him to do what she said. Fatigue engulfed him, and his legs shook as he walked to the adjoining room with Kyle.

He returned shortly, clean and in fresh clothes, hastily chewing a last bite of food. Mother Mavis looked up at him and smiled. "Sit on the far side of the bed. Speak softly in her ear; you will know what to say. Try to get her to react so I might induce her to drink water and potions. Speak to her often, but under no circumstances are you to touch her."

I can't touch her! MomMav said she's doing everything possible. Can that be true? He settled on the far side of the bed, leaned down and whispered to his wife, "My life, my future, my love, I'm here and I need you."

His voice softened, and was lost to those standing nearby. Lady Deanna quietly slipped to a far chair, tears trickling down her face.

* * *

JAROD'S pleas, heavy with grief and pain, cut into the Mother's heart as no knife could have done. He looked into her eyes. His voice, raw with anguish, ached through her. "Is there nothing else you can do?" Mother Mavis fought to stay calm.

The corridor door opened, admitting the High Healer, Tobias Sternwood. He too, showed signs of a long journey. Mavis watched him closely for his first reaction. His aide came forward with his supplies and equipment. He smiled at Mother Mavis and bowed to the Zenith Lord, but his eyes widened when he first viewed the Zenith Lady.

"Mother Mavis, is this—" She cut him off with a look that could shatter stone. Her eyes flickered toward the Zenith Lord.

Tobias looked around and with a slight motion of his hand, his aide left after placing his burdens near the bed. Tobias waited until the door closed behind him. "I have Flower's Syrup with me."

"Not now, perhaps later," Mother Mavis whispered. She then spoke softly to the Zenith Lord. "I will go out with Tobias for a few minutes. The door will be ajar. Call at once if she stirs." Jarod nodded slightly without taking his eyes from Maress.

The two healers stepped into the corridor. Mavis' voice showed the strain she'd been holding back from the Zenith. "She has been this way for over four days. The severe pain comes and goes. Some distress is always there. You know what I fear! I have said nothing to the Zenith Lord of what the outcome is likely to be."

Tobias nodded. "We should send for the Pinnacle." Mother Mavis nodded once, her face grim.

Screams from the bedchamber shattered the stillness. They hurried back to the bed. Mother Mavis looked at the reddish purple glaze in Maress' open eyes. Mavis and Tobias' eyes briefly met before she turned her attention to her Zenith Lord. "Jarod, my son, I think it would be best if you sent for the Pinnacle and your High Councilor."

Jarod's realization of Maress' pending death registered in his mind. His barely discernible voice stumbled. "Send the messages." Tobias hurried from the room.

The Zenith Lord's face paled. He pleaded, "MomMav, what can we do?"

The nickname was from his early years, when the pronunciation of "Mother Mavis" resisted coming from a babe's mouth, and the use of his private name for her brought more grief than she could bear. Quickly wiping a tear from her cheek, she dug her nails sharply into her hand as she hurried to Tobias' supplies and returned with Flower's Syrup and a short reed. Maress began to writhe in the first jerking motions of a seizure.

Mother Mavis grabbed a small clean cloth from the bedside table, rolled it and placed it in Maress' mouth. The seizure lasted a few moments; its toll became clearly visible as Maress slumped into the bedcloths, fighting for breath. The Mother carefully drew up a small amount of the syrup in the reed and released the dark potion at the rear of Maress' throat. The insensate woman choked, but swallowed the thick syrup, growing still almost immediately. Her eyes lay open in an unseeing glaze.

Mother Mavis pulled Jarod away from the bed. "My son, I know what is attacking her. The symptoms are those induced by a poison I have seen once before." His face showed disbelief, then shock, and finally, anger. The veins of his neck visibly pulsed, and his shirt grew tight around his arms and chest. He let out a soft, low moan, and his body relaxed to normalcy except for his face. His features hardened, and his eyes held a fierceness the Mother had never seen before.

"I don't know of an antidote. Tobias is working hard to stem the poison's effects, but—I fear it will only prolong her agony." Mother Mavis' voice cracked; she fought to continue. Jarod looked past the Mother to Tobias kneeling beside the bed, grasping his graystone; beads of sweat covered his forehead. "Little is known of this poison, only that it is highly transferable through sweat. You must not touch her without a protective cloth between you, and it must be changed before it becomes damp." The Mother pointed to a stack of clean cloths beside the bed and then indicated a cauldron containing discarded cloths steaming in a liquid over the fire."

"I...can...not...touch her?"

"No, my dear one, you cannot." Unmistakable pain filled the Mother's voice. "Comfort her, my son; stay close to her. She may sense that you are near, and draw strength from your words and closeness. It's the most we can do now."

* * *

JAROD stared into Kyle's eyes. "How?"

Kyle dreaded this moment; still, he returned his piercing gaze. His voice, filled with pain, answered slowly. "We do not yet know. An investigation is under way. I...I..." Jarod cut him off with a motion of his hand and returned to the bedside.

Zenith Lord Jarod Greatstone made no noise while he lay next to his Maress; tears ran across the bridge of his nose, disappearing into the bedclothes between them. His tears ceased within a few minutes; he lay still next to her, her head cradled in his arm with a padded cloth between them.

Kyle watched his Zenith Lord, his friend, while barely contained rage flowed through his body. *I will kill whoever did this with my bare hands. I have failed in my primary duty! How will he ever trust me again?* Kyle's shoulders slumped.

* * *

THE first contraction came an hour later.

Mother Mavis pulled the bedclothes high up from the bed's foot to tent over the abdomen and examined Maress' spreading. She lowered the bedclothes. No sound came from Maress, and Mother Mavis gave thanks for that small miracle. Tobias said nothing, merely looking at Mother Mavis and slightly nodding once. Jarod rose and came around the end of the bed. His face was set in determination and finality, and his gaze never left his wife.

Mother Mavis turned to Kyle. "Take the Zenith Lord to the next room and close the door." With her heart breaking, she looked into Jarod's eyes, smiled, and forced as much strength into her words as she could. "Fathers are not supposed to be present when a babe comes. It's too hard on them." She hoped he did not see the despair in her heart written across her face.

He was too exhausted and strained to do anything but go with Kyle; they disappeared into the adjoining room. Tobias stood at the bedside. He looked up at Mavis. "Will it affect the child?"

The old woman looked haggard beyond her many years, her voice so quiet that Tobias had to lean forward to hear. "I don't know. Her spread is too fast. The babe will come soon. Once the poison takes hold, it moves slowly allowing the damage to range rapidly. It may be her early delivery will save the babe. "

Tobias only nodded and leaned forward to administer more Flowers' Syrup and continue the flow of power from his graystone. He looked at the adjoining room while the door closed. Hearing the latch fall, he shook his head. Mavis went to her supplies and pulled a small pouch from the bag. She looked at Tobias.

"Tea of ease?"

Tobias nodded once.

She walked to the outside corridor and knocked quietly. Kyle answered, looking surprised. She motioned him into the corridor and spoke softly, "Jarod must have some relief. It will do him great harm to see what is to come unaided. I have felt the depth of his love for Maress since they first met. What is going to happen next could do never-ending harm. Have tea brewed with the contents of this pouch and urge him to drink. It has a pleasant taste; it won't harm him. His mind will remain alert, but it will calm him and help him handle what is about to come to pass."

Mavis looked defeated. Surprise appeared on Kyle's face. "I do this from compassion, as he would for you. Her death is assured within a few hours. She will be unrecognizable. I don't often keep a loved one away at the end. The Zenith may not be granted such a dispensation, no matter how justified it is."

Kyle put his arms around Mavis and held her close. The Mother saw the same determination and stalwartness built from great strength of character that Jarod possessed, though Kyle's and his bloodlines differed. Mavis suspected it came from Kyle's mother's side of his family.

The mother bowed her head and returned to Maress.

* * *

KYLE watched the Mother leave, knowing the devotion Jarod and she felt for one another.

He called a guardsman from the door of Maress' room. "Have tea brewed from this for the Zenith. See to it yourself, make sure they do it properly, and return with it quickly. Tell the duty officer to pass the word that the Pinnacle, High Lord Lockley will arrive in a few days. Tell him to have the usual preparations completed in time." Kyle's quiet tone emphasized the importance of his order. He watched the guardsman hurry away and then went back to watch over Jarod with a heavy heart.

A few minutes later, the tea arrived in a small pot with an empty mug on a silver tray. Kyle filled the mug. Jarod sat on the side of a chaise with his head braced in his hands, his elbows on his knees. Kyle placed a hand on his shoulder. He sat still at first; then he looked up seeing the proffered mug. He took it and sipped the hot brew without acknowledgement of his actions. After a few sips, he sat the mug down on the floor and stretched out on the chaise. Kyle went to the adjoining door and stood in the doorway. Mother Mavis turned to him. Kyle jerked his head down in a single nod.

"Stay with him; he will need you this day." Mother Mavis' attention again centered on her patient, and Kyle returned to Jarod's side.

6

KYLE heard a faint cry from Maress, and the shrill squeal of a babe as the first rays of dawn shone through leaded glass doors leading to the balcony. He opened the adjoining door to Maress' room in time to see the Mother holding a babe, flanked by Tobias.

Jarod appeared at his side. The stench from miasmic air assaulted their senses. Tobias' right hand fluttered in the air around the child while his left grasped his graystone. Lady Deanna attended Maress, wrapping her body with clean bedcloths. The flesh over the stark bones of her body split and peeled away. She was near death, and the continuing loss of blood would kill her within minutes.

Horror filled the Mother's face. "Jarod, please, stay away!"

He pushed Kyle aside and approached the bed. His face reflected the torment he felt, and he vomited. He stood looking down at the twisted, raw flesh of his wife while bile soaked his shirt and splattered on the floor.

Tobias jerked his head around to Maress. "She has gone to Light's Source!"

The Mother wrapped the babe in clean cloth, checked its life signs, and placed the child in the cradle brought in with her supplies. She then pulled a hard substance wrapped in a cloth from her pocket. "Jarod! Eat this, now!"

Kyle forced him away from the bed toward the Mother. His eyes looked as dead as his wife's. The

30

Mother forced the substance into his mouth and motioned to Tobias. Tobias grabbed his graystone and lightly touched Jarod's head.

Jarod collapsed into Kyle's arms. Tobias sagged and nearly fell. Beads of sweat covered his forehead, and he could barely walk to the chair. Kyle adjusted Jarod's weight and carried him to the chaise in the adjoining room. He slept peacefully. Kyle rang for Rolo, Jarod's steward, and walked slowly to join the others with Maress' body.

The Mother went to the bedside and knelt, her voice low, "Light's Source, take your child Maress into your abode." Lady Deanna stood with tears flowing down her cheeks; her usual regal bearing smashed.

The Mother motioned for Kyle to come forward. She looked up into his eyes, "Lord Kyle Byrne, Captain of the Zenith's Guard, witness the passing of this part of the Zenith into the Light." Mavis had said the same words when Jarod's mother died after his birth, and again when his father died two years ago. Now, she had spoken them three times; to say them again would undo her.

Kyle looked down and grimaced at the putrid mass replacing the once beautiful woman who had lain there. Raw, crimson flesh replaced her face, the whites of her eyes had turned black, her mouth was distorted in agony, and her upper body had bloated, with signs of corruption already pushing its way out. He kneeled, as did Tobias and Lady Deanna. His face, hardened to stone and his voice reverberated the pain in is heart. "Light's Source, as guardsman of the Zenith, I release her spirit to you." Kyle's predecessor said these words two years before.

The Mother addressed herself to the three kneeling beside her. "Lady Deanna, I must swear you to secrecy. Announcement of these events must wait until the Zenith commands it. We swore to protect the Zenith, as you did. I serve on you now, that oath will be violated if premature knowledge of these events is made known before the Zenith Lord wishes it."

Lady Deanna held out her hands, palms upward, "I so swear by the Grace of Light's Source."

Mother Mavis rose unsteadily to her feet and walked slowly to the cradle. The others stood and followed, encircling the child. The mother intoned, "Light's Source, we pray for the protection of this child as part of the Zenith, and we swear our oaths to protect this new part of the Zenith."

All four stated firmly, "I swear!"

7

TWO heard the babe's cry.

Travis Grant, the Holy One, looked up from his book. Realization, and then shock registered on his face for a small part of a moment. Others around him showed no evidence of hearing the cry.

Travis stood. The men in the room stood and bowed their heads while he walked quickly to the door. Upon reaching the tower's highest level, he rang the bell for the Birdmaster. Cally appeared within seconds, and immediately bowed. He looked remarkably like the birds he kept: tall and thin, hooked nose, a shock of hair that resembled plumage, and strong arms.

"It has been a long while since you last visited, your Holiness."

"Too long indeed, Cally. Bring me your strongest eagle."

Cally did not hide his surprise. Eagles, hard to train and with their task completed, often never returned. He bowed and hurried away.

Feathers danced over a hooded eagle perched on Cally's leather wrapped arm when he returned. The Birdmaster held the eagle facing His Holiness and removed its hood. Bright eyes focused on Travis and locked in place. His Holiness held its attention for several long moments; then the bird shook its head.

"Release the bird. He will return with a message. Call me, night or day, when he returns. It should not take more than a day."

His Holiness missed Cally's bow and hurried back down the stairs. Cally slowly shook his head. No one sent messages this early in the day, especially His Holiness. He carried the impatient bird up the stairway and released him to deliver its charge.

His Holiness reached his rooms and yanked the bell pull. Moments later, the head steward knocked once and entered as clothes flew in the air. His Holiness went to his small private bookcase, and the rain of clothing ceased.

"Your Holiness, please, is there some way I can help you?"

"Three of us will leave within a day. We will need supplies for a three-day trip, traveling hard. Two guards will come, too. Call the Prelates to my study in a half-hour. Have their stewards start packing; they will be going."

"At once, your Holiness." Handford had worked in service to the Holy One for ten years and had never seen him in such a state. He hurried to the door; the signs promised a busy day ahead.

* * *

THE second man to hear the babe's cries frowned and continued preparing his morning meal.

8

MOUNTGLEN entered his private suite and closed the door behind him. Teal blue pants and tunic with white shirt clashed with his mottled complexion, and did nothing to disguise his thinness or height. The black, highly shined boots with pointed toes made his feet look even longer. Dark half-moons gave his brown eyes a feral appearance, similar to the face of a rodent.

Vertigo overwhelmed his mind as his body hurled into the air in the middle of the room, suspended halfway to the ceiling and several feet above the door's top edge. As he dangled there, helpless, his clothes ignited along the entire length of his body. No sound escaped his lips, but his mind screamed in agony. His ashen clothes flared and dropped toward the floor, consumed by fire before reaching the thick rugs below. Mountglen could cock his head enough to see his flesh was not actually burning as the bright flames danced over his skin. His flesh felt cooked to the bone; the pain should have rendered him unconscious, and he prayed for his mind to stop feeling. Pain and his conscious state held for what he considered an eternity.

His body was slowly lowered to a few feet above the floor, and then fell to the thick rugs below. He could not tell the burning had stopped at first. The intake of air seared his throat anew, and he felt like he had been screaming for hours. His body lay naked, even his boots had been completely destroyed. The thick, soft rugs tortured his skin. He remained there, unable to lift a finger.

His body jerked upright to a standing position. The harsh odor of singed hair prompted him to look at his body. A visible sign of burning remained; his normally hirsute torso and limbs now glared dark pink and hairless. His testicles ached and throbbed, as if a horse had kicked him. Mountglen wanted to curl into a fetal position, instead, his body muscles stretched painfully in the air.

Shadure's black, hooded figure formed. Only blackness lay beneath the hood. *"You failed! The brat still lives! Now you or one of your consanguinity must kill the imp. I held you in pain for a mere three minutes. You will spend eternity wishing for pain as gentle if you fail me again. You have less than a month until the Naming Day ceremony. The brat must be dead by then. Fail me again and you die. Then, you will come to know what real torment is, for all eternity."*

Mountglen slumped to the floor like a puppet whose strings had disintegrated. His mouth opened, but nothing came from his raw throat when he tried to moan. He managed to crawl to his bed and pull himself halfway up before darkness filled his mind, and he slumped to the floor.

9

THE Mother spoke softly to Lady Deanna. "We have much to do before the Zenith wakes. It won't be pleasant. I ask your help."

"I will do what you require, all that I'm able." Lady Deanna recaptured her composure as she looked through the open doorway and smiled sadly at the sleeping Zenith Lord.

The Mother nodded and returned to the blood-soaked bed. "If you will get fresh linens, Tobias and I will clean and prepare her for wrapping. The Zenith Lord should not see her as she is now."

Tobias left to find white canvas while the Mother attempted to bath Maress' remains, but soon gave it up as hopeless. Lady Deanna went to the housekeeping area, and Kyle returned to Jarod.

The child slept peacefully.

Fresh air flowed through the cleaned room two hours later. Maress' body lay in the middle of the clean bed, wrapped in bright, white canvas. Golden threads woven into a sunburst pattern on a black linen scarf lay centered across her forehead. The black banner placed across the chest of the murdered was missing.

Mother Mavis went to Jarod's door and waved at Kyle to join her. He entered looking as haggard as the rest of them, and his words showed the strain. "The Zenith still sleeps."

She looked at Tobias and Lady Deanna. "He will wake soon. We must be ready for him. I think it will be best if Kyle and I talk to him first in the adjoining room. Lady Deanna, you need rest, too. Please retire, and find me when you wake."

Lady Deanna kneeled before the bed for a minute, briefly touched the child's cradle and left the room without speaking, a tear filling her eye once more. She closed the door silently behind her.

The Mother took Kyle's hand. "The time for our own grief must be put off. We must be here for Jarod when he wakes, and see him through these next few days. Have you started a murder investigation? Yes, of course you have."

"It will be enlarged soon. The Spires is sealed."

"Tobias, where are the food and drink we found yesterday?"

"I placed everything in separate containers, and have them there on the small table."

The Mother followed his eye, unaware he had accomplished several tasks that only now she began to see. Her concentration had rested solely, completely on Maress and later, on the child. "Kyle, take portions of anything edible or potable, and test it on animals. Be extremely careful of what you touch. If you can isolate something, bring it to me sealed. Wear gloves and burn them after you are finished. I will watch over Jarod while you are gone." She smiled and looked at Tobias, "And Tobias will watch over me."

10

KYLE donned a pair of gloves before gathering the containers into a sack. He carried them gingerly toward the entrance to the Chambers. A Pikeman pulled one of the two heavy doors open. Ten men snapped to position and saluted in unison. Returning their salute with his free hand, Kyle asked for the Duty Officer. He appeared from around the corridor's intersection and saluted.

Users of poison don't make a frontal attack, Kyle surmised. "Return the men to regular duty on the two floors below. Keep the Spires sealed."

Then, hardly aware of the man's salute as he rushed by, Kyle hurried as fast as the sack's encumbrance allowed down five flights of stairs to the first warehousing level. He entered the nearest door where provisions for the nearby kitchens formed upward to the ceiling. There, he found the rat cages.

The warehouse cats killed some mice and rats. Their remains and cages lay uncollected for the day. Kyle selected five cages, one with two victims. He was stacking the cages when a troubled voice asked, "May I help you, my Lord?"

Kyle looked around to see a man of senior years with white hair and the armband of a warehouse keeper. "Is there a private room nearby?"

The man looked surprised at the request; he pointed to a door in the middle of the near wall. "That is our marking room. No one will be in there now, and it's the nearest, my Lord."

Kyle went to the door and found a small room with one table and a chair. He sat the sack on the table and looked into the old man's curious eyes. "There will be guardsmen in the mess hall. Send four to me."

"Yes, my Lord." His running steps echoed until he passed through the warehouse door.

Kyle carefully picked up the cages and stacked one on top another until he held five cages with six pairs of glaring eyes filled with hate. He had carried them to the small room and set them down when he heard running footfalls coming toward him. He stepped outside the room and returned his men's salute.

"Two of you guard this door, the other two guard the main door. No one is to enter." His voice remained calm, but carried a force his men seldom heard from him. They snapped to position when he returned to the small room.

Kyle unsnapped the locking wire on the first cage. He took the first container and carefully opened it, finding a whole slice of apple with dark discoloration. He picked it up and slid it into the wire cage. The rat pounced on it, devouring it in seconds. He placed the cage on the floor and put the container of apple slices in front of it. The rat tried to get to the container, lunged to the cage's middle and looked up at its captor with renewed hate in its eyes. Kyle repeated the process with each remaining container of food until he came to the last. He found a clear liquid, probably water. Maress seldom drank wine, and he knew of no time when she did so that early in the day. The container did not fit between the spaces of the wire cage. He needed to distract the mouse while he placed the container inside. *Good thing that you are young, unlike your friends.*

Kyle tilted the cage backward and opened the door. The frightened mouse stayed at the cage's rear when he lowered it and set the container of liquid inside, locked the cage and drew a sigh of relief. He positioned the chair where he could sit and watch the five cages. The rats ate the food and the mouse sniffed at the water. Finally, the wary mouse drank a few sips of water then gulped down the rest.

Before the mouse finished the small amount of liquid, it shirked one time, its eyes bulging and fell dead. Quickly, its underlying flesh went from pink to crimson and its eyes glazed over. Something seemed to be eating its flesh from the inside. Then, the rat in the middle cage jerked and died with the same symptoms. Kyle looked at the container of sweets in front of the dead rat's cage. Maress loved the sweets, but strictly rationed them to one a day. Kyle resealed the containers of remaining sweets and water.

Kyle sat for half an hour longer observing the live rats while they fought for freedom. The scent of death drove them into a frenzy of clawing at the metal around them. Kyle carefully placed the sealed containers containing poison into the sack. He left the others in front of live animals. His men snapped to position when the door opened. Kyle carefully set the sack on the floor, away from his feet and his men. Pulling one glove from his hand, he dropped it into the sack. Carefully hooking his finger inside the remaining glove, he pulled it inside out and off his hand to join its mate. He asked for and received gloves from the closest guardsman and donned them.

The quartet of guardsmen stood stiffly at position with eyes staring straight ahead when Kyle rose. "You are to remain here on guard. No one is to enter that room without my being here. You are not to discuss any part of what you have seen with anyone including yourselves. Violation of this order will be swift and painful." The men never heard their commander issue such a threat, nor heard of it happening. They exchanged glances and stood rigidly at position. Kyle picked up the sack and started his return trip. He heard the guardsman whose gloves he had borrowed relaying his orders as he went through the warehouse's exit.

11

KYLE found the Mother in Jarod's room, where Tobias had taken the cradle, gently rocking it back and forth. Tobias sat at the table, his head resting on his folded arms, his eyes locked on Kyle. Kyle set the sack inside the room and silently closed the door. He looked at Jarod, still sleeping in fresh clothes without boots on the chaise where he had left him. *Tobias is a potent healer!* he realized.

"He should sleep an hour or two more," The Mother said softly. "You can speak. It won't wake him."

"The sweets and clear liquid quickly killed," Kyle said. "The others were still alive when I left. I brought the poison containers in the sack. The others are in front of the cages used for that item. It took a small amount to kill the rats. The corpses displayed the identical signs that Maress showed. Her meals arrive on a food lift from the kitchen. Her ladies-in-waiting take them to her room. We should start our questioning with them. There is a small study down the hall. Tobias, can you tell truthfulness through your stone?"

"If the lie is great enough, or the liar scared enough, it will give me an indication. Many times, when one thinks I can catch the lie, their fear will break them. Certainly, I can try."

The Mother's soft, resigned voice said, "Kyle, have someone go to the bakery near the outer wall's east entry. There you will find a woman, girl actually, in sorrow's clothes. Her name is Trina Gabbles. She suffered a stillborn delivery, two weeks ago. We will need a wet nurse soon."

Kyle looked suspicious. "Can she be trusted?"

"She's my great-granddaughter. I trust her."

Kyle's mouth gaped; the Mother had raised Jarod for ten years and he for six years, and neither knew she had ever been married, nor that she had children. Tobias' slight smile faded quickly.

Kyle went into the hall, shaking his head. A guardsman saluted as Kyle closed the door. "Quickly send me the first five officers you can find. Have Rosh brought as well." He returned to the room.

No one spoke for several minutes. A soft knock broke their concentration. Kyle stepped into the hall and sent the first two officers to find the ladies-in-waiting that had served Maress the morning before. One he ordered to stay with him. Confessions needed two witnesses. Tobias made three. The next received the Mother's directions to the bakery. He whispered to Rosh, "Bring Gaz to the study." He ordered the last officer to stay in the room with the Zenith Lord, and to wake the Mother if either the child or the Zenith stirred. The Mother's smile faded as sleep took her. Kyle, Tobias and Lieutenant Damish quietly stepped toward the study; each lost in his deliberations.

Lady Gayle Strand, daughter of Lady Deanna, arrived first. She looked nervous and tired, her eyes swollen and red. Kyle arranged four plush chairs around a square table only slightly wider than the chairs. He led Lady Gayle to the chair closest the door. The strong sunlight through sheer draperies opposite framed her features without blinding her. The two men rose and Kyle formally introduced them. She curtsied, and her face flushed a light pink when her eyes fell on Lieutenant Damish. She seated herself and tried to smile. Lieutenant Damish sat erect, looking more than a little self-conscious. Tobias had his left hand inside his tunic, firmly grasping his graystone. Kyle slumped in his chair, looking tired and tense.

"Lady Gayle, can you tell us what you did yesterday?"

Kyle asked quietly and slowly.

She went through a list of her normal, daily routine of duties, flustered at first, ending somewhat at ease.

Kyle used the same gentle tone. "Did you see anything unusual?" His eyes bore into the girl, and she chose to look at Tobias from time to time.

"No, the Zenith Lady took ill early in the morning. We work in pairs helping her. Lady Suzan Dermouth is my partner. We take turns rising early to get the Zenith Lady's morning tray of fruit and water, and Lady Suzan had the honor yesterday." Kyle, aware of everything she had said, knew everything that touched the Zenith's life in any way. Lieutenant Damish also knew Lady Gayle's routine from the look on his face.

Kyle's voice and demeanor never changed, "Lieutenant Damish, see that Lady Gayle is escorted to her room and a guardsman placed at her door." Kyle looked at the young girl, "Lady Gayle, you will wait in your room for us to send word. It won't be long."

Lady Gayle rose, looking a little uncertain. She took the lieutenant's arm and the two awkwardly stepped toward the door.

Kyle looked to Tobias, who shook his head.

Lieutenant Damish stood half in and half out of the room. "My Lords, Lady Suzan is here."

Kyle motioned for them to enter. The interview went like the one before, until the last question.

Lady Suzan's voice fell an octave, "Well yes, a girl from the kitchen brought up the Zenith Lady's tray as I waited by the food lift. She said something about a broken pulley. The food lift worked fine when I fetched a tray for the Zenith later in the day. They must have fixed it."

Kyle and Tobias shifted in their chairs. "Can you describe the girl?" Kyle asked.

"She wore a white shift like they wear in the kitchen, with her hair wrapped in a blue cloth. She spoke quite rudely. I wanted to reprimand her, but I needed to hurry and deliver Mar… the Zenith Lady's tray." Lady Suzan's face colored; only family dared refer to Maress without her title, and never in public. "The tray, strangely, had the sweets the Zenith Lady likes so well. They always come up on her night tray, never in the morning."

Kyle's voice, calm and precise, lacked the emotion he felt. "Did you notice anything else?"

The girl shook her head. Kyle gave her the same admonitions that Lady Gayle received. He asked the lieutenant to see her escorted to her room with the same orders.

Halfway to the door, she looked back, "Oh, there is one thing more, my lords. Part of her little finger had been cut off, her right hand, I think. Does that help?"

Kyle masked his excitement, keeping his tone flat. "Yes, Lady Suzan, that helps." She continued to the door, her face showing more confidence.

Kyle watched them leave the room. Lieutenant Damish reappeared at the door, "My Lord, Lieutenant Rosh is waiting with a gentleman."

Kyle waved at them to enter, "You too, Lieutenant."

Lieutenant Rosh pulled a fifth chair over and adjusted it into the circle. Michael Gaz and Tobias exchanged greetings with a nod. Kyle waited until they sat. "Gentleman, this is High Healer Tobias Sternwood. You are ordered not to divulge any information to anyone except those of us in this room, the Mother Mavis, or to the Zenith Lord."

The officer's reply came in unison, "Yes, sir!"

Kyle went on, "The Zenith Lady has been murdered by poison." The officer's shock broke through their professionalism. It was their duty to protect all parts of the Zenith. Kyle's upraised hand stopped the questions on their lips from being voiced. "Every man under your command and every person on this floor over the last two days shall be sworn to secrecy when we leave this meeting. That means all one hundred men and anyone else noticed or reported being here: housekeepers, servants, ladies-in-waiting, anyone. The most important piece of knowledge is that an heir survived. At this time, *no one* is to know that! It will be treason if that knowledge escapes, and the person responsible dealt with accordingly. Those officers and men will serve here, effective now, with their billets on the floor below. They are restricted to these two floors until further orders are received from the Zenith or me. Lieutenant Damish, take care of the logistics. Lieutenant Rosh will organize the men, see to their orders, and notify the officers in the inner ring that I have scheduled a meeting at the ninth hour tonight in the Great Hall, guarded inside and out from the men assigned here. They are not to talk to anyone while on that assignment, and won't discuss any event they are privy to under the pain of treason." Kyle's eyes left no room for misunderstanding. "They are to say they are under my direct orders if an officer stops them, and to see me if there is a problem. Lieutenants, you have much to do before sunset, you are dismissed."

The lieutenants stood, saluted, and made for the door before Kyle's returned salute came to rest on his chest. He waited until the two lieutenants left and looked at Tobias, "This is Gaz; he performs many sensitive duties for the Zenith and me. Tobias nodded at the small, wiry man. Kyle went on to describe the two interview's particulars. "Gaz, find out how and who smuggled her into the inner circle. That also means there is an agent, a traitor able to pass through the gates!" The coldness in Kyle's speech brought an edge to the room. "You know what to do better than I." The man rose, bowed to Kyle and left the room as if going to a social function.

"Is he always so talkative?" Tobias asked.

Kyle smiled for the first time since seeing the babe. "He's a good man, and does an excellent job for the Zenith." The smile did not last. "What did you determine from the ladies?"

"Both are more frightened than they wanted to let on. I had a strong reading, and I believe they are telling the truth. I felt no deceit. In fact, I felt more than usual when feeling another's intentions. It's probably the tension from the circumstances; it went well for me. Lady Gayle is quite taken with Lieutenant Damish."

Tobias had a small grin on his face that Kyle did not reflect. Kyle started to comment when a knock came and the door opened. Lieutenant Rosh said only five words, "My Lords, he is awake!"

Kyle stopped Tobias on the way out. My Lord, you will remain here for a few days. Rolo will see to your needs." Tobias took the command with good grace.

Kyle asked the others to wait outside, and went alone into the room. Jarod still looked sleepy. Mother Mavis pulled a rocking chair close to him. The cradle sat in a far corner behind them. A beautiful woman Kyle had never seen sat beside the cradle on a small rocker suckling the babe, rocking gently and seemingly unconcerned about her bare breast. She casually pulled a cloth over the babe and her breast, showing no sign of embarrassment.

* * *

JAROD'S mind rose to consciousness. He felt relaxed. Memories flooded over him. *Maress! What could have done that to her?* He felt tightness grow in his chest and his hands balled into fists; fingernails bit at his palms. *Great Light's Source, how will I live without her? No! That cannot be. She must live!*

Jarod focused on the Mother. "Maress?"

Kyle stood, came to position, and spoke while staring straight ahead. "Zenith Lord of the Seven Realms." His face was stone again, a wet stone. He choked back a sigh and started again without any sign of propitiation or obsequiousness. "I, Apex Lord Kyle Byrne, Captain of the Zenith Lord's Guard, give over to you my life."

"Nooooooo…" Jarod moaned.

Kyle finished the ancient ritual. "I have failed to protect a part of the Zenith. My life is yours for all time."

Grief welled up again in Jarod's heart from the agony he saw in Kyle's face.

Mother Mavis looked up at Kyle. "Sit down! Jarod, my dear one, look at me."

His eyes rose up to look into the Mother's soul.

"I will grieve with you, my son, but now is not the time. Maress died of poison!"

Jarod looked from Mavis to Kyle. Kyle stared straight ahead, his facial muscles growing hard once again. Then, he knelt in front of him and took his hands. Jarod watched the anger build in Kyle and it seemed to transfer to him by touch; their faces set with deadly determination.

Jarod rose. "What arrangements have been made?"

Mother Mavis laid her hand on top of Jarod's hand. "Would you like to see your son before you go?"

His face softened slightly. "Where is he?"

The Mother looked at Trina, already moving to the chaise.

Jarod stood, looking and acting like new fathers have since time began. Then, determination and purpose returned, and his body stiffened.

"This is Trina. She will wet-nurse your son. She's a sweet child, although a bit unconventional at times."

Trina bowed her head and pulled the blanket down to expose the babe's sex. Jarod's conflict consumed him. *I want to take my son and hold him, love him!* He saw Maress at the time of her death in his mind's eye, and his stomach churned.

Trina held the child toward the most powerful man in her world, like offering candy to a child. He took his son in trembling hands. The babe started at his touch, and he handed the child to Trina who wrapped him in his blanket.

He looked at the Mother, "How can one person feel the depth of despair and the height of joy at the same time? I feel only despair now. I will wait to hold him when I can make room for him in my heart with joy."

The Mother smiled, but her countenance shouted despair. "Seek a balance, my son. Either great joy or great despair can cause harm at this time."

He watched Trina carry his son to the rocker, humming a tune. He focused on Kyle. "What has been done?" Kyle went over the day's events. He stopped with the Guard Officers' meeting called for ninth hour. Jarod looked at him with new eyes. "When did you last sleep?"

"I don't know, the day before…"

He took his best, true friend by the shoulders, his voice direct, flat. "The meeting is over five hours off, and it will be a long night. Sleep now, and meet me in the anteroom. The last thing I need is you too tired to function."

Kyle embraced Mavis and kissed her lightly on the cheek. She slowly sat down as the door closed behind him.

Jarod fought the anger and rage that filled him. He refused to regard Maress or his son while those emotions guided his actions. He found the peace he sought deep inside him; it surfaced slowly, and finally he took a deep breath without shaking. He looked at his son for a moment, and then walked through the door to the adjoining room to be alone with his wife for the last time.

12

JAROD brought the candles closer to the tome before him in a dark, subterranean room deep beneath the Spires. The sadness in his face slowly hardened into determination, and a stone-like façade captured his features. He slowly closed the tome, wrapped it in its protective covering and placed it in the towering bookcase. He had not noticed his stomach growling, and the pangs of hunger took him by surprise.

After finishing lastmeal in his room, he visited the nursery. The child grasped a silver ring that had once been Jarod's from Trina's hand while gurgling and thrashing with glee. Small amounts of tension drained away when he saw his son.

Trina curtsied, smiling warmly. "My Zenith Lord, have you decided on a name?"

"Yes, but it's not supposed to be publicized until his Naming Day. You are not the public, are you?" The obvious and pleasant mirth in him lasted but a moment. Sharpness and impenetrability returned to his face. Trina smiled and shook her head. "His name will be Marc."

She looked at the babe critically. "You chose well, my Zenith Lord."

A soft knock at the door, followed by Rolo's entrance, tensed him up again. Rolo spoke softly. "The Captain and Master Gaz wish an audience, my Zenith."

Jarod frowned, returning his attention to his son; he lightly stroked Marc's head before nodding once. Rolo bowed himself out. Jarod glanced at Trina, who was tending to Marc's latest need. He took the babe and cradled him in his arm when she finished. The babe's eyes focused on him, and Marc made the gurgling noises babes make. He handed Marc to Trina and walked away.

Kyle and Gaz saw the babe when the door fully opened. Kyle grinned from ear to ear. Gaz smiled too, a rare sight. Jarod led the way to his small study. He went to the armoire on the near wall, retrieved the finest brandy in the Seven Realms, and carried it and three glasses to a group of plush chairs around a table. Kyle and Gaz joined him when he motioned, handing them each a glass when they reached him. "To my son, gentlemen." The three men touched their glasses together and each took a sip of brandy.

Kyle spoke first after Jarod sat. "Gaz and I have been discussing yesterday and today. We feel only someone already within the Spires could have accomplished Maress' murder. It had to be someone able to get into the inner circle. That took help. The strict procedures keep someone unknown from getting that far without an escort. The only clue we have at this time is a wagon belonging to a man that delivers wine to us. The wagon was found abandoned, and the man is missing." His sigh conveyed his frustration.

"Lieutenant Rosh went to inquire at the dock where the man named…" Kyle looked at Gaz.

"Kirsh."

Kyle nodded and went on, "Kirsh has not been seen since he left on a delivery the morning of the poisoning." Kyle stopped his report abruptly, looking at Jarod's reaction. The Zenith Lord's demeanor did not change, and he motioned for Kyle to continue. "A warehouseman said he visited the common room every night located in the inn where he let a room in the attic. He hadn't been there either, and missed one night a week ago. The innkeeper hadn't seen him. Nothing in his room proved of consequence to our investigation. We are now searching the inner and outer circles. The Guardsmen and Spires' staff have all accounted for their movements. We suggest you keep the Spires sealed until we can finish our search. We have ordered the men to report to one of the search's supervising officers if they find anything, and to touch nothing. We have more than two hundred men working on the search between Gaz and myself. I will let Gaz comment on an additional point."

Gaz spoke confidently. "My Zenith, I have reports of three murdered prostitutes found in the canal at different times, within a few feet of each other, over the last ten days. Each had her throat cut by the same type of blade and in the same manner. My men are making inquiries, both officially and unofficially. We have not had murders of this type in the City for over two years; to have three in one week now and have the treachery here is suspicious. We don't know if they are related, and until we know for certain, we cannot discount a connection. My men are also checking for anything else unusual in the City. I will keep you apprised as things develop."

Jarod nodded, somewhat overwhelmed by the amount of activity going on around him. He wondered; *how do they find the time?*

He looked at the man he trusted most and a man he had begun to trust. Kyle's trust came from a lifelong friendship, mutual respect, love and a proven ability. Gaz' trust came from his previous deeds and his father's recommendation. He believed himself lucky to have such men to serve him and the Seven Realms. "Thank you. I'm pleased with your efforts." He looked at Gaz. "Will you excuse us? I have a personal matter to discuss with Kyle."

Gaz sat his empty glass down, rose and bowed his head. "Of course, my Zenith."

He left before Jarod could replace his glass with one of water. He noticed Kyle had taken only that first sip when he toasted Marc. The rest of the evening deserved a clear head.

"You look rested, a bit. Did you sleep?"

"About four hours, enough for now."

"Kyle, what do you know about Gaz?"

"The same as you, I guess."

"Me? I know very little about the man. Father said he would discuss Gaz with me, but he never did. He told me I could trust his skill and that he did a good job. I have been working to complete the efforts Father started—and those damnable inspection tours—for the last two years. I never had time to delve into Gaz' function. Of course, now I can see some of those functions. I still know little about him."

Kyle tried to hide his look of surprise. "He's the top spymaster in the Seven Realms, and reports directly to me. He heads two rather large forces, one officially and one unofficially. It will take a good while to go over everything he does. Ask him for a briefing later in the week when you can set aside some time. He genuinely respects you, and I think he will be pleased to discuss his current projects with you. He's proud of his accomplishments, although he does not express it often. Letting him know you are interested will be good for him."

Jarod sipped a little of his water. "Make the arrangements. Now, I need the bath Rolo is preparing before the meeting tonight. He should have the hot water ready soon. I don't think I have ever been this tired. We will both need rest by the time this night ends."

Kyle took a final sip of brandy, leaving nearly a full glass. "The sleep this afternoon helped, but I'm sure I'll sleep soundly the next chance I get." When Rolo came to fetch Jarod for his bath, Kyle excused himself and left.

The bath helped ease his tension. He reluctantly pulled himself from the tub after the water became tepid. He dried; put on a robe that he left untied and appraised the mirror's reflection of his face, looking for physical changes caused by pain or grief. He saw none. Somehow, he found that strange. His muscular, defined body reflected back at him. He and Kyle exercised most days, when possible. Many called his rugged face too handsome. Thick, sandy colored hair fell to his shoulders. Sparse hair spread across his upper chest and then made a line to his navel and beyond. He kept his face clean-shaven except in the field, when time and circumstance did not permit.

Rolo laid out his dress uniform, marking him the Supreme Commander of Military Forces in the Seven Realms. The title came from the last war with evil. Their recorded history mostly destroyed during the conflict, left fragments of predominantly useless information hinting at a marvelous civilization with technology far beyond their comprehension. The form of government for the Seven Realms and the Zenith's position survived from that time. Jarod did not mind wearing that uniform; he hated the State Regalia.

He dressed quickly in black calf boots over black pants, a padded, white leather baldric over a long-sleeved white shirt with cuffs and banded collar trimmed in gold, a black vest, and a gold sash that bound his waist. The vest had a finely embroidered deathcat the size of his fist over the heart. He swung a heel-length, crimson cape lined in gold wormcloth across his shoulders, fastening it with a gold braid from his right to left shoulder. The cape displayed the same embroidery as the vest, emblazoned over the left side of his chest, except much larger, with the deathcat's eyes holding the fire of red rubies. His crimson-plumed, gold helm, yet another symbol of his position, was always carried indoors, not worn.

The ceremonial sword hooked in place on the baldric through eyelets in the sash, vest and shirt. The weapon's hilt and scabbard, heavily overlaid in gold and jewels, looked impressive, belying its true condition. A sharp blade made from inferior steel centuries ago, and never meant for use; the Zenith would have needed to be a midget with arms like tree trunks to compensate for its balance. He prayed an attack never came while carrying such a weapon. Its purpose to impress achieved its function. His battle sword weighed three times its weight and cut fine linen in two pieces as it floated across the blade; it could decapitate a man's head with minimum force and he could have used it for shaving if not for its size. The baldric, worn outside the shirt and protective clothing in battle dress, provided increased functionality with places for various pouches and additional weapons.

Tonight would be difficult for him and his men. Their oaths to guard the Zenith lay shattered. *They failed in their primary responsibility and duty. Five thousand men in the strongest fortress in the world couldn't protect one woman! The last assassination attempt against a Zenith occurred over five hundred years ago. Lulled into a false sense of security was not an excuse. No excuse will suffice!*

Jarod would take the oaths of over a thousand men tonight: The same oath Kyle tried to give earlier that he had cut short. He owned their lives from tonight on, until every one of them died. The oath's absolute finality served a purpose. If he ordered a man to cut his own throat, he would obey. Anyone who refused betrayed his sworn oath, and would probably face death by his own fellows. The Zenith, the only power that might defeat the Dark's Source in the next war, demanded protection. The death of the Zenith promised a serious setback that assuredly spelled defeat by Dark's Source. Great need required great sternness and greater determination.

The Zenith was comprised of more than one person; he and his immediate family, wife, and children made up the whole, the Zenith. The male ruled over political affairs and the army in most cases, like Jarod had done. The Zenith Lady took a more active role at times, and in some incidences ruled as he now did. Maress sponsored many causes for the general populace throughout the Seven Realms. The populace would greatly mourn her. The family, was loved by the people for many generations, and respected by the realms' High Lords for their high standards of conduct and benevolence. Jarod had not considered who might replace Maress to continue the projects she started for the people's benefit. But he promised himself he would not let them fall by the wayside.

Suddenly, the vacancy overwhelmed him. He tried not to think of Maress' death. He knew the Mother had been right when she told him about balance and could not obtain that balance by denying her death, but tonight, he wished not to think on it. He made a final appraisal of the mirror's reflection and hurried out, his rage hidden.

Jarod stopped in the nursery before going to the Great Hall. Trina walked the floor with his son on her shoulder. She glanced up at him and put one finger to her lips. He stood for a moment, looking at the wonder of his son. In his mind's eye, she became Maress—not Trina—for a split second. He straightened and quietly left the room.

The uneventful trip down twelve levels with the light of one small lamp passed unnoticed, His deliberations focused on his realm, Stonefire. Not the biggest of the Seven Realms, however, the city of Stonefire grew to be the largest ever known. The remaining six realms, ruled by High Lords, swore allegiance and fidelity to Stonefire, or rather, to the Zenith Lord.

Jarod opened the door and stepped out into the anteroom. He saw anguish had returned to Kyle's face now, and he looked at the Zenith Lord with difficulty. Kyle snapped to position and saluted. Jarod walked to him and put his arms around him in a tight embrace. Kyle's face had softened when he released his grip. His face had not changed, but his voice softened. "It is not your fault."

"It is my duty, and I failed you—"

Jarod raised his hand; stern coldness returned to his speech. "I need you tonight, as I always have and always will. We need to survive this last death. Tomorrow, we work for life. The life of a new part of the Zenith, and the life of a new spirit joined with Light's Source."

*　*　*

KYLE had a faint smile on his face when he went through the door at the rear of the Great Hall. Tapestries hung from high up to the floor, concealing the anteroom's existence, scarcely three feet away. The tapestry's design overlapped, with the pattern repeated in front of the door to the anteroom. It gave the visual impression that one materialized from thin air by moving between the tapestries into the Hall. Only the Captain of the Guard could approach within twenty feet of the dais, enhancing the tapestry's illusion.

The dais was set immediately on the tapestry's display side. Seven levels represented the Seven Realms in a stepped, pyramidal design, as did the seven kinds of gems set into the gold throne centered on the highest level. The gold and gems mined in Stonefire remained unequaled throughout the rest of the world.

The positional title of Captain of the Guard belied Kyle's importance; in fact, he held the rank of Apex, Supreme Commander of Military Forces for the Zenith Lord and the Seven Realms. In addition, Jarod's father had elevated him to Lord of the Seven Realms for exceptional performance to Stonefire. His older brother's inheritance of the familial titles and lands would make an unusual situation of two brothers with the title of "Lord" in the same immediate family at the same time. Although Kyle would not inherit lands, Jarod and his father had made sure he might never want for anything. He could retire at any time and live in a High Lord's sumptuousness. In Kyle's mind, that option did not exist. He felt certain that Jarod knew he would not leave his service until age or death forced him out.

Kyle stepped between the tapestries. The Great Hall swallowed the one thousand two hundred and forty three

Guard Officers from the inner circle and hummed from soft whispers scattered about. The Great Hall's acoustics proved phenomenal. Speaking in a voice slightly raised in volume from normal speech carried throughout the great room. The men aligned by rank, standing fifty abreast stood in loose formation. The men's uniforms resembled Jarod's, except for his golden and Kyle's silver trim. They wore crimson; they also did not have rubies sewn into their clothing.

An Apex officer from the first rank saw Kyle emerge and yelled, "FOCUS!" One thousand, two hundred and forty three pairs of heels snapped to position, and fists crossed over hearts.

Over a thousand men can make a real thunder of noise. What would it be like filled with five times this many people? Kyle wondered. He went to stand beside a plush chair located in front and right of the dais to wait for the Zenith Lord and then returned his men's salute. The guardsmen's fists dropped in unison to their sides.

Jarod did not keep them waiting. He slipped between the tapestries and into the room's light. The same man as before yelled, "FOCUS ON THE ZENITH LORD!" All present dropped to their right knee, fist to heart and head bowed.

Kyle did not hear Jarod's approach, but did not start when he felt a hand on his shoulder. "Stand!" Jarod whispered in his ear. "I want them to know you are not in disfavor."

Kyle followed the order with lumps in his throat and heart. Jarod ascended the seven steps, and stood facing his officers. "I am one with the Stones, and the Stones are protected." The men stood to focus position. Many noted that their commander already stood beside his chair.

* * *

JAROD looked out over his officers. He had talked with every one of them at least once over the last two years.

He knew and respected them all. "Lord Kyle and Gentlemen, what you will hear tonight is the Zenith's business. No one outside the Guard is to know the facts I bring to you, save one fact alone. The Zenith Lady Maress, part of the Zenith, is dead." He tried to keep the pain of those words from showing to his men and found partial success. "The Zenith Lady died of poison early yesterday morning." Rustling voices sounded throughout the men.

"FOCUS!" Kyle shouted. His men went rigid once again. Kyle faced his Zenith Lord, drew his sword, knelt with the blade lying across his outstretched hands, and bowed his head. His voice carried throughout the Great Hall. "My Zenith, I and the officers of my command offer you our lives for the failure to protect the Zenith Lady. My life is yours!"

Every officer bent his knee and repeated Kyle's words, "MY LIFE IS YOURS!"

After the deafening sound subsided, Jarod ordered, "RISE." His eyes went around the room making eye contact with many of his officers. His men's dour faces remained frozen in place. "Your lives are spared."

The men's faces changed little from before. They all felt that they had failed in their highest goal, order, and duty: to protect the Zenith.

"My wife died a horrible death," he continued. "Her murderer will die a death of agony beyond description. You will be my instrument in causing that death. There are two facts that are not to be repeated outside the Guard until we make the announcement. First, a new part of the Zenith has been born; I have a son."

His men's faces broke their dour expression and a few even smiled.

"Second, no one outside this room is to know how the Zenith Lady died. There will be a meeting of senior staff at ten tonight and messages sent shortly to the realms' ambassadors to summon them to a High Council of

State. The Zenith Lady will be celebrated into Light's Source tomorrow morning at sunrise." Jarod raised his hand to the hilt of his sword.

Gaz pulled away from his vantage point far above and waved a white cloth at the closest of three bell towers. The great bell pealed, followed one minute later by the next and one minute after that by the third. The bells pealed in rotation, the sounds would carry to the every part of Stonefire one minute apart until sunrise. The mournful ring caused by the bell's padded striker had the desired effect on his men. The bell's first note sent messengers from the outer gate to the ambassador's residences located on the Circle of Villas; a circle of lavish embassies a scant mile from the outer walls.

Jarod continued while the first bell's sound died. "The Guard will provide full honors. I will receive the ambassadors and their guests here. The ambassadors' Chairs of State, thirty feet from the Dais, the archer's covers above manned with our best marksmen. Every person entering the Great Hall will be assigned to an officer for observation at all times, as discretely as possible and at a distance. Your detailed orders will come shortly after the senior staff meeting later tonight. Apex Lord Kyle will recount the manner of the Zenith Lady's death in detail." Kyle's muscles tensed, but he did not blanch. "No detail will be left out!"

He went down the rear of the dais and disappeared through the tapestries.

* * *

THIS is the least I can do to save him some of the pain, Kyle decided. *He must have been busy while I slept.* He started an account of the last day and a half. The room remained deathly quiet as he spoke.

13

THORD finished his first small keg of wine as he heard the bell. Not sure at first, he listened as another bell sounded farther off a minute later. He threw the window open as the third bell rang from the closest proximity to the inn where he had been for the last two days. Its melancholy sound filled the room, bringing relief and joy. The right side of his mouth pulled into a gruesome smile while he shut the window. He did not like the idea of staying in the City any longer than necessary. *It damn well took them long enough,* his mind screamed in protest. *Now, where are those fools, Kirsh and his bitch? Why are they not here?*

Thord knew they had not seen his face. The cowl and the candle's placement had not allowed Kirsh or Claudia to see much during the one time they'd met. They could not identify him if caught. Still, he wanted to be away, preferably with them dead.

Claudia had the attributes for the job; nondescript features and a mild voice. She looked respectable enough dressed like the kitchen's staff, or so he had considered her at the time. Now, Thord's mind questioned his judgment. He had covered his tracks: changed inns—and women—three times in the last ten days. *Those women won't talk—it would be hard to do while floating in the canal with their throats cut.* His smile returned with the thought.

Thord reviewed the plan yet again in his mind, looking for flaws. Kirsh drove the wagon carrying the barrels of wine from the loading dock to the Spire's inner circle. His mouthy bitch, Claudia, had balked at the idea of a sealed barrel even after Kirsh's assurances that the small air holes supplied enough air. Thord produced another gold coin that she grabbed and said nothing more. Kirsh would let her out of the barrel at a corridor's unguarded section leading to the lifts frequented by the kitchen staff. She would make her way to the seventh level, report to the kitchen at the proper time and request the Zenith Lady's tray, explaining that the food lift to the Chambers did not work, and she had been sent to hand carry it to the twelfth level. She would add the poison to the water and place the sweets on the tray. Thord wondered what additional events his paid underlings had wrought.

He walked from the City earlier in the day to the road leading to the Spires a mile away. The curving road broke through giant hardwoods, and he saw the outer circle's mammoth wall and the broad, closely guarded gates. The lack of activity unsettled him. A heavily guarded road to the left, led to the Circle of Villas.

Where are they? The question kept nagging at his mind. He could leave. High Lord Mountglen said nothing about staying for conformation. Nevertheless, his lord expected him to be thorough. Thord finally decided to return to Mountglen and immediately felt better. He missed his sport. He followed Mountglen's orders, contacted the person his lord had selected that had access to the inner circle, and set the plan in motion. "Hells to the Dark One, I'm going home."

Lifting his pack over his shoulder, Thord took the inn's rear stairway to the street. He walked briskly, in his peculiar graceful motion, toward the stable he had found the first day in the City. The stable boy led his big stallion from its stall when he saw Thord coming. *The boy has a way with horses. Not many people can handle the brute I ride.* The horse looked groomed and well fed; the boy had him saddled quickly. Thord's good mood, fostered by his decision to leave, grew. "Are my supplies ready?"

* * *

"YES sir; I packed them myself." He pointed to Thord's

pack that had been empty when he arrived, packed to the brim. He thought, *where have I seen a man walk like that?*

* * *

THORD felt wonderful; he would soon be home and have his sport. He fished in the outer pocket of his vest and threw the boy a coin. Thord did not notice it until it shimmered in the light. Gold gleamed like no other metal.

The boy's face froze in shock. His hands, however, had no such problem; he caught the gold coin, bowing deeply. Thord's gruesome smile lasted until after he secured the saddlepacks over the horse, mounted, and rode off at a trot.

* * *

THE boy looked at Thord's retreating back until he disappeared onto the road leading from the City, then, he ran to the inn's rear entrance adjoining the stable. He remembered where he saw him.

He found the innkeeper at his usual place behind the bar. "Master Taggert, sir, I have to leave for a bit. It won't take long, sir. Please."

The boy knew the innkeeper valued his extra work and he rarely asked a boon. He grabbed his pit boy when he passed the bar's end. "Spell Karl for a while." The pit boy started to complain; the innkeeper held up his hand for silence. "He's kept the fires in the pit going for you more times than I can count and spitted the meat when we are busy. Now spell him!" The boys hurried away without speaking. Karl smiled.

He entered the shop two blocks away and went through the hanging drape in the rear and up the stairs to the roof, and walked directly to the old man, Vatore, rather than looking at the birds as he usually did. "I have to send a bird."

Vatore looked into his eyes. Karl thought he might

protest, but Vatore would let the boy reap the consequences of his actions, as he had told him many times, and handed him the small box without speaking. The boy reached in and selected a color. The old man merely shrugged when he took the box and the small red peg Karl chose. Vatore selected a pigeon, attached the peg to the identification band on the bird's leg and threw it up into the air. They watched it circle once and then disappear in the looming darkness toward the Spires.

The old man looked down at the boy. "I hope you know what you are doing." Karl smiled and left for the inn.

14

CALLY knocked for the third time at the door to His Holiness' chambers, three hours before dawn. Handford opened the door and gasped. He had never been so close to an eagle, much less one of gigantic proportions. "You cannot disturb His Holiness at this hour! Have you lost your senses?" Light flooded the room when the door to the Holy One's bedchamber opened. Travis motioned Cally to him.

He carried the bird into the open chambers, his eyes wide. "What is wrong, man? Have you not seen a man in his sleepcloth before?"

Cally stopped short, looking around the room. "Yes your Holiness...I mean, no your Holiness...I never dreamt I might be here...I believed it would be much grander." His face colored as he realized what he had just said, and to whom he had said it.

His Holiness chuckled, "I'm still a priest, Cally. Now, let's have a look at this fine bird." He clutched his Stone through his sleepcloth while Cally removed the hood from the bird. It blinked in the sudden light, then as before, settled his gaze directly on His Holiness' eyes. The two stayed locked—eye-to-eye—a long time for an exchange. Finally, His Holiness nodded and ran a finger over the bird's head feathers and scratched. Cally's mouth dropped open. The eagle actually murmured to His Holiness. He motioned for the Birdmaster to replace the hood after a moment of petting. Cally's amazement grew when the eagle did not fight the hood. His Holiness smiled. "Be sure he's well fed and tell Handford to send the Prelates to me." Cally closed his mouth when His

Holiness went into an adjoining room to dress.

* * *

TRAVIS expected Prelate Daniel to arrive first; he was not wrong. Dressed as ordered in plain riding pants, shirt, boots, and a cloak dyed the same gray that His Holiness wore. Travis looked him over once and nodded his approval. Their clothes matched perfectly, as he had planned. Prelate Thurston arrived moments later. His silver-trimmed collars and cuffs and his cloak emblazoned with a silver representation of the Tower of Stones did not please His Holiness. "We will travel without rank. You will change and we leave within the hour." Prelate Thurston's face did not break composure, but he bowed sharply, spun on his heel, and disappeared through the door. His Holiness shook his head slowly from side to side.

"Your Holiness, Thurston has not been from the Tower crater in years. He feels comfortable in his station. This will be a hard trip for him."

"I know Daniel; he will see the sense of it during our travel. Tell Handford to see that everyone is ready to depart in one hour. We will meet at the stable." His Holiness went to the far wall, knelt on the pillow and lifted his eyes to the painting above as Daniel closed the door on his way out.

Travis traced the rays of white light falling across the countryside with his eyes. The Tower of Stones stood bathed in Blessed Light. His favorite painting nurtured his meditations for hours at a time. He considered taking it with him; the trip should take no more than a week or two. His Holiness chuckled and shook his head, knowing the falseness of his thought. He savored the painting for one last moment. *I will miss it!*

The guards and stable hands fell to their knees when His Holiness entered the stable. Travis' voice, a full baritone with great resonance, projected a soothing, meaningful tone that fostered good feelings in those who heard it. He did not have the singsong meter of so many of the clerics; instead, a message of force rang with his words. Many believed it had played a part in his election. Travis' essence, character, presence of mind, keen insight, and deep, abiding faith had brought him to the highest office of his religion, the one religion of the Seven Realms. "May Light's Source protect you." He motioned his supplicants to rise.

Prelate Thurston entered in a state of agitation, dressed as ordered. He bowed to His Holiness and went to a stable boy and guard standing next to a horse he rightly assumed was his. "It has been years since I sat on one of these beasts. I will break my neck before I'm halfway there!" Everyone in the stable—that could see him—looked constrained not to laugh. Thurston tried to mount several times with the help of the two men. He finally found his seat, half by chance, on a fairly large but gentle mare. The remaining travelers mounted their horses as Thurston gave the mare a sharp kick. She shot from the stable with Thurston waving his arms and yelling.

One of the guards rode after Thurston at full gallop while the others started out at a trot. They found Thurston a mile ahead with the guard gently giving the Prelate instructions on riding. To his credit, Thurston had somehow managed to stay seated. The guard mounted and eased his horse beside the mare as Thurston gently nudged her forward. She fell in behind the leading horses and Travis chuckled to himself when he saw Thurston practicing the breathing exercises that preceded meditation for calmness. The guard fell in behind, finally able to laugh quietly without the scorn of a prelate directed at him.

They soon reached the crater walls encircling their hidden retreat. The steep cliffs of rock rose four hundred feet high at the lowest, and over seven hundred feet at the highest. They slanted inward from the top, and were too steep to climb inside or outside the crater. The crater stretched approximately nine miles across the center of a nearly perfect circle. The one passageway from the valley proved difficult to find from inside the crater, and nearly impossible to find from the outside without prior knowledge of its existence. It meandered back and forth several times for several hundred yards. They had to dismount and lead their animals through sections where rock formed arches and overhangs, with some parts of the trail enlarged to accommodate horses and pack animals. Thurston mounted on the first try when they emerged from the passage; if he was trying not to show his satisfaction, he failed.

The terrain outside the crater dropped steeply into a small valley next to the mountain range that led eventually to the backside of the Spires. Their journey skirted the mountains, and they would approach the Spires from the northeast. Few people outside the Tower crater's occupants knew of its location. There was no reason for anyone to seek out that part of the mountains and unlikely anyone could find the entrance to the crater if they did. Still, guards kept a close watch on the crater's inner slope.

The Tower's largely self-supporting community of about three thousand hid from the outside world to be at peace and without its cares. Its scholars, priests, and workers had sworn to protect its location and purpose with secrecy. The Tower's staff carefully screened possible newcomers to fill whatever current vacancies they had. They looked for those priests who liked and appreciated a small community cut off from the rest of Stonefire and the world. They left the comfort and security of that cloistered life at the entrance to the crater.

His Holiness, Travis Grant, felt eyes watching him, and a new and strong presence. Surprisingly, he didn't feel threatened.

15

THE first rays of the new dawn glistened through the darkness onto a small section of ground, a space two hundred feet long and fifty feet wide, resting between the face of a Spire and the Keep's walls. The garden had been incorporated into the design for the latest expansion to the Spires, five centuries ago. Its only entrance passed through a tunnel from the Zenith's Chambers. Jarod, Kyle, Apex Glen Strong of the City, Apex Richard Dews of the Outer Circle, Apex Gerald Wright of the Inner Circle and Apex Dexter Young, Kyle's second, carried the Zenith Lady's litter. The High Priest of Light's Source for the Spires and his counterpart from the City, waited on the far side of the enclosure. The bells of the Spires stopped. The eerie silence after the mournful tolling throughout the night did not last. Kettledrums sounded in perfect cadence from the top of ramparts: ten beats, followed by one beat, followed by two beats, pausing five seconds before the next series. Rock bounced the sound, mixed with echoes, projecting resounding waves of booming thunder outward over the City.

The two priests, one at each end of the funeral pyre, turned as one and bowed toward the light, not worshipping the sun, but the goodness of Light's Source it symbolized. The drums struck an additional triple beat at the end of the series. The pallbearers slowly approached the pyre. Maress, resting on white canvas, glided over the mound of cut wood at the end of the short journey and was gently settled into position. The drums added another beat at the end of this series: four this time. Mother Mavis, Tobias, and Lady Deanna entered the conclave. The party fanned out behind the Zenith and knelt on crimson cushions. He remained standing. Five beats.

The Dialogue of Closure began. The priests intoned a chant together. "Who brings one to be joined to Light's Source in eternal Light and Goodness?"

"We, Jarod Greatstone, Zenith Lord of the Seven Realms, bring My part, the Zenith Lady Maress Greatstone, daughter of the High Lord and Lady of Northmount. We present this part of Ourselves, taken before her time by foul means. We pray that Light's Source receives her in a state of Grace and Purity." Six beats.

"We, the servants of Light's Source, join this child, taken before her time, to be with Light's Source. We plead for her to be in the brilliance and joy of Light's Source forever.

"We feel her Light upon our spirit; to live with and know she is with us." Seven beats.

The priests took the torches from holders drilled into the Spire and lit the pyre. Flames shot skyward. The incense-soaked logs burned brightly. The drums stopped. Triple fanfares from a hundred trumpets sounded from the walls of the Spires out over the City, announcing a new spark added to Light's Source. The priests and guests slowly retraced their steps into the Spires. Jarod stood for several long moments before walking toward the passage. In going, he looked up and saw large birds carrying messages in six different directions to the High Lords of the Six Realms. One of them also went to a mother and father.

16

THE old man stood outside his son's shop, listening to the drums, counting the end beats. It had been only two years since the old Zenith went to Light's Source; *"may he rest in eternal peace."* He hoped this ceremony had not taken the Zenith Lord, but he feared the worst. The Zenith had done wonders in the two years he had held the Dais, his Lady, too. The trumpets pulled him from his deliberations. They would be here soon; would have been here already except for the ceremony at the Spires. Hardly ten minutes passed before he heard horses' hooves coming at a trot.

The officer wore the rank of a Gal, a commander of over eight hundred men. One Lieutenant and two pikemen rode with him. They wore dress uniforms; again, the old man looked toward the Spires. The Gal reined in beside the old man who looked up into his dark eyes, "The Inn of the Red Bull, two blocks down on the right, stable boy named Karl." The officer saluted the old man and the four guardsmen rode off. The old man shook his head at his misgivings. *What has that boy got himself into? I should have questioned him. He may end up in the courts if he doesn't know what he's doing.* The old man walked into the shop rubbing the back of his neck.

* * *

THE innkeeper swore, irritated from the constant pounding on his door. Did the fool outside, with his incessant pounding, not care that his guests could hear? "Stop that pounding and go away, I have no rooms!"

The Gal's voice boomed like the pounding. "Open in

the name of the Zenith's Guard!" The peep door jerked open and closed just as fast, the door's heavy bolts slid free. The Gal spoke before the man could begin sputtering his apologies. "You have a stable boy named Karl. Where is he?"

"Over the stable. The stairway is in the rear. I will take you."

The Gal held up his hand. "We will find him. He won't return today. Thank you for your trouble."

Master Taggert closed his open mouth and looked at an empty road as the three guardsmen disappeared around the corner.

* * *

THE guardsmen climbed the stairway and knocked at the door, though not as loudly as before. Karl spoke sleepily from the other side. "If you want a horse, it will be a minute. I have to dress." Minutes later, he opened the door and nearly fainted; a Gal with a contingent of men in full dress uniform exceeded his expectations. The officer's face softened. "Just come with us lad; you're not in trouble if you had a good reason for sending us the message."

"I did have, you will see." Karl grabbed a rolled paper from his room, followed the men down the steps and took the offered arm. The pikeman steadied Karl while he used the stirrup and swung his leg over the horse's neck in one smooth motion. No one had to tell him to hang on. They left at a full trot at once, riding halfway up the gradual, twisting slope, passing the hardwoods to the Spires entrance before the enormity of his actions entered Karl's mind, making him shiver.

17

JAROD saw Lady Deanna leaving the suites of rooms known as the Chambers when he returned from the conclave. He called to her. She came to him and curtsied low to the floor. He motioned for her to rise. "Lady Deanna, the Mother told me of the work you did to arrange the ceremony this morning, and the effort you put forth while Maress lay ill. I want you to know how much I appreciate your efforts on her behalf. I request that you remain in service to me for a while longer. I understand you know the workings of the staff and how to get things accomplished. Maress handled those things for me...before." His voice lowered as his self-control took over. "I want you to take charge and be my secretary, at least for the next several weeks."

"Zenith Lord, I'm honored to help in any way I can. I worked with the Zenith Lady on many of her projects, and I know the staff. I will do whatever I can."

"There are several guest suites outside the main entrance to the Chambers. It might make it easier for you if you took one of those for your own," he continued, letting his ideas run together; something he rarely did. "There will be a High Council meeting combined with a High Council of State. I want only the ambassadors, no guests. We will use the 'State' room instead of the Great Hall. The High Council will have preference in seating. I will leave everything else to you. The Pinnacle, Lord Lockley is already in route to the Spires. I greatly appreciate your efforts."

Lady Deanna smiled. "You honor me, my Zenith. I will start at once."

Jarod went toward the suite he had taken over since he returned. He could not yet sleep in *their* bedchamber. Halfway there, he heard steps running toward him. He turned to see Lieutenant Rosh approaching. Unknown to Jarod, Rosh worked for Gaz in an attachment his father had set up for special investigations. According to his father, they had been quite effective in various operations, but his father never explained more before his death. Jarod had no idea what those operations entailed. Rosh saluted and handed him a note:

MUST SEE YOU AND CAPTAIN AFTER STATE – URGENT! ~ GAZ

Jarod nodded to Rosh, "Agreed. Anteroom." Rosh saluted again and retreated the way he came.

* * *

ROLO, the chief steward, had laid out his uniform and robes of State as Jarod entered and started undressing. Rolo had been taking care of him since the age of six, and had bathed him in ointment for sunburn when he had fallen asleep lying in the sun on his balcony, nude. Over the years, the steward had seen him nude a few times by chance. It still embarrassed him, and his bald head grew scarlet from the top downward, including his ears. He felt his job included the Zenith's privacy. Jarod's uninhibited nature meant nothing to him. However, Jarod soon learned the fastest way to get Rolo to hurry with his duties was the impression of impending undressing. He went into the closet area from Rolo's sight to save the man any uneasiness. Rolo left the room in less than three minutes.

* * *

JAROD stripped to his privatecloth and donned a floor length robe of gray linen, tied with a crimson sash. He returned to the reception room of his suite, sat in a plush chair, put his feet up on a matching footstool and closed his eyes for a few seconds before the knock came at the door.

"Enter."

The door opened and Rosh stepped into the room. He acted as if seeing the Zenith Lord at his ease happened everyday. *Rolo should be more like Rosh,* Jarod decided.

Rosh crossed the room, saluted and handed Jarod another message. He broke the seal.

> *Lord Lockley arrives - three days. I arranged for a guard to escort.*
> *Pinnacle arrives - five days. He travels with his own guard.*
> *Fresh mounts sent to speed the trip.*
> *Gaz*

"Is there a reply, my Zenith?" Jarod looked up at the man, who was staring straight ahead.

"No. Rosh. Where did you train?"

"At the Academy, my Zenith."

"Nothing else?"

Rosh relaxed a little and his eyes looked down to Jarod. "Gaz trained me, my Zenith."

"Thank you, Rosh." Rosh snapped to position and saluted before leaving, closing the door behind him. Jarod started to relax again. *Gaz trained him. In what?* He had inherited Gaz two years ago, when he took the Dais after his father's death from a riding accident. The accident still bothered him because his father's horsemanship exceeded the best riders in the Seven Realms. Richard told his son several times that he would talk to him about Gaz, but he never had in any detail. He did let him know that Gaz could be trusted, and could handle most anything that came up. He just never told him what kinds of things he handled, and after his death he continued the projects his father had started. The inspection tour came next.

Kyle had asked if Jarod wanted him to continue

working as he had for his father. Jarod readily agreed and then got lost in his coming marriage to Maress. Now, he understood his function, and began to realize his excellence at what he did. *I need to spend some time with Gaz,* he decided, looking forward to the briefing.

Jarod gazed over his balcony when he heard a trumpet. He saw the huge inner gate swing open and a carriage roll toward the entrance. His men surrounded it in double file; an officer on horse led the carriage slowly forward. Men in full dress uniform stood in every possible place a passenger could view, spaced three feet apart and at position. The realm's fanfare sounded again, and its flag raised as the carriage entered through the inner gates. The flagpoles circled Stonefire's flagpole, five feet taller than the rest. He could not make out the crest on the side of the carriage, but the fanfare and the white horses identified it as Northmount's ambassador. They bred the best horses in the Seven Realms.

He returned from the balcony and started dressing. He had not worn the State regalia since his wedding. He tried not to think about that day. Rolo would be there with the coat, robe, and crown shortly. He pulled on white stockings, then skintight pants. Slipping the shirt over his head, he was tucking in the excess material when a knock came at the door.

Rolo entered with an armed escort, the Robes of State, and the box containing the Crown of State. Ten men, called a pebble, took up posts outside the door as Jarod struggled into his boots. The mirror reflected the brilliant white of his clothes and boots. Rolo held the calf length coat for him to slip his arms into. It fit him snugly from the waist up. The bottom of the coat flared below the waist, permitting a long stride. The buttons, formed from the same light wool fabric as the coat and shaped into small orbs, ran from the banded collar to the waist. Everything he wore matched the same brilliant white until the last items: The outer robe of purest white ermine, trimmed in crimson fox and fastened with a heavy gold chain from right to left. The front of the robe bore the image of a deathcat fashioned from precious gems from waist to shoulder in amazing detail. The robe came to a half inch above the floor. State Protocol required this meeting of notification and with it, the symbols of rule. Jarod hoped this would be a short session; he would soon be running with sweat.

Rolo went to the box holding the Crown. He pulled the tie and removed the top; the sides fell outward, revealing the crown. Lapis lazuli fashioned the bottom row of gems, representing Deepwells, continuing upward in rows shone garnet for Westwood, opal for Trueridge, sapphire for Eastfall, diamond for Northmount, emerald for Mountglen, and ruby for Stonefire. The stones' setting formed a domed cap seven inches high that held a five-inch deathcat rampant worked in gold with ruby eyes on top. The crown's history covered over two millennia, and the craftsmanship that had made it had been lost over time. Rolo reached into the compartment under the crown and removed the dagger. Its scabbard was made of blood red rubies, and its handle of one five-inch faceted ruby. Its blade held a mystery.

The Zenith's battle sword, the dagger, and a battle sword he had never seen possessed the same inscribed metal. No other traces of the metal surfaced in the Seven Realms. The blade of his battle sword had the same etching as the dagger. Jarod wondered more than once what had produced the etching. Nothing he did to the sword had any effect on the polish of the blade, nicked, or scratched it in any way. The significance of the symbols on the blades remained unknown. His battle sword could pierce metal shields and break swords made of the finest steel. The dagger hooked to the front of his coat. Rolo attached it and reached for the crown.

"Rolo, follow me to the anteroom with the crown. I want you to wait there until after the audience." His servant frowned, he hated the lift; he secured the crown in its box without hesitation. Jarod started toward the lift, with Rolo and the guard following.

He emerged from the lift to find Kyle waiting. The Apex Lord looked up at Jarod's head. "Rolo is bringing it." The sounds of the moving lift started; a few minutes later an ashen-faced Rolo stepped from the lift, removed the crown, and handed to Jarod. "How long?" His voice sounded sad.

Kyle's voice reflected it. "I guess it is a few minutes after the hour. The State chairs had filled when I last looked through the spy hole."

Jarod looked as if he already wore the heavy crown. He looked in Kyle's eyes, "Come, let us get it over with." Kyle walked to the tapestries and disappeared between them. Fanfares sounded and died, and then major domo's voice announced Kyle, hardly audible behind the tapestry. Jarod waited three minutes and placed the crown on his head. Rolo knelt before the Zenith. Jarod found the pride on Rolo's face reassuring. He reached forward and pulled the man to his feet, and skirted around a shocked Rolo to the tapestries.

Three levels above the floor of the Great Hall, recessed alcoves placed ten feet apart with a cloth covering that matched the color of the stone walls, held archers. They connected to a hall that encircled the great room below and then connected to an outside, heavily guarded, staircase. The alcove's covering, not discernible from below and recessed enough that the low lights from the connecting hallway maintained their secrecy even to the ambassadors. The archers could see the floor below with little difficulty. Three trumpeters, each in a brightly lit alcove midway down the long walls, faced three others on the opposite wall.

Jarod signaled the major domo from between the tapestries, who closed the fist of his right hand. The trumpeters sounded the Zenith's fanfare. Every man in the room knelt on their right knee; the ladies went into a low curtsey, with all heads bowed. No one noticed the Guard's officers had not stirred from their observances. They continued their watch; their scabbards hung loose, unhooked and ready. Archers stood at the ready with arrows notched and slight pressure on the string, unseen from below.

The Zenith climbed the steps of the dais; pulled the robe up slightly so the white ermine fell over the arms of the throne, exposing its crimson fox lining. From an outside balcony at ceiling height, a mirror focused on the sun directed the light on the top square of the Dais.

Jarod pronounced a single word like a sentence of death. "Rise!" The breathtaking effect caused gasps throughout the Hall. Even those who had attended his wedding looked awed. It had only been seconds since the fanfare; no one saw him enter, no one heard him enter. The jewels sparkled like small suns. He had achieved the effect he wanted, and at the same time hated this part of his job. The protocol and show consumed more time than he wished.

Formalities came first. "We the Zenith, recognize the ambassadors of Deepwells, Westwood, Trueridge, Eastfall, Northmount, and Mountglen." He called the realms in order of the crown's bands of jewels, according to ancient tradition. "Have any present grievances to bring before the Zenith Lord?" The room remained quiet. "We will hear the oaths of the Realms."

Men rose in the same order he had called. "I, who speak for our realm, reaffirm our realm's loyalty, fidelity, and service to the Zenith Lord." Jarod looked each man in the eye with a cold stare while the ambassadors made their pronouncement. Some found his look disturbing even from the distance between them.

As the last ambassador regained his seat, Jarod spoke; his voice carried command and sorrow. "The Zenith is saddened to inform the Realms of the death of our part known as the Zenith Lady Maress Greatstone." Moans and several gasps clearly sounded from in front of him. The ambassadors looked grave. "That part of Us joined with Light's Source this morning. The High Council will meet in six days. The Council of State shall attend. These statements being made and the Law fulfilled, this audience is at an end." Jarod rose, standing still while the assembled guests bent their knees or curtsied low with heads bowed. He stepped down the dais and between the tapestries into the anteroom.

Kyle gave the order to rise and as the guests began filing away, he followed after his Zenith Lord. Several of the lady guests had tears on their faces. One fainted while rising from the last curtsy. Two officers appeared at her side and helped her regain her composure.

Gaz stood at the anteroom entrance. A boy about fourteen years old stood in the corner with a guardsman next to him. Rolo stood by the lift; looking uncomfortable.

Karl's jaw dropped when he saw the Zenith. The guardsman snapped to position. Gaz had a smile on his face. "My Zenith Lord, I have someone for you to meet." Gaz faced the boy and his smile widened. The boy stared at Jarod as if frozen in time, nothing moved.

The guardsman nudged him, "Kneel, you idiot!" The boy shook his head as if waking from a dream. He dropped to both knees and touched his head to the floor. Jarod walked to the boy, bent down and raised him to his feet. Placing a finger under Karl's chin, he closed his mouth.

Returning to Rolo, he removed the dagger, and handed it to him. Next, he removed the crown. Taking the crown Rolo secured it in its box after he placed the dagger in its compartment. Jarod unfastened the robe; glancing at an uneasy Rolo, he unbuttoned his coat and removed both at the same time, laying them over Rolo's outstretched arm. Kyle pulled the bell cord in the lift as the Zenith Lord turned to the boy.

Karl's mouth dropped again when the lift started its ascent, his eyes following Rolo's disappearance. This time, he closed his mouth on his own.

Jarod looked at Gaz, obviously having a good time at the boy's expense. "Who is this fine-looking lad?"

"My Zenith, this is Karl Matthews. He observed an interesting person coming to and leaving the City. Karl was eating a meat pie near the canal where we found the murdered women when he saw someone hurrying from the river with blood on his hands. He did not see his face when he passed, but he did see a hand with a scar he recognized, and a gait he had seen once before. He confirmed the identity when the man came for his horse at Karl's stable. I asked him to describe the person he saw. He did much better than that." Gaz handed Jarod a rolled piece of paper. He unrolled it to reveal a detailed likeness of Thord.

Karl had done the drawing with charcoal, and had managed to get every detail of Thord from the waist up. The bottom of the drawing contained a detailed description of Thord's voice, language, his unique gliding walk and demeanor written in neat lettering. It listed the supplies he had purchased for him. Rufus, the name Thord used, figured prominently in the top right corner of the paper. Jarod noticed the handwriting; it flowed with precision, better than most by far. "Who wrote this at the bottom?"

"I, I, did Sir, uh…Zenith Lord."

Gaz took pity on the boy, "Karl is a stable boy at an inn on the edge of the City. Our mysterious stranger paid him well."

"May I see what he paid you?" Jarod held his hand out.

Karl's manner caved inward. He reached for a pouch, opened it, and reluctantly handed a heavy gold coin to Jarod. "Zenith Lord, I don't think he meant for me to have this coin from the surprise on his face, but he smiled and rode off."

Mountglen's profile etched deeply into the gold on the obverse, on the reverse the name "Mountglen" shown in relief. He handed the coin to Karl.

"You mean I can keep it?" Relief flooded through Karl.

"You received it for honest work, did you not?" Karl nodded. "Then what right have I to take your payment? Tell me Karl, where did you learn to write and draw?"

"My Zenith..." Karl looked to Gaz for approval before continuing. The man's smile urged him to go on. "...being a stable boy leaves a lot of time with nothing to do. I learned to read from my priest so that I could read the tracts from the Holy One. Then, I just started practicing writing the words of the Holy One. The drawing part came naturally. I got charcoal from the pit and drew on a part of the wall. The stable has a leak at that one spot. The rain washed it off, or in the winter the melted snow cleaned away what I'd drawn; sometimes before I had a picture finished it ran down the wall." Karl took a long breath. He had run his words together without breathing.

"What else do you do at the inn?" Jarod asked.

"I taught myself numbers. Colleen helped me. She's the fishmonger's daughter. Sometimes when Master Taggert—he's the innkeeper—has too much to drink, he has me do the day's tally. He said I do as well as him. I think I do it better because I catch his mistakes in the book, but he hardly ever catches a mistake from me." Karl looked a little embarrassed, perhaps from his bragging.

Gaz said simply, "The Squares?" He used the nickname of the Academy derived from the black and white pattern of the marble floors.

Jarod took in the boy's presence with new eyes. "What do you want to do when you are grown?"

"Oh…well, Sir…uh, my Zenith, I figured I would save this gold coin and try to work out a way to make more."

"If I sent you to a school for several years, so that you may learn ways to better yourself, would you want to go?"

"Oh yes, my Zenith, yes." Karl's eyes sparkled with excitement.

"It will be hard."

"I will study hard, my Zenith. I will give you my gold coin."

"You give me your gold coin and I will give you two in return. And, I will give you a silver coin for every year you do well at the Academy."

Karl looked a little dazed. He held out the coin to Jarod. Gaz stepped forward, took the coin and put it in a vest pocket. He took two gold coins from his leather bag and handed them to Karl who looked as if he might pass out at any moment.

Gaz waved the guardsman forward. "Take the boy through the passage to Lieutenant Rosh. Relay the Zenith's orders. Tell him also to get the boy student's garb. Send him to Priest Cannon for testing and placement." Reaching behind him, Gaz touched a stone that released the stone door in the wall. The door swung into place after the guardsman and Karl passed through with no trace of its presence.

Jarod looked at Kyle and Gaz. "Gentlemen, it might be good to know what activity comes from the Circle of Villas in the next few hours."

He half expected Gaz's reply, and it did not surprise Kyle at all. "My Zenith, I have men in all the villas and I will notify Lord Byrne if something is reported that negatively effects the realms. Neither birds nor messengers have left the Circle of Villas. I have increased the men watching the activities at Mountglen's villa. They have reported nothing, and nothing has come from my man inside the villa. I do have a report on our mysterious stranger. One of the murdered girls described, big brute of a man that matched the drawing, to her neighbor working in the same profession. They made a habit of checking with one another. This, of course, is circumstantial, but it's what we have at this time. I will keep you appraised as things progress."

Jarod's admiration for his spymaster climbed even higher. "Gaz, I have long neglected your operations. My father spoke highly of you. I want to meet with you and Kyle to go over your workload and assignments. In addition, I want to hear your concerns. Is two days enough time to get your priorities together?"

"My Zenith, I would be honored to give you a briefing any time you wish, most of the information is in my head. Two days will be fine."

"Good, let's leave the time flexible, but plan for the afternoon two days from now. Kyle, did you notice anything of interest from the audience?"

"No, everyone seemed a little nervous, but I expected that. Everyone I saw looked genuinely saddened, or so it seemed from where I stood. Any one of the ambassadors from the Circle of Villas could certainly hide any emotion they wanted if they felt threatened. After all, how many faces does a diplomat have?"

Jarod did not comment on the remark, he only chuckled. "Thank you gentlemen. I will be in the Chambers if I'm needed." He walked toward the lift, not seeing their bowed heads.

18

CLARENCE Mountglen waited in the family dining room for his father, a rarity. He stood at the windows, looking down at the gardens. Eric Mountglen entered and went to his seat at the head of the table; Clarence took his usual seat to his father's right. Neither spoke.

The servants brought food within a minute of Mountglen's arrival. Clarence knew his father wanted something from just looking at the meal. Mountglen had ordered a light meal and must have known his son had not been long awake. Pork cooked as they both liked it and fresh snips from the garden made a pleasant meal, not the heavy meal with different sauces his father favored. Mountglen ate lightly; his son ate less. His father never liked wine with his meal; he preferred water, with wine afterward. The servants cleared the table and brought decanters of wine and glasses. Mountglen waved them out and poured his son a full glass of his favorite wine then poured himself a half glass of his favorite. He turned his chair at an angle to allow better eye contact with his son. Clarence did the same to cover his uneasiness. He rarely had a pleasant meal with his father, and certainly not one catered to him. Clarence took a swallow of wine and his tense face relaxed.

"My son, what do you think of an afterlife? Do you think there is one?"

The question took Clarence off guard. His only conjecture, *Great Dark's Source, he has lost his mind!* "I have never been religious, father. I read some of the tracts from the Holy One several years ago, but could not make much of them. I know many of our subjects believe in

Light's Source. I don't believe there is anything else. When you are dead, you are dead."

"And if there is an afterlife, how do you think you will fare?"

"Father, you know my peculiarities; I don't think knowledge of my desire's fulfillment would please 'The Great Holy One.'" Clarence sneered as he said the last words. "You only have a few years on this world, so one must make the most of his time here, there is nothing else."

Mountglen patiently—something he had little of—stated, "You didn't answer my question. How will you fare?"

Clarence squirmed a little, but did not evade the question this time. "Not well. As I said, you know my peculiarities, and what happens afterwards when Thord has his sport. I have done no more than you have. Are you changing your opinion? Do you want me to take up Holy Orders?"

Mountglen's stoic face remained set. His eyes left his son for a moment. He swirled the wine in his glass. "If only it could be so simple." Mountglen's smirk let Clarence realize he knew the truth of the things he had said; he might have known for a long time. "What would you say if I could prove to you there is another existence?" Mountglen asked.

Clarence's uneasiness with his father's questions increased. "I have never regarded the subject to any degree. I don't believe there is anything after death. I will have much to answer for if there is, as will you, I might add."

His remark had little effect on his father, surprising Clarence. Mountglen had slapped him more than once for being flippant, but not this time.

Mountglen seemed lost in though for a moment before continuing. "I have believed much the same as you for most of my life. I have had dreams over the last year, some good and some bad. They had one thing in common: They dealt with death and its consequences to me. I believed it paranoia, at first, but I began to wonder as the dreams became more frequent. I asked myself, what would I do, could I do, if the dreams came true? Frankly, I began to worry. I knew which I would see when dead if Sources of the Light and Dark exist. I obsessed about it for a while, and then considered it more a fact. Then something happened that gave me hope a little over a month ago. Not the conditions I wanted, but it did offer hope for something better than I had imagined. I had a chance and I took it. It has dearly cost me. However, I still think I made the best choice. I had another dream last night. The nightmares I had before are gone. The same offer is available to you and you may choose. I want you to come with me now. I want you to see for yourself. Come." Mountglen started for the door without looking at his son. Clarence would not dare directly disobey him.

The man is a fool, or crazy, or both! Clarence followed his father up the stairway leading to his private rooms, not knowing what to believe.

He caught up with his father, and they entered Mountglen's bedchamber together. It had been over a year since he had last been here; it held too many unpleasant memories for him. He followed his father to the table, and they took the same positions as before at the study table.

Mountglen took the Dark Stone from inside his shirt. Clarence knew he always wore it; he did not know its history or how his father got it. Mountglen locked his hand around the stone and leaned into his chair with his eyes closed. Several minutes went by. Clarence believed his father would be completely insane before long, if not already.

Clarence felt the air moving like a breeze, at first. The light in the room began to fade. The currents of air grew progressively stronger by the minute. A shadow formed across the table in front of him. Cold chills ran through his body. He looked at his father, his eyes closed and his face ashen. Shadows took on the appearance of a tall man dressed in black robes. Blackness, that pulled the light from the room into itself from where the face should be. Clarence had never seen anything as black or as dead. His father let out a sigh and opened his eyes.

They both heard whispered words in their minds. *"You did well calling me for the first time. It will become easier with practice and as the power of the Dark Stone grows. Clarence, your father has done my bidding in bringing you to me. The power of Dark's Source is growing on your side of the void. Before, Light's Source won the great battle. This coming battle will be Dark Source's victory. I give you the same chance to wage war on Light's Source that I gave your father. Your reward will be great if you do not fail me. Your father can tell you about failure. You have this one chance, as did he. What say you?"*

Clarence could hardly believe his senses. The apparition in front of him looked real; he had no doubt of that. His mind raced over the conversation during their mid-day meal; he knew that he had no choice, as his father had had no choice. He tried to think of a way out for several minutes; he became resolute with failure. "I agree."

"You have chosen wisely. Your father failed to prevent Jarod's brat from being born. Now, you both have a task to fulfill. The idiot you sent to the City is on his way here. You cannot wait for him. The Naming Day is in a month. The brat's death is imperative before then, at all costs. Those costs include your lives! Fail me again and your punishment will not be gentle."

The shadow figure faded. Light poured into the room. Both men blinked at the sudden brilliance. Mountglen looked at his son. "Have the servants make ready for our trip to the City. I want ten men with us. We can use a coach; we have the time. I want Timmons with us. Tell him to bring his equipment. We leave at first light."

Mountglen stood and walked slowly toward the big bed. He looked exhausted in both mind and body.

Clarence came to his wits with a start. "Father, what did he mean about the price of failure? What is it?"

His father stepped to the side of the bed. "I will tell you on the trip. Now go. We leave at first light." Clarence saw his father lay down and his hand motioned him away with an irritating flick of the wrist. Clarence left the room, thinking, *Timmons?*

Clarence delegated the tasks of organizing the trip, and lounged on a plush chair in his room with a decanter of wine. His deliberations took on a foreboding urgency. *What have I done? I believe what I saw. Father called that...that being. It knew me. I could feel it in my mind. Even if I wanted to say no, I don't think it would have let me. Could it have killed me? Would it have killed me? I think it could, but would it? It has a need for us! We have to do something it cannot. That has to be it. Why has father missed this? Why Timmons? He's the best archer in the Realm, but what good will that do us at the Spires?* He finished his glass of wine and went for a walk to ponder what had happened to him and what might be ahead.

Clarence walked by the stream. He looked back at the mansion and saw his father at his window, looking at him. Mountglen moved slowly, reaching up to wipe his cheek. The action shocked Clarence. *Surely, he's not weeping.*

19

JAROD sat at his desk when he heard the commotion outside, then a knock at his door. Rolo entered, as quietly as always, and hurried to his side, definitely not as always.

"My Zenith, the men have found something on the seventh level. The Captain sent word asking for you to join them as soon as it's convenient."

Jarod reached the warehouse in less than fifteen minutes, with Kyle's officer in tow. A heavy contingent of guardsmen in front of the warehouse entrance came to position and saluted as he entered the warehouse and saw Kyle and Gaz standing over two bodies.

Kyle waved the Zenith away and came to his side. Gaz was examining the bodies with a cloth tied over his nose and mouth. Jarod could smell the stench well before entering, and once inside, it became overpowering. His stomach turned; thankfully, he had had a light meal.

Kyle lowered the cloth from his nose when they stepped from hearing range of others in the room. He still spoke softly. "A guardsman noticed the smell and had the barrel unsealed. They were in there for at least two days. Their murder coincides with the time they finished their part in what took place. The man is Kirsh; a guardsman identified him. The woman is not known, but she has lost part of her little finger on her right hand, severed at the first knuckle and not recently."

"You and Gaz come to my rooms when you are through here. Don't hurry through this, find everything you can." He realized the superfluous nature of his order as soon as he'd said it.

Kyle saluted and returned to Gaz and the bodies.

Jarod retreated, returning the way he had come. He noticed nothing in his path as guardsmen and household personnel scurried to get out of his way. Fury filled him; he wanted them alive! Back in his room, he started reaching for the brandy, but reconsidered and poured himself water. It helped his stomach, but not his anger.

Two hours passed before Rolo's knock came at the door. Kyle and Gaz came across the room and stood near where Jarod sat in a plush chair. "Sit, gentlemen, and tell me they died a horrible death."

Kyle nodded. "My Zenith, as a matter of fact, they did have a particularly nasty demise. They suffered torture and mutilation before death. A slow acting poison caused their death. The poison works on the nervous system. It renders them immobile and affects the throat so that they can make no sound. It's a bad death from what I understand. I have only seen the results, but I know it takes hours to die. They died after the barrel was sealed. The man's wounds, cauterized by fire, died from the poison, not from loss of blood. The woman had small cuts over her body, again seared closed by fire. Their wounds fulfilled their purpose to cause prolong suffering. They entered the barrel still alive. There are scratch marks inside the cover and their fingernails were ripped and torn, consistent with the marks. Whoever did this had help or is quite strong. He had to lift them up and into the barrel and then manhandle it into position. We believe it happened in the warehouse. The barrels are checked into and placed on the warehouse tally and checked again on a routine basis. No one could take one that size without notice. There are three hours between first and midmeal requisitions when the warehouse is empty. We found an area behind the barrels where the torture happened. Their clothes were there. Also, there were five gold pieces for him, two for her, hidden in their shoes. Mountglen minted them.

"I have asked High Healer Sternwood to look at the

bodies using his graystone. He said he would try and lately he has had improved results and is hopeful of finding something useful." Gaz had a quizzical look when the Zenith frowned. "We couldn't find anything that could lead us to the person responsible. My men are checking assignments now for anyone who could be a likely perpetrator."

Jarod looked up while Rolo came through the door with a tray of chilled wine in decanters and glasses. He poured them each a glass and set a plate of fruit and cheese on the table in front of them. "Thank you, Rolo." No one spoke until he left the room.

"There is not much more I can tell you at this time." Gaz leaned forward and started to reach for a glass of wine. He stopped short and eased back into his chair.

Jarod looked at Gaz with slight amusement. "Go ahead, help yourself. I don't stand on much protocol in the Chambers." Gaz still looked a little hesitant, but he took a glass of cool wine and a piece of cheese.

Jarod raised an eyebrow at Kyle. "I cannot add much to what Gaz has said. I have assigned the men he'd requested to help with sorting out the, who, where, and why. We may have something figured out by tomorrow. It's strange the killer didn't take the gold coins."

Gaz added, "The poison is rare and can be effective by just touching it. I had the men wear gloves; perhaps the killer didn't want to touch the coins. The High Desert People in Deepwells produce it, they do not sell it on the open market, and it's usually given to outsiders for performing a great deed for the good of their people. They look on it as a show of respect and trust. They are giving someone a way to kill them. I have only seen it used once before; the symptoms are the same." Jarod and Kyle took a glass of wine.

"Gentlemen, you have done well." Jarod said. You are also on the edge of exhaustion. I want you to retire for the day and get a good night's sleep. I will meet with you at mid-morning tomorrow." He did not wait for comments. He refilled his glass and left the room.

Kyle knew he went to his small study with its portrait of Maress, he knew his Zenith Lord well. Gaz knew where he went as well; after all, he excelled at being the best spymaster in the world.

20

THE guards returned from their scouting. "Your Holiness, there is a good area just ahead. We have an hour of good light. I suggest we make camp for the night." Travis nodded his permission. The two guards pulled the pack animals from the line and trotted back toward the campsite.

The three clerics rode their horses over a small rise to find the guards unloading supplies. Travis and Daniel rode to the hitching line, dismounted, and tied their mounts. His Holiness started undoing his saddle packs when one of the guards saw him and came over to help. Travis waved him away. "We will help as much as we can, we don't expect you to do everything." The guardsman started to protest, but instead bowed his head and returned to unloading the pack animals with a smile.

Thurston managed to get his mare to the line next to Daniel's horse. "How do I get off?" Several bouts of laughter choked off, faces red. Adam, the guardsman who'd helped him before, came around and started quietly talking to Thurston. In short time, Thurston stood on the ground and took his first step. His eyes widened and he bit his lower lip to keep from crying out. "Oh dear. Light's Source, help me."

Travis looked over, his face showing genuine concern. "Thurston, try walking around a bit to work the soreness out. It will help to keep you from cramping."

Seeing the man's degree of pain, the smiles of the others fell away. Adam's voice held the concern they all felt. "Prelate Thurston, we have used this site many times. There is a pool about fifty yards from here. The water is heated from underground. You will find great benefit from a good soak. Be careful of the rocks at the center and on the bottom of the pool, they are quite hot." Thurston threw his saddlepacks over his shoulder and gingerly walked toward where the guardsman pointed.

His Holiness called the guardsman to him when Thurston disappeared well beyond hearing. "Adam, you have been much help to Prelate Thurston. I want you to know I appreciate your efforts."

The guardsman looked into Travis' eyes, "Your Holiness, the Prelate did a great kindness for me some ten years ago, the only time I ever spoke to him before today. I don't think he remembers, but I do. I will help him as I can, whenever I can."

"Your actions do you in good stead, my son. I won't forget." They turned to the chores of setting up camp.

Thurston came through the woods over an hour later, smiling. He had fresh clothes on, his riding clothes still wet from washing. Richard had just started the fire. To everyone's surprise, Thurston arranged a lean-to from branches he'd collected on his return. He draped his wet clothes over it, close to the fire and away from the smoke. His actions favored certain muscles; his face showed signs of lingering pain.

Adam and Richard returned from their hunting from opposite directions. They spoke briefly. Adam walked to His Holiness. "Holy One, we have not been able to find any game. It's unusual; there are animals here, even in the winter. I don't understand. Something has frightened them away."

Travis nodded. "I think I will take a walk." His hand silenced Adam's unspoken objection. He reached through his robe and grasped the Stone. The sensation of a presence nearly stopped him in his tracks. He hurried toward the direction of the strongest vibrations.

Travis' vision blurred, and he dropped to his knees, unable to see. His vision cleared, and he saw underbrush passing as if he was running waist-high to the ground. The fast pace slowed. Warmth escaped into his hand from the Stone. Gentleness, with quiet assurances and peacefulness, circulated through him.

Slowly, the vision of land he saw moved again. He spotted a figure ahead in the trees. Travis' body jerked; he was looking at himself! He blinked, wishing the vision away, and slowly, his normal sight returned. He looked around for what had produced this vision. Ten feet away stood a deathcat with tawny colors and black stripes that camouflaged it in the underbrush, looking at him with eyes of golden fire. Travis had never seen one before. It looked larger than he expected, and must have weighed well over a thousand pounds.

Emotions of gentleness and protection again soaked into his essence. His mind whirled with images of him and his traveling companions at various places earlier that day. The deathcat had trailed them from when they'd first entered the tree line outside the Tower crater. He saw many more images: two cubs playing, grooming them, feedings at her teat, prey stalked and the kill, him entering the woods. He projected images of pleasant things through his life leading to this time, and stopped on the image of first seeing her. She crept forward without a sound until her head stopped in front of his, barely six inches away. Travis considered it strange not to be afraid. She leaned forward, pushing her forehead against his. He felt her soft, warm fur and an overpowering feeling of well-being.

He thought she was growling at first; then he smiled, recognizing a deep, loud purr. He stood, reached out and scratched her behind the ears. She rubbed against him, almost knocking him to the ground. His stomach growled with hunger. The deathcat looked at him, turned, and walked a few feet away. She stopped, turned her head to him for a few seconds, and walked on. Travis got the idea and followed her.

She stopped and put her head in a hollow about fifty yards away. Her head rose with the throat of a small deer in her jaws. She lifted the carcass with ease and started toward the camp. The deer seemed to weigh nothing to the deathcat, and she carried it with ease. Travis found he could feel her emotions now, even without touching the stone. He stroked her head while they entered the camp.

Daniel looked faint. Thurston shrieked, stumbled backwards, and sat down hard, pain and fear covering his face. The guards reached for their swords.

"Wait!" The two men stopped with their swords halfway out of their scabbards. They both looked at His Holiness. "Our new friend has brought us lastmeal."

The big feline carried the deer near the fire and dropped it. She walked a few paces away, lay down, and started grooming herself, paying no more attention to them. The horses, on the other hand, had fits. The smell of the fresh kill and the sight of the deathcat became too much for them. Adam and Richard stroked their necks and spoke softly to them. One by one, they calmed.

The guards returned to the fire and found Thurston skinning the deer. Surprise covered their faces. The Prelate caught their look. "Priests do many things before they become priests!" The guards approached, walking on the opposite side of the fire from the deathcat, and helped the Prelate dress the deer.

Daniel came with supplies for cooking and a pail of water Adam had retrieved from the spring feeding into the hot pool. They both looked amazed when they saw Travis sitting quietly next to the deathcat, stroking her neck. Her throaty purr rumbled across the campsite.

21

THE angle of the sun declared mid-morning. Glen, the capital of Mountglen, consisted of Mountglen's Keep, nestled at the base of Mount Glen; the city itself; the Moonbright River running from the Glen mountain range; a warehouse district; and the docks. Three-story buildings formed the sprawling city, numbering over two hundred thousand souls. No wall surrounded it. Caches of supplies, hidden in the mountains in case of attack and mostly forgotten—any attack remained highly unlikely—supplied a small degree of protection. The Glen mines had played out long ago. The realms never warred among themselves to any degree since the Great War.

The mainly self-supporting realm lacked grain, certain medicinal herbs, some spices and farming machinery; imports from Stonefire and Deepwells satisfied those needs. Mountglen exported leather goods and the best wines in the realms. The need for commerce kept the two main roads to Stonefire well traveled, and the road tax kept it in good repair. Still, the coach ride would be hardly better than being on horse.

The trip by coach would take the better part of three weeks, a long time to share a small space between two people who liked one another. Clarence believed his father did not much like him, and his feelings for his father remained ambivalent. The truth may be far different than one might suppose.

Mountglen had never been able to share his true emotions with those he loved, not to his wife, who had taken a lover, or to his son, who had taken his teaching and discipline styles as displeasure in everything he did.

Little brought the two together. Clarence's mother had thrown her affair in Mountglen's face; he'd had them both killed in a fit of rage.

Clarence never knew for sure, but he'd always suspected his father of the murders. He tried, unsuccessfully, not to listen to the gossip. The two lovers had been found in a summer cottage on the far side of Mount Glen, with their throats cut and the man mutilated. Clarence once asked his father what had happened. His reply was one word: "Justice." The subject never came up between them again.

Clarence had wondered if Thord had been the instrument of his father's rage. A few years after the deaths, he'd asked the huge man if he had any part in the killings after Clarence became the main supplier of Thord's sport. The scarred man's answer had been a resounding, "NO!" without hesitation. Thord was a skilled and thorough man, able to apply himself and follow directions to the letter; however, he did not hide things well when confronted by Clarence or his father. Clarence doubted Thord had participated in the crime. His loyalty to his father caused Clarence to wonder what price had he paid for it. Regardless of what he thought, Clarence had made his mind up that he would not bring up contentious subjects during the trip in order to keep the peace.

Still, he needed answers about Shadure, even if it meant a fight. His father said he would tell him on the trip, and he usually kept his word. *You will never get the bird if you never let the arrow fly.* "Father, tell me about Shadure. I must know the ramifications of what I have entered into—"

Mountglen's raised hand stopped him from going further. "You are right about your suspicions. You never believed I loved or cared about you. The truth is that I have and do, overly much. I also loved your mother. Her relationship with her lover brooked on open flaunts.

Glen's magistrate planned to take the knowledge to the Zenith. The Zenith would have no recourse but to have a public trial. I couldn't have that. More than sufficient evidence abounded to find them guilty. The magistrate let me know he had no plausible recourse. The knowledge had spread too far. News of the Zenith's sister involved in anything traveled rapidly, this traveled faster than any birds. I knew the old fool had it right. The knowledge would reach the City another way if he didn't bring it forward. The sentence is death, a public death. The humiliation would have been unbearable for both of us. I went into a rage. I ordered the only woman I ever loved drugged and murdered with her lover. They died without the pain of disclosure, a public trial, and a public beheading. I tried to keep the facts from you. I knew, of course, you would find out in time."

Clarence sat in shocked amazement, trying to come to terms with this sudden confession.

Mountglen pulled the stone from his shirt. "Curious things began to happen after that. The Dark Stone somehow comforted me. In my darkest times, I held it and knew peace. I held it in sleep and had unbelievable dreams, some erotic and so detailed to the point that I believed they really existed, others came more pleasurable to the remaining senses, taste and smell in addition to touch and sight. None of them had a dream quality; they felt alive. My father gave me this stone on his deathbed. He tried to tell me something about it. He died before saying anything except the word 'keep.' I believe he was trying to say 'keep away.' I know it sounds bizarre, but I soon found the Dark Stone had power. You know how the graystones work. Healers use them in their art, and priests send messages through the minds of birds. Short messages they are, but they still control the bird's mind. The Dark Stone always told me when someone betrayed me, in ways that left no doubt. I tested it many times, and found its warnings always true. However, as in all things, there is a price for something given.

"That price is rage, anger, deceit and hate. I found myself doing things I never dreamed I would—or could—do, your mother's death, for one. I took the Dark Stone off and hid it away when I realized the extent of my actions. I have had better experiences. The dreams that followed became the opposite and not so tantalizing, nightmares woke me screaming and soaked in sweat, instead of knowing when someone meant to cheat me in business deals, or how I could take the advantage, I became gullible and lost a fortune. Not long afterward my every waking moment consumed me with desire for the Dark Stone, my nights remained a hell. Finally, I put it back around my neck. Immediately, I regained the covert knowledge I had lost, recovered the lost fortune twice over, and had nights consisting of nothing but one long orgasm and woke refreshed and with a clear head."

Mountglen brought his eyes from the Dark Stone to look at his son's shocked face. "I believe the Dark Stone's influence is transferred to you by our consanguinity. I watched you grow from a gentle boy into a man with what you call 'your peculiarities.' I felt completely helpless. The evil that had changed my life manifested in you."

Fascination broke through the numbness Clarence felt as his father continued. "Only Dark's Source knows how many bastards you've brought into this world. Then, your attentions went elsewhere. How many children have you killed after defiling them? How many young boys and girls have you given to Thord for his sport? Think, my son, what did you aspire to three years ago? Could you have done those things then? I don't believe you could. I think that person would be horrified at what you have become, as I'm horrified at the things I do. Still, we have free will. Do you want to defy the Dark Stone's power—Shadure's power? Do you want to fail Shadure?" Clarence's near daze shut out all but his father's voice.

Mountglen squirmed uneasily in the seat facing his son. "The price of failure. That is what you really need to know. I felt more pain than I could ever imagine when my agents failed to kill the Zenith's child. I felt sure my heart would stop from the torture. My clothes literally burned off me while I hung in the air. It felt like it went on for hours. Shadure told me later that it had lasted three minutes! My body hair had burned off from the neck down when he released me from the pain. I think Shadure did that to provide a constant reminder. It won't grow back. My skin showed no signs of the burning, but I truly burned. The next few weeks my body seared in agony that I never knew existed. That was the price of failing one order, and the price of ultimate failure is an eternity of pain far worse than I endured." The color drained from Clarence's face.

Mountglen's voice whispered. "I would have destroyed the Dark Stone when I first saw it if I had known its influence on you or me. I know no way to escape from this evil. Shadure claims we will be highly rewarded—in both this life and the next—if we don't fail him, and Dark's Source wins the coming war.

"Our history of the last war is mostly lost. We know the horrible devastation that followed. Thousands upon thousands died, and at the end, Light's Source won. You and I won't fare well if Light's Source wins this time! I considered being a martyr, sacrificing you and me for the Seven Realms. Just thinking about those ideas produced a blinding pain in my head."

Mountglen considered a moment before continuing. "Shadure said the power of the Stones grew. It controls me now, and I suspect you also, or it will soon. Martyrdom is no longer an option. I don't think there is a way out, either for you or me. Shadure wouldn't permit our deaths except by his doing.

Clarence watched his father stare at him with haunted eyes. "Tell me about your dreams of late. Do you realize a difference? Do you think you could become a gentle, kind person again?"

Clarence's face paled. He did not know the answer to his father's questions. He feared the rightness of his words and that gentle, kind person only lived in distant memories now. He sat for several long moments before speaking. "Father, Shadure needs us for something. It cannot do what it needs and wants us to do to accomplish its requirements. If it could complete its goals by itself, it would not need us. There must be a way to fight it."

His father seemed drained. When he replied, his tone showed no emotion. "First, I wouldn't let him hear you call him 'it.' Shadure is not human, but he's tremendously proud. Yes, he needs us now to accomplish his ends, but how long will it be before his power can influence us without the benefit of the Dark Stone or our bloodline? What will we do then to escape his wrath? No, I see no way out. The power of the Dark Stone conditioned me for years, you indirectly, but you are still influenced. The only way out that I know of is one of eternal pain and damnation. Know this, my son: I grieve for myself, but I grieve more for you!"

Clarence set dumbfounded. His head spun, going to one conjecture, only to race off in another direction before the first had finished forming. Then, at last, he tried not to think at all. They rode until midday without speaking.

The coach pulled to the wayside and stopped for their midmeal for an hour. The guards and coachmen would have a few minutes to themselves, and the horses would drink from the stream adjacent the road. Mountglen and Clarence hated the routine before it began. Clarence told the coachman he and his father had things to discuss and to make a place separate and private for them. Mountglen made no comment. The midmeal of bread with cheese and wine refreshed him. This was the ideal way stop, a gentle slope to the stream covered with shade trees, spring flowers scattered about, and fluffy white clouds against a deep blue shy. Neither Clarence nor Mountglen ate much or noticed their surroundings.

Mountglen had wine after eating when Clarence edged closer to him. "Father, I forgave you long ago for what happened to Mother. I do believe you are right about the influence of the Dark Stone. Is there anything you have not told me about Shadure?"

"You forgave me? You knew? How?"

"As you said yourself, common knowledge and gossip. Children can be cruel. Maybe that is why I have such contempt for them. What about Shadure?"

Mountglen's face showed his puzzlement. Clarence continued, "Can he come into my dreams without me knowing? He says he can see into our world that way. I'm not sure if he sees reality or our dreams. I'm not sure he can see mine. I know he sees yours."

Clarence sat against a tree with a full glass of wine, watching the sunlight sparkle on the crystal. He swirled it, deep in concentration for a moment. "What does he see when you are drunk?"

Mountglen looked startled. "I don't think he comes when I have been drinking. I feel an influence not to drink that I think is from the Dark Stone. It may be Shadure at work, or perhaps my imagination; I don't know."

Clarence sat with his father until it was time to return to the coach. He embraced the older man for a long moment before his father climbed into the coach, something he had not done in recent memory. Mountglen wiped tears from his face before his son entered. Neither spoke until they stopped again at the first of many inns to come. Riders had left as soon as Clarence had given notice of the trip. Their rooms would be waiting for them.

Inside the coach, Clarence felt his emotions close and hardness suffuse him. He wondered if his father felt the same. The stoic look on his face confirmed he did.

* * *

CLARENCE'S drinking had him well on the way to a drunken stupor when Mountglen last saw him. He rejoiced that he and his son had finally talked, if nothing else good came from this tragedy. He even felt a bit better about himself than he had since his wife died.

However, his self-hatred remained as strong as ever, and he wondered if he truly could have led a different sort of life.

22

JAROD went to the nursery early in the next morning. Trina and the babe lay on the floor atop an ermine throw large enough to cover a bed. Marc made happy, cooing sounds. Trina looked up when he entered and waved him over to them. She remained in her sleepcloth and nothing else, obviously. The thin material didn't hide much, but somehow he didn't find it strange. His embarrassment upon first seeing her nursing his son was the first and last time it bothered him.

He walked to the throw and sat down on the floor next to Marc and opposite Trina. "He looks happy today." Marc stopped playing with the corner of the heavy cloth laid under him to protect the fur, gurgling and reaching for his father.

"He's happy most of the time. I have not heard him really cry. You know he birthed a month early, and I don't know of another infant so advanced at his age. I have seen nothing wrong, but I have sent for great-grandmother. She has far more experience than I have. He's such a good babe. You see the way he's trying to get to you. He does that whenever you come in the room. If you really want to see him smile, lay beside him so that he can touch you."

Jarod did as requested, and the gleeful response proved her right. Trina left and returned within minutes, fully dressed. Marc focused completely on his father, grinning from ear to ear. He lay on his back with his legs working in a crawling motion. He grabbed Jarod's finger when he offered it, and held tight onto his father. Jarod tickled his son's tummy to make him giggle. He said, "Are you as hungry as me?"

He went to the bell pull and gave it a yank. Minutes later Rolo knocked softly, opened the door, and bowed to Jarod, and then to Marc. It surprised Jarod, but he had followed exacting protocol. He grinned, more to himself than the room. "Rolo, please serve firstmeal here for Trina and myself. Also, send a message to Gaz that I want to speak with him as soon as he's available. The Mother is coming, have her admitted straight through to us. Thank you, Rolo." Rolo bowed, his eyes resting on Trina a little longer than necessary. Jarod chuckled. *Rolo, you are a sly one.*

Gaz knocked at the door before they finished their meal. He came into the room a few steps and stopped. Jarod and Trina had both lay down to eat so they could play with Marc at the same time. Jarod rose to greet him.

He led Gaz to the door and spoke softly. "I think I figured something out last night. Maress died in an attempt to kill Marc!" The baby's giggle provided a strange counterpoint to Jarod's statement.

"My Zenith, I came to that conclusion two days ago," Gaz replied. "The poison used could easily have taken your son's life too, if it had been fresh. It must have been stored for years for it not to work on the babe. I requested a meeting to cover this subject with Kyle this morning. It's important that we don't show our concern too soon. I have men constantly watching your son. He's not been in danger. Needless to say, I think you are right. I waited until now, searching for conformation, but have found none." Jarod felt a flash of anger.

Gaz continued without pause. "The only answer I can deduce at this time is that someone wants to stop the succession, and you are intended to be the next victim. I have men watching you, also. I want to discuss this with the Captain to determine the possibilities of my being right and if so, the ramifications."

Jarod's anger cooled. "Notify Kyle that we will meet at

mid morning in my small study." Jarod looked puzzled. "I have not noticed extra men."

Gaz smiled, "Have you recognized any of the housekeeping staff lately?" Jarod stood dumbfounded, then grinned; he nodded approval and returned to his son and Trina. His hunger gone, he stayed a while, playing with Marc. Every time he put his finger close, Marc took it, smiling and making the funny noises that Jarod assumed all infants made. He again felt the lump in his throat and heart. Rolo's knock brought him from his musings. The door opened and the Mother entered.

* * *

"GOOD morning, my son, and to my new son, too. And how is my great-granddaughter?" Trina smiled. The Mother knew she felt unsure about calling her, afraid she might say she should not have been bothered. She went to Jarod with her arms outstretched. He embraced her warmly and kissed her on the cheek. She went to Trina and repeated her actions. Lastly, she went to see her reason for coming, Marc. Mavis smiled and spoke while playing with the babe. "You want to know why he's far beyond where he should be in development. I don't know the answer, I just know he is and he is completely healthy." She looked up to Jarod. "Am I right?"

"Mother, you always amaze me. Trina sent for you. I wouldn't know if he developed a year beyond where a normal babe should be. Some remaining issues need discussion. I request that you stay until mid-morning, and attend a meeting with a few others and me in my small study."

Mother Mavis nodded. "I have canceled my appointments, and will return to the Spires with your permission." She looked at Trina. "It has nothing to do with you or my confidence in your care, my dear. Now, I want a better look at my new son."

His pleasure showed. "MomMav, you may stay here

whenever you wish, as you well know. I must attend to something; I will see you at mid morning." Jarod smiled at Trina and Marc. "And I will see you and my son later."

Trina's smile broadened to match his.

23

GAZ followed Rosh to a room in the first under-level. An old man sat next to the lift controls, his head in his hands, rocking. Gaz looked questioningly at Rosh.

"We told him he caused no trouble," Rosh said. "But he's still like this. Perhaps, if you spoke to him..."

Gaz walked to the man, "You run the lift controls?"

The man nearly jumped from the chair. "I didn't do anything, my Lord."

"We know you didn't do anything wrong, try to relax. I'm not a Lord. Are you the man who runs the lift controls?"

"One of them, sir. I sleep in that room there." He pointed with a shaking finger to a room next to the controls. "I work at night, sir. No one ever uses the lift at night, sir. There is no light, you see. Most people don't want to be in the lift cage with no light. The light comes from up above. There is a window way up on top. It's very clever the way they did it. There are a series of mirrors on the roof and inside the lift shaft. From sunrise to sunset, there is light focused on the inside of the shaft.

"The other night, someone used it several times. The machinery woke me. I assumed it must be the repairmen, because the bell didn't ring and it's quite loud. The first time in years I can remember it being used at night."

"Fine, as I said, you didn't do anything wrong. Please tell me your name?"

"Chester, sir. Everybody knows me, sir. I worked at the Spires nearly all my life. Just ask anyone, sir, they all know me."

"Good, Chester, now you just relax like I said," Gaz

said as he placed a hand on the man's trembling shoulder. "I may have a question or two in a few minutes. You sit down and relax for now." Chester followed the instructions. He looked a little calmer, but not much.

Lamps lit the area around the lift operator. Gaz followed Rosh to a door at the opposite end of the dimly lit room. The torches here felt cold. Gaz felt each of the two lamps hanging by the door. They were cool to the touch, and the wicks looked unused for a long while. Inside the small room, splatters of dried blood covered some of the walls and ceiling. "How did you find the room?"

Rosh answered. "Kelson here, found it. He returned here with lamps. He had no light when he first inspected it, then brought the two lamps inside."

Gaz acknowledged Kelson's salute. "If you keep an eye on our friend Chester there, Rosh and I will look around."

The room held no furniture. The two lamps Kelson had brought lit the small room well. They found ropes with blood worked into one side of the hemp. The victims had strongly fought their bonds, with no result other than cutting their flesh and the rope burns Gaz observed the bodies; they'd fought hard to get out. Knotted pieces of cloth lay a few feet away. Gaz supposed they had been used for gags. A vial, broken into several pieces, lay near the gags. Gaz knelt, carefully picked up a shard, and smelled the inside portion. He looked up at Rosh and nodded.

"Focus on the Zenith!" rang through the outer room. Gaz nearly fell back onto his butt. Rosh grabbed his hand and pulled him up, both men smiling as the Zenith entered.

"What is this?" Jarod took in the room and its contents.

"It looks like the torture happened here," Gaz replied. "Rosh tells me they inspected and cleaned the room weekly. The victims probably received the poison here. I'm not sure why, as of yet."

Rosh looked at the box Jarod carried. "My Zenith, may I carry that for you?"

"No Rosh, I have it."

"I have a few questions for Chester, if he didn't faint when he saw the Zenith."

Jarod smiled. "Why Gaz. I've known Chester my whole life." The three men returned to where Chester sat. "Chester, we have a few more questions for you, then we will be gone and you can go home. I know you should have been there long ago, and Ethel will be worried. You be sure and give her my apologies." He stepped aside to let Gaz ask his questions.

"Chester, how could someone get something heavy from that room over there to the seventh level?"

"Use the lift. That is what I would do."

"The lift goes to the seventh level and to this level?"

"Oh yes sir, the lift can stop on this level, the main level above, at the rear of the Great Hall, and on the fifth, seventh, and twelfth levels. No one ever uses it any more except for the twelfth and main levels. Nevertheless, you can still get off on those certain levels if you have the controls set right down here and know how to trigger the hidden doors. They added those doors four or five hundred years ago; whenever they added the top five levels. We bring the cage down here once a week to clean it. I do that on the night shift. I have not noticed anything unusual as of late." Chester had become more at ease with the Zenith present.

Gaz kept his voice calm. "Chester, who has knowledge of how the lift works besides you and the other people running it?"

"Oh my, let's see, us that run it like you said, also that machinery lot who test the ropes, pulleys, chains, and things. I report to the Steward of the Great Hall—I think because they didn't know whom else to have supervise us.

We hardly ever see the man. I don't think he knows, but he might. I guess if someone accidentally pushed the right stones in the right order, they could open one of the doors, but I don't think it likely. They have to be pushed in exactly the right order."

"Do you know how it's done?" Gaz asked.

Chester looked a little nervous again. He looked at the Zenith, and calmed when he saw him smile and nod. "Yes sir, the old shaftkeeper trained me before he retired. That is what they used to call us, shaftkeeper. He said it had been passed down to him, and he felt we should pass the information on to the next man. When the lift stops…" Chester looked at the Zenith as an afterthought, as if wondering if he should be telling the Zenith's secrets. Jarod smiled and nodded again. "…you feel at the bottom of the cage until you find a letter 'Z' carved in one of the stones. It's not big, and is easy to miss. That stone is the bottom right of a larger 'Z.' You push the one with the 'Z' carved in it, then the one to its right, then the one over the first stone, but you skip a stone, push that one and then, the one to its right. See, it forms a 'Z' written backwards." Chester busily made Z's in the air, frontward and backward. "Oh and well, you would have to know how to set the levers down here, or you could have a nasty fall until the safety chain catches you."

Gaz's expression contained most of his excitement. "Thank you Chester, I think you can get home to Ethel now." Chester bowed his way out and gave Jarod a big grin. The day liftkeeper came in a moment later; his jaw dropped when he saw the Zenith. He gave a low bow and went to the levers to see their settings, and then tried to disappear.

*　*　*

JAROD did not know his name. They looked about the same age. "You can bring the cage down here?"

The sound of the Zenith's voice startled the man, and

he bowed again. "Yes, my Zenith."

"Fine, then please do it for me." He turned to Gaz. "I assume you are going to check this out?"

"With your permission, my Zenith." Jarod knew that Gaz could hardly wait to try one of the doors. He had a good guest which one.

The cage made its usual sounds as it stopped. Jarod entered the cage and turned around to face outward. The liftkeeper closed the gate and began to push and pull levers. The cage rose from sight. He stepped out at the twelfth level and pulled the cord to signal his arrival. The cage started its descent. He went to his small study to ponder some questions before his meeting.

24

THE Mother arrived first at Jarod's small study, small only in comparison to the main study in the Chambers. She found him in a plush chair, staring at the portrait of Maress. Life-sized, it well caught more than her likeness.

Mavis came in quietly; she almost reached him before he noticed her presence. His eyes showed moisture. "Mother, is it time? I didn't realize the hour. Would you like some chilled juice? I have your favorite, mixed berries."

The Mother went to the credenza and poured a glass of juice. "Not time dear, I just wanted to come by a little early and see how you're feeling." She started to return to her chair and saw the wrapped box on the table and froze. "Jarod, is that the Box of Stones?"

He became instantly alert; his reply came out sharper than he'd intended. "Yes, how do you know about it?"

"Your father and I discussed it many times. You must not open it today. In fact, put it away before the others get here. This is important, my son. Please do as I ask."

"I don't understand MomMav, why?"

"There will be someone here tomorrow that knows how to handle its contents. You could do great harm in opening it today. The inside is sealed with wax that you must not break."

"Who is coming tomorrow? I will do as you ask, but who is coming, and how do you know?"

"His Holiness will be here tomorrow. I don't know what time, but he's getting nearer as we speak. You must not say anything to anyone about his arrival. I know he's coming because I can feel his presence, as he feels mine."

"But, how is that possible?"

"Oh my dear, I imagined your father must have told you. His Holiness is my husband."

"WHAT?" He had not meant for his voice to be so loud. "But, but, but—Mother, how do you know he's coming? Your husband, when, how, I mean—"

Mavis stopped him with a smile and lightly put a hand on his arm. "It's not forbidden for priests to be married, my son. I will tell you about it sometime. Please, put the box away until tomorrow. You will see that I'm right in asking that of you. You are smart to think of it. May we have midmeal together? I will answer your questions then." The Mother's usual calmness became evident, as did her stress.

Jarod tightened the cloth wrapping on the box and went to the wall by the small fireplace. He turned a small gargoyle's head, releasing a door that concealed a small space in the stones. He placed the box inside and turned the gargoyle's head again. The door closed, disappearing into the wall, and yanked the bell pull for Rolo, then went back to his chair. He told Mavis what had transpired over the last few days while they waited. The Mother had been a loyal and trusted advisor to his father. Richard had told him she had a quick mind, and could often see what others could not. Jarod had found that to be true.

Rolo's soft knock came as he finished telling her about the lift. Jarod requested that his midmeal include the Mother. He also requested the Mother's belongings be transferred to a suite inside the Chambers. "So, any ideas?" he asked after Rolo left.

"Yes, my dear, but let us wait for the others if you don't mind."

The others arrived within a few minutes as Mavis told the progress of a new hospice. She went to Gaz and grasped his forearm. "It is good to see you again, Gaz. Are things well with you?" He nodded and the two joined the others in a circle of plush chairs.

"Mother Mavis and gentlemen, there is chilled juice, water, wine, and some pastries on the credenza. You may get them as you will," Jarod began. "I have included the Mother in this meeting. She has a keen insight and helped my father on several occasions. I want each of you to summarize your experiences over the last few days. We may discover something others of us don't know. Gaz, please start and bring us forward to this morning?" *Is there anyone MomMav does not know?* Jarod wondered as he watched the spymaster.

Kyle followed Gaz. A long discussion regarding Marc being the target of the poison followed. They all agreed at the end that the child's protection came first. The discussion wound down when someone other than Rolo knocked at the door. Jarod frowned; he had left orders not to be disturbed. "Enter."

Guards struggled with a man led by Lieutenant Rosh. The guardsmen bore the man's weight, while Rosh's face reflected his concern. "My Zenith, Captain, he insisted and gave the proper command signal." Kyle knew that meant there was the possibility of risk to the Zenith.

The distressed man, his color drained to a deathly pallor, went straight to Jarod and slumped to his knees. "My Zenith, please forgive this intrusion. It's most urgent that I speak with Gaz. Please, my Zenith, forgive me; your steward tried to stop me. I must see…" He fell over on the thick rug. Blood began flowing from his head. Gaz knelt beside him. Rolo, seeing what happened, rushed out and returned a minute later with a pillow, cloth and a water basin.

The Mother asked Rolo to bring her medicine bag. Taking the cloth from Gaz, she cleaned the man's wounds, and then asked for help getting him undressed. Jarod, Kyle, and Gaz removed everything but his privatecloth. Dried blood caked over a stab wound in his abdomen. Rolo returned with the Mother's bag. She selected several things and mixed them in a glass with a little water and wrapped them in a strip of cloth to form a poultice, applying it over the stab wound. She then mixed another poultice for the man's head, slipping it in place under the cloth. She looked up at the men around her.

"He has almost bled to death! We cannot move him if you want him to live. He suffered the stab wound, first then the head wound. My aide is with Lady Deanna. Rolo, please send for him and I will need blankets. His chances are not good. He still may die. We must have him drink a small amount of a potion I have. It will tell us if the knife punctured his stomach, although there is not much we can do if it did. I don't think the knife hit any of the vital organs, but I won't be sure until later. Gaz, can you tell us about him?" The quick and efficient manner the Mother took charge of matters in her domain amazed Gaz, not the Zenith.

"He's Arthur Garret, the man I have working inside Mountglen's embassy. He has strict orders on how to communicate with us. He broke every rule of his training by coming here, but he must have good cause. He's one of my most reliable men. I went through his clothes. I found this ring. It's heavy gold and if I'm not mistaken, that is a rather large emerald."

Jarod took the ring and examined it. "It is an emerald, one of the best I have ever seen. I don't remember seeing this." He handed it to Kyle.

"I cannot put a face with it, but I think I have seen it before. I cannot remember where. You don't forget a ring like this. I will think on it. It will come to me."

The Mother's aide, Duncan, came through the door with another voluminous bag. The Mother gave him a quick report. "Do you think you can use your tube?"

"He's in shock, it may kill him."

"He may die if you don't!"

Duncan went to his bag and started pulling things out. He turned to Rolo. "Bring me some boiling water as fast as you can." Rolo exited the room running.

The Mother went to Jarod. "We will be some time. There is nothing else you can do now."

He frowned. "Kyle, Gaz, let's get out of the Mother's way. We will adjourn to the small reception room. Mother, ask Rolo for anything you need." The Mother and Duncan, already lost in their art, barely noticed when the men left the room.

*   *   *

JAROD, Kyle, and Gaz, each lost in their deliberations, walked to the small reception room. Used primarily for small, intimate receptions where strangers found it easier to meet, the space could hold about twenty people, seated in plush chairs arranged in small groupings. A warm room, it was painted a pale yellow and decorated with soothing colors in light pastels, and faced out onto a balcony with glass-paned doors. Many of the meetings held there became more social than business.

Jarod stopped a steward on the way and requested midmeal for the three of them. No one spoke the rest of the way there.

Strangers passing by would not know what to think. Jarod dressed in his usual black calf-high boots over black trousers, a white, long-sleeved pullover shirt with eyelets for lacing from chest to throat and trimmed in crimson or blue at the cuffs and collar. Blue reigned today, with a matching sash hanging to his right knee: the clothing of a common soldier, not the outfit one expected to see in the Zenith's Chambers.

Kyle wore his regular uniform, much the same as Jarod's attire. The boots and trousers came from the same providers. Kyle's white shirt had a banded collar and cuffs with silver trim. An officer's tunic in crimson trimmed in silver and a silver embroidered deathcat over the heart, still not as grand as the dress uniforms worn by the guardsmen in the Chambers. The deathcat designated his rank of Apex.

Gaz, a small, wiry man whose clothes seemed too big on him, wore tones of brown; soft boots, with the trousers out, a long sleeved shirt with banded collar, all in light tan, and a coat near the deep brown shade of his trousers. He could easily be lost in a crowd. His overall appearance reminded one of a small shop owner or vendor, definitely not one would expect to see in the Zenith's Chambers, not at all.

Jarod opened two of the doors to the balcony to let the cool spring air into the room. The men settled into three of the chairs, arranged in a semicircle facing the balcony. Jarod spoke first. "If you are ready, Gaz, I would like to start the discussion of your operations, unless there are any questions concerning recent events."

Gaz removed a paper from inside his coat. "My Zenith, as you know, the Guard maintains ten outposts at sites throughout the Seven Realms on the coast. These outposts are located at the places we feel are capable of sustaining a landing force by sea. I have men in those units that fulfill more than their Guard duties. These men work with priests, and can send messages through them. The Guard commanders are not aware of that fact. Assigned to become friends with a variety of people in the port cities, these men comprise reports on several subjects. What the people think of your policies, their relationship with their High Lord, the presence of the Guard and how they perceive us, conditions of the realm's army, cooperation between us and them, illegal activities, who lands at the port and what their business entails." Jarod's face became a mask of calmness.

"I work with High Lord Long in much the same way. I have men placed in magistrate's offices throughout the Seven Realms. While the magistrates are loyal to their realm, some of their clerks are mine. In this way, we learn much about how they transact business within the realm, and how well the criminal laws are enforced. Several years ago, your father had to step in to stop the then Lord

Wells from lopping off too many heads for lesser offensives. Shortly afterward, he died in a fall, and his son took the realm. The reason for the succession never became public. You know how superstitious the Deepwells people are about accidents. I have never had much luck infiltrating the High Desert People in Deepwells." The last sentence was said more as an afterthought.

"I have one or two men in each of the High Lord's keeps. It's difficult to find these men. The High Lords generally want staff from their own realm. Therefore, I usually find a need for a specialist each realm does not have, and fill it with a man trained by my staff at the Academy." Jarod looked surprised, but he said nothing. "We train these men in customs of the realm of their assignment, what to look for, and how to report to us. I have profiles on all of the High Lords, including their likes and dislikes, from food to women or men, their duty, and especially how they feel about you. We also know the intrigues in the keeps most of the time."

Gaz continued as if he was naming his favorite children. "I have a team of men who do nothing but investigate crimes against you and Stonefire. We share information to allow the realm to take action, prevent further injustices, and save embarrassment. Most of the realms have some type of organization like ours. None of them know I have men in their realms. We cooperate and share intelligence to our mutual benefit, and they believe me to be a rather weak administrator. I have spent a long time to build up that reputation. Most don't believe that I'm capable of running such an operation as what I have put together.

"In short, my Zenith, I'm your eyes and ears throughout the Seven Realms. I also have a mean bite if required. I coordinate my operations with Kyle, and obtain his permission before any operation. I funnel information through him to you. We have a rather loose working relationship that works well. I understand my operational limits."

The Zenith's expression had not stirred during all of this.

Gaz let out a sigh of completion. "Is their anything special I can answer for you, my Zenith?"

Jarod sank farther into his chair, a bit overwhelmed. He saw at once how Gaz' activities served him; he had never considered that aspect before. He also deduced why his father had never discussed it with him; he naturally felt he would have plenty of time to discuss matters between the realms and other lands. Jarod had been twenty-three when he took the Dais and he married Maress later that same year. He knew he still had a long way to go to master the Zenith's role. He brought his thoughts back to current events. "What do you know about my Uncle Eric?"

Before Gaz could answer, the door opened, and the steward brought in a tray of food and chilled wine that he placed on the table in front of them. He poured the wine and set an individual plate near each of the men. Jarod nodded to the steward. He gave each a clean starched napkin, bowed and withdrew. The meal consisted of roast pork, sweet vegetables, bread, fruit, and cheese. "Gentlemen, this can wait until after we have eaten if you wish."

Gaz picked up a piece of cheese and his glass of wine. "I don't mind continuing. Your uncle, Eric Mountglen, is forty-seven years old. His base of operations is his keep above the city of Glen. He married your aunt twenty-four years ago. His son, Clarence, is twenty-two years old. He also resides at his father's keep. Lord Mountglen is brutal in his business dealings. He only lost a large amount of money one time, and then recouped almost twice as much from that same person several months afterward." Gaz hesitated, "My Zenith, this next part of my report is highly critical of your uncle."

"Go on."

"Your uncle is suspected of arranging your aunt's death, and that of her lover. They found the lovers bodies murdered at a summer cottage on Mount Glen. The magistrate had become aware of the affair. Mountglen knew it only a matter of time before the news came to your father's attention. Your aunt received a strong sleeping potion before the killer cut her throat. She bled to death in her sleep. The man fared much worse. Mutilation of his genitalia occurred prior to administration of the sleeping potion. We don't know if your uncle's orders included that. He did receive the potion and was dispatched as your aunt was, but he suffered a while first. He would die anyway from blood loss, but the throat cut hastened his death. I make the distinction because we don't know if a perceived time problem occurred. Why mutilate him and then speed his death? They never solved the crime. The throat cuts are similar to the three prostitutes recently found here, except the killer in Glen used his left hand, and here it was a right-handed slash, with the same up stroke at the end. The knives had an unusual claw projection at the point in both cases. It's quite possible that they received their training from the same person, or one may have taught the other. This is the only crime we suspect your uncle of committing. That said, he's also known to be unscrupulous in some business dealings."

Jarod remembered his aunt fondly. She had played games with him as a child. He'd heard her saying to his father that Mountglen had become a hard man to love. They had quit the conversation when they discovered him nearby. He never forgot the anger on his father's face. Kyle sat without commenting, his face as emotionless as Jarod's.

Gaz continued, using his reporting voice that let no private emotions show. "His people don't know much about him or the son. Lord Mountglen has delegated the running of his realm to able men who, as far as we know, do an honest job.

"Your uncle rarely has a woman, and when he does, she's brought to him in secret, seems to be paid well, and leaves in secret. He has seen the same woman, on and off, for several years. He rarely gets drunk. He's said to have a quick and violent temper, however his staff is compensated well and staff changes are infrequent." Gaz paused a moment before continuing, and sipped his wine.

"Your cousin Clarence is another matter altogether. His reputation as a caring, somewhat sensitive boy ended at the age of nineteen and took a dramatic turn afterward. We have found no proof of any wrongdoing. Nevertheless, we believe he has committed child molestations and murders of both sexes on numerous occasions."

Jarod's immediate response of anger and concern showed on his face, but he said nothing as Gaz continued. "The bodies are never recovered. Clarence's links to several of the children in various ways is very suspicious. No one has questioned him due to lack of proof. The chief magistrate of Glen is worried, and has had the boy watched covertly for over six months. Clarence is either not the guilty person, or he has been extremely clever. I believe it's the latter. Lord Mountglen seldom drinks to excess, whereas Clarence drinks for days at a time. There has never been a problem with a missing child during these episodes. Clarence has also developed a mean streak like his father. We believe that he had suffered strict and sometimes harsh treatment from his father.

"Your uncle employs a man named Thord—Thord! By the light of the Source, that's him!" Gaz rushed on in a gush of words. "My Zenith, the man in the picture, the one Karl Matthews drew. That is the exact description of Thord. He has been in your uncle's service for several years. We don't know exactly what his duties entail, but I think I'm beginning to understand."

Jarod's face, sad and angry, lost its composure. "You are confirming my suspicions that a member of my own family is responsible for my wife's death. Go on with what knowledge you have of this man." His voice did not show the sadness or rage he felt in his heart.

"My Zenith, I apologize for my insensitivity to your feelings. I'm sorry."

"No, go on Gaz. I'm not angry with you. Please continue."

"Thord is reported to be a brutal man. He has scars from many fights. It has been rumored he fought across the sea, but we have no proof of that. We know nothing of him before he appeared in Glen and worked for Lord Mountglen. Clarence is in his company on many occasions. Thord keeps wild dogs, and uses them for what he calls 'his sport.' He has them fight for food. At times, he takes bets on the winner. That is the only crime we know he has committed. He usually travels with Lord Mountglen. My last report states he's in Glen. I should have updated information in a few days."

Jarod stared at Gaz with a gaze that could bore holes through a battle shield. "What happened to the bodies of the missing children?"

"That is one of the problems, my Zenith. There has never been anything left for proof. No bones, nothing."

Jarod stood and walked toward the balcony with a new glass of wine. His voice became cold, mournful. "Thord's dogs wouldn't leave much bone!" He walked out on the balcony. Kyle motioned for Gaz to stay there, and followed Jarod outside.

"The Dais has always been good to the High Lords, especially to Mountglen," Jarod mused aloud. "How could he hate me so much to kill my wife?"

"Perhaps he does not hate you, Jarod. It could be greed, or any of several emotions that drives him. If he is the one behind this deed, we will need absolute proof to bring him to justice. If we can lull him into a false sense of security, he will make a mistake. We will be there to see it when he does—that, I promise you."

Jarod finished his glass of wine in one gulp and threw the glass toward the adjacent spire. He never heard it shatter on the ground far below. He turned, passed through the reception room and out into the corridor, and was gone.

* * *

WORRIED for his Zenith, Gaz found Kyle on the balcony. "I handled that badly. I have caused him grief. Kyle please let him know how sorry I am."

"He does not blame you. I will go to him later today, and we will talk. Maybe go exercise with the stones. I know him well—he will work through his feelings and take the appropriate action. I bet he's right about the dogs." Kyle felt a shiver creep up his spine.

Gaz spoke as if talking to himself. "I will get a message off to Glen. The magistrate may be able to get more proof with some of these pieces." The two men left the room together, going in different directions.

* * *

KYLE went to Jarod's room and listened at the door. He opened it and entered without knocking. Jarod did not become aware of Kyle's presence until he put his arm around his Zenith's shoulders.

Jarod's quiet sobs continued for several minutes. Kyle felt Jarod had not truly expressed his grief until that moment. He led Jarod to sit on a plush chair, until his sobs died.

Then he went to the credenza and poured Jarod a small glass of brandy. He took it without comment. Kyle went to another chair and sat with him for a long time.

Rolo knocked, once. Kyle ordered him away. Neither man spoke.

Finally, Jarod looked into Kyle's eyes. "Thank you." The pain Kyle saw nearly choked him with his own.

Fighting to hold himself in check, Kyle asked. "Do you feel like exercising?"

Jarod looked into his friend's face and tried to smile. "I will meet you there in an hour." Kyle left with a sad smile.

Outside, Rolo stood across the corridor. "Captain, the Mother sent word that she believes the man will live."

"Thank you Rolo, I will let the Zenith know. Don't disturb him for now." Rolo bowed his head and went off to his other duties. Kyle went to his quarters, one level down, to exchange his uniform for his exercise garb.

* * *

THE Zenith Lords who had good health and were physically able spent one year at Stonefire's mines to learn its management. They studied administration, mining techniques, lessons in command, the art of working with people in a manner that produced the best results and the operations of a large undertaking. Jarod's father, Richard, had gone when eighteen, and Jarod went at seventeen, after completing the Academy ahead of schedule. Jarod's father had observed the men working at the various tasks of mining. He noticed how certain repetitive jobs increased different groups of muscles.

He used that knowledge to produced exercise routines, utilizing stones as weights, after returning to the Spires. He converted a room at the far end of the Chambers for nothing but exercising. He refined the routines until his death. Jarod and Kyle had used Richard's techniques since their Age-of-Man years.

Jarod, envious of Kyle's inclusion while he had to wait, wanted most to join his father and Kyle in their exercises. They grew up using stones of different weights in strong, woven hemp sacks attached to various pulley configurations. They had also helped refine the exercises. The results had been excellent for them, producing men with extraordinary physiques. They said they felt better from following their exercise routines, and missed the exercises when they could not arrange the time. None of the three had ever been seriously ill, which they partly contributed to regular exercising. Kyle escaped the many ills his mother had endured, including the one that ultimately took her life.

He arrived at the exercise room as Jarod started warming exercises. Kyle noticed the hourglass had just started filling with sand, and matched his pace. They went on with their individual routines, working with the stones for one-and-a-half hours after running in place.

Jarod's father had the water from a collector on the roof diverted through a viaduct into the room and a drain to take it away. A lever controlled the water flow. Finely woven wire mesh immediately under the flow of water dispersed it into a fine spray, like a light rain. Jarod had another arrangement of this type built for Maress and he in the refresh room, off their bedchamber. He may have made it for Maress, but he used it daily, as she had. It flowed from a collector designed to heat the water, not like the one in the exercise room that caused Goosebumps.

They stripped and approached the rainmaker, as they called it. Kyle liked the water cold; he went first, the water at the bottom of the collector being colder than at the top. Soap solution provided a fine lather. They knew the timing of the water flow from the collector and could determine the approximate halfway point when Kyle jumped out and Jarod jumped in. Kyle had nearly dressed when Jarod pulled the lever to stop the flow and started to dry himself.

"Jarod, what do you think of Trina?" A sheepish grin appeared on his face.

"Well, she's pretty. She seems to be doing an excellent job with Marc. She has been considerate and kind, although she has an impish side and is a free spirit. All in all, I think she could be quite a handful, but well worth the effort. You could do a lot worse."

"Me—no, not me, I just…wondered."

Jarod chuckled. "I know that look. Wondering like a vulture wonders about prey. I think she could be a lot of fun. MomMav told me that her husband died shortly after she came with child. Why not spend some time visiting my son? It might do the three of you some good."

Kyle considered the invitation for a moment before his sly smile returned.

They left the exercise room joking, with Jarod prodding Kyle to follow up on seeing Trina. The exercise had done what Kyle had hoped; it gave Jarod a respite from the troubles he had been coping with for the last week.

25

THE second day of travel ended, at least the riding part. The party rode in single file; Richard led, followed by His Holiness, then Daniel, Thurston, and Adam. The group had started up a gradual hill leading to a plateau when they heard yells from above and ahead.

Richard and Adam had drawn their swords, and Adam had swung out and around to pull his mount alongside Richard. Two riders approached from the plateau at full gallop. They reined in when they approached His Holiness' party.

"You don't want to go there," the first man said between gasps, pointing up the hill, "you will be eaten alive!"

Travis eyed the two men, who seemed to be no threat. "Please, try to calm down and tell us what happened."

Both out of breath, they gasped for air before the first one began telling their story. "We took the short way across the plateau, as you are about to try. We came across a fresh kill at the last good camping site before leaving the plateau. It seemed a pig-like animal. It's hard to find game up there. We believed whoever killed it must be gone, so we dismounted to get a better look at the carcass. That was when there came this deafening roar from a deathcat! I've never seen one before, and don't wish to see one again. It's the biggest animal I ever saw! It must weigh two, three thousand pounds."

His companion nodded. "The horses half dragged us to the edge of the plateau while we tried to mount. You don't want to go up there. It'll eat you alive for sure. You have fine protection in your guards, but ten like them won't save you." His companion glanced fearfully over his shoulder as he spoke.

"My son, we are doing work for Light's Source. No harm will come to us." Travis' voice rang with confidence.

Disbelief came over the newcomers' faces. "Begging your pardon, father, but you might want to tell us which town you are from, I mean, well, so we'll know where to send the remains, if there are any."

"My son, we are in no danger." His Holiness spotted the deathcat loping along at an easy pace behind the frightened men. When it saw the group, it headed straight for them. Richard and Adam put their swords in their scabbards, smiling.

The second man turned around and saw the deathcat bounding their way. He let out a shriek as both men spurred their horses down the hill at a full gallop.

His Holiness dismounted and waited for the beast he had named Lady. She came to a stop a few feet away, and he went over and scratched her behind the ears. She pushed her head into him in greeting, staggering him.

* * *

THE two men arrived at the bottom of the hill by the time Travis had mounted. Lady fell in beside Travis and they continued on as before. The first man stared in disbelief as he saw the men, plus one deathcat slowly going up the hill. The second man wiped his brow. "I guess they had better protection than we assumed." The two men looked again from time to time until His Holiness' group disappeared from sight over the edge of the plateau. The second man shook his head. "No one will ever believe us."

* * *

THE group soon reached the campsite, and the peccary

Lady had killed. The guards started making camp. Travis went to Lady and knelt in the grass next to where she lay. He grasped his graystone. Lady looked at him in concentration; the images came slowly and not in as much detail, but they came. Travis became delighted beyond his dreams. He would sleep tonight, a happy man. Thurston came over and sat next to Travis. Lady looked over at him and sniffed the air.

"Do you think she will let me pet her?"

"Take your graystone and meditate on some of the most pleasant memories you have. I wouldn't dwell on anything that had to do with killing animals."

Thurston grinned shyly, but followed the instructions. It took about ten minutes, but eventually Lady approached Thurston in a crouch. She gave his face a lick with her broad, rough tongue and laid her head in his lap. Thurston scratched her behind the ears, and before long she voiced her loud, deep purr. Minutes later, she crawled to Travis and put her head next to him. Thurston grinned from ear to ear.

"Thurston, we will keep our experiences with Lady to ourselves for now. The prelate nodded as he rose and went to the campfire to help dress out the peccary.

Later that evening, Daniel tried his hand with Lady. It took a little longer than with Thurston; but soon, they could hear Lady's purr. Travis gave Daniel the same warning as Thurston.

* * *

LATER that night, the men gathered around the campfire. Travis caught Thurston's eye. "We should be in sight of the Spires by mid-morning and to arrive there by mid-day. You should be able to get a hot bath immediately. It will help your discomfort a great deal. I believe the Mother will be there, too. I'm sure she will also have something for you that will help."

Thurston just smiled at the advice, feeling no

embarrassment since the men had begun to sympathize with him. Not long afterward, Travis circled to the side of the camp, away from the horses. He knew that Lady slept for a while next to him. He also felt that she might well be gone when he woke the next morning. *It will be some time before I see her again.* He regretted that. Still, on the morrow he would see his Mavis. Sleep came easily that night.

26

JAROD had not eaten well since his return to the Spires. His hunger after his workout with the stones prompted a large lastmeal and he went to bed early, the first night he did not have a wet pillow. He dwelt on Maress, but finally managed to put his memories aside. Then sleep came quickly.

*   *   *

KYLE also felt the results of his workout. He liked seeing a little of the old Jarod breaking through the gloom and depression. Then, his mind drifted to images of Trina. He too, found sleep easily.

*   *   *

TRINA fed Marc and walked him until she heard a burp, followed by a giggle. Smiling, she put Marc down in the cradle next to her bed. She considered Kyle as she stretched out under her covers, fantasizing about what he might be like in bed, then giggled. She always found sleep easily.

*   *   *

MOUNTGLEN and Clarence visited one of the smaller inns. Mountglen watched while his son went to bed with his clothes on and his head at the wrong end. He had not heard any remarks from Clarence that he'd had dreams or felt Shadure in his mind. He drank a glass of wine hoping he might find sleep easier that night. He would only find dreams of death, his death, and of the endless torture that lay in store for him if he did not succeed at his appointed task.

* * *

LADY Deanna put away the plans for the High Council meeting, late. She enjoyed the new duties the Zenith had given her, and she strove to carry them at as best as she could. She wished she had a son like Jarod or Kyle, as she had many times before. She had a genuine love for her daughter; still, she was not a boy. Sleep came quickly for her. The dreams of a nude man that she recognized pleasured her. She would not remember them the next morning.

* * *

LIEUTENANT Damish wrapped his arms around Lady Gayle's nude body. It had been a big risk coming to her room so often. Their lovemaking, that special kind, the love of young lovers with their whole world and life before them, enhanced by the danger of capture, held them in joyous intrigue. They had secretly promised themselves to one another. Discovery would ruin both their lives. They both slept extremely well.

* * *

PINNACLE Geoffrey Lockley, second only to the Zenith, remained more than irritated. The ride that day had been over hard terrain, and fresh horses promised that they might continue. He preferred going on as long as they could that evening, but decided against it when he saw the fresh horses. They had only just arrived, and looked almost as worn out as the steeds they were replacing. A cool, running stream a short distance from the camp at least provided a chance to bathe. His musings went again to Jarod. He believed his love for him approached that of his own two sons. The message only said that Maress had died, and to come at once. A trip like this would take a toll on any man, even a strong, robust one. Wading into the chilly water, he tried to relax his powerful muscles and let his irritation wash away. He remembered playing with Jarod as a toddler, and wondered where the years had gone. He'd watched him grow into a fine Zenith, and had rejoiced in Jarod's marriage to Maress. He knew the wives and lovers of leaders of great countries seldom numbered two people. Now, Maress' murder required a secured line of succession. Richard had never allowed anyone to bring the subject of another marriage to him when the Zenith Lady Danora died. If only Jarod had been able to provide issue. Maybe, just maybe, they saved the child. He would find out on the morrow. He hated these trips. His mind settled again on Jarod and the succession until his physical demands lulled him to sleep. He slept well.

* * *

HIGH Healer Tobias Sternwood had worked with the Mother and Duncan all day. Duncan would stay with Arthur tonight, and the nights to come until he either woke or died. The three had done all they could for the man. The rest would be up to him. The lack of an infection played an important part and amazed them. Tobias had not seen Jarod that day, and wondered how the young man was faring. He liked the Zenith, considering him a good ruler. He wished him well. Arthur's condition troubled Tobias, and his mind kept returning to him. He finally found a troubled sleep.

* * *

GAZ blew out most of the candles late that night. He had been rereading reports on the movements of various individuals known or believed to be the type of person they were looking for. The last few days had taken a toll, and fatigue gnawed at him. He fell asleep running names through his head. Even so, he slept well, as always.

* * *

MAVIS lay down with a sigh, tired beyond her ability to think. She let her mind settle on the child. An adorable babe, and he looked exactly like Jarod had looked at that age. Well, not exactly, he had not reacted like Marc until he was two months old. She'd been worried about the advancement of the child at first. Now, she relaxed; he acted like a normal babe in every way, happy and good-natured. He certainly did not take after his father in that respect. Before she knew it, she drifted into sleep. Her last musings envisioned meeting her dear Travis the next day.

27

THE next morning, Kyle sat up in bed as if stung by a bumblebee. "Lawrence Burcock!" He shook his head, clearing the cobwebs in his mind. *Lawrence Burcock wore the ring. Of course, he'd worn it when Lord Mountglen returned to offer his sympathy to the Zenith Lord Richard and explain his wife's death.* Kyle rose, went through his morning routine, and dressed in record time. He sent for Gaz who arrived only moments later. The man did not look as if he had slept well, although he stated otherwise.

"Gaz, Lawrence Burcock wore the ring when he accompanied Lord Mountglen to explain his wife's death. I'm sure of it. He always accompanied Lord Mountglen, but I never noticed the ring until then. He made only one more visit after that, and had it then, too."

Gaz instantly sifted his mental files. "I will try to locate him, find out where he has been, and if he had the ring then. This is heady, some progress at last. I will keep you informed as soon as I hear anything." He left before Kyle could respond. Kyle smiled; he'd never seen Gaz so enthused before. He had come to doubt if the man ever showed his feelings. After checking his uniform in the mirror one last time, he started for the Chambers.

He expected Jarod to be in the nursery, and went there first. He found Trina, who admitted him with a shy grin. He did not think she had a shy bone in her. "How is our future Zenith this morning?" he asked. Trina answered pleasantly, and let him know that Jarod had not visited, yet. Kyle watched as she changed Marc, then the two of them took turns playing with him. Kyle assumed he made a fool of himself.

* * *

JAROD slept late. The sun was well into the morning sky when he finished his bath and dressed. Today he wore a guardsman's shirt with crimson at collar and cuff. He had the type of neck for banded collars; he liked the look, too. He never wore the crimson vest, covering most of the white shirt that usually completed the uniform.

He called for Rolo and ordered a light firstmeal, then went directly to the nursery when finished. Marc lay on the ermine throw spread across the bed, with Kyle on one side and Trina on the opposite. They laughed, and Marc giggled. They both had sheepish grins on their faces.

Kyle approached Jarod and waved him outside. "I remembered who wore the ring, Lawrence Burcock, Lord Mountglen's bodyguard for so long. He had it when he came with Lord Mountglen after your aunt's death."

Jarod reflected a moment. "Yes, I do remember now. I wondered at the time if Mountglen had become generous to a fault. I think I didn't place it because Burcock is so big. It didn't look as imposing on his hand. Good thinking, Kyle. I always knew I had a good reason to give you that position." They both returned to Marc's nursery smiling. It became a morning ritual for Jarod.

Rolo's knock preceded his entrance. He bowed his head. "My Zenith, Lord Long has arrived. He awaits your pleasure."

"Rolo, has my small study been put aright?"

"Yes, my Zenith, the Mother told me that the man rested comfortably outside the Chambers; he has not regained consciousness. Jarod felt Rolo acted a bit stiff this morning. "My Zenith, may I stay with the babe for a moment?"

Jarod looked serious. "Rolo, are you considered the public when it comes to my household?" Trina stifled a giggle, and Jarod could not hold his serious mien as a smile crept along his mouth.

Rolo looked perplexed. "No, my Zenith, I don't think so."

"Well that settled, you may know my son's name will be Marc. Moreover, yes, you may visit with him whenever you have the time. Tell Lord Long I want him to join me for midmeal in the small study. Let him know that I can see him later today if he wishes. How did he look, Rolo?"

"Lord Long looked rested, but he is feeble."

"Lead him to understand that his well-being comes first in this case." Rolo bowed his head. As he closed the door, he saw Rolo leaning over the babe, making silly faces.

High Lord Mathew Long had been High Lord of Law and Justice for Jarod's grandfather, father, and now him. Ever since he was a child, he had always searched him out for solutions to his problems. Problems at that time consisted of getting away from the Spires to catch frogs. Lord Long always took time for him, and even told him how he might try. He also alerted the guardsmen of how he might try. He wanted to see if Jarod made it outside the inner circle. He did—right into the guardsmen's hands. Lord Long and an attachment of guardsmen took him on a picnic by the river later that summer. They just happened to pick a spot near many frogs. The boy captured several big ones. He did not understand why he could not take them to the Chambers. Lord Long also pretended not to see or hear the one Jarod hid in his shirt. He really did not understand why someone wanted to eat its legs. Nor, why the maid dropped a serving tray of dishes the next day when the frog jumped on her foot.

Past eighty, Lord Long traveled in a sedan chair whenever possible; and rode in a specially designed coach for longer journeys. His frailty excluded riding a horse. His servitor, Hinston, carried him from the sedan chair and up any stairs. He also stayed at his elbow whenever he walked. Jarod doubted if Lord Long weighed a hundred pounds. Hinson always took the lift to the

Chambers with the lord cradled in his arms, and the Zenith kept a suite for him there. Recently he had spent less and less time at the Spires. Jarod did not begrudge him his retirement; he simply missed seeing him.

Lord Long had been instrumental in renegotiating the treaties between the Realms. He had proved the value of the central power remaining in Stonefire. He found compromise where few expected a good outcome, and all of the High Lords knew and respected him.

Jarod knew Rolo had ordered Lord Long's favorites for midmeal. He also found a lap tray waiting for him to use. Promptly at high noon, Rolo's knock preceded Hinston, with Lord Long in his huge arms. He deposited his charge in his usual chair, and kneeled before his Zenith Lord with head bowed. Hinston had always been in awe of the Zeniths. Jarod thanked Hinston, and asked him to wait in the hall. Rolo had ordered a fully loaded tray for Hinston, and had placed a chair by the door for him.

Lord Long shakily bowed his head to Jarod. "My Zenith."

"Thank you for coming, I realize the effort it requires. The High Councilor will arrive later today, and the Pinnacle arrives two days later. I hope you can stay that long. I want you to know that your health and comfort means more to me than seeing you stay from a sense of duty that makes you uncomfortable or ill. You must promise me that you will do as I wish in this."

The old man's face lit up and his eyes sparkled. "My Zenith, you have always been kind. I will do as you say. I believe I will manage quite well. I have Hinston and your staff has always helped in any way they could to make me as comfortable as possible. Rolo has always taken a personal interest in my needs and supervised my care well.

"I want you to know how deeply saddened I'm over the death of Maress, my son. I can truly say—" his eyes reflected his emotions, "—I never heard a bad word said of her. Your happiness enthralled us all. Men, who bear your responsibility don't always find love and a political match in the same woman. I wish you well, and a quick recovery over your grief, albeit, that too, rarely happens." Lord Long relaxed into his chair.

Jarod had a lump in his throat the size of a melon. He had never heard Lord Long talk about anyone's personal feelings before, certainly not his own. He had always been the perfect senior statesman and consummate reader of the Law. "Thank you, my lord, your kind words mean a great deal to me."

Jarod started to say more, but Rolo's knock interrupted him. Rolo and a maid brought in the food trays and served them, placing Lord Long's lap tray in the most comfortable position.

Once alone with Jarod, Lord Long became the senior statesman. "Now, how may I serve you my Zenith? Have you any questions about the marriage pack or the will?"

Jarod's voice took on the sound of a man who had lost his spirit. In a way, he felt he had. "No my Lord. Maress was murdered."

Lord Long's fork fell to his tray. His face, already white, turned ashen. Concerned, Jarod poured him a glass of water, taking it to him rather than waiting for him to reach out. He took several swallows and waved him away. "You are sure? No…no, of course you are sure. Tell me what happened."

Jarod sipped his wine and told the entire story, from when Maress took ill to their present conversation. He included the part about Lawrence Burcock. "There is no conclusive proof we have that will hold up in a High Lord's trial at this point. The High Council will meet later today. His Holiness will arrive today. My question to you is what is the best way to proceed concerning Mountglen? I wanted you to have time to consider before the meeting, and I'm glad you saw me before the others arrived."

"My dear Zenith, I, too, am glad you talked to me first. I will reflect on the ramifications to you and the Seven Realms. If your suspicions are proved correct, you must plan for the eventual takeover of Mountglen."

Jarod had not considered beyond the capture of Maress' murderer. He realized, at once, the impact that course of action might have on the rest of the High Lords. He needed to do some reflecting, too.

They said little else over their meal. Afterwards, Jarod poured them each another glass of wine. Smiling, Lord Long took the goblet and said, "One thing about being my age is that no one looks when you take a second glass of wine."

"And just exactly what is your age? I need to know how long I have to wait."

Lord Long chuckled. "My Zenith, I assumed you knew. I will be one hundred and four in two months."

Jarod nearly dropped his wineglass. He knew when he celebrated his birthday, just not how many there had been. *We must make that a celebration*, he promised himself. *Hells to Dark's Source, every day must be a celebration!*

As if he had read Jarod's mind, Lord Long said, "The first thing I do when I wake is to make sure I'm still alive." Before Jarod could respond, he continued, "My boy, I'm sorry to have lived so long to see a day like this one. I need to rest now. Please let Hinston know I'm ready to go to my room. Call me when the others arrive. I will be ready."

Jarod watched while the big man gently carried Lord Long down the corridor. He hoped that the High Lord's quality of life hadn't been diminished by the effort given to the Seven Realms. He knew the work had been grueling at times. He also knew it provided him a feeling of accomplishment and joy at being in the center of important events. *How could it not have taken a toll?* He opened the door to his study when he saw Duncan hurrying his way.

"My Zenith, Arthur is awake. He can barely speak. He asks for you." Jarod rushed to Arthur's room.

Tobias and Mavis stood next to the bed. They started to speak; Jarod cut them off with his hand. He went to Arthur's side. It took a while for the man's eyes to focus. He became agitated as he recognized his Zenith Lord who leaned close to his ear. "Try not to move around," he said softly. "I'm here, and I will stay until you can tell me what you need to say. Please try to relax, breathe slowly, and speak when you are ready."

"Your son...is in great danger," Arthur gasped. "A man has...killed a Gal. They both... stood well over six feet. I followed them...from the embassy to the river. I heard the Gal say...he wouldn't hurt the Zenith. I never saw anyone...strike so fast. He slit the Gal's throat. I watched while...he stripped him of his uniform. He used the Gal's privatecloth...to tie his feet together with some rocks...and pushed him into the river. The man said that now...he would 'kill the brat.' I'm sorry, my Zenith...that is the phrase he used. I tried to return...up the path. He must have seen me...going toward the bridge and the Spires. He must have! I went slowly...fearing discovery. He waited for me...at the bridge. He stabbed me...but not where he intended. I jumped up...onto the wall of the bridge. He reached for me...and I grabbed his hand. I fell into the river. His ring came off. I knew the wound's...serious nature. I saw some reeds...when I surfaced in the water. I snapped one, used it to breathe through under water...and stayed beneath the bridge in the dark... He couldn't see me. He must have believed...the current had carried me...downstream. I could see him...searching for me along the bank. He started running...along the bank, downstream. I pulled myself...to the bank, still under the bridge...and must have lost consciousness... I woke in sunlight on the bank... I saw a Guard officer...and a Lady walking toward the river...when I came from the dark shadows.

The officer helped me. I told him I had to…warn you of danger. He got some men…and brought me to you…" Arthur's voice became raspy and weak.

Jarod kept his voice low and soothing. "You have done me a great service. I understand what you have told me, and I will take action. Now you must rest. You have done what you can. Mother Mavis, her assistant Duncan, and High Healer Sternwood are here to take care of you. You couldn't be in finer hands. I want you to relax as much as you can. Try to keep your breaths slow and do what they say. Don't talk for now. Just rest, and let them help you." Jarod shook Arthur's limp hand gently. Arthur's eyes closed as he slipped away from the bed. The Mother followed him into the hall.

The Mother's professionalism surfaced, again. "His wound is serious, though I believe he will live. Duncan got his tube in his stomach and we gave him water and medicine. He had syrup of the flower, too. He won't have much pain. My son, have you ever considered becoming a healer? You did well in there."

Jarod kissed her on the cheek before she returned to her charge. Noticing someone dusting portrait frames that did not need dusting, he approached the man. "Do you work for Gaz?" The man nodded and kneeled before him. "Have him come to the small study at once." He turned and went down the corridor to his study. The door opened within a few minutes.

"My Zenith?"

Jarod looked up from his writing. "Arthur is a brave man. He didn't describe Lawrence Burcock as such; he just said both men stood over six feet. He saw him kill a Gal and take his uniform. Arthur pulled the ring from his hand when he fell into the river."

He deliberated for a moment, looking perplexed. "Gaz, you said you did a project for my father, something about mapping the secret passages. Does the nursery have any way in besides the one door?"

"No my Zenith, not has far as I know. I will have the room checked carefully, and I will double check my maps as well."

"Arthur confirmed that Marc is the target. Let Kyle know, and tell him I want increased guards at the entrances to the Chambers. I also want every door to a secret passage inconspicuously guarded at both ends. The contingent of guardsmen must be big enough to fend off a surprise attack from a large, muscular man who will strike without warning. He will probably be wearing a murdered Gal's uniform. The one thing that puzzles me is why the hurry? Why did they take those kinds of risk to kill a child? I feel an unknown sense of urgency in what has been done."

"My Zenith, you would make a good agent. I feel the same urgency in these actions that you do. I will see that your orders are immediately carried out."

"Good, I'll be here for a while if I'm needed. Please give me advance warning of Lord Lockley's arrival. Tell Kyle that the Mother is convinced that His Holiness will arrive today, and I have found that she's rarely wrong. I don't know how she knows, but have full honors ready for him if he approaches. I don't know how many will be in his party, since he does not like traveling in a large group. I think it will be best if they had rooms in the Chambers. It has been a long time since I have seen His Holiness, I hope he's well."

"I will see that it is as you wish." Gaz bowed and turned toward the door.

Jarod's voice stopped him before completely left the room. "By the way, Gaz, I'm afraid I cannot be one of your agents. The Mother has already spoken for me to be a healer."

"Of course, my Zenith." Gaz had a puzzled look on his face as he went down the long corridor.

28

KARL Mathews waited at the office door of Priest Cannon, the head academic for the Academy. The man opened the door from the inside precisely as the Academy's bell rang the hour of nine. Karl jumped, thinking the room empty.

"Come in Mathews, don't just stand there." Karl followed the priest and took the chair where he pointed. "Lets see now, it's a matter of placement, umm yes, placement. I gave you a book on the organization of the Guard, your assignment for yesterday. Now, I want you to explain to me what you read, umm yes, tell me what you read."

"Priest Cannon, I found it most interesting. The names have to do with stones: A Pebble is a group of ten men, and is led by a Skimmer. Three Pebbles or thirty men are a Rock, led by a Rocker; he's the first level of officer. Three Rocks or ninety men are a Trass, and are led by a Lieutenant. Three Trass or two hundred and seventy men comprise a Scree, and are led by a Thrower. Three Screes, a Boulder, led by a Gal; a team of forty support personnel supplements them, bringing a Boulder to eight hundred and fifty men. I found the name 'Gal' strange. I looked for it in your library. It took a while, but I found it. It means an iron-bearing rock. There is a small Boulder of six hundred with no support team also led by a Gal, used on short missions when speed is important. Three Boulders make a Tor; they have an additional support team of fifty, bringing it to twenty-six hundred men, led by a Looker. Two Tors or fifty-two hundred men are a Mount, led by an Apex.

There are several levels of Apex. The first level is a Fang, and its badge is the head of a deathcat. The second is a Claw, and its badge is the head and one leg of a deathcat with its claws extended in a striking pose. The highest Apex wears a badge with a full deathcat reared on its hind legs. There are three of them: the Zenith, the Captain of the Guard, and the Pinnacle. If there are more, they left them out. All Apex officers are referred to as simply 'Apex,' and known amongst the men. Detailed drawings are circulated throughout the Guard." Karl sat still, feeling a little breathless.

Priest Cannon nodded throughout Karl's dissertation. "Two more hold Apex rank, my son. One is a crouching deathcat, and the last is a springing deathcat. I hope you will never see those badges; they are used only in war." He rambled on. "Looked up Gal, looked it up, well that shows initiative, shows initiative, good, very good. You can do sums too, umm…yes.

"You will start in the next class, which begins in two months. I will give you several books to read before then, as you have a lot to learn before your first class. I will test you often to see your progress, yes umm, progress. The Zenith sponsored you personally. It has happened before, but not by this Zenith or his father. The remaining students will be from families of the Lords of the Seven Realms, umm realms, yes. You are required by law to wear a badge yourself." Karl looked surprised.

"Any student sent by the Zenith wears a badge of a deathcat cub in the same stance as a Claw Apex. It signifies that you are under the protection of the Zenith. Any attack on you represents an attack on the Zenith. Our students can get a bit rough sometimes, especially with someone they perceive to be in a lower social class. One could lose their head if they accidentally harmed you! It will make things more difficult for you, umm yes. The books I want you to study will give you some of the knowledge they already have. It's my hope, umm yes hope, that it will allow you to better fit in with them."

Priest Cannon selected several books from his collection and handed them to Karl. "Be off with you now, umm yes, now. I will see you in one week at the same time. I have placed your gold coins in the lockup, and entered them in the books under your name, safe, umm safe. Your uniforms will come to you by tomorrow. Be gone now, umm now."

Karl took the books, bowed and headed for his rooms, anxious to see what they contained. *I wonder if he always talks that way.*

29

HIS Holiness rose at dawn and was surprised to find Lady lying nearby, washing her face. Travis assumed the wild game in the area had decreased by at least one. He grasped the opal stone as Lady looked at him with sad eyes. He flooded her with gratitude through the stone. Lady's purr would wake anyone still sleeping. Travis scratched the back of her ears. Magnificent feelings of peace washed through him. He let her know she should not come any farther with them. She sent back worry. He countered her feeling with ones of safety and gratitude, then sent an image of returning. Crawling the short distance to his face, she gave him one very wet lick, then rose and disappeared into the woods.

They broke camp early. None, more than Thurston wanted to arrive as soon as they could. The hospice sat to the side of the city, with the Mother supervising the healers and herbalist as well as the general staff. She also kept apprised of the hospice houses throughout the Seven Realms, run with monies from the Zenith. Travis planned to stop there first to refresh and change into their more formal attire. They arrived at mid-morning.

He felt Mavis' presence close by, and knew she waited for him at the Spires. Travis asked the steward to inform the Spires that he would arrive at mid-day or shortly thereafter. The five men each had a hot bath and dressed in fresh clothes.

Travis asked to see the main patient area. He went down the long rows of beds, blessing all, talking to a few. The steward approached and informed him that the Spires had sent an honor guard. He turned to head for the entrance when his eye fell on a giant of a man overflowing his bed; not only tall, but heavily muscled as well. He asked the attendant about the patient's condition, and learned he had an arrow wound, and lingered near death. The wound is too great for our healers to heal. They cut the arrow's shaft at his skin level and stopped the bleeding, but the arrowhead is too close to the heart to be removed. He gave only one piece of information, his name, Lawrence Burcock. Travis blessed him as well.

His Holiness' group, accompanied by an honor guard of thirty, approached the gates of the Outer Circle at mid-afternoon. Trumpets sounded from each of the parapets in succession, making three rotations of fanfares. Travis saw a sea of men and women kneeling before him when the gates opened. It had been a long time since his last trip to the Spires. He had forgotten—or tried to forget—most of the pomp and ceremony accorded him on his visits. It became quite overwhelming at times. He felt the weight of those souls on him, and for a moment, wished to be a simple priest once more. Then he realized: *You are a simple priest, you idiot!* He dismounted and walked through the crowd, giving his blessing, knowing the same actions would be required again when they entered the inner circle.

The head steward of the Great Hall knelt before His Holiness and took the proffered hand to his forehead. He informed him that their entire party had quarters in the Chambers. He led the party to the lift at the rear of the Great Hall. The size of the Great Hall and the idea of a lift dumbfounded the guards. A tight squeeze for five men and the creaking chains drained the color from more than one face.

Jarod, Kyle, and Gaz were all waiting to meet him. The two priests from Maress' cremation ceremony stood in the background. The Zenith Lord started to kneel before His Holiness, but Travis stopped him, and kissed the younger man on the cheek. Jarod put his arms around his old mentor and hugged him. The two priests at the rear of the small crowd gasped. His Holiness went to each of the others, giving his hand to be touched to their foreheads while they knelt.

He went to the priests last. Travis had not missed their reaction when the Zenith embraced him, and pitched his voice for their ears alone. "My sons, I raised the Zenith for over ten years. I know the tenet of forbearance of touch. That is to maintain distance between the faithful and the priest. There is no distance between the Zenith and myself. The tenets of the faith are there to guide, not to impede." He stopped their attempted protests with an upraised hand, and then turned to see Jarod coming to him.

"Your Holiness, Lord Lockley is arriving in a few minutes. I request you attend a meeting of consequence when he has refreshed himself. I think there is someone else that wants to see you until then. Rolo will show you the way. The Prelates have rooms adjacent to yours; your guardsmen's rooms are on each side of them. I will send word when the meeting will start. The Mother is invited also." Rolo led Travis toward the Mother's suite.

The same general routine followed for High Lord Geoffrey Lockley. The Zenith and The Pinnacle walked toward his suite, telling him about the meeting, and that he wanted to convene it as soon as Geoffrey felt prepared. Geoffrey nodded and they agreed on a half-hour hence. Jarod asked Lady Deanna to have the participants notified. Pages swept past him, running in different directions to deliver his requests before he walked a few steps from her door. He saw Kyle, and asked him to go with him to the council chambers ahead of the others.

"Did Gaz tell you what Arthur said?" He went on at Kyle's nod. "It seems this man Lawrence Burcock is involved in many things that will interest us." Jarod's mind leapfrogged. "I have requested guardsmen for the secret doors. I never knew so many passages existed. I think it will be wise for us to familiarize ourselves with them when we have time."

"I agree. I have had a search started for the identity of the Gal that Arthur saw killed. We found the privatecloth still at the bottom of the river under the rocks it held. The current must have carried the body down to the river. You know how strong it is at the small bridge. Finding the body will be difficult. Gals are in and out of the Spires all the time, and many are over six feet and powerfully built men. Messages have been sent to the outposts, but if the Gal was on leave, it may be weeks before we hear. Still, the effort has begun."

They reached the council Chambers and sat in their usual seats: The Zenith at the head of the table, Lord Apex Kyle Byrne to his left, and The Pinnacle on his right. Ten large, plush chairs surrounded the table, four on each side and one at each end, with enough room for twice that number should the need arise. The three-inch thick tabletop, cut from a massive slab of marble, reflected light in smoky tones. Seats and small desks lined the wall for scribes, and an open area took a quarter of the room for twenty guests. The meeting convened with Jarod, Kyle, Gaz, His Holiness, the Mother, Tobias, Geoffrey and Lord Long, without scribes. Gaz sat ready to take notes he would flush out later and give to Jarod. Only Geoffrey and His Holiness did not know the complete circumstances surrounding Maress' death. They began arriving within a few minutes, and found seats. Hinston deposited his master in his usual seat, bowed to The Zenith and left the room.

Jarod looked around the room before speaking. His voice showed his strain. "We are here to discuss the death of the Zenith Lady and its ramifications. Most of you already know the details of her death. Your Holiness, Geoffrey, I am sorry to inform you that my wife died by poison. She was murdered."

Shock registered on Geoffrey's face, but the Mother had already prepared Travis. The coldness in Jarod's eyes reflected in his speech. "We have concluded that the most likely suspect is a High Lord of the Seven Realms, and the ultimate target is my son. We have only circumstantial evidence that precludes bringing formal charges against this person at this time. We believe the perpetrator of this crime is my uncle, Eric Mountglen. A man named Kirsh and an unknown woman committed the crime. We believe that a man known as Thord hired them. A man we believe to be Lawrence Burcock murdered Kirsh and the woman."

Travis' voice rang with disbelief. "Zenith Lord, what name did you say?"

"Lawrence Burcock—your Holiness, do you know this man?"

"I don't know him, but I went to the hospice before coming here and inquired about one of the men before I left. They told me he was near death and his name, Lawrence Burcock."

Jarod's voice took on eagerness. "Your Holiness, which of your Prelates will be the most capable in convincing this man that he has a chance of redemption?"

"That is Thurston. He could talk a deathcat out of its fur."

"Gaz, I want you, Tobias, Duncan, and Prelate Thurston to go to the hospice house and see what you can learn from him. Write down every word he says. Do whatever you must to keep him alive. Find out everything you can from the hospice people about him. Hurry, as fast as you can get there!"

"At once, my Zenith." Gaz and Tobias left the room on the run. Gaz shouted orders to his men in the corridor as he raced by.

* * *

DEEP sadness touched Travis' next words. "Jarod, my son, I'm so sorry. Please allow me to give an invocation for her."

The Zenith only nodded. His Holiness, spiritual leader of the Seven Realms, stood with his palms upward, level with his heart.

> "From Light's Source-
> Let Light stream forth into the minds of men.
> Let Light descend on the entire world.
>
> From the point of love within Light's Source-
> Let love stream forth into the hearts of men.
> May Peace, return to the entire world.
>
> From Light's Source, where the Plan of the Light
> is known-
> Let purpose guide the wills of men,
> The purpose of which the Masters know and
> serve.
>
> From the center which we call the race of man-
> Let the Plan of Love and Light work out.
> May it seal the door where Dark's Source dwells.
>
> Let Light and Love and Power restore the Plan on
> our World."

Travis sat down with a heavy heart and heavy conjecture. *It has already begun. We have no more time.* He looked down the table at a man too young to carry such a burden, *as if any man is old enough to save his world.* "I must see you as soon as possible on a matter of extreme urgency. It's not something that can wait."

Jarod said to Kyle, "Please fill Geoffrey in on what we know. Lord Long brought up a subject earlier today, and

I request your ideas and opinions about it. I will be with His Holiness in my small study. We will continue in the morning, if not tonight." He noticed Geoffrey's moist eyes when he got up to leave. He and Maress had been fast friends from the day they met.

* * *

JAROD went to the credenza and poured two glasses of wine. They had not spoken on the way to his study. He really did not want to talk about Maress, not now, and hoped Travis would not bring up the subject. The last few days had been troubling enough. He felt emotionally drained. Events were happening so fast, and most of it he could do little about. He did not know how much more frustration he could take. He took a glass to Travis and sat across from him. The worried look on His Holiness' face concerned him.

* * *

"THANK you, my boy, I know the meeting we left is important. However, the information I have will impact everything you do in the future. You reply, 'The Stones are protected,' in the formal ceremonies you perform. I doubt that you, or any Zenith before you, for two millennia, knew the real significance of the phrase. I only discovered the meaning a few years ago from reading old personal histories and manuscripts. I learned most of you believed that it meant the Stone you wear or the Box of Stones you guard. It's neither."

Travis wondered at the amount of despair and joy a death and birth could bring as he continued. "The first Zenith's name is an appropriate name for your son. Mavis told me the name, and the increased development in cognitive and physical skills he displays. These things tie together from many parts. I will try to describe it logically. Then we can discuss whichever parts you wish." The mention of Marc seemed to lighten Jarod's spirits.

Travis' voice, anything but condescending, held its usual warmth. "An object from the heavens crashed in Stonefire where the Tower is now, many millennia before the Great War. It crashed into an area of solid rock, creating the Tower crater. We don't know where it came from or why it came, probably a random event. No matter, it crashed here in Stonefire. Crystal formations began forming around the crash site shortly afterward. They broke into many shards while cooling, revealing a Stone lined with gold veins like the one you wear. The people of that time soon learned that the Stones had power. They imbued the wearer with increasing insights over time. Later they discovered the wearer had the ability to use physical force with their mind and to speak directly to minds by feelings or images. The deathcat became one of the most receptive beings to this form of communication. They soon bonded to the Stone-wearer who first called them, and protected the bonded person as it protected itself. Laws protecting them remain.

"The existence of a Dark Stone became known as a tool of Dark's Source. The evil manifested through the Dark Stone overcame the Stones of color by influencing men to do evil.

"Then an amazing thing happened. Links to Light's Source developed when men came together and acted as one, combining their strengths and working for good. They learned that the person wearing the Dark Stone supported Dark's Source. The one Dark Stone channeled power from Dark's Source, while Stones of many colors channeled power from Light's Source. The Dark Stone influenced people to do evil while the other Stones influenced events, helping in communication and healing. The Dark wanted to rule, to destroy Light's Source on this world. The gold veins disappeared when someone wearing a Stone willingly gave that Stone's power to another. The powers of the transmitting Stone greatly diminished, transferred to the recipient Stone whose powers increased. Not only did the recipient receive the power, so did his consanguinity, in some cases to sons already born! The power flowed with the man's seed.

"The power of Dark's Source used many devices to bond men to the wearer of the Dark Stone. In time, armies arose to conquer Light's Source and did much evil. With their power fragmented over so many, the men of Light's Source became easy prey. They found they could win if they combined as much power as they could in one man. They did not have much time to fight amongst themselves over the choice of who should lead. They quickly and unanimously agreed on a great fighter, noble in intent, devoted to Light's Source and respected by his peers. As you well know, I mean Marc, who became the first Zenith Lord. The armies and forces of Light's Source and Dark's Source battled for years. The forces of Dark's Source, defeated in the last great battle, diminished the power of the Stones to an almost unfelt level. The Dark Stone couldn't be found after the last battle." Travis sat uneasily in his seat while discussing the great evil that had almost destroyed their homeland.

After a sip of wine, he continued. "Marc received a vision. In it, he saw that the Stone's power would return and that his line, his seed, would be needed again. He took the name Greatstone, and took the land that became Stonefire. He built the Tower in the crater at the seat of the Stones' power, and formed an order of priests to teach the way of Light's Source and to keep the secrets of the Stones within the priesthood. The reference to the Stones given in our teachings is that they are part of Light's Source: a gift. The history of the Stones became lost to everyone over time—except to the priests." Jarod frowned. "Even they excluded their lower ranks, so that knowledge of the Stones was earned by devotion to Light's Source and good deeds. Only seven know the Stones' story, and only four know it completely in our time. Language changed over time. Today, only four of us can still read the old writing. I have one of our most devout translating the tomes."

Travis tried to recognize an emotion from Jarod. He'd never seen him close himself off so much before. He went on. "The six men who led the armies for Light's Source received realms. That is how they formed the Seven Realms."

I must get on with it, he realized, *he has known most of this since he was a child. But not the history of the Stones though, surely not.* "The true history of the Great War, systematically reduced over time, is hampered even more by the changes in our language. It has been the duty of each Holy One to determine the power of the Stones, and to test for an increase of that power. The power is returning to the Stones now, and rapidly. The writings tell us that the power will return to one born to be great. I believe that person is your son, Marc! I also believe I can confirm it."

* * *

JAROD'S rejection continued against hope and reason. *I pray you are wrong. I gravely fear you are right.* He had not stirred, and his face remained calm while his insides tore apart.

His head spun with this confirmation, not knowing if he could speak. He buried his head in his hands. He knew the confirmation was necessary, yet, he dreaded it. The slim doubt he clung to would disappear with his hope. He looked into the Holy One's eyes. "If what you are saying is true, I'm to believe that my son is to fight another Great War, and that it's the influence of a Dark Stone that is responsible for Maress' death?"

Travis nodded solemnly. "Yes, someone bound to the Dark Stone caused her death. It never resurfaced that we know of, and it is not mentioned in our documentation— that we can decipher—who held it last. Well, maybe now we have a good idea. We have a lot to confirm and if I'm right, a lot to do. We won't know for sure until I can test Marc."

Concern finally showed in His voice. "Test him how? I won't see him hurt. Maress gave her life for him. I won't see her or his life wasted."

"He won't be hurt in any way. In fact, we believe it will be quite enjoyable for him."

"Travis, you help raise me. You know I love and respect you. It's just…it is just, so much as happened to me in the past week. I have spent my days chasing after information on Maress' death." His mind formed what he did not say. *I'm scared to* confirm *what you say!* "You will need to bear with me. I need some time to think. Let us return to the meeting. I will want to talk to both you and Mavis when it's over." His mind resolved itself. *I don't need it confirmed, you do.*

They did not speak on the way to the council chamber. Everyone rose when they entered. He waved them down with his hand and took his chair. Kyle finished his briefing to Geoffrey and Lord Long. Jarod pulled the bell for Rolo.

He ordered refreshments for everyone, including Hinston. Geoffrey looked at him with an expression of such sadness he had never seen before. He stood and poured himself and Lord Long a glass of wine. Lord Long had a twinkle in his eye when he took it to him. Lord Long took his hand, the twinkle gone. "I cannot express the sadness I feel for you, my Zenith." He gave his trembling hand a light squeeze and returned to his seat, then looked around the room.

Jarod indulged himself by not moving forward on the current information at the moment. No matter how much he wished it did not have to be, Marc's future lay open and defined. "I have known each of you my whole life, except Kyle, who I met at age four." Geoffrey's chuckle broke some of the tension. "He and I are closer than any two brothers could be, I think."

With a glance at Travis, he made his decision. "His Holiness and the Mother have something we must do and discuss. I don't think it will take long. It's my request that you stay here until the three of us return. We won't be disturbed. Have Gaz wait here when he returns, regardless of the news. He rose, motioning again for those staying to keep their seats.

Jarod looked at the Mother when they entered the corridor; "We are going to the nursery." She made no comment and took Travis' hand as they started for the nursery.

He was lost in apprehension on the way. *Please, let it be someone else to open the Box of Stones. My Maress is gone; I can't bear to lose Marc as well. Give me strength as well if he's the One.* His mind rejected his desperate pleas almost as they formed. *I know he's the One.*

Trina, in a pale yellow dress, had dressed Marc in light blue. They lay on the floor playing. Trina held a locket made of silver on a chain. She swung it over Marc's head. He tried to grasp it and when he succeeded, he giggled. Trina ran and threw her arms around Travis. He held her for a moment, then drew back to regard her. "This cannot be Trina; she's just a little girl." Trina laughed and hugged him again. "My dear, please wait outside for a few minutes. The Zenith and I have something to do with Marc. It won't take long." Trina suddenly looked worried. She bowed to her great-grandfather, curtsied low to Jarod, and quietly left the room, closing the door behind her.

Feeling as though he might burst, he held his emotions in check. "What is this test you mentioned?"

Travis drew a pale stone from beneath his robes and over his head. "You see the gold veins in the Stone. These gold veins will transfer into Marc. They won't harm him in any way. They should give him a feeling of peace."

"But, you are not sure. You have not done this before

to anyone. How can you be sure?"

"Jarod, no one has done this in over two millennia. I have faith in the writings, and in the things I have seen and felt recently. Marc let out a lusty cry at his birth. I heard that cry as plain as if I had been standing in this room next to him. I sent an eagle to the only person I suspected might have heard, also. His reply confirmed my suspicion. He's on the way here now, although I don't expect him for a few more days. The Mother told me how Marc likes to hold on to you. How he seems to know you, even at this early age. I believe that the power of your Stone draws him. You may not feel it, but you will. I think he does now."

Jarod did not know what the transference might do to Marc if they had misjudged him. His speech became measured and quiet. "You are asking me to let an unknown power invade my son's body. I know you are both loving people, and I know you believe in what you say. Are the two of you agreed in this?" The Mother and Travis both nodded. "Then know this: I will never forgive either of you or myself if any harm comes to Marc." He took a deep breath. "Do what you have to do."

Travis went to Marc and removed his tiny dress. The babe's eyes focused on the old man, and he tried to reach for him. Travis held the Stone, swinging slightly back and forth, over Marc's head. He let it grow still over the babe's chest and then let it slowly progress downward. Tiny golden arcs left the Stone and entered the babe when it got about two inches away from Marc's chest. The babe giggled, then reached up and grabbed the Stone. The room started to fill with a golden light that radiated from Marc, not the Stone.

Travis knelt and lifted his hands. "Thank you, Lord of All, for sending us this child to help us in our hour of need."

Jarod stood, troubled. *It is Marc! He will be the Darkslayer, and there will be war!* He stood in a daze while the light slowly retreated into Marc's chest. The babe looked up at his father and gave his little, cheerful laugh. Jarod took his son in his arms for a long moment; Marc was his usual bubbly self. Mavis went to the door and asked Trina to come in. She saw the last of the light receding into Marc. Her mouth opened, but no sound came from her. Jarod laid him down in his cradle, with Marc asleep before his head hit his pillow. Travis looked down on the sleeping child.

His words held a power neither Travis nor the Mother had ever heard. "He is the Darkslayer!" Shock registered on Travis' face. "He will have heavy burdens placed on him. Come, we have a lot of planning to do. This is something that affects the Seven Realms. I will need advice on our plans. I want those at the meeting fully briefed. You will restrict knowledge to them. We...I, need you."

"My son," Travis said, "how do you know this?"

"You are not the only one with ancient writings, and ours have be retranslated every ten years."

Shock, and then resignation registered on The Holy One's face.

"And, what am I to do?" Trina asked.

Travis turned to her with a smile. "Why child, do what you have been doing all along. He's only a babe. But try not to drop him on his head; someday he might have to save us all." He turned and left with Jarod and Mavis. Trina did not look nearly as free spirited now.

All eyes turned to them when they entered the room. Jarod turned to Gaz after they sat. "The man claiming to be Lawrence Burcock is dead. He died of an arrow wound close to his heart. Duncan, Tobias, and the Prelate said they didn't know how he lived as long as he did. The Prelate heard only one saying from him, over and over: 'Have to kill the brat!'" Gaz looked at the Zenith Lord apologetically. "Someone stopped us a few beds away as we left. He wanted to know if the Zenith paid for his care at the hospice. After we affirmed that all the hospices fell under your largess, he said he knew the man. We asked that he tell us what he knew of him. He said he had known him briefly in Mountglen. Burcock had stated that he refused to leave Mountglen again and his surprise at seeing him rang true. We hadn't mentioned Mountglen, so I think he told us the truth."

Jarod signaled for Rolo and requested the Prelates join them while the room buzzed in quiet conversation. Travis nodded.

His voice to Rolo had been forceful and his eyes cold. He addressed the room in the same way. "Gentlemen, shortly I will ask the Holy One to recount for you what happened a few minutes ago in the nursery, and its ramifications. I request you to retire for the night after you hear what he has to say. You may deliberate alone or with one another, but this information is not to be shared with anyone else. Tomorrow at mid morning, we will reconvene, and I will hear your suggestions. I want to see Kyle and Gaz in my study when we are through here." He neared the door while it opened to admit the Prelates. He passed them, barely seeing their nods.

He went to his study and pulled a plush chair where he could see the painting of Maress. *I wonder my dear, did you know somehow, feel somehow, that our son would carry such heavy burdens. I will do my best to protect him. I give you my word that your fate won't befall him.* Suddenly, his convictions became too painful when looking into those eyes. Any vestige of hope that Marc might escape his fate evaporated.

He poured himself a glass of water, and then walked to the window, watching the sun fall in the sky. His deliberations centered mostly on his regrets for the pain and trials his son would have to face. *Marc must have time to find some joy in life before the killing starts. Will the channel to Dark's Source cease if we can capture the Dark Stone? Does Mountglen or Clarence have any humanity left to act on an appeal to stop the reign of terror to come?* He decided they must not have much reasoning left. Especially, if the Dark Stone had already influenced them to do the unspeakable deeds reported to him.

The last Great War had killed more than half the population of the Seven Realms before Dark's Source withdrew. Disease and starvation took half of those left. Great skills and knowledge had been lost. They lost centuries of accumulated knowledge, including the ability that built marvels of machinery and many disciplines, including the study of medicine that had not been duplicated yet. He prayed that it would not happen again.

He sat in a darkened room when Kyle and Gaz entered. Even in the low light, he could see their strained faces. Rolo followed on their heels, lit several candles and then left quietly.

Kyle looked into his eyes, "My Zenith, I don't know about you, but I think Gaz and I could do with a glass of your excellent brandy, with your permission, of course."

Jarod smiled, "I think you are right. You may do the pouring." The three men talked long into the night. Rolo brought them lastmeal and then fruit and cheese about midnight. Kyle and Gaz had discussed various options until the drink dulled their deliberations. They did not make a decision.

Neither man noticed that Jarod had switched to water after his first drink. He did not want, could not, be drunk in case something else happened. He wondered if he had been foolish, and then discarded that idea and decided on caution's road.

After he and a few guardsmen put Kyle and Gaz to bed in guestrooms, he sat at the side of Kyle's bed for a moment, looking down at his sleeping form. "I cannot lose either Marc or you...I think either might kill me." He pulled the covers up farther around Kyle and left the room.

He found Travis waiting for him in a chair outside his suite. "My son, it may not be as bleak as it might seem.

Tomorrow, we must open the Box of Stones. The book inside may be of great help. "*Lord* Deion" may be able to help too, when he arrives."

It took a moment for it to register in Jarod's mind. *Ah, the Protector comes!*

Jarod's warm voice softened. "Until mid morning then, you and Mavis sleep well." It felt strange thinking of them in bed together. He let the image go and went to bed within a few minutes.

30

JAROD woke early, and found it strange that he felt so well. He went out on the balcony in time to see the sun casting its first rays on the City. The City, a jewel as much as any in his crown, laid out in perfect squares with wide streets. Entire blocks made beautiful with green parks with flowers from each of the Seven Realms, at least, the ones that thrived in Stonefire. At the center of the City was a green park four blocks square with fountains, play equipment for children, and hide-a-ways for older children. The shops around the Center Square offered the best goods produced in the Seven Realms and imported from across the seas.

Jarod wondered if the attack from Dark's Source might come from the sea. The Seven Realms had no navy. Traders had learned of the riches in the Seven Realms and ships from the eastern lands came frequently. No doubt, due to the rich deposits of gold and precious gems mined in Stonefire. The mines remained hidden to anyone from across the seas. In fact, very few people knew their location inside Stonefire. Traders, not allowed beyond the ten port cities, saw little of the larger, inland cities. Rumors spread across the seas over time, the way rumors are likely to do; the amount of Stonefire's wealth grew with each telling. The Pinnacle negotiated trade agreements with foreign countries based on the guidelines established with the High Lords of the Seven Realms. He did an excellent job keeping goods of many types flowing to and from distant lands. He had men that could hire on as seamen for short periods, usually one round trip voyage. They had sufficient time to check prices at the warehouses and gather information about who did business with the Seven Realms. Gaz also had men that went farther inland to gather more information. These activities, always completed as covertly as possible, remained an ongoing effort. Jarod wondered if the rulers of distant lands knew as much of the Seven Realms as he did of them. Stonefire discouraged visiting seamen from exploring beyond the port cities, but that did not mean it did not happen.

The sun reflected off the wide river and its two canals. The canals, dug over three hundred years ago to facilitate the transport of goods without fighting the raging currents and many rapids of the river. The flow from the river regulated the barely moving water. Mules pulled barges to and from the City using the canals. The river flowed in a generally eastward direction to the sea. The canal to the south of the river brought barges to the City to be unloaded at the east docks. The barges then entered a flooding lock that opened into the river when filled. The barges transversed the river to another lock on the north side, and repeated the process in reverse. The same arrangements had been constructed at the port city of Outreach; there, the transverse distance became much greater, spanning the wide delta to take advantage of the dissipated current. The canals worked well moving commerce in and from the City; he speculated if they would work just as well moving an enemy. Some of the port cities had the same arrangements without the need for locks: Devinswood in Westwood, and Elizabethville in Mountglen.

The high ground surrounding some ports made the use of canals unworkable, and only ships and seamen from the Seven Realms serviced them by taking goods and supplies to and from the three main ports. He made a mental note to discuss the idea of a fighting navy with the council; it would also be good to know the naval strength of lands trading with the Seven Realms. Outreach,

Stonefire's major port city, put few ships out to sea despite its name. Now, perhaps, that isolationism would end. That would be another subject for the council on another day, and he already had plenty to go through on this day as it was.

Dressed in his privatecloth and robe, Jarod looked in the mirror and saw a devilish grin form on his lips while an idea formed in his mind. Rolo's soft knock, followed by his entrance with a firstmeal tray, set his mind. He ate well and fast.

After dressing, he went to the guestrooms where Kyle and Gaz still slept. He motioned for a guardsman, and borrowed his sword and shield. The guardsman looked puzzled as he handed the items over to him. He quietly entered Kyle's room, pulled the drapery to fill the room with light, and then banged the sword against the shield in rapid succession.

The deafening sound jerked Kyle straight up in bed, his eyes wide and his arms fending off imagined attackers. Kyle stumbled toward his sword before he saw Jarod standing by the window. The look on the Apex Lord's face forced him into a howl of laughter. Kyle's face went from dismay to anger, to a smile and finally to laughter.

Gaz rushed into the room with a drawn dagger, completely nude. Jarod laughed even harder at the expression on Gaz' face. "Why Gaz, I daresay you are a bigger man than one might suppose." Gaz turned various shades of red, as he and Kyle returned to gales of laughter. Slowly, Gaz joined in after pulling Kyle's bedclothes around him. Jarod looked at Kyle when their laughter died down. "I told you I would return the favor."

"That happened what, five years ago?" Kyle saw Gaz's questioning look. "I did the same thing to him the morning after his first time being drunk. He swore he would get me back. However, Gaz, I wish you could have seen the expression on your face. Please, forgive us." He could barely get the words out before starting to laugh again. Gaz did not join in as quickly this time. Seconds later, he laughed with them.

"Kyle, the room of stones in ten minutes, you need a workout."

"Have mercy, I didn't make you do that, too."

Jarod's eyes went to Gaz and winked. "You are not the Zenith, ten minutes."

He walked to the door with Gaz smiling and following along. Outside, with the door closed, he returned the sword and shield to the guardsman, trying his best not to laugh. "My Zenith, please don't tell him you used my sword and shield." He nodded; he heard the guardsman chuckle before he started for the room of stones.

Kyle reached the exercise room within the time proscribed. "This is cruel punishment." He got the words out in a serious tone, but then could not keep a straight face. The two worked their muscles much the same as the day before.

He put his hand on Kyle's shoulder after showering and dressing. "I want you to give serious consideration to the consequences of an attack by sea. Be ready when the subject comes up. I don't know when I will raise it, maybe today, also, your ideas on building a navy and training the men to sail it. Travis said the Dark Stone's power grew. We don't know how fast or where Dark's Source has the influence to harm us, nor do we know by what means. I just think it should be discussed, at least." Kyle nodded and the two men started for the nursery.

Kyle knocked softly and they entered the nursery. The Mother smiled and came to embrace one and then the other. "We have exciting news. Trina called me this morning to see Marc perform his latest trick." The Mother's bright smile warmed them. "You have already seen him grasp and hold objects. That usually does not happen before about two, two and a half months. This morning he rolled over two or three times on his own. Again, that does not usually happen until about two months of age, and that is in only a quarter of the babes born. Some babes can take as long as four or five months to reach that level. You have quite a remarkable child."

Both men beamed from ear to ear. Jarod went to his son and did what most fathers had done since the dawn of time, but he did not know that. Kyle took a little more interest in Trina than he did Marc.

* * *

THE Mother sat in a rocker doing needlepoint. She did not remember being this happy in a long while. Maress' death hurt, but she knew that sort of pain, and could handle it with loving care. She had the man she had loved for as long as she could remember together again with Jarod, Kyle, and now Marc. It had been two millennia since a real war occurred. There had been a few skirmishes by feuding High Lords from time to time. Most settled without too much bloodshed by the Zenith. *Full-scale war will take a lot of healers and herbalist we don't have.* She began mapping out plans for training in her mind, a reflex action, started without thinking. She shook her head. The scope of such a project took much more planning than she could do from a rocking chair, and she looked up at the water clock. "My sons, it's time for our meeting."

Jarod and Kyle said their respective good-byes to Marc and joined Mavis going toward the door. They looked at Marc when he raised his head and let out an angry cry, looking directly at Jarod. Trina took the babe in her arms and distracted him while the three left the room.

* * *

THE participants waited in the same seats as before when Jarod entered. They all stood except Lord Long, who bowed his head. He did not wave them down as he had done before. He sat and looked at each person as they regained their seats. None looked like they had slept well. "Mother Mavis and Gentlemen, shall we begin? First, we need to discuss your conclusions on the matter of Mountglen?" He leaned into the chair and let the others get their ideas focused.

Lord Long answered first. "The law is quite clear: Mountglen will forfeit his head, as will his son, if the allegations are found to be true. There is no one left in his line of succession. The Zenith has the right to take the lands and merge them with Stonefire. However, I advise against it at this time—I feel the High Lords will be leery over any stratagem of that type. They view the central government as good, overall. There has been no default of fidelity to the Zenith by any High Lord in the last two millennia, until now. It will be the end of the Mountglen dynasty if we prove their crimes. I strongly believe that the other five realms will support a new dynasty with little or no resistance. All of the High Lords are in your debt. Some won't admit it openly, however, each of them owe their fortunes to the Zenith's line. It's the Zenith's decision, ultimately. By law, he can take the realm and keep it separate from Stonefire, or merge the two into a larger Stonefire." Lord Long let his words sink in before continuing.

"Great care must be given to the selection of a new High Lord. Our goal is to be seen as a benevolent benefactor rather than acting from self-interest. The Zenith has great power in this under the law and he can do as he pleases in this matter.

"It might save a lot of time to be pointed in the right direction if the Zenith has contemplated this matter." Lord Long looked at the Zenith. No hint of a twinkle resided in the old man's eye.

Jarod spoke without hesitation. "I'm in favor of a new dynasty based on what I now know. First, we must get absolute proof of Mountglen's wrongdoing, proof that will stand up in a High Court. That won't be found easily." Several nods rippled through the room.

"The bigger question is the effect Dark's Source will have on the realms. If it can control my uncle, it may be able to control anyone. In fact, we must assume the worst case and plan for those possibilities. What do we do with the Dark Stone if we are able to capture it? Can we keep it from influencing others? Is there a way to protect the general populace and us? Those questions—and probably a thousand more—must wait until we know more about the Stones and how they work.

"However, I'm getting off-topic. The answer to your question is simply put: I have no designs on the realm of Mountglen. There must be an overriding consideration to force me along that path." He sat for a moment, watching the reactions to his words. "Perhaps it's time to make a formal agenda of actions needed, ranked by importance to the Seven Realms. We must devise a way to protect Marc until he takes his place, if His Holiness is correct about my son, and unfortunately, I believe he's right. I detest the idea, however, we must also train him in the skills he will need."

His voice filled with strength and cold resolve, "You all must accept the fact that we are now at war!" The abrupt change in the Zenith Lord's voice drew alertness higher. "Its declaration happened when Dark's Source had my wife killed. I expect everyone here to act as if those statements are true until we can prove them incorrect."

He looked at each person at the table before continuing. "I'm clearly in a biased position on the subject of Marc. I will excuse myself until you can list the things that will protect the Seven Realms. I have discussed the possibility of attack from across the seas with Kyle. I believe it's something else we must consider. I will leave you to your work."

Jarod left the room. Everyone except Lord Long stood and bowed their heads.

He went to his study and paced while his deliberations swirled. *I swore to put the welfare of the Seven Realms above all else when I took the Dais. How could I know the effect that vow would have on my family? Is there any way to protect Marc? There must be! We must have time to prepare. I will put the Seven Realms above all else, but I won't jeopardize the life of my son. He's the protection of the Seven Realms! He will always be my first priority, and the greatest concern for me.*

With that decision made, he began to calm down. He wanted a distraction; he wanted some fresh air, to see happy people, to escape. He put his battle sword baldric on, took his sword from its hiding place and slid it home in the scabbard. He finished dressing in a black cape and hat. The hat had a wide brim that curled slightly downward, with a long black feather slanting to the edge of the brim. He reached the lift without encountering anyone other than guardsmen, whom saluted smartly.

He remembered the stone Gaz had pressed in the anteroom to release the passage door. He had never used that passage before, and was surprised to see light at its end; not much, but enough to see by. The source turned out to be a small window looking out onto a courtyard. One stone on the left wall looked worn at its bottom edge; he pushed on it. The door swung open onto a dark alcove, and closed after he passed through. He looked at a plain wall. He found he could not see down the passage from the outside. The window had bars every three inches like the others on the first three levels. He smiled. *Who conceived the idea of putting a window looking down a secret passage?* He walked out into the adjacent courtyard; one that he knew well.

His hat pulled low and its long black feather made the distraction he wished. Those he passed by did not have time to get a good look at his face after looking at the feather. He went directly to the only stable inside the inner ring, the Zenith's stable.

He found the stable empty except for a stable boy he

had not seen before. His clothes showed little rank, feather, or no feather. The battle sword and its scabbard made it a completely different matter. He walked to the stable boy as if he owned the place, which, of course, he did. "The Zenith is sending me on a mission. I will need the big black."

The boy looked doubtful until his eyes saw the sword. He ran off to get the horse ready. Jarod went to a box beside the first stall and removed two sweetstones. Blackwind gave him a gentle nudge when brought to him. He gave him the two chunks of sweetstone as he always did. He thanked the boy and mounted. He realized, *This is a lot easier than the last time I slipped out to bring a frog home.* He wanted to laugh, but restrained himself.

The inner-ring gates opened for wagonloads of supplies. The practice of both gates not open at the same time except on special occasions needed revision. He went against the flow of the supply wagons and no one gave him much attention. The outer-ring gates opened to allow entry to the next set of suppliers when the inner gates began to close. He rode through, again without much notice; the inspection focused on those that entered, not the ones that left.

*   *   *

THE pikeman looked at the concern on his lieutenant's face. "Is something wrong, sir?"

"I could have sworn I saw the Zenith. In fact, I know that is the Zenith's horse. Oh Blessed Light!" The lieutenant began running toward the inner gates.

*   *   *

JAROD rode at a leisurely pace into the city. He purposely took roads he had not traveled, working his way toward the Central Park. He found the stable on its western side, exactly where the plans called for it to be when he had approved the funds. He dismounted; a stable boy dressed in a fancy livery ran out to meet him and took the reins. He reached into his pouch for a coin.

"Oh no sir, I cannot take a gratuity. The nearby shops pay me. This is about the best horse I have ever seen. I will brush him down for you, sir."

"Wait! I believed the stable serviced those visiting the park."

"Oh it is, sir. However, you see the shops on the western side are the finest in the land. Most of the better trails in the park are on the eastern side. It does not matter if you don't go to the shops. Most people that come here do shop, though. But sir, none of them have a horse this fine." The boy went toward the stable, leading Blackwind.

He thought. *Well, this won't make it onto the council's agenda, but I will see what is going on here.* He walked across the wide avenue to the facing shops. The first shop, a man's clothier, drew his interest. He had never been in a shop. He considered it strange that he owned much of the land in Stonefire and never once had been where his subjects lived out their lives.

Tinkling bells sounded when he entered and a man rushed from the rear of the building. He fought not to laugh at the man's clothes. He had purple trousers with a yellow shirt, a gold sash, and he wore sandals with no stockings.

He rushed straight to his new customer. "Oh my, oh my, oh my, you do need help with all that black! We must put you in something with a little flare. I don't believe you have been here before. Now, don't worry; I dress the finest people in Stonefire, the country! Our clothes are the best made from the finest materials in the world, but that is why they are so very expensive. That won't be a problem, will it?"

He let his cape slide away from the sword. The shopkeeper saw the gems set into the top of the scabbard;

his eyes widened. "Oh my, yes, well, I can see price will be no problem. Let me show you the latest things being worn at the Spires on formal occasions."

He did not hide his surprise. "Are there many formal occasions at the Spires?"

"Oh my, yes, our Zenith is quite the one for entertaining. If, of course, you know someone that can get you invited. I might be able to arrange an introduction to someone who could help in that department, for a small fee, of course. Now, if you will step right over here, I will show you the finest clothes in the Seven Realms. I'm Jessup, might I inquire as to your name?"

This should be interesting. He followed the man toward the rear of the store and took the ornate plush chair the tailor offered. "My name is Jarod, after the Zenith." His sword swiveled around athwart his lap. Jarod wondered if Jessup might drool when he again saw the gems set in the scabbard.

"Yes, I see, let me show you a few things." Jessup disappeared into a side room and emerged with the most garish outfit Jarod had ever seen. "This is being worn at the Zenith's formal occasions by only the very elite. I heard by the few, who have had the deep sense of fashion and the daring to wear something so new, which the Zenith himself commented on the man's good taste. It comes in different color schemes. No two are alike."

Jarod looked at the horrible mix of colors and said simply, "That is good. I think, perhaps, something in white." His conscious gave him a slight twinge when an idea arose, a very slight twinge.

"I'm afraid I have nothing already made up, which is no problem. I use only the best seamstichers. Can you give me an idea of what you have in mind?"

"Well first, white boots." He went on to describe the formal State regalia in minute detail, with Jessup writing as fast as he could. "I think ermine will do for the robe, trimmed in crimson fox, and held by a heavy gold chain.

Also, I would like a dagger made with the scabbard set in rubies and the handle fashioned from a single ruby."

"Oh my, my, my, surely you are not serious. Oh, my, you cannot be serious. You are jesting with me, are you not?" Fingers tapping his gem-hilted sword, Jarod shook his head. "Oh, I see, well, oh my, I will have to make some inquiries. I'm afraid the ermine and rubies will be a problem. They are very rare, you know."

Sounds of many horsemen interrupted the conversation while he considered letting Jessup off the hook he had swallowed. He stood and saw the stable boy pointing to the shop. Apex Stephen Goldlion entered the shop within seconds. He walked toward the rear where The Zenith Lord stood.

"Apex, how good to see you again, I have just been describing the clothes we talked about. Come and sit a moment while Jessup tells us about getting the outfit made. Now, I don't want to hear a word. Come and join me for a minute, and then we can be on our way. Go on Jessup, you said something about cost, I believe." Stephen looked somewhat perplexed, but went over and sat next to Jarod.

Jessup's shock showed. "Well, oh my, let me see, the robe in white ermine, trimmed in crimson fox, held with a heavy gold chain. The ermine will difficult to get. I suppose you will want only the purest white?" Jarod nodded. Jessup began to sweat a little, although cool air circulated in the shop. "Well, my dear sir, Jarod," The Zenith put his hand on Stephen's arm, which stopped him from coming out of his chair. "I can only give you an estimate on the robe, a very broad estimate. Made, as you have specified, will be somewhere between five and six gold pieces. The rest of the outfit will be no more than a gold piece, excluding the dagger. I will have to refer you to someone for that. I fear the cost would prove prohibitive to anyone except a High Lord or..."

"Stephen, Jessup has been showing me outfits worn at

the Zenith's many social functions, like the colorful one, there. You are at those functions, what do you think of it?"

Stephen looked at the outfit. His face contorted to keep from laughing. "I can honestly say, my...my friend, I have never seen an outfit to match it."

"There, you see. I deliver only the finest. Do you not think that outfit might suit your needs? I could have it fitted to you in no time."

Jarod stood. "Perhaps, another time. Apex, we are leaving."

"At once, my Zenith."

The two men walked to the street. An honor guard kneeled in salute. The stable boy held the horse and gave the reins to the Zenith Lord. Then, he too, kneeled as the guardsman had instructed him.

Jessup's mouth hung open from the time Jarod left the shop, but when the honor guard knelt, he fainted.

Jarod and the Apex rode at the head of the guardsmen. "My Zenith, you gave us a scare."

"I know Stephen, but Jessup made it worth the time. Do men really wear those outfits? And, if I'm not mistaken, you caught me leaving the Spires to catch frogs?"

Stephen laughed, "Yes, my Zenith, on both counts."

"Well, perhaps we can throw some business his way for the imposition I caused him. Perhaps, some of the Apex dress uniforms." Apex Stephen Goldlion only smiled ruefully at the idea.

His fanfare sounded when the outer gates opened. The ceremony surrounding the Zenith resumed its high protocol. He handed over Blackwind to the stable boy. "Did you accomplish your mission, my lord?"

"That I did. He's a fine horse; take good care of him. He likes sweetstones, but don't overdo it."

Jarod watched for a minute while the boy returned Blackwind to his stall, wondering if he may ever again have such a lark. Sadly, he doubted it would be possible. He wanted to leave the Spires one time before the pressing events completely forbade going anywhere but to war. *It was foolish perhaps, but it did me well, and I will never have another chance.*

He entered through the Great Hall and went straight to the anteroom, turning the day's events over in his head on the ride up. *Jessup didn't know me. How many people in the Seven Realms have any idea of what I look like? Coins carry father's image. Besides, you really cannot tell much about a person's features on coins. I could go virtually anywhere in the Seven Realms without being known. The Guard will know me; the High Lords and Lords will, but the general population won't. They certainly won't know Marc if they don't know me. What if Marc grew up outside the Spires, and only a few people knew who, or more importantly, where he resided?* His deliberations trailed off as the cage reached the twelfth level.

Rolo caught up with him and asked about midmeal. He told him what he wanted and started toward the small study, where he felt most at home.

He looked up at Maress' portrait. "My dear, it's a different world out there, did you know?" He poured himself a glass of wine and sat looking out the window at the City below. He felt sad. Then, the remembrance of Jessup's clothes broke his mood. Perhaps he *could* send some business his way. *I'm sure he would think the orders quite mundane.* He chuckled again.

Rolo found him looking at the portrait of Maress when he brought his food and wine. Jarod went to the small table where Rolo placed his meal. "Rolo, have any of the Zeniths entertained, had banquets with entertainment, that sort of thing?"

"Most have, my Zenith. Your grandfather had banquets and spectaculars known throughout the land. The Great Hall filled to overflowing on many occasions. Your mother and father gave several before your birth. He refused to have them after her death. At first I believed it was due to his grief, then one day I overheard him say he disliked the fuss. He did a lot of hunts and fishing trips with the High Lords, however, and sometimes their sons went along too. I remember that you went on several of those. You are aware of your father's private nature. Does that answer your question, my Zenith?"

"Yes Rolo, it does. How much time is required to prepare for one of those banquets?"

"Several months, my Zenith. The invitations need to be sent in time to make arrangements. Some will take four weeks to get here. They usually stay a week, at least and will be away from their realms for over two months. The minimum amount of time should be three months; I recommend four."

"Thank you, Rolo, you have been a great help. Please ask Lady Deanna to come to me." Rolo bowed and left on his errand.

Four months should be about right, he considered. He attacked his meal; he felt good about his morning. He had finished when Lady Deanna arrived.

"My Zenith, how may I serve you?"

"I believe we keep an active list of the High Lords, Lords, and important personages from throughout the Seven Realms. How long will it take to devise a guest list for a banquet where there will be ample time to speak with certain people in private during the week they are here?"

"My Zenith, there are many activities scheduled for the guests during the whole of that week, too many activities for everyone to make an appearance at half of them, much less, all. You could request one's presence without any problem. I looked at some of the old records on this subject for the Zenith Lady. She wanted one after the babe's birth. She had planned to request one for the week of your birth in eleventh-month. I had completed some work on it before..." Deanna's face paled as she realized what she was saying. "Oh, I'm sorry my Zenith, I didn't mean to bring your Lady's—"

"Don't distress yourself, Deanna; I have accepted the fact that Maress is dead. I have to put her death away for a while. I believe she's with us in Light's Source. Go on with what you were saying."

Clearly, Lady Deanna had not been reconciled to Maress' death, and neither had he.

"I have a preliminary list of guests drawn up, and had started a list of activities. The guest list presents some unique problems; the titles and responsibilities vary between the realms. I think I have most of it worked out. I can find it for you in an hour or so. It was put away…"

Jarod nodded. "Tomorrow will be fine. I probably won't have time to do much with it until then or next week. I would like to have it at hand, but tomorrow is in plenty of time. Thank you, Deanna."

* * *

LADY Deanna stood and bowed her head, with a sly smile on her face that Jarod missed, and went out. She smiled fully in the hall. She rather liked the Zenith calling her in the familiar. *Now where is that box?* she wondered.

* * *

JAROD walked by the council room, and heard loud voices from behind the thick door. His father had told him on several occasions, "If you want something done in a hurry, get out of the way so they can yell. They will be too restrained if the Zenith is present."

It must be working, he thought with a smile.

31

THE knock came late in the evening. Jarod had already bathed and was relaxing in his suite, reading. He had nothing on but his robe for modesty. He opened the door to find a tired but smiling Kyle and Gaz. The three men found seats, and Jarod signaled for Rolo before anyone spoke.

"Before you both start, have you eaten lastmeal?"

Kyle looked at Gaz, and then to Jarod. "We did have lastmeal several hours ago. Something light would be nice. Maybe some cheese, fruit and definitely some wine."

Rolo's timing remained perfect. Jarod gave the order for food and drink, and then turned back to the two men.

Kyle continued, "We have put together an agenda of ten items for your approval. Also, the members of our group, including Lord Long, request to stay here at the Spires until after the Naming Day ceremony."

Jarod began to relax, only then realizing how stressful the waiting had been. He nodded at Kyle to continue. "Marc's health, protection, and education must be provided for. That is paramount in everyone's deliberations. We need to start a concentrated effort by a select group to study the old books, and begin a search for lost books. The council members said to search their libraries first while they are here at the Spires. Take no action against Mountglen until the evidence is conclusive. The procurement of that evidence will be a task for Gaz. We also recommend the preparation of the start of a new dynasty in the event that Mountglen's guilt is confirmed. Gaz is to investigate the murder of Lawrence Burcock. I will start the preparations for war. We will do it quietly at first, until you are ready to make an announcement. Priests are to start counseling sessions with the persons they can reach to identify any who are having the type of disturbances described in the old books. They are also to increase their involvement with the communities they serve. They will forward any pertinent information to the Tower. Most of the priests don't know that it's one of the reasons the Tower exists. I will call in seamen we can trust to lay out plans and discover the cost and requirements of building a navy. Finally, Gaz will have his agents infiltrate the lands across the seas in all directions. They will look for rulers who reign with tyranny and abuse their subjects." Kyle leaned into his chair, folded the paper he had read from, and let out a sigh of relief and fatigue.

He reached over and took the parchment from Kyle's hand. He opened it and briefly, read the list before returning it. It did not take long for him to see the sense to it. "I veto the infiltration of the keeps until I have had time to meet with the lords myself. I don't believe we can trust anyone outside the Spires, and at least one person inside the Spires. I agree that we need to investigate the possibility of a navy, but suggest we do it as covertly as possible. Disguise it any way you can, and don't let those we talk with leave with the idea that we are considering the building of a fighting navy."

Jarod relaxed a little before continuing. His tone remained the same. "I'm planning a banquet," Kyle and Gaz registered their surprise, "in four or five months. The outside reason will be to pay tribute to the Zenith Lady. I don't want any mention made of Marc. The real reason will be to get certain information from the guests. We will define the extent of that information over the next few weeks. I approve of the council staying here in the Chambers.

"Gentleman, the council has done a good service to the Seven Realms and me. I commend you, and it will be by proclamation. Now if Rolo will get here with some refreshments—"

Rolo's knock punctuated his sentence, and the three men chuckled while the steward entered, paying no attention, setting the food and drinks on the low table within reach of where they sat, bowed, and left.

They talked and laughed over convivial subjects for an hour, giving themselves a break from their problems. Jarod recounted his events of the day. The part about Jessup's clothes and shop had them all laughing. Neither Kyle nor Gaz said they disagreed with him going into the City alone, but he was sure they thought it.

Rolo's knock brought them alert. He entered and took a message to Gaz on a silver tray. Jarod knew that Rolo did not disturb them for something unimportant. Rolo bowed and stood nearby, waiting for a reply.

Gaz read the message and looked at Jarod and Kyle. "Mountglen is on his way here. The message says Clarence is with him. They are traveling fast by coach. A postscript says the bird is almost dead. The person sending the message must have scared it badly."

Jarod sat into his chair in deep concentration. Kyle and Gaz did not disturb him. He looked as if coming out of a dream after several long moments. "Kyle, I want you to send a detachment to Mountglen's keep and search for two things, the old books and evidence of their involvement in Maress' death. Gaz, you will have men in Guard uniforms. If the need arises, I will excuse it by saying the description of Thord prompted the action, and that we felt it prudent to rule out any possibility of someone from my own family doing such a thing, no matter how remote. We won't have to excuse anything if we find what I expect. Have your men meet with Travis and the Prelates for a brief on what to look for and how to identify the old books. Some parts of the writings are the same in all the books. They will leave for Glen as soon as their training is completed.

"They are to say they are a relief group for the dock garrison if they encounter Mountglen's coach on the road. They are to avoid any conversation with him or Clarence. The Gal will do the talking if a confrontation takes place. I will brief him personally. There is to be no misunderstanding that this is my direct order to the men. The troops are to be respectful at all times. They are not to break anything, and are to leave things as they found them. A small group of men should not cause alarm. Of course, if a scree of men are performing exercises nearby, that too should not cause concern. Those activities are quite common."

He frowned, "They won't be able to return before Naming Day. Have them take a graystone. Mountglen's keep and our garrison will have fast birds. They are to send a message as soon as they find anything. I will detain Mountglen and Clarence here until I hear their report. We will watch him in secret if he arrives and does not let us know he's here. Gaz, do you have a replacement for Arthur inside Mountglen's embassy?"

"Yes, my Zenith, he started today. Mountglen financially destroyed his father, and he committed suicide. William hates Mountglen, so he will be quite diligent. I questioned him for a long time to insure that he won't take revenge himself. It turns out that he's devout to Light's Source. He told me he wants to see the agony caused by a public trial for Mountglen's business dealings. He knows nothing of what we suspect. He will do well."

"Good, get word to him that Mountglen may be arriving in two to three weeks." Kyle nodded his agreement. "Kyle, you select the Gal. He must be someone you have known for a while.

"If Lawrence Burcock killed Kirsh and the woman, who killed Lawrence Burcock outside the Spires with a Guard arrow? I saw the arrow on its route to Gaz from the hospice. I want the Gal to vouch for every one of his men. Gaz, I want you to vouch for the ones you send.

They are to meet the guardsmen they will be traveling with and know one another's faces, at least. I will issue the order for their mission personally."

He considered a moment before continuing. Kyle and Gaz sat in silence. "It will be acceptable if they don't find anything. They won't have an axe hanging over their heads and I will make that clear. I want them to go as soon as possible after the two of you are certain they know their mission, they know one another, and they know what they are looking for. Now, gentlemen, I find myself tired. Please excuse me, I will see you both in the morning."

Kyle stood at once and saluted his commander. Gaz bowed his head and started for the door. Jarod acknowledged them with a nod and slowly walked to his bed, not seeing Kyle's concerned look.

* * *

GAZ stopped Kyle halfway to the stairs. "I have never seen him like that. Does that happen often?"

"Zenith Richard realized he had a mind of a genius early on. Few people know he completed the academy in a third of the normal time. The rest of the time, he spent studying advanced subjects including everything from combat to philosophy. He's even a fairly good artist.

"I have spent my life studying the military and leadership. I have received honors from the Seven Realms for the work I have completed. You know my background. I earned my Apex deathcat by doing what some called impossibilities. He would give me an idea more than once, and let me work it out in the field. He's an amazing man. It's a shame you have not been able to observe him in action the way I have."

"I knew his brilliance, but I had no idea he had such a decisive command. I'm impressed." Kyle smiled at him and the two went their separate ways.

32

DEION approached the Spires with eagerness and hope. His first trip to the Spires, the size and grandeur of the City awed him, but nothing could prepare him for the overwhelming presence of the Spires. He understood now how it had become the central point in the last great battle.

He felt the presence, his heartbeat and his breathing, when he concentrated. He would soon feel his complete presence if the Old Books reported correctly. One question among many hung in his mind. *Will the Darkslayer know me in the same way?* The babe's strong telepathic skills still grew daily. He had never believed since he took the vows of the Protector that the Darkslayer might come in his lifetime. He could not imagine that much power at such an early age. He had felt his own powers steadily growing for the past year.

His clothing looked immaculate. He had changed into a fresh outfit, neatly packed for this day, at the inn where he'd spent the night. The boots, trousers, tunic, and cloak, all dyed the same shade of gray. The cloak spread out around him, hiding his size. He pulled the cowl from his head when he approached the outer gates. His snow-white hair glistened in the early morning rays of the sun, contrasting with his deeply tanned face. He sat upright and erect in the saddle as if he had just started his trip. In truth, he had been traveling almost non-stop since a few hours after he received the Holy One's message.

The lieutenant at the outer gate had never seen the emblem sewn into the cloak. He believed only the Holy One wore a gold tower. The white deathcat curled around the base of the tower surprised him the most. He had never seen anything like the man. A great air of calmness and power swirled about him. His features, almost too fine for a man, he might describe him more beautiful, than handsome, but not to his face. The piercing blue eyes belied the man's countenance and held visible power. The Lieutenant felt stripped to his spirit for this man to see and read the good and bad within him. He did not realize how close to the truth he came.

"I'm Deion Russell; I come in answer to a summons from the Holy One." The quiet power that radiated from his deep voice astounded the lieutenant.

The lieutenant would not have known the proper address for this strange man if word had not preceded his arrival. "Your Grace, you are expected." Deion had heard his title so seldom it startled him. The Lieutenant did not know or suspect the peaceful man in front of him commanded the skill of the most accomplished warriors in the Seven Realms. Coupled with his many powers, he was the most deadly man alive, for a while.

The lieutenant called for an honor guard with orders to escort His Grace to the Holy One. The men presented their pikes in salute. Deion certainly had never had that kind of treatment. He gave his blessing, replaced his cowl, and allowed the guardsman to walk his horse to the main entrance inside the inner walls. His true size became evident when the cloak fell close about him after he dismounted. He amazed the guardsmen; his six feet, four inch heavily muscled frame fitted his true mission.

He followed the steward of the Great Hall to the lift in the anteroom. He gave Deion instructions on the lift's use, and where to find Travis' room. He kneeled, waiting for his hand to place on his forehead. It took Deion a few seconds to realize what the man expected. He gave the steward his hand and blessing.

* * *

HIGH Priest Aubusome entered the Chambers when he saw another priest emerge from the lift enclosure. "You there, priest, wait, you are not allowed in the Chambers without being called. You have no right to be here."

Priest Aubusome caught up with Deion as he turned to face him. Shock registered throughout his whole body. He felt the full impact of the presence before him, and fell to his knees and bowed his head. Realization of the priest's identity hit him as hard as the force that took him to his knees. He looked up at the man exuding great power and finally saw the emblem on his cloak. "Your Grace, I'm sorry. I didn't realize..." What happened next totally surprised him. He slowly rose to his feet without any effort on his part or seemingly from His Grace. Sublime peacefulness filled his mind.

"You need to work on your pride. It does not fit your rank, High Priest." That said, Deion turned and continued his way to Travis' room as if he had lived there all his life.

* * *

TRAVIS awakened with the same feeling as when he heard Marc's first cry. Dressed, he paced the reception room off his bedchamber. Peaceful and calming feelings flooded his being. He clutched his graystone and concentrated as hard as he could. His door to the corridor slowly opened. Deion walked in as the door slowly closed. "How wonderful to see you. You look grand. I see the Stone has been working on your body over the past year." He embraced his visitor before he could kneel. His arms did not go completely around the big man's chest. He stood apart and admired him as a father admired a lost son. "May blessings from Light's Source be on you and all you do."

"And on you, Holy One. I must know if the child is

the Darkslayer. I'm sure he is, I can feel it. I just want to hear it from you. I had heard the babe's cry and started preparing before the eagle came. Did you know he likes his crest feathers rubbed? I started as soon as I sent the reply."

"He is the Darkslayer, and I knew the eagle liked his head scratched. Much has happened that you must know before you speak with anyone else. They just brought pastries and juice. Come and refresh yourself while I tell you what I know about the child. His name is Marc, by the way, named before the Zenith knew. I have a feeling he knows much more than he admits."

Deion sat and refreshed himself as Travis walked backed and forth, telling of what had happened from the time of Maress' death to his arrival. After a while, he sat in the plush chair across from Deion and continued until he recounted the whole story. He pulled the bell pull next to the chair and leaned into the soft pillows, thinking of what, if anything, had he left out.

His steward came a few minutes later. "Roger, we will need some more pastries and juice." Roger looked from the once heaping tray to Travis. Deion emerged from the refresh room with his cloak and tunic off; he looked to be a mountain of muscle. The steward bowed his way from the room and returned shortly with a loaded tray of fruits, cheese, hot bread, and more juice. The Holy One sat chatting about the Protector's trip. Roger placed the tray on the low table between them and bowed his way out.

Travis spoke calmly. Still, urgency encompassed his words. "The Zenith does not know about you or the role of the Protector. *I think.* I wanted to wait until you arrived and tell him in your presence. You must probe Marc to make sure. We know it won't hurt the babe; the Zenith will be unnecessarily worried if he knows. I suggest we leave that part out until you are sure. Jarod has grown into a dynamic Zenith. He's exactly the type of person we need to prepare for what is to come."

Travis sipped his juice, thinking. *According to the ancient parchments, we should have sixteen years to ready our forces for the first major attack. Not even a day of that time may be wasted.* "I brought the old books with me. We should be able to piece together a plan for Marc's training with those and the one you have. The Prelates are here, too. The four of us must make headway as quickly as possible." Travis paused, his face determined. "The Zenith must be won over to the plan. You will play an important part in convincing him, and may have to demonstrate some of your special skills. I don't think it will take a lot for him to be convinced. I can feel a protective instinct alive in him of great magnitude. We must be careful not to bruise or diminish that feeling as we exert our protection."

Travis' face and voice smiled. "Now let's go find the Zenith and let you meet the Darkslayer. I think they will both be in the same place at this time of the morning."

They donned their tunics, and Travis led Deion toward the nursery, knowing that he knew Marc's location, exactly. He knocked softly at the door and the two men entered quietly. Jarod, Kyle, and Trina all looked amazed on seeing him. His Holiness made the introductions. "My Zenith Lord, I would like to present His Grace, Deion Russell, of the Tower. He's the person that I mentioned would come." Deion returned Marc's stare from Trina's arms. The babe giggled once; he nodded once to Travis.

Jarod's voice answered wryly. "Ah, the Protector has arrived." Shock spread across Travis' face, and Deion chuckled.

He stepped forward to within a few feet of the Zenith. Jarod started to bow his head. Halfway, as if in answer to his remark, he found himself floating in the air. His feet, a foot from the floor, and no one had touched him. Deion slowly lowered him back down an inch at a time. "My Zenith, I vow upon all that is Holy, I will fight to protect you and your son with the power and abilities the Source of All has given me."

Jarod stretched out his arm and felt himself filled with peace as Deion took his forearm in his grasp; not able to speak for a moment until the rapture seeped away, "I never believed you really existed until recently." A look of total surprise registered on Travis and the Protector's faces.

Kyle went to a plush chair and sat down heavily. Trina took Marc and sat on the bed. Both continued staring at Deion as Jarod continued. "I hoped you would come, and that Travis had sent for you. I'm glad you are here." Jarod turned to Kyle. "This is Lord Kyle Byrne, Captain of my Guard." He motioned toward the bed. "This lovely lady is Trina, His Holiness' great-granddaughter and Marc's wet-nurse. I believe you have already met my son, Marc."

Now, Travis and Deion found bewilderment swirling within them. Travis spoke first. "How could you know? The position of the Protector is the most closely guarded secret we have. Only the Prelates and I are aware of his existence. Except now, those in this room know, too."

Jarod smiled. "You are not the only one with old books. I have one in the old language, one in the new. I have learned, as have the Zeniths before me, the books are the same. I meant to discuss this with you today. I believe they will aid you in translating your books. I know my books by rote; they don't contain anything that could have helped us so far. I will introduce Deion to the council this morning, when I discuss the agenda with them; then the two of you can spend time afterwards with my books. Then, I think it will be appropriate to open the Box of Stones." Now Travis had to sit while Deion smiled.

Kyle caught his eye. "I'm glad you are on our side." Kyle rose and grasped Deion's outstretched forearm.

Deion's reply had a ring of steel. "Don't underestimate Dark's Source and its minions. They will have their own special powers and creatures, as I'm sadly aware of, and you already know. Dark Source's influence alone can be extremely powerful. His power and that of a few of his minions goes well beyond influence, and will continue to grow. We must guard against thinking the Dark's Source is less than what it is. That will be a fatal error on our part if we fall into that trap. I wouldn't say these things without knowing every person in this room is devoted to the Darkslayer." Heads turned to look at Marc without thinking. No one spoke. Jarod kissed his son's forehead and got a giggle for his effort. They took their leave of Trina and Marc with minimum conversation. Deion let Marc take his finger in parting and their smiles lit up the room.

* * *

JAROD entered the small council chamber, followed by Kyle and Travis. Deion entered next and captured every occupant's attention. The room became quieter than he ever remembered; he looked slightly amused at the reaction. "I present His Grace Deion Russell. He's here at the request of the Holy One. He will do all he can to protect Marc and me. You will learn more about His Grace shortly. If everyone will be seated, I have an announcement to make."

He stood at the head of the table and repeated the orders given to Kyle and Gaz the night before and then continued. "Security and loyalty to me and the Seven Realms are paramount in this venture. I know how to handle my uncle and cousin if we find nothing. This subject is not for debate. We will appreciate hearing any comments if anyone here has ideas on how to speed the search."

He sat. Deion took the chair at the opposite end of the table, alone. Eyeing the members of the group, he scrutinized everyone except Jarod, Travis, and the Mother.

Again, Lord Long spoke first. "Will it be possible for

one of the Prelates to accompany your men?"

His question started a round of comments before Travis could speak. Finally, he stood. The room became quiet once more. "The Prelates may not take any part until the evidence is returned here. Sending members of our Order not only presents a problem with their vows, it could supply Mountglen with a device to use on our Zenith if no evidence is found." Lord Long nodded his agreement.

He waited for additional comments. Finding none, he continued. "I have approved your agenda with one exception. I don't want the keeps infiltrated by Gaz's men just yet. I'm planning a banquet in four to five months. I will reconsider my decision if the matter has not been resolved by then."

His mien and voice projected as solidly as the stone around his neck. "You have all done a good deal of work in a short period of time. I want each of you to work logically on the items that fall in your areas of expertise. I know you will cooperate if information requires interchange, and we should strive to keep the council informed of our progress. I appreciate your requests to stay until after the Naming Day ceremony, and they are approved with my sincere gratitude.

"The Pinnacle arrives tomorrow. I suspect I will be with him most of the day. We will most likely be in my small study if any of you want to talk with either of us. I think Geoffrey likes it as much as I do. Lord Long, I will come to you if you wish to see me.

"I believe we have little time to consolidate our plans. Let me know if I can do anything to speed your efforts. We may reconvene on an as needed basis. If there are no pressing matters, we are adjourned."

He told Travis to bring Mavis and the Prelates to the Zenith's study at midday. He gave the same message to Kyle as he left.

Jarod went to the entrance to the Chambers.

Lieutenant Damish had just entered. He stopped and saluted. Jarod nodded in response. "Lieutenant Damish, I believe you are the duty officer for the Chambers today. I'm going down in the lift. I want a pebble of men here for escort duty when I return. It will be an hour or more."

* * *

SUSPECTING little, Lieutenant Damish saluted as Jarod went into the lift. The Zeniths used armed escorts within the Chambers infrequently, but it did happen from time to time. Lieutenant Damish assumed the Zenith must be bringing up part of the State Regalia, and added it to his duty roster. He might have been a bit more excited if he knew Jarod brought their future in his bare hands.

Emerging from the lift, Jarod headed to the under level stairway. He went down three levels and continued through several passages, each guarded, to a twenty-foot square room. Two guardsmen ate at a table in the center of the room. Two more stood at their post on either side of ornately carved doors. They snapped to position when Jarod entered. He knew the four men. "Go on with your meal."

The two guardsmen guarding the door stepped forward five paces and stood at position. Jarod pulled a small key from his pouch. The intricately carved pattern of the door hid the keyhole. Jarod glanced over his shoulder; the four guardsmen faced away from him, following their standing orders. He turned the key, opening a panel in the carving. He reached inside and pulled a lever. Bolts slid back into the door. Jarod closed the panel and locked it, replacing the small key in his pouch. The keyhole located at the handle had not been touched. Jarod opened the door, took the torch next to him, and entered the passageway. He closed the door, opened a panel on the backside of the door, and threw the lever to the locked position. He then navigated the dark passageway with the light from the single torch, bypassing deadly traps as he went. He pushed a certain stone at the midpoint of the passageway, causing a door to open with little noise.

Jarod lit the torcheres beside the entrance to the room and grimaced at the stale air. He opened two small shafts, one led down to the river and one led to an opening above ground, starting airflow. He waited a few minutes for fresh air to circulate throughout, then lit a few more torches. The room measured exactly one hundred yards on each side and twenty feet high. Half the room was filled floor to ceiling with gold ingots, reflecting the torches' light. Tubs containing the seven types of gems mined in Stonefire took three quarters of the remaining space. The mines produced what seemed a never-ending supply of its precious output. Not even the High Lords had any idea of Stonefire's—that is to say the Zenith's—wealth.

The day-to-day running of the country and the Guard came from taxes, but mostly from additional revenues. Stonefire produced an overabundance of wheat, oats, herbs, legumes, cloth, iron, steel and many products manufactured throughout the realm. Jarod owned most of those holdings and enterprises. Stonefire had the lowest taxes and enjoyed the highest standard of living in the Seven Realms.

The vast accumulation of wealth remained totally unknown outside of the Zenith. Most of the High Lords believed that the mines paid for the charity the Zenith provided throughout the Seven Realms. Actually, the High Lords tax payments provided most of the funds used for those services. The gold or gems provided monies for the various business ventures of the Zenith and hadn't been depleted in centuries, moreover, his wealth grew steadily. The Zenith controlled the price of the gems sold through simple supply and demand. His gem cutters exhibited expertise without equal. Their needs were fulfilled and they were well paid and cared for near the complex of mines. It had been that way since soon after the Great War.

Jarod went to a bookcase against the wall next to the entrance and selected three books. One, he read for nearly an hour and returned it to the bookcase, frowning. He carefully wrapped the two remaining books in cloth and placed them in a plain leather sack. Next, he took a small, jeweled box from the top shelf and placed it inside his shirt. He capped the torches and candles except the original torch. He left the airflow open to cleanse the air, took the sack, and retraced his steps to the guardroom.

He passed through without speaking, nodding to his guardsmens' salutes. Opening another secret door he was sure no one knew about, Jarod climbed a circular staircase up three levels and through another stone door into the anteroom. He came out exactly opposite the secret passage he'd learned about from Gaz's actions the day he met Karl.

His armed escort met him when he arrived in the Chambers. He posted the men outside the two entrances to the Zenith's study and went inside. Jarod took the books from the sack and set them on the table. He took the small box from his shirt and placed it behind one of the books in the bookcase, out of sight.

He gave orders that no one should enter before he returned, and ordered two of the guardsmen to follow him. He left them outside the small study. Inside, he removed the Box of Stones from its hiding place, secured the box in its cloth wrapping, and returned to the Zenith's study. He placed the wrapped box on the table next to the books he brought earlier. He rang for Rolo and told the guardsmen to admit him. He found a plush chair where he could look out and see a small part of the City between a Spire and the outer wall. Jarod ordered a midmeal for eight with juices and water to drink when Rolo arrived.

His fears consumed him. *Is this the right thing to do? The first warning in the book is not to reveal the secrets too soon. Everything points to this being the right course. How can I be sure? It would be so much easier if we knew the Dark Stone played a part. It has been dormant for two millennia. I cannot be the cause of disseminating the knowledge too early, but I may be putting Marc's life in danger if I wait. The golden veins going into him and the responding glow should be the proof I need to go on. Still, I must be as sure as I can.*

Without thinking, he reached up and grasped his own Stone as he pictured Marc in his mind. Jarod nearly jumped from his chair when he distinctly heard Marc's giggle. *Thank you my son, I love you, too.* Jarod heard a small laugh, and felt a warm sensation run through his body. No longer unsure, he dreaded what would happen in the years to come.

The door opened, bringing Jarod from his conclusions. Rolo entered with a cart loaded with food and drink. He laid out a buffet on a long credenza. "Rolo, I want to have a lastmeal tomorrow night in the small dining room. There will be ten of us. The Pinnacle should be here by then, too. I think fish and crustaceans will be a good choice. I seem to remember it's a favorite of Lord Long, as well as the Pinnacle. Have the kitchen prepare something special for sweet-time."

"As you wish, my Zenith, and your memory is correct." Rolo resumed putting a cloth over the food he had laid out. He bowed and went through the door, stopping halfway. "My Zenith, the Mother is here."

Jarod motioned for her to enter. "Mother, I'm glad you came a little early. Actually, I expected you a while ago."

Smiling, she walked over to him, leaned down and kissed his forehead before seating herself opposite him. "My son, I hoped you might want to talk a while before the others arrive. These past six days have been a strain on me; I can only guess how it must have been for you.

How are you?"

"I think the fast pace has allowed me to accept Maress' death gradually. The shock of that day is now a fact in my mind...it's something I can deal with, not an ongoing nightmare. I don't think anything will cause me that much pain again." Jarod's mind rebelled at the statement. *There is still Marc and Kyle.* "It is a pain I can almost see. I can shut it away for periods, and then it surfaces again. I remember the counseling you gave to the families of those dying at the hospice as good advice, and I have tried to heed it. I think it will be a long time before the thought of her death won't feel like physical pain, along with the additional feelings of sadness it brings. Nevertheless, it's something I can see past. I couldn't do that when we talked before."

The Mother simply nodded and took the conversation to lighter ground. Several minutes passed before the guardsman announced the rest of the group had arrived. Jarod gave permission and they entered, waiting until everyone took their seats, and then went to the head of the table by the books.

"I will make a few comments, and then there is food for midmeal. We will open the Box of Stones afterwards. You must be told what I'm doing before that, and what it means."

He pointed at the two volumes on the table. "These two books have been copied every decade since the Great War. The copiers cannot read, and they have no idea what they have copied. The first book is in the old tongue, the second is current usage. They are supposed to be an exact translation from the old language to the new. The books are proofread and edited for changes in our current language by both the Zenith and his heir, since the whole process began with the first Zenith. The previous copies are kept for five years. Those copies are re-examined against the new copies once more, and then burned." Jarod walked to the credenza, poured a glass of juice, and continued speaking after a few sips.

"The first part of the book describes the process I just described. The second part of the book deals with the need to continue the process. That graphic part will scare the hide off you. At least, it did for my father and me. The third part contains information concerning the Stones and how to protect them. Your Holiness, they are the physical Stones described here, not our consanguinity. That book addresses that in the last part. I know the book by memory. The Protector is described also, Your Grace." Deion could not hide the surprise on his face, nor Travis, nor the Prelates.

Jarod continued. "The Zenith is charged by the book with the responsibility of not divulging its existence or its contents until the proper time. I believe this is the proper time. I cannot be absolutely sure of my emotions after the events of the last six days..." His eyes showed his distress, and he glanced down at the books. "And my thinking may be flawed. The books are not long; they take less than an hour to read. I request that His Holiness read the book. His thoughts will be open to you if he believes the timing is right. If not, I will demand your oaths never to reveal what you have heard today. This too, is a procedure in the book, and calls for your presence. I believe the whole thing is devised to protect me, but I'm not sure, there may be more to it than that."

Jarod reflected a moment. "There is food and drink on the credenza. Your Holiness, I will sit with you while you read the book. The rest of you may get what you will to refresh yourselves."

* * *

TRAVIS rose. "You have my oath that I will do as you have requested in this matter." He went to the credenza and took a plate. He found his hand shaking as he pulled the cloth from the food. Taking a little food and a glass of water to the plush chairs where Jarod waited, he set his things on the low table between the chairs and looked into the Zenith's eyes as he took the book. He had never seen such strength or coldness in the man before. Jarod had nothing from the credenza; he sat quietly as Travis read the book.

*   *   *

THE others in the room got plates of food and something to drink, although they did not seem to have much appetite, but it gave them something to do. Jarod looked around the room and realized. *I'm the one with the most to lose; yet I think I'm the calmest person here.*

Travis read the book rapidly, eating bits of cheese while he read. He slid forward in his chair when he finished, and took Jarod's hand. "My dear son, I had no idea you carried a burden such as this. I believe you are absolutely correct in opening the Box of Stones at this time." His voice pitched low for Jarod's ears alone. Jarod simply nodded.

Jarod went to the head of the table. "There is one part of the book that refers to Lord Deion." He looked at the large man. "You must make no further use of your powers until you are named Protector. You are in great danger until then. I suggest we complete the Naming ceremony shortly. You might have died this morning. In fact, I'm surprised you were not hurt. I think somehow, Marc protected you. You will understand more when you read the book."

Deion looked shaken to the core. "I agree." He went to the credenza and filled his plate full. He turned around to find the rest staring at him. His blush looked totally out of place on his huge frame. "I eat when I'm nervous." The responding laughter caused some of the tension to fade.

Jarod went to the door and gave orders to the guardsman. His Holiness followed and spoke out of earshot of the others. "I have brought what he will need."

"You knew?"

"Let us say I guessed. Marc's birth cry filled my head with reality. I have heard with the Stone before. It always had an unreal quality: the voices or sounds, off just enough that you know it didn't come from your surroundings, not that time.

"We search the priesthood first for candidates to train for the position of the Protector. If we do not find someone suitable, we go to the general population. Deion started training for the priesthood when he came to our attention. Any new priests who show unusual abilities come to the Tower's attention. The Prelates and I are the only ones in the Order that know why. A prelate will visit the site where the priest is working to see how strong his telepathic powers are, and if the priest is malleable to the training. In his case, the prelate's shock at finding a twelve-year-old boy who had just gone through his Age-of-Man time left no doubts. His power's strength urged the prelate to take him to the Tower without hesitation." Travis looked a little sheepish. "That prelate stands before you now." Jarod smiled and nodded.

"Deion is an orphan, and had lived with the priests since his second year. He showed a real interest in the priesthood at twelve years. Many boys do at that age and in those circumstances, especially when they have never known the outside world. Most grow out of it in a short time. He never did—it's as if the Tower's and his creation had the same harmony. I think his destiny is to be the Protector. His hair turned white at his fourteenth year. He began growing rapidly and putting on mass soon after, and every year his strength and abilities grew. He devoured the training so fast that he amazed the entire Tower. He went into the mountains to study and meditate at nineteen." Jarod and Travis slowly made their way to plush chairs in a private corner.

"I saw him once a year during that time. We measured him for new clothes to see him through the next year.

They would be so small on him by the following year he returned in rags. It took only one year to determine we had to add more inches than for normal growth. His body hair disappeared when he returned after the first year, except for his pubic hair and what you can see here. His skin started to gain the luminescence it has now. His telepathic powers had increased tenfold. The two of us discovered that we could communicate with the help of the Stones. I sent an eagle to be sure the message reached him when I heard Marc's cry. I knew the messages I received from him came much stronger than the ones I sent. I didn't want to take any chance of his misreading my projections. The eagle took longer, but it's the surest way." Travis calmed as he continued his outpouring of thoughts he had never been able to utter.

"Deion found a Stone in the mountains. It's a blue Stone and had many gold veins. I received a query from him one day: he wanted to know what it meant when the veins in the stone made little arcs that entered his body. I could hear him well from that day on, not as well as Marc's cry, but close.

"In the fall, I ordered him to the Tower. It took him nearly three weeks, traveling through first snows to reach it. He has not changed for the most part. He has continued to add muscle mass and I think he grew another inch." Jarod remained calm, belying the storm of concepts and questions raging through his mind.

Travis took a breath and reflected a moment before continuing. "He's one of the most devout men I have ever met, however, he's subdued about his faith. He seems to know how and when to talk to someone about their faith. He's one of the most gentle men I know; I have never seen him become angry with anyone or anything.

"The past year, he has resumed his training with the sword. He knows battle techniques and logistics well. He's not yet as good on a horse as you or your father, but he could give you a ride to remember. His martial arts skills are beyond anything I could have ever imagined. Jarod, he has a fire in him that I have seen in few men. He will protect Marc with his life, better than that, he will find a way to save them both."

Travis sighed. "I can see only one reason for this to come together at this time. It's collaborated in the books I have and yours. I don't know how much time we have. I hope it will be enough."

"Thank you, Travis, I feel better about entrusting Marc's safety to him when the time comes," Jarod replied. "That is an additional subject we need to discuss. Maybe we can find some time early next week." The knock at the door ended their quiet conversation.

The guardsmen brought in a wooden bathtub lined with porcelain over sand, and put it at the open end of the room. Trina arrived with Marc, took him to Jarod, and left to wait outside. She did not seem happy. Travis went to fetch the things Deion needed. He returned before the tub completely filled with hot water. The Protector had a puzzled look on his face as the prelates read the third part of the book for the third time, talking in low whispers.

Travis took Marc from Jarod. Kyle had no idea of what was transpiring around him. Jarod paced off twenty paces from the rear of the room opposite the tub and placed a glass of water at that mark on the table. He ordered everyone except Deion behind the glass of water. He ordered the prelates to remove anything containing metal from their persons, including their boots. He believed Kyle must have believed him mad at this point. Jarod had the partially clad prelates follow him to where Deion stood, near the tub of hot water. He spoke to the three of them at length. Finally, Jarod went to the far end of the room, leaving the prelates in place and followed his own orders. He returned to big man's side minus his belt and boots. He wore the solid gold chain holding his

Stone. Jarod told Travis to keep Marc at the rear of the room when his participation ended, and for Kyle to remain there until the ceremony ended. The prelates lit candles and pulled the draperies over the windows, leaving enough light to see clearly.

The prelates held a sheet up in front of the tub, facing the others at the far end of the room. Deion went behind the sheet, stripped off his clothes, and entered the bath. He took five minutes to bathe. When finished, he took the sheet, folded it in half, and wrapped it around his waist before nodding to Jarod.

Jarod looked at Marc nervously. "I will remind you not to talk to anyone except as required by the ceremony." He retrieved the small box from the bookcase and nodded to the prelates, who went to stand on either side of the Protector.

Jarod picked up the folded clothes and a long object wrapped in linen from the table that Travis had brought earlier. He laid the beautifully bejeweled Box of Stones on top and carried them to a table near Deion. The prelates placed three torcheres to from a triangle: two on either side and slightly behind him, the third, in front of him and behind Jarod, spaced equilaterally.

Jarod nodded and Deion dropped the sheet. His skin took on the translucence of fine porcelain. His bronze complexion covered his entire body. The candle's reflections and the translucence of his skin became more amazing when his muscles flexed. He bowed to Jarod and Marc, then to Travis. Part of his long white hair fell over his heart when he rose up. Jarod gently put it over his shoulder and stepped away, and then nodded to Travis.

"I, the spiritual leader of the Seven Realms, ask this. Do you, Deion Russell, claim to be the Protector?"

His voice came strong and clear. "I do."

"Who is it that you are sworn to protect?"

"The one who will defeat Dark's Source."

Air currents began to stir in the room. Slow, agonizing

moans wailed out of nowhere. The wind grew until its fierceness blew through the room with the vengeance of a gale, except for the inside of the triangle formed by the torcheres. That area remained perfectly calm; the candles barely flickered while storm winds assailed the rest of the room.

Travis continued over the din. "How will you be known?"

"By my deeds, by my badge, by my name, I will fight to the death to protect the one I guard. I will wear the badge of the Deathcat and the Tower. My name will be Protector."

The wail rose in pitch and became louder.

"How will the one you protect be known?"

"By his deeds, by his badge, by his name, he will fight to destroy Dark's Source. He will wear the badge of the Deathcat. His name is Marc Greatstone. He is the Darkslayer!"

The moan became a howl. The wind tore at the others. They had to hold their hands in front of their faces. Kyle could hear the guardsmen trying to enter the room. The doors were unlocked, but they did not open.

Travis brought Marc from just inside the triangle to Jarod's side as Thurston stepped forward and picked up the small box. He opened it and presented it to Jarod. Jarod removed the Guardian's Stone, a huge ruby, three inches long and heavily veined with gold. He gave it to Marc, and helped him hold it up in the light of the candles.

The ruby left Marc's hand and floated upward. When it reached the level of Deion's heart, he too, began to rise. He rose four feet off the floor while streams of light flowed from the candles to the ruby. The light started as a golden tone, and gradually increased to the purest white. The wind and howling outside the triangle disappeared. The ruby and He hung in the air, while the light became too bright to look at without pain. No one turned away.

Suddenly, a bolt of gold light the size of a man's arm shot from the ruby to Deion's chest, over his heart. He absorbed the light for over a full minute, his feet slightly apart, his arms slightly out from his sides and his head thrown back. He made no sound.

The light disappeared. Slowly the ruby and he floated to the floor. The room remained quiet. Kyle went to the door and opened it. He ordered the guardsmen to stand at the ready, and assured the Mother and Trina that all remained well inside. He closed the door behind him and looked at Deion.

He stood on the floor in the same pose that he held in the air. Daniel stepped forward and took the privatecloth from the stack of clothes beside them. He and Thurston held the cloth at Deion's abdomen, ran it between his legs and fastened the cloth with its strings. They righted a small, overturned bench from the floor behind him and gently guided him to a sitting position. As they did, he began to become aware of his surroundings.

He took his clothes when they handed them to him and dressed without further assistance. He put on everything but the tunic and the cloak. His garments retained the gray of the Order except for the black shirt. The colors of his badge had reversed the Tower to white and the deathcat golden, the mark of an Apex.

Thurston and Daniel pulled the draperies, flooding the room with light. Around Deion, a golden aura radiated several feet in every direction. Jarod slid the Guardian's Stone into a gold frame attached to a heavy gold chain. The gold sealed with the Stone. He knelt and Jarod placed the chain over his head, to rest on his shoulders. It lay next to the blue Stone.

Jarod's next words came softly. "The Stone cannot be removed except by the force of three or more Stones of equal or greater power, or your death." The prelates returned the torcheres to their original place. The Protector smiled at Marc. Then they both laughed with relief of tension.

Travis held the tunic out to Deion, the same gray as the rest, piped in black with the same badge as the shirt. Travis picked up the linen-wrapped parcel when he had the tunic on. "Does the Protector accept the challenge?"

"I do." Deion kneeled before Marc, Jarod and Travis. Travis let the linen fall to the floor. He held out a battle sword that looked identical to Jarod's own. Later, they would find the etched characters slightly different. Deion took the sword in both hands. The golden aura around him coalesced, and then flowed into the sword.

Jarod looked down at Marc, smiling, "Well, my little Darkslayer, say hello to your Protector." Marc held his arms out, and Jarod handed Marc to Deion. Any doubt in Jarod's mind about the suitability of the pairing disappeared. The babe and the giant somehow looked strangely similar. Marc held his arms out to Jarod, who took him to the door and gave him to Trina. "I think he might be hungry." Trina's worried look washed away as she took Marc and headed to the nursery, guarded by a pebble of guardsmen. The Mother rejoined Travis, and he began explaining what had happened.

Jarod went to Deion and embraced him tightly for a moment. He released his grip and stepped backward. "Thank you. I will give you both all the support I can."

Deion smiled. "I know."

Two stewards came in and with astonished looks, began putting the room aright. Kyle approached Jarod. "Why did the wind that tore the room apart not upset the glass of water?" Jarod looked over at the glass, and the water inside that remained at the same level, and shrugged. "I don't know. I only used it for a marker, nothing else."

Jarod looked around the room for damage to any of the other books when a realization struck him: *Many of the books contained commentaries on Light's Source.* He looked at the glass of water. *Could there be a connection?* Tucking the implication away for now, he requested more food, juice, and wine. He saw that the water pitchers on the credenza were also undisturbed. *There has to be a connection!* he concluded. The jeweled Box of Stones set undisturbed like the water. The same as his books; they sat on the table by the chairs, exactly where the prelates had left them. He explained his observations to Deion while the others began returning to the table. Everyone that professed not being hungry earlier made short work of the food there.

The conversation remained brisk. They discussed the ceremony and recounting parts over again. Jarod saw they had forgotten the Box of Stones, or perhaps assumed its part was over. In fact, he wondered if some had forgotten it completely. He went to the box and began to unwrap it, moving slowly. Not a single voice uttered a sound by the time he completed unwrapping it.

The jewels set into the box showed their true magnificence. The sunlight reflected off the glittering gems, casting patterns of light throughout the room. Jarod pulled the Stone he wore from beneath his shirt and over his head. Letting it hang over the center of the Box of Stones, he twisted the chain, causing the Stone to spin. Golden arcs leapt from the box's center jewel to Jarod's Stone. Gold veins began to reappear on the Stone. The arcs vanished, leaving the Stone heavily veined with gold in less than a minute. He pulled his shirt open over his heart. Golden arcs flowed into his body when the Stone drew close to his skin. He took the Stone and let it hang over the box in the same place as before, which now caused a loud, cracking noise. The top of the box floated up into the air under the Stone. Jarod shifted the Stone to the right and the lid followed to a vacant place on the table next to the bottom half of the box. He let the Stone drop down until the lid rested on the table. He put the Stone around his neck and looked at the rest of the people at the table; almost laughing at the expression on

Travis' face. Jarod's tone conveyed his pleasure. "We have a few secrets, too." Travis nodded with a smile, conceding the point. "Deion the next part is yours."

He stood next to Jarod and listened to the instructions of exactly what to do. He took his ruby and placed it into his palm, holding it with his thumb. He then passed the Stone over the open box. The emptiness became clouded. An old book surrounded by seven Stones appeared as the cloud dissipated. Each stone different, the Stones of the Seven Realms not seen in two millennia, sparkled in preternatural brilliance. Jarod's voice became somber, "Thank you, Deion. Your Holiness, the next part is yours. You will need your graystone, the one you have worn the longest."

Travis had the graystone off by the time he reached Jarod's side. Its shape reminded one of a coin: almost perfectly round, flat, two inches across and a quarter-inch thick. Jarod whispered to him for several moments; Travis' face registered shock at one point. Then Jarod stood out of His Holiness' way.

Travis let his graystone descend into the circle of Stones. The graystone began to spin. A vortex of silver and gold light sprang up around the spinning stone. It swallowed the graystone in bright, opaque light. Gradually the vortex began to descend into the box. A beautiful emerald still spun slowly where the graystone had been. Travis pulled the chain up and looked at a two-inch long, one-inch square, perfect Stone. It had several gold veins running through it. The golden arcs leapt into his chest in the same manner that Jarod's had done. He placed the Stone around his neck and returned to his seat, smiling.

Jarod lifted the Book with his bare hands. No one noticed the sweat on his forehead. When he had the Book completely free of the box, he placed it over his heart. He closed his eyes and whispered words no one could hear. The Box of Stones began to fade from view; the Seven Stones of Stonefire remained. Jarod took the small, jeweled box the ruby had been in and carefully placed the Stones in it, closing the lid.

His voice rang strong and clear. "I, Jarod Greatstone, Zenith Lord of the Seven Realms, proclaim to Light's Source that the Stones are free and are to be used in the protection of Light's Source and the destruction of Dark's Source."

He placed the book in the sunlight. Thunder sounded throughout the room. Bright light radiated outwards at the same time. The light, only visible for a minute part of a second, traveled through the Spires, through Stonefire and then, on through the Seven Realms. The light's journey to the far seas took only a second.

* * *

SEVEN hundred miles southeast of the Spires, Shadure had materialized in Mountglen's coach in a rage. Mountglen and Clarence's alarm locked on their faces. Suddenly, he moaned and twisted in agony for several minutes. Bright light blinded them for a small part of a second. Shadure vanished with the light. Mountglen and Clarence looked at one another for a long, silent, moment. Neither could speak; they paled as they stared at each other, white with fear.

33

JAROD sat in his favorite plush chair in the small study, trying not to be overwhelmed by the day's events. He looked up into Maress' warm, green eyes, wondering if she could possibly be aware of his thoughts. *Well, my love, it has started. Our son has been named Darkslayer, and he has his Protector that the Old Books promised. I only pray that we can find a way to help him and maybe spare some bloodshed. My darling, I miss you so much.*

Jarod felt the ache of her loss in his heart and throughout his body. He got up and was pouring himself some juice when he heard Mother's voice from the open doorway. "May I come in, my dear?"

"Of course, would you like juice?" Jarod saw the smile on her face and poured her a glass of her favorite mixed berry juice. They seated themselves, and he said, "Tell me about Trina."

"Oh, she has had a lot of sorrow in her young life." Mavis settled herself in a plush chair across from Jarod and accepted the glass he offered her. "She married Paul, the baker at the shop where your men found her. They owned the shop and did well; their business remained good and their personal lives remained happy. She told me often that the only thing that could make her happier would be a babe. She yearned for one with all her heart." Jarod's concern grew. The Mother sounded resigned.

"She finally conceived, making them both ecstatic with joy. Oh my, you should have seen her then. Her radiance, her spirit floated above the clouds, and pure joy bubbled from her. Being around her became the bright spot in my day, although I didn't see her often, not nearly as often as

I wished. I shared their happiness when I did.

"Paul went down river to visit his parents during her third month. Trina stayed behind to mind the bakery. Paul should have returned in three days. Trina believed he had simply stayed an extra day when he didn't return on the fourth day. She came to see me on the afternoon of the fifth day."

Mavis looked down into the glass of juice, swirling it around. She continued without looking up. "I sent one of my young workers to inquire about Paul the next morning. He returned that evening with bad news. Paul had been working at his father's farm, doing some of the chores his father could no longer do. He had a team of horses pulling up a tree stump. One of the chains snapped and flew at him. The frightened horse lunged forward, and the chain caught Paul's leg, throwing him to the ground. He landed head first. The fall broke Paul's neck. I'm sure he died instantly. His father saw the entire accident."

Jarod felt a pang of grief for Trina, and then for himself. He shook it off, holding his emotions in check. "The father became consumed with grief. He died in bed sometime during the night. Paul's mother, in grief and beside herself, didn't know what to do. She had never sent messages, and had no idea how. The local priest oversaw the cremation ceremonies; he had called for a messenger when my messenger arrived from the City. The priest couldn't use a graystone and couldn't send a bird.

"Luckily, the boy had a good head, and sought me out before telling Trina. I feared she might lose the babe, it being her first. I didn't know what kind of reaction she might have. She saw the boy and me coming through the east gate and knew instantly that Paul had died. She became beside herself with grief. My fear about her losing the babe increased. She came and stayed with me at my home beside the hospice for a week. I gave her soothing teas and herbs. She worked out her grief enough to return to the shop."

Mavis sighed; and went on at a slower pace. "She adjusted normally over the next months and began to think of the babe and her happiness returned to some degree. She made baby clothes and bought those things she couldn't make. A cart hit her in the street when its wheel broke three weeks ago. She had minor injuries that did no damage to her or the babe, or at least, she didn't think so. The contractions began that evening, and she sent for me. I knew something had gone drastically wrong the moment I saw her. She was pale, and sweating profusely. Her contractions continued throughout the night. I never heard the babe's heart when I listened. The babe lay stillborn early the next morning."

The Mother's professional façade faded, and Jarod saw the depth of her sadness. He hurt for Trina and the only mother he had ever known.

Mavis' voice held steady. "I stayed with her for a few days. She handled it better than Paul's death. She told me she believed she would do better if she could work a little in the bakery. I hesitantly agreed, but she well knew her limits. She started work a few hours a day, making change and greeting customers. She told me she had reconciled both of the deaths and began to think of what to do next. Paul and she owned a small home in a nice area of the City and they had managed to save more money than I would have imagined.

"She received a generous offer for the bakery the week before I sent for her to come here. Paul had done most of the baking and excelled at the work, but it became more than she could handle. The buyer promised to keep the staff; he would pay her to stay a while and show him its workings. He learned the bakery routine in a few days, and it became clear that he had considerable experience with the work. He didn't mind her leaving to come to the Spires when I sent for her."

Mavis sipped from her glass and became lost in concentration for a moment. She roused herself and continued, having made a decision. "I have been watching her closely for any sign that might not be a healthy attitude toward Marc." Jarod made eye contact with her and held it. "I have not seen any indication that she sees him as a replacement for the babe she lost. She seems quite happy taking care of him. She enjoys seeing the two of you together. Most of her zest for life has returned due in part to Marc, and maybe it has a little to do with Kyle too. She seems genuinely fond of him." The Mother's warm smile brought a smile to Jarod, too. "I will be surprised if she does not continue along the way she's going now. She has always been a happy person, and I see that part of her returning."

Jarod had listened intently. *I know some of Trina's sorrow but how could I possibly know the grief from losing a babe? She's suffered more than I have.*

Mavis saw the despair in Jarod's face and continued. "And now, I will tell you about Travis and myself, although there's not much to tell. I met him early on, and we fell hopelessly in love. Travis completed his final studies for the priesthood, and we married shortly after he took his vows. He traveled often like most new priests.

"When I became interested in hospice work, Travis sent a letter to your grandfather proposing a hospice for the City. The Zenith agreed, and construction started soon afterwards. Travis started his rapid climb in the priesthood at the same time. I don't how we had time to have two children, but we managed." Smile lines played at the corner of her mouth. "The Zenith built me my little house next to the hospice that I truly love. I didn't permit the children in the hospice, and I took a bath and put on fresh clothes before returning home. My youngest son died in his fifth year. I'm still not sure what caused his death.

"My second son died from a fall at thirty-two, but not

before having Trina's father. He and his wife are still alive, and live in a village not far from Paul's village. Trina is their only child. We send them messages often, and they have given Trina much support over the last year. Trina has agreed to keep her involvement here a secret. She realizes something of importance is happening. She swore to me that she would say nothing of what she sees or hears to anyone, even before I brought up the subject of being discrete. Jarod nodded at Trina's thoughtfulness and grasp of what happened since coming to the Spires.

Now, Mavis truly smiled. "Travis and I are still so much in love." The smile on Jarod's face broke his somber mien. "It has matured with us over the years. We send messages back and forth with the priests. I have visited him at the Tower for a few days on several occasions. He stops at the hospice when he's passing by on one of his trips. I guess you could say we are like two old crows: stuck together for life, and would have it no other way." Jarod felt the joy radiating from Mavis.

"I took great pleasure in being here with Kyle and you. We loved you as much as our own children. Travis' elevation to prelate near the end of that time forced him to go to the Tower. It became clear that I couldn't go. I had opened several new hospices throughout the Seven Realms, and had far too much to do to be that far from the Spires. Travis, like your father, saw the work I did as important and worthwhile. They both supported me in every way they could. Many of the priests never marry, so a priest without a wife is not unusual. Over time, our marriage was forgotten except by a few." Mavis sat deeper into her chair and sipped at her juice. The twinkle in her eyes had returned.

Jarod became lost in indecision for a moment and his voice was hesitant. "Will you tell me about Kyle? He has never talked about what sent him here. I asked him about it once, maybe ten years ago. He became angry, and would have nothing to do with me for a week. I never brought it up again."

* * *

MAVIS spoke cautiously after a long pause. "I suppose you should know now, especially in light of recent events. Kyle's mother caught a respiratory disease from him. He recovered quickly as children do. She became deathly ill, and lingered for a long time. I received a message well past the time that a healer or I could have arrived with any hope of a recovery. She died the day we arrived. Lord Byrne and his son's grief wrought a bitter herb for Kyle. His father and brother began to blame Kyle for his mother's death. Travis got reports from the local priest of Kyle's severe mistreatment."

Jarod's expression darkened.

"Travis came to the Spires often to counsel the local priests in those days. The prelates rarely venture from the Tower's crater anymore, but I think he still wanted the contact with the people. Your father heard his teachings on several occasions and took an interest in him. They became friends and discussed all matter of things. Your father made the statement that he wished he had someone at the Spires for you. Travis told the Zenith that he believed Kyle to be a good choice, despite the difference in years. Your father said nothing. Travis told me a look came over his face, as if he had heard of Kyle's mistreatment. Three weeks later, Kyle arrived at the Spires in horrible condition. Lord Byrne had no warning. My heart broke when I saw him.

"Since Kyle's treatment didn't involve a matter of State, your father couldn't punish Lord Byrne directly, nevertheless, he suffered indirectly from lost contracts.

"Children being, what children are; he rapidly put on weight and seemed to be happy. None of us could think why he had such a strong attachment to you; we could see it as genuine caring. Then it began to make sense. He had lost his mother, and had been lonely and isolated at home. He knew those feelings well, and we realized he felt empathy with you. At age four, you saw him as someone wonderful. His needs and your natural feelings for that age worked to benefit you both. We watched the two of you grow and become brothers in heart over the years. I believe he feels extremely protective of you, much beyond his duty and responsibilities."

Concern became evident once again in Mavis' voice and Jarod's face. "Kyle has never been home since he arrived at the Spires, and his father nor brother has ever been invited here as far as I know. It wouldn't surprise me to find that they blame that on Kyle, too. His rank is far greater then his father's. I don't believe that would set well with them. There have been times over the years when the Zenith had them called to account for some of their actions toward their own people. The Zenith never became openly involved, but he kept a watch on their conduct. I believe Gaz still has a man in their keep. Kyle does not officially know any of the happenings since his arrival here. I think your father felt it would do no good to burden him with the knowledge of his family's misdeeds."

Mavis sighed again, but continued, realizing she had made the right decision in answering Jarod's request. "I'm telling you this, my son, because of the recent troubles. You will need to know whom you can trust, and who might hold bad feelings against you or your men. Lord Byrne is not one I'd trust. I believe it will embarrass Kyle and do no good for him to know we have discussed this."

Jarod's response came quickly. "I agree, however, Kyle will be told if Lord Byrne does not fully support me, not that you and I discussed the matter, but that his family is not loyal and their history. Gaz and he are close, and I suspect he has followed his family's activities. I hope I won't have to say anything, and I don't think I will. There is always the chance of outside influence. We learned that, already. I—" Rolo's knock cut him off.

He entered with a message on a tray in Kyle's hand. The Gal he had selected, Gaz and their men waited in the Great Hall on his pleasure. Jarod explained that he must go to Mavis, kissed her on the cheek and left.

* * *

"**FOCUS** ON THE ZENITH!" The men snapped to position and then knelt. Jarod ordered them to rise, and motioned for Kyle and the Gal to come to him.

"My Zenith, this is Gal Jerome Kess. He's the man I selected to head the mission you planned." The Gal saluted, and Jarod acknowledge it with a nod.

"I know the Gal. How have you been, Jerome? If I remember correctly, you have six, or is it seven children?"

"My Zenith, I'm honored you remember. Actually, it's eight now, another son born two months ago. I have six sons and two daughters." Pride showed on the Gal's face; pride Jarod understood, and a mental picture of Marc flashed in his mind. He could not help but smile.

"Jerome, your orders are these: You, a few of your men, and an attachment of Gaz's men are to study how to identify writings from our past. The Holy One will have a document for you alone that will tell you if you have found the right books. You will have a three-week journey, and the men you pick will have to know the material well enough to remember it when they get to their destination. You will be going to Lord Mountglen's keep. He's on his way here, and you may pass him on the road. If your outriders see a coach, give it the road and keep riding as it passes. Try to avoid any contact with Lord Mountglen or Clarence as best you can. If you cannot avoid a conversation, you alone are to speak to him or his son. You are to say that you are on the way to Elizabethville with troops for normal rotation.

"Some of Gaz's men and your picked men will go to the library in Lord Mountglen's bedchambers when you arrive at his keep. There is a wall of books there. Gaz's men will go over the exact things you will be searching for in detail. Lord Mountglen has always kept a diary or journal. He hides it well. The old books we are searching for should be in plain sight. He does not know their value. The journal is a different matter. "You are not to break any of his belongings, and leave the room as you found it if at all possible. Now, I must ask your oath that you personally vouch for each of your men."

"Upon my life, my Zenith."

Jarod motioned for Gaz to join them and looked at Kess. "It may mean your life if Mountglen finds out what you are about through you or your men!"

Gaz joined them, and Jarod continued in the same quiet voice. "The sound in this room travels much too far. What I will say to your men will be somewhat misleading. You will tell your men their orders in private, where there is no chance that you will be overheard. I suggest using some of the rooms at the academy." Jerome nodded.

"I also suggest you keep the search group to no more than a pebble of men. The bedchamber suite is large; still, if you bring more than ten, you will be falling over yourselves.

"There may be an old steward there. I don't remember his name. He walks with a slight limp, and he would be in his seventies now. Tell him the Zenith wants to know if the irises still bloom if you find him. By this he will know I mentioned him to you. I went there once about eight years ago, and had meals with Lord Mountglen and Clarence in his chambers. The steward put irises on the table every day. Mountglen gave him the limp. He may be of some use."

The weight of Jarod's countenance, his quiet, authoritative voice, and the manner in which he issued his orders must have left an impression of respect on Kess from his affect. Jarod continued. "Kyle has a warrant he will give you, signed by me. It gives you the authority for the search and carries my seal. Keep the information about this assignment close to your heart. Let only Gaz's men who make up the search party know all the details.

"His men will ride with you in Guard uniform. Make sure your men know them by name and treat them no different from your own guardsmen. Some will assist you at the keep, while others have additional tasks to do. Gaz will coordinate his orders with you.

"Lastly, there is a retainer of Mountglen's named Thord. You will have a detailed drawing of him. He is vicious and dangerous. Arrest him, and put him in Glen's lockup under heavy guard. Do not let him see your force at the keep, and then escape."

Jarod paused for a few heartbeats. "I'm sending a force of your size to deter anyone guessing your real purpose or to oppose you and to give you enough men to meet any challenge. You are not to let Mountglen's forces or household stand in your way. You will have another order from me that puts you under my direct command. I don't think you will have any trouble. Good luck, and remember the iris."

Jarod returned the Gal's salute and walked to the dais. The men came to focus position as he climbed to the top. He gave a short talk with several key phrases that would have meaning when their briefing continued in smaller quarters. He passed the duty to Kyle and headed to his Chambers.

He changed his mind on the way and went to the exercise room instead. Stripping to his privatecloth, he warmed his muscles with stretching and then attacked the stone weights. He worked hard, pushing his limits with each set of routines. A full two hours passed before he began light exercises to cool his muscles.

He slipped off his privatecloth and started toward the rainmaker when he caught his reflection in the mirror. Something held his gaze to his reflection. His damp hair hung limp and the sheen of sweat glistened over his body's muscles. He felt a tug at the edge of his mind. A slight dizziness settled over him, and he let his mind drain of any negative feelings. He had never felt the feeling of such gentle peace that came over him.

He heard a voice like Maress' smoky purr whispering in his ear. He could almost see her when he closed his eyes. The words, hard to distinguish in the beginning, formed and became embedded in his memory as her face materialized. The mental words sounded clearer as he relaxed...

"The emerald stone, the Sire's Stone, from the Box of Stones, is yours. Use the Box and take the power you will need. Marc must and will find his own stone. You have done well. Trust your instincts. I cannot come to you often, or when I wish. Don't fear if I don't come to you when you think you need me.

"The Protector's skills will merge with Marc. Marc will find his Stone and the Darkslayer will surface after his Age-of-Man time.

"Dark's Source cannot invade the Tower crater. Marc will be safe there.

"That is all I may tell you. You will have my love for all time."

The image faded into nothingness. Jarod could see Maress' warm, green eyes clearly in the last few seconds, and reached for her with heart, mind, and body. He slumped to his knees, exhausted. His own blue eyes stared at him when he finally looked into the mirror. He had never felt so weak, and then strength flooded through him as he rose. His mind became clear and alert. He did not know how long the message took to impart; his body still glistened with sweat.

The cold water felt good for once, he washed away dirt and sweat while his mind washed away its doubt. After drying, he took fresh clothes from his cupboard and dressed. He felt strong, his fatigue gone and his mind sharp. The vision of Maress' eyes lingered in his mind. His own eyes became moist.

He sent a message for Travis to join him on the way to

his study. He nearly finished a full picture of water in the short time it took Travis to get there. He waved him to a seat and joined him with the last of the water.

"Travis, I'm sure you know from what happened this midday that I and the Zeniths before me know far more than you believed. The Zeniths trained to perform the tasks I did this morning, and taught that the priesthood's challenge not only involved the teachings of Light's Source, but also the keeper of knowledge until its need surfaced.

"That time is now. I don't know what the books you have are about, completely. I have two additional books kept in the same fashion as the one this morning describing the role of the priesthood from now forward. I will give them to you to read. Simply put, the priests who can channel power from their graystones will become teachers to men and boys who manifest the ability to channel. I expect an increase in that ability. The Tower crater will become a training place for that purpose. I also believe that the crater is free from Dark's Source. You will have to accept my word on that point." Jarod's intensity seemed to manifest in Travis.

"It is written that the coming war will be fought by armies of power. I don't know if that is channeled power, or man's armies, or both. I feel that it's both. There is no doubt that channeled power will be involved. That suggests this war will be much different from the last one. This one will start where the last one ended." Travis' fear showed plainly.

"Several passages in my tomes mention the main attacks from the Dark will start in the Darkslayer's sixteenth year. Nevertheless, there will be skirmishes and attacks from the Dark like the attack on Maress and Marc. Even though we have years to prepare, and it will take years before we are ready, I fear we won't have enough time. Marc's training will be paramount in our efforts. He won't begin to reach his potential until after he reaches his Age-of-Man time. It's my hope that he will be able to learn what he needs in the intervening years. That task is also yours. The Protector must teach him the skills of man's warfare with men and the use of his power; you must teach him the skills of warfare with channeled power. Your priests will become an army of power!" Travis' look of disbelief vanished into resignation before it had fully set on his face.

"The biggest obstacle is that I'm not clear on the way they will be used. We know that in the last war, the Dark Stone influenced men to spread hate and war on the rest of us. I don't know how the power's escalation on either side will help and hinder us. Your priests must test their limits as they grow in strength; they must find ways to control and use the power given to them.

"You saw the power Deion absorbed today. That much power didn't evolve until the end of the war and that, to only the first Darkslayer. I have no idea how much power Marc has now; I suspect it's a good bit more that we can determine. Deion lifted me in the air and communicated over hundreds of miles before he received additional power today. Do you have any idea how strong he is now? I can only guess that it's a great deal more than even he realizes. We must determine his strength. I believe it wise to wait until he's in the Tower crater before that determination is made." Smiles played at both men's lips.

"You read the book today; it's quite clear: Deion should be dead now! Using the power as he did without the protection of a Major Stone leaves him open to attack from the Dark. The lack of an assault may or may not be a measure of the Dark's minions' power. The only inference I can see is that Dark's Source is still limited in its actions. How long that will last is unknown and not mentioned in my books. Dark Source's presence has certainly manifested itself. We may have enough time to prepare if Mountglen and Clarence are operating under its influence alone. I believe Dark's Source needs to feed on mankind to exist. Mankind's destruction is not an issue to them! No one can foretell the horror Dark's Source could bring on us all as it feeds on us!" He leaned back in his chair and finished his water.

The possible nightmare Jarod foretold reflected on Travis' face. He remained quiet for a long moment. "My son, it will take some time for the enormity of this to take hold. I must get it in perspective and devise a plan to accomplish our goals. It's more than I can deal with at the moment."

He slowly shook his head, before continuing. "The prelates are working on the translation process using the two books you gave us. It's my hope that our books will contain as much useful information as yours and more. What do you know about the books at Mountglen's keep?"

"Not much. I saw them once. Mountglen let me look at them without hesitation. That is why I don't believe he knows their value. Clarence and I started to knock at Mountglen's door one afternoon; an old steward stopped us, saying he should not be disturbed from his writing. Clarence told me later that he kept a detailed chronicle of his life. The steward interrupted him once, years ago, and Mountglen broke his leg with a fireplace poker. The man walks with a slight limp from the way the leg set. I gave this information to our men.

"They should be ready for their instructions from the Prelates by this evening. The Gal will have a pebble of men for training in the old writing. Gaz will have seven men attached to the Gal's unit. Three will be looking for the chronicle. I don't think it's something Mountglen would leave lying about." They smiled at the understatement. "The remaining four will be in Glen gathering information on any unusual activities in the realm. I hope that they will be at the keep no more than half a day. If all goes well, we should have a message before the Naming Day."

Travis nodded. "I will check on the progress of the prelates, and tell them to expect a message from the Gal. May the Source of All give you strength."

Jarod looked perplexed. "Travis, I have heard you and Deion use that expression a few times. What exactly is the 'Source of All'?"

"Exactly? I have no idea, my son. We know that Dark's Source and Light's Source are a dichotomy within the Source of All in the old writings and in our books of knowledge. Good and Evil evolved and manifested from the same Source. There have been debates over the concept for centuries. Our oldest written teachings say they each grow in their separate planes or worlds. The Stone's power was given to man for his protection to seek a balance as evil began to exert its influence. The questions raised in theology over this have made work for many a priest's lifetime. We in the priesthood that believe it, take it on faith. Many don't embrace the concept, and we have not released it to the people; rather, we use the dichotomy as example. I have lately begun to question that practice. It's still under debate whether to release the concept to everyone or not, we do not use the term in public meetings. I have only permitted it at the Tower. The debate about it may go on for years.

"Now, if you have nothing else, I must check the progress of the prelates and let them know they will be needed later today."

The two men said good-bye, and Jarod tried to relax once more. Rolo's soft knock sounded like thunder to him. He took the message from the tray. *What will happen next?* Rolo sensed his mood; he bowed quietly and walked toward the door. Jarod's voice stopped him midway. "Thank you, Rolo." He faced his Zenith Lord and bowed again.

"Is there something I can get you, my Zenith?"

"Do you think the kitchen might have berries and cold

sweetcream?"

"I will see what I can do, my Zenith."

Jarod smiled at Rolo's quiet departure. He knew he would get berries and sweetcream if Rolo had to pick the berries himself. He opened the message with apprehension. He felt that way about any message now.

It was in Gaz' neat hand:

> *My Zenith, I have a man I would like you to meet. He's a man that I have found reliable and loyal, and I think he will be a good person to have for the future. I can have him here with an hour's notice. He will be gone by morning.*
>
> *Gaz*

He folded the message and laid it on the table next to the chair. He looked over at it after a moment, picked it up, and tore it in tiny pieces. He no longer felt berries and sweetcream would lighten his mood. Rolo brought his refreshment a half-hour later. Jarod told him to send a message to Gaz, and handed him the sealed reply. He needed something to break his mood when the refreshment failed. He did not think he could get away with another visit to Jessup's shop.

Leaving his study, he knocked lightly on the nursery door. Trina opened the door and smiled when she saw him. He began to feel better. Marc lay awake and giggled when he picked him up. He spoke baby talk without realizing it. Trina stood close and smiled. The two played for a quarter hour and he left a yawning babe in Trina's arms. It had worked; he did feel better.

34

BOTH Mountglen and Clarence were relieved that the traveling day grew to an end. They had started early. Everyone and the horses felt fatigued by mid-afternoon from the fast pace.

Shadure materialized without warning: No wind, no light dimming, in one split second he sat next to Mountglen. The blackness remained around him as it always had, with slight variations forming a face under his cowl, a sharp, cruel face with an odd beauty. The space around him grew bitterly cold.

"You have one chance to reach your goals. The brat and his father must die before the Naming ceremony is completed. I will see you installed as the new Zenith. Fail me, and you both will die."

Clarence looked at the apparition. "Who will do your work for you if we die?"

Shadure stared at him for a long moment, and Clarence felt his very soul shrivel under that pitiless gaze. At last the shadow spoke. *"You have some courage, at least. I doubt it will make up for a lack of intelligence or common sense. Many will take your place if you die. You think I need the Dark Stone; you are mistaken. If you ever question me again, I will take your head as easily as I took this."*

Shadure vanished. Pain shot up through Clarence's hand and left arm. Flames flared up for one brief second; that pain, too, hit his consciousness and remained. He bit off a scream, letting a loud moan escape. He raised his left arm. His small finger was gone, leaving no stub, the flesh seared with fire where the finger had once joined the palm. So precise, not one drop of blood had fallen or one part of his clothing had been scorched.

Mountglen used his cane to thump the roof of the coach, bringing it to a quick halt. He leaned out of the window. "Is the river near?" The driver pointed through a stand of trees to the river about thirty yards away. Mountglen wrapped Clarence's hand in a scarf from his neck, helped him from the coach and through the trees toward the river while two guardsmen trailed behind.

Clarence rested on the bank and thrust his hand into the swift current. The cool water sent more pain through his hand. It took a conscious effort to keep it in the water. The pain began to ease within a few minutes. He slowly pulled his arm from the river and rolled over on his back. The burning sensation dissipated, leaving a distant ache and exhaustion.

His father gently retied the scarf around his hand. They returned to the coach with Clarence bent over in pain. He entered the coach on his own. Mountglen shouted one word as he entered. "Hurry!"

Clarence lifted his head. The look on his father's face caused him to forget the pain for a brief second. Mountglen's eyes were wet; his face openly showed concern. Clarence had never seen his father show those feelings. There might have been a time when it would have given him great joy instead of great contempt, but he did not want to remember that far back.

One tear made its way down his face. "I'm sorry, my son, truly I am."

"It's all right, father." Clarence tried to smile and sat deeper into the cushions. The beginnings of a plan began to form in his mind, and that diversion further eased his pain.

35

GAZ met his man at the outskirts of the City, his words crisp. "We go to the Spires."

"Not even you can get in there!" Forrest Workman's predicable response afforded Gaz a rare chuckle.

Gaz did not reply and started toward the outer gates at a trot. One gate opened enough for them to ride through without stopping. The same procedure followed at the inner gate. Gaz's companion had a new look of respect when they stopped at the Zenith's entrance and dismounted.

Two guardsmen escorted them to the grand staircase, as Gaz had previously ordered. He watched as Forrest looked up the circular stairway to the top, twelve floors up. They started the climb. Guards stood at the entrance to each floor as they passed. Two more guardsmen waited at the top and escorted them to the entrance of the Chambers.

Forrest's mouth gaped open. The doors to the Chambers, intricately carved and overlaid in gold and precious jewels, formed a life-size mosaic of a deathcat emerging from a forest. A Lieutenant sat at an ornate table beside the right door. Five guardsmen flanked the end of the corridor, also by Gaz's order.

Gaz nodded to the Lieutenant when he reached the table and faced his visitor. "Give him your weapons." Gaz saw uncertainty flare on the questioning face that stared at him for only a second.

* * *

ONE question came foremost in Forrest's mind. *How*

could Gaz have gained access to the Spires? He paid me well for my work in the past; I have no idea how he built a connection to the Spires, but there is no doubt he holds sway here.

He certainly did not want to give up his weapons; it went against his grain. The look on the guardsmen's faces as their hands caressed the hilts of their swords changed his mind. He decided. *If this little rat gets me in trouble, I shall make him pay!* He started taking off weapons: a sword and several knives of different styles. The Lieutenant laid them out before him on the table, points facing Forrest.

Two guardsmen opened the heavy doors outward. The inside of the doors formed a picture as beautiful and elegant as the outer doors and filled with power: a beautiful pastoral scene with vivid colors and delicate shadings. Gaz proceeded down the corridor toward the study. Everywhere Forrest looked, he saw something beautiful: statues, paintings, tables, chairs, even more beautiful doors. Yet, nothing forced itself beyond subtlety, everything was subdued; it gave you the correct impression that if you lingered to look, you might see treasures hidden from a cursory view.

A guardsman knocked once and opened the door to the study. Jarod and Kyle sat at the end of the long table. Gaz walked halfway to the table and bowed. "My Zenith, I present Forrest Workman."

Forrest's mouth fell open; the look on Kyle's face brought him to himself. He knelt on his right knee and bowed his head.

"Rise. Forrest Workman, are you a man of his word?"

Forrest did not stand gracefully. He had not often kneeled to any man. Women! Well, that was a different matter altogether. He looked at the young man facing him at the end of the table. He looked so young, but his voice had strength and his eyes bore into him. "My Zenith, yes…the answer to your question is 'yes.'"

"Then give the weapons that you kept at the entrance to my Chambers to my guardsman."

Forrest looked at Jarod for a moment with a startled expression and then slowly a wide grin formed on his face. The guardsman came up beside him and took four knives and a short rapier as he handed them over, hilt first. "My Zenith, I stand before you as helpless as a babe."

Jarod smiled. "I sincerely hope not, Forrest."

Kyle left the table at the sound of a soft knock. Deion entered and stood behind Jarod. The grin on Forrest's face vanished on seeing the Protector. "This is His Grace Deion Russell and the Captain of my Guard, Lord Kyle Byrne." Deion leaned down and whispered in Jarod's ear, making the Zenith look at Forrest and frown. "I want your word that you are unarmed."

The grin returned to Forrest's face. "My Zenith, you are a man I like, if it's permissible to say so." He reached behind to the nape of his neck and pulled a short, throwing dagger from beneath his shirt with two fingers. The guardsman took it before he could bring his arm around in front of him. "My Zenith, you have my word, I have no more weapons on me."

Deion walked around and took the seat beside Kyle. Jarod motioned to Gaz and he took Forrest to the seat at the end of the table, facing him. Gaz took the seat to Forrest's right.

Kyle's voice sounded as cold as his eyes looked. "I have heard you are a paid agent; do you owe loyalty to no one except those who pay you?"

"My Lord, I owe great loyalty to the Zenith. My father's accusation of theft put him into the prison near the great delta. I must have been no more than ten or eleven at the time. My mother died earlier, and I went to live with the priests. I persuaded my priest that I knew what actually happened; the magistrate's son did the theft. I told him about another witness, a horse-leader on the canals.

"No one listened when I tried to protest at the

magistrate's calling. Then the magistrate had me thrown out of the calling." Forrest spread his hands in front of him on the table in full view. "The priest found and talked to the horse-leader; then he approached the magistrate saying there may be new evidence. The magistrate refused to call the session again. He told the priest to mind the faith and let him take care of the law. Now, I realize the magistrate must have known of his son's guilt. Recalling the session wouldn't only have him admit his error, but he must also condemn his son."

Forrest took a breath before continuing. "A priest named Thurston—bless him—said he wouldn't let it end there. As I recall, he became quite angry, and wrote to High Lord Long. The High Lord had traveled to one of the realms. His assistant sent the letter on to your father.

The Zenith sent men to talk with Priest Thurston and me, then to the horse-leader. It took a few weeks, but everything got set straight. I heard the magistrate died in prison by the hand of another prisoner, his own son! The son lost his head a month later. My father blessed the Zenith every day for the rest of his life. I owe your line a great debt, my Zenith. In my dealings I have never done anything to hurt Stonefire, and I never will."

The expressions of the men opposite Forrest had not changed during his story, giving away nothing.

Kyle continued. "Gaz tells me you have heard of a certain Dark Stone that the ruler of Ozlid seeks. Tell me what you have heard."

Forrest shifted in his chair. "My Zenith, Arestead and Hamptor are in an uproar about it. Ozlid has offered a huge reward for the stone. Part of the proof is in knowing its description. I had never heard of such a thing and didn't pay much attention to it."

With a look of deep concentration, Jarod said, "From what I have read in Gaz's reports, we may have need of your talents. We request you to be our guest for a few days. Gaz will see you have comfortable quarters. We will return your weapons when you leave the Spires. Gaz, join the Captain and myself in my small study after you see to Forrest's accommodations."

* * *

JAROD asked Deion to confirm the man's tale with Thurston when the door closed behind the two men. Kyle started to the door, looking around when Jarod did not stand to leave. He placed a restraining hand on Deion's arm and nodded permission for Kyle to go on to his small study.

He turned his chair toward Deion. "We have not had a chance to talk since your Naming today. How do you feel?"

Deion reflected for a moment; his words came slowly at first. "It is most difficult to put into words. I seem to have many feelings at once. Earlier, when I told you Forrest still had a weapon. I felt the knife, the physical knife itself and more, I know the blade, I knew it had killed. I also know that it killed in self-defense. It's more than a feeling. I know the emotions Forrest felt when he threw it—he believed he would die if he did nothing. I also know he spoke the truth to you."

Deion's voice held a touch of awe as he continued. "I feel Marc as if he's part of me. I know when he's awake or sleeping. I knew when you visited him earlier today. There is a different kind of emotion from you. It's like no one else he contacts." Jarod smiled.

"I meditated in the mountains. Sometimes, a light enveloped me. I felt blissful, in rapture, during those times. This morning I knew I floated in air, and then even that awareness left me. I felt that same bliss in every part of me. The times before measured like a drop of water, but today, the ocean engulfed me. I felt bonded to Marc before; it's much more than that now. It feels like our spirits have joined with ropes of rapture. I know no way to describe it. He brings me great joy, and I think he feels that from me. Your presence brings him the same kind of emotion, that I know."

"I'm greatly relieved you are here," Jarod said. "I have a strong feeling that Marc needs a safe, hidden place for many years, and I feel the best place for him is the Tower. I know from my books your charge to protect and to teach. Will residing in the crater present any hindrance?"

"I don't believe so. There is great power in the crater. It may be of help. I don't think I'm stronger there, but perhaps more aware of my powers. I began to feel natural with them in the crater. It may be the same for Marc."

Deion's countenance took on concern and reticence. Jarod did not disturb him. "My Zenith...Jarod, I would like to try something with you. I think it will be of help. Please give me your hands."

Deion took his hands and closed his eyes. Jarod felt a great peacefulness spiral through him. He closed his eyes and felt nothing of his surroundings. His grief formed in front of him as a huge, black ball. He felt it course through him, its full power consumed him. Slowly a light formed around the ball, turned crimson and began to burn away the black. He could smell the stench of decay while the ball diminished in size. He watched in awe while it reduced to nothing, the stench gone, and the air fresh and clean.

He remembered the grief in his heart, but the pain diminished to a remembrance. The experience ended as quickly as it began, or so he assumed. He opened his eyes. Deion dripped with sweat, looking weary and depleted. His huge frame slumped, but he smiled. "I'm fine. My strength will return in a few minutes. You must go my Zenith; Kyle and Gaz have been waiting. We have been over an hour."

"An hour? It seems like only a minute, two at the most."

Deion released his hands, leaned back, and closed his eyes. Jarod left him in peace and started for his small study. It felt strange: The remembrance of his loss remained, the feeling of loneness remained. None of that had changed. But his terrible pain and grief had been replaced by memories. He felt he had emerged from a thick darkness into the fresh, cool, clean air of a spring day.

Kyle and Gaz awaited his arrival. They stood when he entered the study.

"Gaz, how is our guest?"

"My Zenith, he's a little overwhelmed at present, and perturbed at me for not answering his questions. His room is on a guarded floor and he has an escort assigned to him. I believe he will work out well for our purposes."

Jarod's question came as no surprise. "Can your men tell us when Ozlid made the offer for the Dark Stone?"

"The last man returned four months ago, and his report didn't mention it. Zack Stand should be returning at any time. I will ask both."

Jarod began speaking while he motioned them to their plush chairs and joined them. "Let us look at what we know. In the west, we have a tyrant who has heard of what we think is the Dark Stone. The kingdoms across the eastern seas feud over trivial matters with minor skirmishes." He looked perplexed. "It would seem if Ozlid knows of a Dark Stone, the ruler there must have designs on other lands. They are in the west. What is the threat from the east? We will need ships."

"I heard of a ship sunk off the coast of Deepwells in a storm. The ships from the east seem better built and manned compared to the western ships of Arestead and Hamptor. They are not in a class of the sunken ship. They reported her larger and faster than ever seen before, bearing a different design and carrying three masts. It seems the lands to the south are where we should look for our shipbuilders. I think this is a possibility we must explore. Do we know anyone who has been there? Have we heard of any lands trading with them?"

Kyle and Gaz said nothing. Kyle slowly walked to the window and peered out over the City. Jarod knew it as a good sign. Finally, he spoke without turning. "Gaz, do you remember anything about a man found washed up on the beach, nearly dead, that later joined High Lord Wells' service? He's an accomplished soldier, not a seaman, but a soldier. He gave no information about his land. The Guard taught him our language and interviewed him as I remember. I heard about it at a reception held at the Academy. He posed no threat, and Lord Wells offered him an officer's post."

Gaz did not hesitate. "Yes, I recall a report on him. We kept watch on him for some time until he swore fidelity to Lord Wells. He then became Lord Wells' responsibility, but I still get reports on him. They state his accomplishments in many areas, and he has a formal education. He still does not talk about his home."

Jarod's voice took on the low, quiet, cold tone that Gaz began to expect when a decision loomed. "Gaz, ask one of the guardsmen to send His Grace to us. He may still be in the Zenith's study. I think we need to speak with this man. Kyle is there anything else you can think of concerning him?"

"It has been two years at least, since the reception. I think he's the one I heard had improved Lord Wells' troops by half again their previous performance. But I may have him confused with someone else."

Gaz returned and Deion arrived a few minutes later. His appearance reflected his usual self. Before he could speak, Jarod asked, "How do you feel?"

"Fine, my Zenith."

"I take it that your power over birds is the best of anyone at the Spires?"

"My Zenith, it's the strongest in the world until Marc gains the training in that aspect of the power. I can feel power from great distances; there is none as strong as ours."

"The Birdmaster has five birds trained to go to Segquo, the leader of the High Desert People. I need you to assist Gaz in structuring a message and give it to the birds. Add one additional message: I will visit Segquo before the year is out.

"Segquo will forward the message to High Lord Wells the fastest way. Fill the birds with urgency, but not to the point they harm themselves. See if you can determine the time their flight will take, and send a message by Rolo of what you find. That is all, gentlemen. Kyle, stay a minute, please."

He waited until the door closed. "Kyle, some wine?"

"Yes, I will pour." They settled in their favorite plush chairs.

Jarod sipped, then said, "I have been keeping three ministers busy doing the realm's business since this nightmare started. How is the Guard?"

"I have assigned three Gals to help Apex Wright. I have heard no complaints that are not being addressed in the daily reports."

He tried to relax without much success. "Two weeks ago, I would never have believed this week possible…it seems as if it has gone on for years. The bad has to end soon. There will be balance!"

"I hope it comes soon, we are going forward mostly on determination at this point." Kyle took a deep breath, then a sip of wine.

Jarod grinned slyly. "Have you seen Trina lately?"

Kyle's mischievous grin answered the question before he spoke. "I make a few minutes for her in the morning. Sometimes we have a morning sweetbread together."

"I have it on good authority that she might have some interest in you. I will say no more on the subject."

The two continued to chat for nearly an hour when the Pinnacle's fanfare cut through the night. Jarod looked toward the open window. "He's not due until tomorrow; come with me to greet him, and then we will come here for a short time. Neither of us can stay up all night talking."

* * *

GEOFFREY stepped off the lift looking exhausted; covered in road dirt, his hair matted to his scalp. Jarod and Kyle both embraced him with a slap on the back as if he was dressed in a sparkling uniform and ready to inspect the troops. They went to the small study. On the way, Rolo glimpsed the Pinnacle and hurried off. They got through the high points of the week's events, with a few glaring omissions, in less than an hour.

Light taps on the door, followed by the Mother's entrance, drew a smile from Geoffrey. She looked at him and shook her head. "Just as I suspected. You will have your usual tea before bed, put two drops of this in before you drink it, and you will easily find rest. It won't harm you; it's from the tea of sleep. More than two drops, however, and you will sleep until noon. Good night my sons, at least one of you will sleep well."

The Mother left as Rolo entered. "My Pinnacle Lord, your rooms are ready with a hot bath waiting. Lastmeal will come up in about thirty minutes. I ordered your favorite fish; if you prefer something else, I can change it."

Geoffrey's broad grin told of his wants before he shook his head.

Jarod stood. "We have given you the base of it. I will speak with you in the morning. There is much more to tell and planning to do. Rest well tonight."

Kyle added his concurrence for a good night, and a weary Pinnacle went off to his quarters. Kyle looked to Jarod when Geoffrey had closed the door behind him. "Do you think we should have told him about Marc and the war tonight?

"Why not? The Mother's tea would have little effect if we did. He needs the rest, and so do we. Have firstmeal with me, if you are not too full of sweetbreads."

Kyle's special smile lasted through their leave taking, and he too went off to find rest. He finished his wine on the small balcony, and looked out over the City. Then he joined the other's quest.

36

JAROD arrived the next morning, and ate little. He smiled at Kyle's sheepish grin when he entered. After firstmeal, Rolo delivered several messages. The first came from Deion. "The birds have flown; he estimated three days to their destination." The rest came from ministers requesting resolution on one thing or another. He made notes on them, and marked them for Lady Deanna. He requested a mid-morn meeting with His Grace, and sent Rolo on his way. He asked Kyle to join him for an exercise session. He changed into his exercise garb and the two went to the room of stones, discussing much of nothing. Kyle stripped to his privatecloth and joined him running in place.

They had been at it for about twenty minutes when Jarod spoke. "Yesterday, I received a vision and message from Maress while here." He said it as if he told Kyle what he had to eat that morning.

It took a moment for Kyle to comprehend. He stopped moving completely. "What did you say?"

He had said the message to himself so many times that when he stopped running, he told Kyle the event verbatim between gasps for air. Then he said, "I want you to give Geoffrey a full report this morning of everything we know. I have requested a meeting with Deion at mid-morning to seek his advice about joining with the Stone Maress mentioned. I know what it means. I want to hear his concerns and advice. I will ask you both to attend the Stone's joining if he agrees with my interpretations. I will want the Holy One there, too. You are not to mention that part to Geoffrey ahead of time." He started his exercises with the stones.

Kyle said, "I have never seen you quite this way. What can I say? I know your mind is made up." Kyle walked over to where he exercised. "Is there any danger in this for you?"

"I'm not sure. According to one of the old books, it could kill me if I'm wrong about this. Nevertheless, how could I be wrong? Deion's ascension to Protector proves it." Jarod's voice remained matter-of-fact. Kyle knew he had already set his mind to go through with it, and the decision bothered him.

Kyle took him by the shoulders. The exercise stone he used crashed to the floor when he released the tension rope. Their eyes locked for a moment, and then Kyle pulled Jarod into his arms and held him tightly. Neither of them wanted to let go. Kyle kissed his brother—in all but blood—on the cheek when they did. "You won't die. There is too much to be done, and no one but you to do it. But take no chances, it could mean Marc's life, too. You are the Zenith. The High Lords wouldn't like overrule by anyone but you, until Marc reaches his Age-of-Man time, at least. No one but you can prepare us for war. Take care. You are more than the Zenith to me—you are my family." Kyle's eyes moistened. He stripped off his privatecloth and went directly into the rainmaker, pulling the handle to its strongest flow.

Jarod stripped from his clothes and walked into the water when Kyle went to dry. Neither man spoke as they dressed. Each was lost in his deliberations.

As they headed for the door, Jarod took Kyle's arm and turned him. "You are my family, too."

37

WHILE Jarod looked at the sun playing tricks with shadows in the City below, his thoughts ranged much farther away. He looked up when Deion entered through the open door. "My Zenith."

"Your Grace, we call you as counselor to the Zenith."

His smile vanished, and he closed the door behind him. The two settled into chairs, and Jarod told him about the vision and message. He gave him an old book opened to the right page. Deion read the few pages as he got them both glasses of juice. Finally Deion closed the book and placed it gently on the table between them.

"I cannot tell you much. You have set your mind to join with the Stone." Jarod noted he had not asked a question. "I feel it won't harm you or any of your line. However, it may not join with you. Mine didn't join with me." He felt the ruby next to the smaller blue Stone against his chest. "But I'm not of the line. I believe that the worst thing to happen would be the dispersal of its energy and the time required restoring its power. How it disperses its power is anyone's guess. We will know more when we see the effect the Box has on the Stone. I can counsel you no further."

Jarod reached behind him and pulled the bell for Rolo. "Thank you, Deion. You are right; my mind is set. I think I'm just being nervous. There will be no doubt when the Box of Stones reacts. I hope it brings me some of the insights you have. *If it joins with me...*

Rolo arrived and hurried off with his messages before Deion continued. "You may gain much more than you bargained for. I cannot imagine it not joining with you after what has happened. The signs are there, and I believe you have correctly interpreted them."

Jarod and he chatted while they walked to the Zenith's study, as if neither had a care. He carried the small box containing the Seven Stones. They arrived together. Geoffrey and Kyle came first to the room, followed by Travis holding Marc. Marc reached for his father when he came close. Jarod took him and held him with his head resting against his neck. Geoffrey smiled broadly as he looked from father to son.

He kissed his son and gave him to Travis. He motioned for them to sit, and stood at the far end of the table, as if the distance might protect them if things did not go as planned. There may have been no protection at all, and that idea jangled his nerves.

"This will be a formal Act of State. No matter the outcome, you will each write a report of what you witness, and give it to Lord Long to be placed in the Journals of the Zenith." He went on to explain the reason for their meeting. Discussions of dangers and effects began to break out. Jarod's quiet voice cut through them like a knife. "My mind is set. You are all here to witness." More than his voice showed evidence of strain. The room became quiet.

Deion walked to him as he took the cloth from around the small box. He placed six of the gems in a hexagon shape, with the emerald in the middle. He took his Stone and let it spin over the pattern. Light blinded them for a moment. The Box of Stones appeared on the table when they could see again.

Jarod's doubts evaporated. He removed his boots, wondering if the small spikes holding the heel would really go through his body and into the ceiling if he left them on. He decided he'd rather not question the advice from the Old Books. He set the boots aside and removed his sash and shirt. His muscles stretched tautly from stress and exercising, mostly stress at that moment. Small drops of sweat ran down his side and chest. Opening the Box of Stones, he withdrew the Sire's Stone. He looked down the table at his son and held the emerald over the center stone of the Box: a diamond as big as the palm of his hand.

The effect happened immediately, as if the power had been waiting for release. He and the Stone shot five feet into the air, the Stone staying level with his heart. His head thrown back, arms out to his side, he floated as His Grace had. Golden energy rose in a thick column from the Box to the Stone, encasing it with power. The energy flow stopped, and the Box of Stones lay dormant. The Sire's Stone looked like pure gold as it slowly revolved in the air.

It stopped revolving aligned perfectly to his heart. Its movement hardly noticeable at first, closing the three feet between them in a flash of light. The emerald, an inch square and two inches long, melted into his chest with its outmost side even with his skin, within a minute. The golden color began to fade, and slowly the dark green of the perfect Stone took presence over the gold. A golden flame remained behind the Sire's Stone, causing it to emit a beautiful green light with golden flecks.

He slowly descended into Deion's arms. The large man caught him behind his knees with one arm and across his shoulders with the other, nestling him—in a limp stupor—against his chest. Deion carried him to the table as if he weighed nothing and gently laid him down. Geoffrey brought a pillow from one of the chairs and put it under his head. He could not take his eyes from the Stone's light dancing in the air above his heart. No one in the room spoke. Jarod's breathing became light and even.

His awareness surfaced from a deep well of rapture. His eyes opened briefly and closed again from the light in the room. Gradually, he sat up and looked around with crystal clarity at the eyes staring at him. The men had auras of color coming from their bodies. He looked at

Deion, encased in a golden light. He heard his voice in his head. *Thank you. You have a beautiful color, too.*

YOU HEARD ME. Deion reeled, and put his hands over his eyes. His response came instantly into Jarod's mind. *Too much power, it takes only a light sending. You can kill with that power!*

The Zenith eased off the table, brushing away helping hands. He went directly to His Grace, pulling his hands away from his face. Blood ran in a small trickle from his right eye. Jarod turned, speaking to the room. "Get the Mother and Tobias, and bring water."

He guided Deion's huge frame to a plush chair and eased him down. "Blessed Light, tell me I didn't hurt you badly."

Deion's weak smile held hope. "I will have a headache for a week, but I'm fine." Jarod believed he might say the same with two feet of steel sticking from his chest.

Jarod had finished dressing when Mavis and Tobias came running through the door. Rolo appeared with a bowl of water and clean cloths. They went straight to Deion. The Mother wiped the blood from his face and looked carefully at the eye. "I can see nothing that caused the injury. How is your sight?"

"I can see a beautiful woman in front of me." Mavis' hands disappeared in Deion's grasp. He opened his hands, leaned down, kissed her hands and whispered, "If you hadn't married, I might send you sweets."

She smiled gleefully and whispered, "I'm married, but you can still send me sweets."

He reached over and took Jarod's hand. "Don't worry my friend, I'm really fine."

Jarod rose and addressed the room. "What you have seen and heard cannot be discussed with anyone until the proper time. I don't know what Dark's Source can hear, or where it or his minions can go. I don't think he can come close to us with the powers we have put into effect, and its concentration in one place. I also don't know how long that will last. My books state that Dark's Source finds our power abhorrent, and won't approach it until it's strong in our world. I'm afraid that if our companions, or we, speak of the events happening around us, we will invite danger and possible harm.

"I'm going to rest for a bit. Geoffrey, when you have your questions answered, please join me in my small study. Kyle, you come, too." He kissed his son and got a giggle for a response. He nodded to the obsequious of those in the room and left with the Box of Stones.

*   *   *

DEION walked with Travis and two guardsmen to take Marc to the nursery. "Is he really that strong?" Travis asked quietly.

"Much stronger than I would have believed. That Stone's power will grow, too. He will be a formidable force. I suspect only Marc will be stronger. I will work with him. He must learn to control that raw power." Travis nodded as they walked on.

*   *   *

JAROD leaned into his favorite plush chair and put his feet up on the stool. He gazed at Maress' portrait, and believed he saw a golden light around her image as his eyes closed and sleep overtook him.

A knock on his door jarred him awake. The afternoon shadows told him the approximate time. On the way to the door, he realized that he felt better than he had in a long time. No trace of the mental and physical exhaustion that had plagued him the last few days remained. He admitted Geoffrey and Kyle, rang for Rolo, and motioned the men to plush chairs. He ordered refreshments, and the three just looked at one another a moment.

Finally, Geoffrey said, "I never dreamed the possibility of what I saw this morning. I can hardly believe what

Kyle has told me of the past week. Is there any doubt?"

Jarod shook his head. "No, the naming of the Protector confirmed my worst fears, and my joining with the Sire's Stone removes any doubt that our course is set. The old writings have proved to be remarkably accurate. Our focus must be to prepare. We must give Marc every possible bit of aid to achieve the knowledge he requires for that time when he's the most powerful of us, and the true battles begin. I suspect it will come in degrees, not all at once. As the Stones grow in power, so will Dark's Source. We have some protections. The area around the Box of Stones and the Tower crater are the strongest points of sanctuary for us. I will send Marc to the crater under the care of Travis, and possibly Trina, until he's weaned. I will direct the Mother and Tobias to start the training required to enlarge the ranks of herbalist and healers. Kyle will begin training a new army. I will direct Lord Northmount to start training a line of battle horses. I doubt if there are more than ten in the Seven Realms. We can explore the possibility of venturing to the southern lands for experts to build a navy and train our seamen when High Lord Wells arrives with his officer. And...I suspect I have much to learn about controlling the power I have been given." Geoffrey recognized a force of authority he had never heard in Jarod before.

"Travis and his priests have to raise another kind of army. Gaz will be investigating foreign and domestic lands. You will discover a wide range of information from Gaz and Lord Long, and it will be your duty, Geoffrey, to keep the Seven Realms united. When you and Gaz uncover influence from Dark's Source, we can deal with it. I will work with Deion to find a way to detect Dark Source's activities; we will find it if there is one. I don't know there is one, but we must try. His Grace may have some additional work to do if Marc will be truly safe in the crater."

He took a moment to collect his conclusions before

continuing. "According to the old writings, we have until Marc finds his own Stone before Dark's Source can wage full war. I have no idea what the books mean by full war. If we are not careful, the war may be lost before it has begun. It would be over now if the attack on Marc had been successful. It will fall on him to fight the ultimate battle. I just hope we are here to help him."

"What about Mountglen and Clarence?" Kyle asked.

His face and voice reflected no doubt in his mind. "They will show their true selves on or before the Naming Day ceremony. I can see no other reason for a rapid trip to the City. Their behavior after they arrive may give us some further indication of their intent. We will take immediate action if our suspicions prove correct. There is a full council meeting tomorrow. I may release some information then. I will announce a banquet in four or five months. I plan to talk with each of the High Lords then.

"Geoffrey, I need you to stay until after Marc has been named."

The Pinnacle smiled. "I would like to send for Elaine and my sons to be here for the ceremony."

Kyle turned from looking at the City with a look of concern that reflected Jarod's own. "There may be danger, and they could be at risk."

Rolo's knock came and the door opened. Jarod rose and looked down at Geoffrey. "Kyle is right, but it's your choice."

He took the note from Rolo's tray and read it. "Ten minutes." He handed the note to Rolo, sending him with the reply. "Gentleman, I will see you at lastmeal tonight."

Geoffrey took Jarod's hand before leaving. "I can think of no one who could lead us better than you. I will give you all the support I can. I don't envy you these coming years."

He squeezed Geoffrey's hand, and felt a surge of warmth and concern flow through his body. He released his hand, and walked him to the door to cover his surprise.

Lady Deanna, punctual as ever, entered and He motioned her to the sit across from him. Her plans for that night's lastmeal pleased him. She reported her activities with a strange smile and a look that he found curious. She had invited the ladies-in-waiting and some of the Ladies of the Seven Realms that visited in the Spires to conduct business for their Lords and arranged for musicians and a juggler from the City. His decision to invite the Apex officers and their wives pleased her. She still smiled impishly as she bowed and went to her office.

He dismissed her actions and emptied his mind while he relaxed into the chair. He felt a comforting presence. He thought first of Maress. He sat up in the chair with a start. The feeling left and he forced himself to relax once more and clear his mind. The warm presence returned to his consciousness. He gently projected, *I'm going to take a nap now.*

Warmth flowed through him like peace itself. He heard Deion as if he whispered. *"Sleep well, my Zenith."* Marc's soft giggle came at the end. He knew that sound, too.

38

ROLO woke Jarod in time to take a bath prior to dressing for lastmeal. He looked at the choice of clothes laid out for him, and decided on the simplest: a white shirt, trousers, and boots with a crimson sash and coat. The white coat had the three spires in black and golden deathcats sleeping at the base of each spire. Typically, he disliked this type of function the most; however, he found himself looking forward to this one. Rolo informed him that the guests awaited his pleasure.

By custom, the guests stood behind their chairs until Jarod entered and sat. He and Maress had departed from that more formal tradition, and entered at opposite ends of the room. They each greeted the guests along one side of the table while heading to their seats. Tonight, he returned to tradition.

Rolo accompanied him to the door, and would later serve only him that evening. He opened the door wide for him to enter. The splendid room promised gaiety; fresh flowers decorated the center of the table for its full length. Giant urns of exotic flowers from the Spire's hothouses stood at a man's height, placed every few feet along the walls of the room. The table's crimson cloths under white plates with a gold band and crystal glasses and goblets with golden serviceware brought smiles to the ladies. Musicians played string, flute, and harp in the far corner.

The musicians played Jarod's fanfare when he entered the room. His guests had arrived dressed as splendidly as the room. He remembered the clothes in Jessup's shop and grinned. His merchandise had not found an invitation.

Trina and Marc had not arrived. Geoffrey sat on his right, Kyle on his left. A lady-in-waiting, wife, or a Lady of the Seven Realms occupied seats between the men on both sides of the table. Even the Mother had forsaken her black for the evening. She wore a pale blue, long, flowing gown.

Kyle and the Apex officers sparkled in dress uniforms. Gaz' formal cut suit in dark blue brought the biggest surprise to Jarod. His normally frizzy hair was combed and contained by a silver clip at the nape of the neck. He could easily pass for a lord. The Pinnacle's taste in clothes ran along the same lines as Jarod's, attired in gray with a silver sash. Travis, Deion, and the Prelates dressed in their finest robes. The lady's dresses ran a rainbow of light pastel colors. Lady Deanna sat near the end of the table, away from Jarod in a pale yellow gown that became her. He caught her eye, smiled, and nodded. Her quite evident pleasure at his compliment brought a blush to her cheeks.

Jarod quietly asked Rolo about Trina and Marc's absence. Marc was sleeping, and Trina did not want to wake him. He ordered Trina to be sent a tray with instructions to come when Marc woke.

The food matched the room in quality. Each course exceeded the previous in flavor and presentation. Soup followed by fowl with sweet berries set the tone of the feast. Lamb with sprigs of mint and root vegetables seasoned with herbs came before cake with cold wiped cream brought more smiles. Cheese, bread and nuts ended the meal. The wines came chilled and full-bodied. The conversation caught quickly as everyone enjoyed the festivities. Jarod became acutely aware that Maress did not fill the seat at the opposite end of the table and again, the pain melted away, leaving something manageable. He looked down at Deion, and found him smiling. The festivities became contagious, and he found himself actually enjoying the evening.

The musicians played an entertainer's fanfare as they finished the dessert. When a guardsman opened the door at the far end of the room, a juggler in a brightly colored costume ran into the room and bowed toward the table. A beautiful assistant followed with a box on wheels that came to her waist. The juggler played a mime, too. He brought out a seemingly endless array of items to juggle and worked it into a mime's story. The guests clapped and called for more.

The far door opened and Trina entered with Marc in her arms. The ladies at the table let out a collective sigh. The sound of breaking glass brought their attention back to the juggler. He stood holding a broken bottle by the neck, its jagged edges pointed toward Marc. He let out a wail and raced for the babe.

From nowhere, two arrows and a knife pierced the juggler's body. He crashed to the floor, blood pooling around him.

The room became pandemonium's retreat: Women screaming, officers yelling commands and the room filled with guardsmen in seconds. Two archers stood on the center balcony with new arrows notched and tension on their bowstrings. The Protector stood, his chair kicked away and a new knife ready to throw. Kyle and his officers had drawn their swords. Two guard officers appeared on each side of Jarod, with two more behind him.

He ordered the ladies escorted to the reception room. The Mother stood over the juggler's body. The juggler's assistant fainted, and a guardsman swept her up and carried her out with Gaz and two guardsmen following close behind.

The Mother's voice cut through the din, "My son, quickly." Jarod raced to the body. The juggler focused briefly on him. Blood seeped from his mouth when he spoke. "My Zenith, I never meant...hurt..." He face went flaccid, turning more into his blood. Deion reached down and retrieved his knife. His face had a look of great sorrow.

The Mother looked into Jarod's eyes, "He said only one more word, Dreams!"

Trina held Marc protectively, staring at the body with loathing. Kyle suddenly stood beside her, leading her and Marc away. Jarod followed them out while a pebble of guardsmen formed around them with drawn swords and started in the direction of the nursery. Kyle had his arm around Trina's shoulders.

Jarod went directly to the reception room. Two guardsmen opened the doors for him to enter. Some of the ladies tried to calm Lady Deanna's hysterics. One helped dab water across her blood-splattered dress. Everyone except Lady Deanna curtsied low. Jarod did not think she knew him—or much else—existed.

His quiet, cold voice bristled with power. "Ladies I require you not to discuss this matter with anyone. Some of my men will talk with you shortly." Jarod started to leave and then said, "My son escaped harm." He continued from the room, feeling Marc's heartbeat and his soft, gentle breath.

The Mother came toward him with a guardsman and Tobias beside her. "My son, Marc and Trina are both fine."

"Mother, see if you can help Lady Deanna." He watched while she and Tobias went on to the reception room. He ordered the guardsman to have the male guests meet him in the Zenith's study when they finished their duties.

39

THE herbalist had told Mountglen that he had done a perfect job of searing his son's wound, that he could not have done better himself. Mountglen had not commented on the irony of the healer's statement. There was no sign of infection. The pain became bearable, and Clarence set sulking in the corner of their room.

Shadure emerged from the fireplace as the door closed behind the departing herbalist. *"You see! I could have given you an infection to eat away your vital organs. It's much more painful than a mere amputation and slight burn."*

Clarence snarled, "You have a curious way of binding people to you, you bastard!" Mountglen tried to get between them.

"Don't concern yourself—I have no intention of harming him further, at least not tonight. Your nephew and the brat live on. Plan well for their deaths." With that said, he vanished.

Mountglen sat by his son and pulled him close. "My son, please do nothing to cause you more pain. The frustration in Clarence radiated to his father.

"You don't really believe he's going to let us live? We will be dead if we fail or not. Do you really think he is going to set you up as Zenith of the Seven Realms?"

"He will still need humans to do his bidding. I want the Seven Realms for myself. We are both going to Dark's Source in the end. If we fight him, we will destroy any chance of ruling there as well as here. I would much rather rule the tormented than be the tormented. Think well on this, my son; do as I say in this matter, and we both will live."

Clarence pulled away from his father and huddled in

the corner of the room with a new bottle of wine. His mind locked more than ever on what he should do. *My father won't rule in Shadure's domain, and neither shall I.* The conclusion made him shiver.

40

JAROD looked over the City from the small balcony off his study. The lack of a moon enhanced its sparkling lights all the more. Kyle started to knock on the open door when Jarod's voice stopped him. "Come in, Kyle. Is everyone assembled?"

Jarod did not speak on the way to the Zenith's study. Believing him lost in concentration, Kyle did not intrude. The men from the lastmeal sat at the table. The room became quiet when he entered. He looked down the long table and frowned. "Lord Long, I'm sorry. I didn't want you to wait up for this. I will be glad to give you a report in the morning. Shall I call Hinston?"

"Your concern does me great honor, my Zenith." Lord Long's sad smile contrasted his sharp, clear eyes. "I hope you won't find it as hard to sleep as I do when you reach my age. My curiosity is as strong as ever. I prefer to stay."

"As you wish, my lord. Gaz, what did you find from the assistant?"

"She's his wife. They have been married five years with no children. She claims she had no idea of what made him do such a thing. He stated to her on more than one occasion that he admired you and your father. They have had no money or marital problems. The Mother told me he had performed at the hospice many times without charge. The wife said that he'd had nightmares for the past few days, and seemed distant at times. His Grace accompanied me in the room. We both felt she told the truth."

Jarod's mind felt a gentle sending. *"She told the truth."*

He looked across from Gaz and saw Deion's slight nod.

He continued. "Gentlemen, some of you must have questions about the events of the past week. What happened tonight is part of a greater conspiracy. I have ordered the ladies not to discuss tonight's events with anyone. I must also include you in that order. There is a High Council meeting tomorrow with the Chairs of State present. I also want the Spire's Apex officers to attend. If there is nothing more, we will adjourn until then."

The sending formed as gently as before. *"My Zenith, we must talk for a moment."* Jarod looked at Deion and walked to the balcony doors. He pushed one door open, and felt the cool night breeze.

"My Zenith, probing another's mind is a delicate process. I have not probed yours, and won't in the future, unless your life is at risk. Communicating with your mind has risks. I had hoped that I would have time to teach you the use of your abilities before this crisis went further. That has not happened. I will learn what I can tomorrow if you wish it. I think it wise if you didn't use your powers at the meeting. I must warn you not to use your powers as you warned me before my naming ceremony. It may well alert evil sources that you now exist on a higher level than before you joined with the Stone. I have shielded your use of power from outsiders, since we don't know who might have hidden and evil talents. I cannot do that, and feel for conspiracy tomorrow. I hope you will consider my wishes in this."

Jarod's countenance took on that far away reserve that only Deion could fully understand. "I won't do anything out of the ordinary tomorrow. Is it possible to be trained by Naming Day?"

"Perhaps in the power's basic use. That is what you need to keep you safe. There is much to learn. I don't think anyone knows it completely. I still learn things almost daily."

Jarod hesitated and then spoke softly. "I will do as you

ask, and we can fix a schedule tomorrow. There is one thing I must know before Naming Day. I don't like asking this and I would like doing it less. It's important for me to know what Kyle and Trina's feelings are for one another, and the depth of those feelings. This involves a matter of State. I will never do anything to hurt Kyle in any way. I must know how to plan events. I…"

Deion took Jarod's forearm. "My friend, I believe you have valid reasons. I will learn what I can as unobtrusively as possible. Put your mind at rest. You are not betraying your friend in asking. He's lucky to have someone who cares so much." Serenity and calmness flowed from him to Jarod. They turned in silent agreement and went their separate ways.

He sat in his room when the question struck him. *Why would Dark's Source risk losing the Black Stone?* He pondered it without finding an answer. His contemplation drifted to Kyle and Trina. *Do I have the right to interfere, or even influence a decision they might, or might not, make?*

The question lingered within him when he woke and joined Trina and Kyle for sweetbreads in the nursery. Marc presented his usual cheerful self with giggles and grins. Jarod played with his son while Kyle and Trina played their word games. He watched the interaction between them with a smile. It might have seemed innocent flirting between two attractive people if he had not known Kyle for most of his life. His instinct told him their relationship remained special. Normally, he would have been more than happy for his friend. He wanted Kyle to know all the happiness life could give him. He also knew that the coming events and his plans for Kyle would place huge stresses on him. He decided it best to wait until he heard what Deion had to say concerning the two of them before discussing anything with Kyle, if ever.

Jarod and Kyle had to change clothes before the council meeting. Jarod asked Kyle if he had time to exercise before the meeting. Kyle replied that he had his dress uniform in the room of stones. They said their good-byes and walked briskly away when the clock reached the seven-mark.

Jarod started to dry from the rainmaker while Kyle finished dressing. Kyle had that grin again. "I have never felt such friendship toward someone in such a short time. Every time we talk, we find more things we both like and enjoy. She's the first woman in a long time that made sense to me."

Jarod's smile became infectious. "Oh, and how many women have there been? Perhaps I should find more duties to keep you from the vices of the City."

Kyle's response came in a matter-of-fact dryness, disputed by his smile. "There is not much vice in the City. I keep catching the participants. Do you know the City has less crime than any major city in the Seven Realms? Besides that, you know every woman I have seen more than once. I cannot say the same for you. How long did you and Maress see one another before I met her?"

Dark clouds fell over Jarod. He said nothing, and turned to dress in pants and robe for the short trip to his room.

"Jarod, I'm sorry. It just blurted out. I said a stupid thing. Please forgive me."

Jarod let his mind go blank, and the inner peace he had felt before flooded through him. He wiped at his eyes, and felt at peace when he turned to Kyle.

"There is nothing to forgive, my friend. Now let's go. Lady Deanna sent word we should use the presence chamber, due to the number of people attending. That means I have to sit on that ridiculous raised chair and look the part of the Zenith. It also means I have to be there first. My dear Kyle, you may find the person responsible for the protocol of the Zenith and dispatch him."

"As you wish, my Zenith. It may take a while. I believe that particular ancestor has been dead for over five hundred years."

I hope it's a long time before you find him, Jarod thought. He smiled and said, "Let's get this over with. I have almost decided what to say." Kyle could not help smiling as he followed him out the door.

When he returned to his room, he sat on the bed, reached over and touched a volume of the Zenith's journals he'd read the night before. His introspection flowed easily: *Now is the time for traps and deceit. I never considered the tales Father told me and the exploits found in the journals, a guide for me. Now I must lay the foundations of intrigue. I don't care for the role I must play, but play it I will. As Father taught, the trick is to accomplish your goals without debasing the Zenith. Well Father, you never said it would be simple. You called it the twists and turns of statecraft. I don't know if I can be that generous in its naming.*

He was only half-dressed when the first fanfares sounded for an arriving ambassador, and entered the lift when the sixth and last sounded. He had not discussed the day's topics with any of his advisors. His mind set easy with what he would say. He used the ride down to the Great Hall's anteroom to think. Nothing his mind considered changed his planned approach. He took his private passageways, and entered through the hidden door to the presence chamber, used mainly for official audiences, not council meetings.

The only others in the room, the major-domo and two Gals armed to the teeth, stood on each side of the throne that sat on its three step dais. The chair lacked the jewels of the one in the Great Hall; although fashioned from gold, its multitude of crimson cushions easily made up for its lack of opulence, in comfort.

Jarod wore a simpler version of the State regalia. Everything white, except for a cape made from wormcloth, white on the outside with a crimson lining.

He wore no crown and carried no scepter. His major-domo hurried to the small dais to make sure he sat where his presence made the most dramatic impression. Jarod rolled his eyes. After positioning the cape to his satisfaction, he and the Gals kneeled before him in salute. The major-domo said the words he'd heard many times watching his father prepare for State occasions. It would be the first time he heard those words addressed to him.

"My Zenith, in this hour of decision, we your servants, stand ready to serve in any way required, even to our deaths."

The proclamation came from an incident many hundreds of years ago when an attempt to kill the Zenith nearly succeeded. The major-domo and one of the guardsmen had hesitated, allowing a knife to wound their Zenith. It became a tradition of words, but he had no doubt these men would give their lives for him. He only nodded, his countenance said more than words. The Gals returned to their positions, and the major-domo went to the right of the two towering, heavily carved doors. He struck the white marble floor three times with his staff.

Guardsmen from the foyer opened the two heavy doors. The major-domo called out. "My Zenith, your scribes of the Seven Realms."

Three men entered through each door and fanned slightly outward, so each scribe had a clear view of the dais. They kneeled in unison on their left knee, signifying they came unarmed, bowed their heads, and then rose in unison. They each went to their own small desk located at strategic points for capturing the words said in the room, bowed their heads toward Jarod, and set down to make ready for their tasks.

The staff sounded again against the marble. "My Zenith, the Pinnacle and his guard." Geoffrey appeared, resplendent in a dark blue suit with a simple golden sash. They approached the end of the table nearest Jarod, kneeled, and then took the seat to his right. His two guardsmen had chairs behind and on each side of him. Each of the High Councilors came forward when announced, sat in their usual arrangement, and then several guardsmen carried the Chairs of State into position. The ambassadors entered in like fashion.

The doors closed after the ambassador's announcements and seating. A select pebble of guardsmen spread across the rear of the room.

Jarod's eyes never left the ambassadors. His voice rang crisp and clear, but not loud. "We are pleased to see the Chairs of State present. However, the information for you is not of a pleasant nature. The Zenith Lady recently died a horrible death from poison, and there have been two attempts on the life of Our son."

Two ambassadors leapt to their feet. The sound of drawn steel rang through the room while guardsmen interjected themselves between the row of ambassadors and the Zenith. The action's quickness and deadly intent drained the color from the ambassador's faces. The two standing slumped into their chairs. Their distinct displeasure at swords pointed at their throats became quite clear once their hearts beat again. The guardsmen returned to the side, weapons still at the ready.

He continued, "We apologize for your discomfort. Our Guard is under strict orders. The attempts on Our lives came in my Chambers. We require any information you or your realms may have, sent to the Spires through you at the fastest possible speed. We will entertain any questions on the subject."

Lord Erwin Gray, Ambassador of Northmount, slowly rose. "My Zenith, how is the child?"

Jarod's voice softened slightly, "We appreciate your concern, Lord Gray. The babe is healthy and thriving. The Naming Day ceremony is in nineteen days. Security will remain tight, and We advise that the High Lords, Ambassadors, and Lords and Ladies of the Seven Realms whom attend the ceremony come unescorted and without guests, for their safety. However, the Law states everyone will be welcomed and none turned away. Any High Lords and all Ambassadors within a day's ride are required to be here. Our primary concern is for your safety."

Lord Garth Dermott, the ambassador from Deepwells, rose next. "My Zenith, if there have been so many attempts on the Zenith, is there evidence of a conspiracy, and is there any help you require from the Circle of Villas?"

"The well planned attacks involved more than one person. That is all We can say at this time. The investigation is continuing. Outside involvement is an open question at this point. We have no proof at this time of participation outside the Spires. We make only the requirement that your realms notify us of any pertinent information they may gather."

When no further questions surfaced, he continued. "We thank the Chairs of State for their attendance, and appreciate their remarks and concern. If there are no additional matters for the Seven Realms, the State audience is concluded."

After kneeling, the Ambassadors filed from the room. Lord Gray positioned himself to be the last to leave. He handed something to the major-domo and continued on his way. All of the guardsmen except the two gals beside the throne left to stand guard outside the two main doors. The major-domo placed a document on a silver plate and carried it to Jarod. He and the scribes withdrew, after which the presence chamber doors closed with a secure thud.

He stared at the note a moment, broke the seal, and read the message signed simply, Earl Erwin Gray.

He stood, removed the cape, and left it on the throne. A Gal anticipated his desire and carried a plush chair to the head of the table. He removed his coat and tossed it on the throne while he came down the three steps.

Jarod looked down the table at the faces, waiting. "Well gentlemen, the realms have been notified of the information I wanted them to have. It does not set well with me, but I believe it necessary if we are to learn who else is involved. This week has been an ordeal for us. There is one more duty facing us; the note from Lord Gray stated that Lord and Lady Northmount are on their way here. They don't know of Maress' death, as far as I know. He generously offered to tell them, but that is my duty. I will arrange for them to stay in the Chambers.

"There is much to do and plan before and after the Naming Day ceremony. You have been working long hours with little rest for the last eight days. I suggest we continue on our paths at a more normal schedule." Little relief stirred in the room.

"Geoffrey, we don't have to wait for the Naming Day to get some things started. I must make friendly overtures to Arestead, Hamptor, and the eastern kingdoms. Do you have someone who could carry a message from me to their rulers?"

"Yes, my Zenith, there is a man living in the City that will be good on a diplomatic mission of that sort. I will arrange a meeting. It won't be so easy going eastward. The lands there are more contentious, and the rulers see any alliances as a possible threat."

Preliminary plans made based on their overall agenda slowly became apparent. It went rapidly; still, Jarod felt relieved when no one spoke after he asked if any additional business required the council. He adjourned the meeting, and asked Geoffrey and Kyle to meet him in his study.

The short meeting yielded Jarod's need to hear their conclusions on the council meeting, and he asked Geoffrey to plan a diplomatic approach to the westward and eastward lands. They decided that one of Gaz' men should make a preliminary report on the eastern lands before an ambassador tried to open relations.

He lounged in his favorite plush chair after they left. He cleared his mind and centered on Deion. He sent a gentle sending. *"Can you come to me now?"* He began to think it had not reached him when he looked up to see him standing in the doorway. He motioned him to a seat.

"My Zenith, how can I serve you?"

"How should we start my training?"

"It should be at the same time every day. I believe that you are in the habit of exercising frequently. I suggest you complete your physical exercises as early in the morning as possible. Then we will need one to two hours alone, somewhere we won't be disturbed, if such a place exists in the Spires." His smile remained genuine, and Jarod chuckled.

"I know a place that should meet your requirements. It's outside, does that make a difference?"

"That is even better. Shall we start in the morning?"

"Your Grace, it will be my distinct pleasure." Jarod's smile set equally wry.

They chatted for a few minutes, and then Deion went on his way. Jarod sent for Gaz and the Mother. They arrived at the same time, both looking anxious. The Mother received the first question.

"How is the Lady Deanna?"

"She's still quite shaken. She blames herself for the attempt on Marc. I gave her tea of sleep last night. She's not much better this morning. She thanked me for the tea. She said she didn't have bad dreams. When I asked about her dreams, she said she couldn't remember much, except that is where she got the idea for the juggler."

Jarod reflected for a moment. "Mother, I request you, His Grace and Gaz talk with her. Make it as casual as you can. Let her know that I'm not upset with her, and I don't blame her. I will send her a note to try to put her at ease before your visit. Find out everything you can about the dreams. Be as gentle as you can with her. I have an uneasy feeling concerning those dreams. Meet with her as soon as you can get everyone together.

"Now, my dear, I have a few things to discuss with Gaz." Jarod walked Mavis to the door and kissed her on the cheek good-bye. He did not smile when he turned to Gaz.

"Gaz, how long will it take for you to set up a course of study for some of our senior officers on the finer points of your craft? The men I have in mind will be of Apex, Looker, and selected Gals' rank. I want them to understand how your men and theirs can combine efforts in a state of war. You will have to convince them that you're a compliment to them and not a hindrance. I have a plan to increase our overall strengths. This will be a part of it. I can foresee a time when a detachment of men trained by your staff and assigned to every Tor and even some Boulders. I will want the commanders of those units to realize their value, and how to use them to the best advantage."

Jarod paused for a moment. "I will be going to visit the High Desert People before the year is out, or possibly sooner. I will want two of your men on the trip with me. They will get extensive training, and will be there up to a year. What do you think of Forrest Workman being one of those men? Can he be trusted to remain for the duration of the training, and then be committed enough to teach what he has learned to some of our men here?"

Gaz' face brimmed with delight. "I have wanted to do exactly what you're proposing for years, my Zenith. Workman has always completed his tasks well, and to my satisfaction. He will see it through once he accepted it. I don't know how long he will stay and teach. He has always been a man looking for excitement doing, not teaching."

"If my suspicions are correct, Gaz, he will have enough excitement for ten lifetimes—if he can live through this one."

The spymaster's face reflected his smile. "My Zenith, I plan to have lastmeal with him today. I believe I can have a good indication for you tomorrow."

"Find out his impression of the Guard, too. You don't have to rush him. We have until Naming Day for an answer, so much the better if you have it before. Give him some freedom in the Spires. Have Rosh show him the Spires and the outside facilities." Jarod started to make it dependent on Rosh's availability, but discarded the idea. "Keep him away from the under-levels and the Chambers.

"One more thing: I want to know at once if you feel Lady Deanna's dreams play a role in the recent events. His Grace will be able to help in that determination."

Gaz left as Rolo brought the Zenith's midmeal. Jarod wrote a brief note to Lady Deanna wishing her well, and that he looked forward to her returning to her duties when she felt she had the strength. Rolo took the note with him when he left.

Jarod poured a glass of wine and selected a book to read after eating. He enjoyed his respite.

41

THE Mother knocked gently at the door. No response came. Deion reached across the Mother and rapped a little harder. When no response came again, he said, "Lady Deanna, it's His Grace. I'm with the Mother and Master Gaz. it's important that we speak with you. You may be able to help us protect the Zenith and his son."

Shuffling steps were heard inside the room, and after a long moment, the door opened a crack. Eyes wide open, she peered out for an instant, then Lady Deanna drew away, allowing the door to swing open. Her hair hung unkempt in long tangles, and she looked as if she had not groomed herself since waking; her condition strayed far from her usual immaculate and stately presence. She sat in a corner of the room by an open window without speaking to anyone. Cold, crisp, air and a dead fireplace left no comfort in the room.

The Mother said, "My dear, how are you feeling this morning? You look as if you didn't sleep well."

Lady Deanna stared out the window. "I...I feel terrible about what happened. I don't know if I will ever be able to face the babe or the Zenith again. I'm so thankful that no harm came to either of them." She continued to sit by the window nervously twisting a bit of hair.

The Mother gently stepped to her side, taking her hand and looking down into her eyes. "My dear Deanna, we know this tragedy had nothing to do with your efforts. You couldn't have known what would happen."

Her voice trembled. "But I'm the one who hired an assassin." Her look of despair was etched around her eyes.

Deion knelt beside Deanna's chair and locked his gaze with hers. "Lady Deanna, please think back and tell us what you can about the selection of the juggler. What gave you the idea of choosing one for the entertainment? Was he someone you had employed before at parties or functions?

Her fatigue seemed to melt away as His Grace continued gazing into Deanna's eyes. "Oh your Grace, I have not entertained in years. No, it just came into my head like a dream. In fact, I believe I did dream something about a juggler. I remembered how they had amazed me as a child."

Lady Deanna's words took on a far-away quality. "I went into the City to make sure the flowers would be ready for the lastmeal. I saw a juggler performing for a few children. His performance held the children and I spellbound. I asked him if he would like to perform for the Zenith. His face hardly changed except for a slight smile. He almost looked as if he had expected me to ask. It seemed strange to me at the time that he showed so little excitement. I believed him merely tired from his performance. His wife became quite excited. She said they had reached the high point in their career by performing for the Zenith.

"His wife's excitement brimmed over when I went to check the arrangements, but her husband seemed sullen and distant. I think his attitude embarrassed her. Last night, his pronounced sullen demeanor worried me. His wife assured me the performance would be fine."

Lady Deanna shivered, her voice barely heard. "And then, that horrible man tried to kill that innocent babe. His wife looked horrified—her hysterical face haunts me still."

Deion's eyes stayed locked to Deanna's eyes. He said, "My dear, you must forgive me for asking, have you had any different or unusual dreams lately?"

Lady Deanna's face colored quickly. "Yes, I have. I really cannot discuss them. They are too personal. I assure you that my dreams had nothing to do with the juggler."

He continued to hold Lady Deanna's attention with his eyes. His voice resonated no more than a whisper. "I have spoken with the Zenith. He does not blame you in any way for what happened last night. You must be at ease with this. He knows that you suffered a great shock and wishes you well." He squeezed her hand. "Master Gaz has a few questions for you then we will let you rest."

Deion and the Mother stepped away. Gaz walked to a few feet from Lady Deanna. She looked up at him timidly, with some of the strain returning to her face.

"Lady Deanna, did you find anything unusual about the man and his wife other than those things you have already mentioned?"

Lady Deanna looked out the window for moment, and then back at Gaz. "No, I cannot think of anything. A beautiful day with a lot of people about, but I noticed nothing from the ordinary."

"Would you mind if I come again, to ask a few more questions about the incidents of that day when you are feeling better?" She slightly shook her head.

Lady Deanna seemed to relax, as if an ordeal had passed and she still lived. As her guests left, she tugged slightly on the Mother's sleeve and whispered in her ear. "May I have some tea of sleep for tonight?"

The Mother smiled and nodded. Lady Deanna allowed a brief smile and closed the door behind them.

A few feet from Lady Deanna's door, Deion said, "I will brief the Zenith on our conversation, if no one objects."

Gaz nodded. "He asked particularly about any dreams she might have had."

Deion smiled, "Our Zenith is most perceptive."

* * *

ROLO returned two hours later.

"Rolo, ask the Holy One and Mother Mavis to join me here in the small study for lastmeal tonight."

"At once, my Zenith. His Grace Lord Deion is here to see you."

He took the plush chair next to Jarod. "My Zenith, Lady Deanna is overly distressed. I detected that she has had most troubling dreams. Her mind is confused, and her thoughts disorganized. She became embarrassed when we asked about her dreams. I probed her mind as best as I could without causing harm. Her recent dreams have been highly erotic. She's ashamed of herself for having them, and she cannot resist their control on her. I couldn't tell if these dreams are hers naturally, or have been somehow forced upon her. In either case, she's beside herself with guilt.

"She consented to allow Gaz to return for more questions when she felt better. In our discourse, she related the circumstances around selecting the juggler. I'm convinced she spoke the truth as she believes it. I'm sorry I couldn't detect more than I did."

"I'm constantly amazed at your abilities. You have confirmed my feeling that she may have been manipulated."

"My Zenith, you have much more power than I."

"I have more power than you?" Jarod's voice sounded incredulous.

"Only your son will ever surpass your power. I will teach what I know on its use and subtleties. I will defend the Darkslayer and you to my death, but make no mistake, your power is far beyond mine, and your son's will be far beyond yours. I had thought I would be second to Marc, but now I wonder if others more powerful will come to our aid. I only hope that our combined power will be enough. I strongly believe that the training program you have requested for our priests will become a deciding factor in the outcome of this war."

Jarod felt as if the weight of the Spires was crushing him. "You must be mistaken. I feel hardly anything of the power."

"You will see tomorrow morning; it will become clear to you. Now, open your mind and find the peacefulness that waits there. You must learn to draw on that strength to sustain you." He reached over and lightly touched Jarod in the center of his forehead.

Power surged throughout his every cell. His mind became clear and his senses heightened. He looked up into Deion's eyes in wonder.

42

JAROD stood at the window, looking down at the City after Deion had gone. Seldom in his life had he felt so sure of his goals, and with such clarity of purpose. Lady Deanna's condition pulled at his mind. He resisted the subject, and held on to the peacefulness.

A knock at the door brought him back to the present. He watched quietly while Rolo and his men set the table for their lastmeal. Jarod suddenly felt a great thirst, and drank two full glasses of juice. The Mother and Travis arrived not long afterward.

Jarod approached the subject lightly. "Mother, how did you find Lady Deanna today?

"She's deeply disturbed. She insists she bear the fault for the attack on Marc. I tried to reassure her that she had no way of knowing what would transpire. She's still withdrawn and angry at herself. His Grace told me afterwards that he felt she believed her feelings are genuine. She looked tired and worn. She became quite agitated when I asked about her ability to sleep. Gaz asked quite gently if anything had disturbed her sleep. She became more distraught; and we left her alone to rest. She asked me for some tea of sleep as I left. I gave her some before coming here."

The rest of the evening covered more pleasant subjects; the lastmeal, wine and conversation were all excellent. Jarod was delighted to have them with him. The clock approached the ten-mark when he kissed Mavis on the cheek and wished them a good night.

In his room, he undressed for bed and studied himself in the mirror. The flickering golden green light came from behind the emerald embedded in his chest. He ran a finger over the warm Stone, feeling no sensation except becoming conscious of power growing within him. He found it quite comforting. He had taken to sleeping nude since the joining with the Stone, feeling encumbered otherwise. He pulled the bedclothes up to his waist and searched his mind for that inner peacefulness. Few minutes passed before he fell peacefully asleep.

* * *

LADY Deanna looked nervously at the tea of sleep brewing beside her bed. Her anguished questions reverberated in her mind: *Will he come to me if I drink the tea? I don't think I can live without him. He must come to me. He didn't come last night when I drank it...*

Lady Deanna drank half the tea and threw the rest out the window onto the rocks far below. She chose a sheer sleepcloth and settled into bed, with only the light from a small fire in the huge fireplace. Sleep came quickly.

The door's opening roused her; she pretended to remain asleep. He circled to the side of her bed where the light from the fireplace would flicker over his body, and let the robe fall to the floor. His voice remained warm and steady. "Deanna my dear, I know you are awake. Look at me!"

Deanna sat up in bed and gazed at the beautiful body in front of her. She threw back the bedclothes and held her arms out to him. He came to her and ripped the sleepcloth away. She encircled him with her arms and pulled him close. "My darling Jarod, I knew you would come tonight."

She used her fingers to trace the hard muscles from his shoulder to the small of his back then went on to caress the fullness below. The taut muscles of his buttocks felt like a smooth melon of warm marble. She gloried in the strength and force of his body. His tongue sent chills through her as he kissed her from neck to nipple and back.

Her head began to swim from the effect of the tea of sleep. The sensations in her body suddenly felt wrong. She opened her eyes, and tried to scream, but could not. The thing on top of her, that had repeatedly taken her, was not her beloved Jarod! The hideous, dark thing writhing atop her body was repulsive beyond words.

She heard a screeching laughter. Then Shadure's minion's thoughts pounded into her mind. *Your precious Jarod is only me, my dear. Do you think the ruler of the Seven Realms would look twice at a cow like you? You disgusting pig!*

Deanna tried to fight the creature off. It began to dissipate, and soon became nothing more than heavy smoke, but that hideous voice continued railing in her mind. Obscenity after graphic obscenity bombarded her senses. She could not breathe, and ran for the window. She threw it open, and the cool spring breeze flowing across her naked body sharpened her mind. Deanna turned and looked at the creature coming toward her, its tentacle-smoke arms reaching for her.

The proposition exploded in her mind. *Come my dear, I will be your beloved Jarod again.* Her mind raced over the many times she had longingly given herself to this creature. She did not hesitate.

Lady Deanna turned and threw herself out the window. No sound came until her body crashed onto the rocks far below.

* * *

JAROD opened the window to let the cool breezes play over his skin, and sat with his legs crossed as Deion had taught. He reached into his core and felt power raging inside. His body felt the welcome calm, and his consciousness merged with it.

Closing his eyes, he centered his mind on Marc. Gray clouds formed in the front of his mind. The clouds disintegrated into a circular border surrounding an opaque form. Slowly, the form cleared. He saw Marc asleep in his cradle. He felt no surprise when his son's eyes opened. Jarod clearly heard his distinctive giggle, and felt a further intensity of power, calmness, and love that nearly jarred him from his position. Marc's eyes closed, and within seconds, he was fast asleep. The increased feelings stayed with him while he let the vision dissolve.

Focusing his mind on the gray void again, he thought of Segquo. Instantly, he found himself in front of his target. Segquo's surprise showed quite clearly. He recovered as quickly, with a broad smile forming on his face.

Jarod looked down at his appearance. He too, smiled when he saw a slight, gossamer representation of his form in an almost imperceptible white robe. There appeared a distortion to Segquo's right. Another form appeared through cool waves of light. Jarod almost gasped at the woman's beauty. Her eyes were a piercing blue, darker than his. Olive skin and long, black hair added to her exotic brilliance. She held the fire of his most perfect jewels.

Segquo's voice pulled his gaze away. "This is Carille. She's our most gifted in many areas, and will be one of your teachers. She has a great mastery of shields, and that must be your first priority if you wish to survive on this plane. I cannot impress the importance this will have for you. We will meet only within shields once you have mastered the technique. The Dark forces either don't have the power to form them, or have never recognized the need. I believe it's the latter, as we would certainly die otherwise. Movement inside a shield causes a ripple through the shield proportional to the movement, and forces us to remain in one place if there is danger about. We can drop the shield and return instantly to our bodies, but can be detected in that moment, and any entity watching will know we had been here. We strive hard for that not to happen. Shadure, and sometimes Wathdure occupy this plane. If they discover us, they could easily kill or injure us."

Small, crackling sounds caused Jarod to look to the side. He saw the rippling effect cascading downward from the level of his head to the pseudo floor beneath them. It flowed like a ripple in the clearest pool of water, and another flowed downward when he looked again at his companions. "Can we speak?"

Carille's voice answered, "Yes, the movement of the lips is usually not enough force to cause a ripple."

Jarod felt awed at her voice. Every tone sounded in perfect pitch, and her words sounded more like a musical instrument than a human voice. The clarity of the sounds she made sounded unlike anything he had ever heard. He felt stunned by the beauty she projected, almost to the point of an assault. Using his inner power, he projected a warm feeling of greeting to her. She staggered, and gave the impression of nearly fainting.

"Highest One, I'm not able to withstand such a level of power that you projected to me. I won't survive, and the shield will be broken, sending me to the High Desert. It's not offensive, but I couldn't withstand it for long."

Jarod immediately withdrew the projection. "I'm sorry I caused you discomfort. Please forgive me."

"There is nothing to forgive, Highest One. You are the supreme among men. I'm pledged to obey your every order to aid you in our fight against the Dark; you have only to ask."

"Carille, you are not in my Guard. You have free will, as all my subjects enjoy."

"No, Highest One, I'm a warrior, perhaps a different warrior than you've know before now, but still a fighter. I have been trained since the age of two for this task. I won't fail you in any way. It's a great honor, and a duty I wish for and am pleased to have."

Segquo said, "Highest One, I suspect that you have a written record of the role my people are destined to play in the upcoming war. Battles fought on this plane have repercussions in the real world. Masters of the Dark could wipe out a whole army from here. It will take great power to counter that influence, and many could be lost."

He considered for a mere instant. "I need to know the extent of my power on this plane. What will happen if I release a surge of power for you to judge?"

Carille's voice answered. "Highest One, we don't know. No one of us has that ability. There are many from Dark's Source on this plane. Few of them have the power to harm us or harm anyone in our normal world. They have not discovered how to form a unity of purpose and, they are reluctant to follow the desires of any of their kind. We have observed three who possess great power, and have generated great apprehension among those of us who have seen them. We don't know the extent of their power, and have not tried to experience it. One opinion is that they will be able to kill our true being in the real world. I don't rule out that possibility. We have been extremely cautious when we have encountered them. We know the names they use from listening to their conversations.

"They are Shadure, Wathdure, and Gangedure. Shadure is the newest, and seems the most powerful of the three. Wathdure seems to be next, and has existed for at least two hundred and fifty years that we know of. Its power has grown rapidly over that time. We have records of Gangedure that cover over a thousand years, but have never seen a demonstration of its power. Its seldom seen, and is rarely called."

The rasp of Segquo's voice was a near distraction after Carille's melodic tones. "We have been here an hour, and we will need another hour to start your training. The ability to determine the passage of time is the next most important ability for you to learn. It's possible for you to be here for weeks, and think it only a few hours."

Segquo's voice pulled his attention away a second time. He felt swallowed up in the sound of Carille's voice alone, never mind her beauty, and felt a pang of guilt. Maress' face flashed in his mind. He had not considered Carille in that way. Still, he felt uneasy. "I must depart soon. I have many duties to perform. You will learn about many of those in due course."

Segquo spoke softly. "Highest One, we hold you in reverence second only to Light's Source. We will never knowingly take any action to cause you distress. We know the urgency and dire circumstances ahead if we don't proceed. Your best interest is our major concern. We cannot win this war without you now, and the Darkslayer in his time. Forgive us if we sound impertinent or overbearing. It is not our purpose."

"Segquo, I have no such feelings," Jarod replied. "I'm aware of the role you and your people are to play. I'm most grateful for your involvement."

Segquo's face registered the slightest hint of surprise. He said one word to Carille, "Now."

The crackling sounded twice within a small part of a second. Segquo vanished in that minute part of time. Jarod found himself alone with Carille, and a bit uneasy.

"He will return soon, Highest One. In the meantime, let me explain about what we call shields. The High Desert People cultivated the ability to reach into the minds of someone sleeping and view their dreams, and we learned the ways of the Gray Plane, where we are now. We, as a people, helped win the last war. Our history tells us that Dark Source's forces resided here when we first visited the plane. Several of our people died before we knew the cause of death. Sealow, Maker of Shields, became the first to create a shield, and it undoubtedly saved his life. The shield protects us from harm by stealth.

"The Three Old Ones could easily kill us if they knew what we did, and they will if we are ever discovered. I once had to stand perfectly still for several hours while Wathdure and Shadure carried on a long conversation nearby. I hovered three feet away, and they would have seen the slightest ripple. We don't really know if they are aware of our shields. They may think it's an anomaly in the structure of the plane, or a sign of our attempt to come into the plane. Their conversations that we have heard on the subject suggest we amuse them, and that they enjoy killing us.

"They produce a force that we call Black Lightning. It flows from their form, usually from their sleeved arm. We have never seen exactly what they look like beneath their robes. We not only can shield ourselves from them on this plane, but we can shield others and ourselves on our plane of existence. They seem to visit there as we visit here. Either place, the shields will work."

His expression changed to a look of wonder. "Wait…you are saying you can shield anyone in our world?" His tone sounded exuberant.

"Yes, that is our belief. We are not positive, but we believe it so."

His spirits surged. "There are several people that need every protection possible. Can you help us?"

"We have anticipated your request, and have begun to recruit our people for that purpose. It will require six of our people for every one shielded. It's much harder to shield in our world than here. Segquo will coordinate those efforts with you. We should find enough to shield ten people completely and a few others at night when they are asleep."

His eyes narrowed. "Segquo is here. I don't know how I know that, but I do."

Carille's smile became as beautiful as her voice. The crackling noise sounded again, but louder. Segquo stood in the same spot as before, and saw the puzzled look on Jarod's face.

Carille looked slightly amused. The inflection of her voice remained constant. "Shields can merge together, and when traveling, the ripples are so fast that they are not visible, and you don't feel the motion of travel. We don't know how any of it works, just that it does."

Jarod turned more serious. "Segquo, you have your history, old books, and above all, talent. The line of Zeniths has the same in different areas. Keep this in mind when you hear my command. You know of the one Cave of Truth. There are six others, one for each realm. They encircle the Cave of Truth from a point due north of the cave's entrance and are equidistant from the center. Three are natural, and three were excavated after the war. I must be present when opened, or they will destruct and that must not happen. The information inside could easily make the difference in winning or losing this war. Have men that you personally trust the most search for these caves. Each cave will have a carved symbol of the Spires above the entrance. No one must go beyond the symbol!"

He continued in a rush of words. "I have two things to do before I can come to your land. One is the Naming Day ceremony, and the second is to make the Darkslayer safe. I will leave for the High Desert as soon as I can. I should be there within ten weeks after the Naming ceremony.

"In the meantime, there are seven people that must be shielded: the Darkslayer; Lord Kyle; Trina, Marc's caregiver and nurse; Lord Deion Russell; the Holy One; a man known as Michael Gaz; and myself. These are the things that must be done as soon as you have the people available."

Segquo answered at once. "Highest One, your commands are my desires, your commands are my life. I won't fail you. We can provide protection for three of those you mentioned. The others have no need. The shields for the nurse, Lord Kyle, and Michael Gaz will take effect within an hour after we part. The Stones already protect the rest, especially for the Darkslayer and yourself. We can do no more to add protection."

Hesitancy fluttered in Segquo's voice. "Highest One, may I ask a question?" Segquo continued after Jarod's nod. "Why are our histories without the knowledge you bring us?"

Jarod took no offense at the question. The ways of the High Desert People required directness to life, and they meant no disrespect. "Marc the First meant the efforts for the second war to be coordinated between certain forces. The line of Zeniths holds the keys to the efforts needed to win. It will be a hard won victory over many years, and even with this knowledge, we could still lose.

"I permitted Carille to hear this because I know she's trusted, or she wouldn't be here. All I do on this plane must be kept between the fewest people possible. No one group is meant to have more knowledge than required to play their part."

"Highest One, you do me great honor in your answer. It will be as you wish."

Carille kneeled with the grace of a swan, and took the hem of Jarod's gossamer robe. The area she held turned into the whitest of fine wool, and she bent forward and kissed the wool. Jarod reached down and took her by the arms, raising her upright. She turned from a representation of a beautiful woman to the essence of beauty, radiating an inner presence of grace and an aura of golden light. The aura forming around her became splendor exemplified. He released her, and she quickly faded to her former degree of ethereal beauty.

Segquo barely whispered, "How…how did you do that?"

"I did nothing," Jarod answered.

Segquo reached forward and touched his sleeve. Instantly, the small confinement of the shield became bright. Small lightning bolts escaped from his form and returned into him. Brilliant hues swarmed out from his robe and returned with increased speed, as a babe runs to its mother and the prodigy returns in glory.

Segquo and Carille both kneeled and bowed their heads toward him. He appeared as he did on his arrival without their touch. They rose to find a questioning look on his face.

"Highest One, I believe it's most important for your training to begin at once." Carille nodded at his words.

Jarod appeared in deep concentration for a moment. "I can spare an hour in the early morning until I come to your land, and that is contingent upon events. How long have I been here?"

"Approximately an hour and a half, Highest One."

Jarod nodded. "Segquo, you said the ripples didn't show when moving rapidly. Can you show me parts of this plane before I go tonight?"

"Yes, but for only for another half hour. We become disoriented after two hours on the plane, and it becomes increasingly difficult to return without notice."

Jarod looked at Carille, remembering her tale. "Take me now, please."

Segquo looked at Carille; she bowed to him and disappeared. He felt no physical signs of what his mind perceived as ever-increasing speed from the minute shadings of the gray surroundings flashing by. He saw a small, dark form in the far distance. They closed at amazing speed, and stopped several yards behind the creature. The man's nude body reminded Jarod of his own, except he had a grotesque face, with the fangs of a heavy boar protruding from his mouth. Short, bristled hair covered most of his head and face, and his black eyes were set deep. The creature danced in a staccato, frenzied fashion, to the extent that he barely stayed on his feet. Sounds of orgasmic pleasure bellowed into the shield.

"Segquo, can you lower the shield when he turns away, and raise it before he comes around into our line of vision?"

"Yes, Highest One, but these creatures are dangerous. We have seen them fight amongst themselves, and they have strength beyond our capabilities."

"Have no fear, my friend; only a fool fights an unknown when he can choose otherwise."

"As you wish, Highest One. I will start a ripple. The shield will be down when the ripple passes your head. It will be fast. I will raise it again before he turns."

"Lower the shield on the turn after I nod."

Jarod concentrated on the power at his core. He let it build slowly, and when he felt it would burst from his every pore, he nodded. The ripple flashed by. He raised his arms with hands clasped in the direction of the creature and released the energy.

Horrible screams assaulted their ears to the point of damage before the creature eroded from the inside out, and dissolved into vapor with the fetid smell of death and corruption. Slight moans lasted a few moments, and then nothing remained of the creature.

He did not know how he became aware of changing position, but he did. Segquo said, "We are about fifty feet above the spot. We must remain quiet and perfectly still for a few moments. We may have visitors, Highest One."

The black-robed form arrived so fast that if Jarod had blinked he would have reasoned it had appeared instantaneously. Shadure pulled his cowl, exposing his head and seemed to sniff the air, looking in every direction. He put black-gloved hands to his temples and had the look of deep concentration. Jarod noticed that the sleeves of the robe did not slide down along his arm. His form remained completely covered except for his head of darkest ebony. The head itself bordered on great beauty, that appeared masculine and feminine at the same time.

"It is Shadure," Segquo whispered.

Another form came into view and closed rapidly. The newcomer pushed his cowl to reveal another face more striking than the first, but different in its composition. Wathdure's face held a hint of human normalcy, while Shadure's face was more rigidly articulated, as if it was stone endowed with speech. Both heads, devoid of hair, gleamed in the surrounding grayness when nothing else had, except inside the shield.

Segquo looked frightened. "That is Wathdure!"

"Can we safely get close enough to hear them?"

"I will try."

Instantly they shot five feet away from the two black forms. Shadure spoke, "—came here. I felt him, first in his revels, and then searing pain came to him. Nothing of him is left. I fashioned him after the father of the brat, and he seduced the woman at the Darkslayer's lair."

Wathdure's surprise reflected in his words. "It is too early for those fools to have mastered the ability of functioning on this plane. The Master took him. It's the only answer that makes sense. Our little playthings are not wise in their actions at times. The bitch is dead. Your creation had no more use to you, and the Master wanted his energy. Think nothing more of it." Wathdure continued on a new subject. "I see that you are becoming acclimated to the light again. How is it affecting you?"

"It will be a few years before I can stay in their world more than an hour or so. Here, it is not too bad. I could leave my cowl down as long as I wish, but the Dark is much more pleasant."

Wathdure's lips barely surged at the corners. "Ah...the beautiful dark. It will always be ecstasy in its perversions. The Master will greatly reward us beyond our imaginings when we triumph. Have you mastered the portal?"

Shadure raised his arm and swung it in an arc between them. The gray parted, and a scene developed as if one looked through a hole in a ceiling to the scene below. The figures came into focus while Segquo minutely adjusted their position to allow Jarod and him to see.

Kyle led his horse to the stable with his groom at his side. He was speaking, "—you will meet him someday. He's a good man, and requires you only to do your best."

Shadure dropped his arm, and the gray returned.

"You are doing well," Wathdure said. "I have ten thousand ready for the fight. We must be ready. Are you sure, they will hide the brat?"

"Yes, but I don't know when they—"

Unaccountably, Jarod sneezed!

Wathdure held his gloved fist up. "Did you see anything? Over there, to the right."

The two Dark forms raised their fists outward toward the shield. Jarod and Segquo shot upward at blinding speed. They soared a mile within a part of a second. Great bolts of black lightning exploded in their empty space. Segquo kept them moving for several more minutes. He looked drained when he stopped.

"Highest One, I must return to rest, or I will endanger us."

"Make the ripple, and I will be gone. Segquo, you are a true friend. I value your spirit." An ancient saying from the old books, was the highest compliment that Jarod could have given.

"Highest One, I'm honored."

The ripple started a little slower than before. Jarod and Segquo disappeared from the Gray Plane at the same instant.

Jarod's eyes fluttered open. Gray forms across from him began to solidify into Deion and his room. His heart raced until recognition settled his mind. "You seem to know when I left our world. How do you sense it?"

Deion's smile was filled with warmth. "My Zenith, I'm not sure, but I felt an emptiness and concern for you. I believe that it has something to do with the power I received. I have felt traces before, but not always accurate. Now, it's a definite feeling of loss that settles over me that is identified with you."

Jarod considered his words with a slight frown. "I wish to try something. Feel your power and let it flow through you. Close your eyes and calmly open yourself to it. Relax, until I tell you to open your eyes."

As soon as he saw his eyes close, Jarod embraced his power. He focused on the Gray Plane, and centered on Deion. The gray formed a circular frame as before, and as the mist cleared, he saw Deion from a few feet above. He sent a soft mental message of one word: *"Deion."*

The Protector opened his eyes to see Jarod's simulacrum staring at him, and they both looked down on their resting bodies. Jarod nodded, and closed his eyes once more while slowly releasing the power. Deion looked at him with wonder when he opened his eyes again. "I think we will be able to communicate that way more easily as we become used to the process."

Deion's obvious question, stayed by a knock on the door, caused him to frown. Kyle entered at Jarod's command and pulled a plush chair to join them.

Jarod smiled, "Kyle, I want to thank you for giving the stable boy such a glowing report of me. I will try to live up to his expectations."

* * *

WHAT? What stable boy?" Kyle recalled his morning for a moment, and then it registered in his mind like a fire springing to life on its own. "I just came from him and I used the lift. How do you know what I said?" He tried not to show annoyance at Jarod's grin.

* * *

JAROD started to speak when he saw a ripple in the space around Kyle. Deion's face suggested he saw it too. Kyle, however, noticed nothing from the ordinary. "Well, they didn't waste any time!" He related his experience on the Gray Plane, and explained what he could.

Deion spoke first. "This gives us another weapon against them. Are you sure the creatures on the Gray Plane don't know they are being spied on?"

Jarod's calm features broke for an instant, showing concern and then, his calm façade returned. "I think they would have attacked if they knew we were spying there—they disclosed too much, and I'm sure to be high on their list of people to destroy. Now I know what evil influenced Lady Deanna. It was one of Shadure's minions made for that purpose. Deion, you and Travis have shields through your abilities, but I don't believe the Mother does. The High Desert People can only shield eight to ten of us. We must keep our plans within that circle until its knowledge cannot cause harm and conversely, we may be able to pass corrupt knowledge to the watchers on the Gray Plane."

Kyle twisted in his chair and Jarod saw a faint ripple cascade down his body. He smiled, but said nothing; Deion's eyes betrayed his awareness. "Why are you two grinning at me?" Kyle asked. "Did that shield make me green or something?"

Jarod chuckled. "No, not at all, when you move a faint ripple slides down the shield, and we are not used to it yet. Others won't see it, or Segquo would have mentioned it. Let me know if someone points at you and runs away." Kyle did not join in their laughter until several seconds had passed.

Jarod's voice flattened when he next spoke. "Deion, we will train tomorrow morning. I will be on the Gray Plane afterward, and request you to watch over me until I feel more comfortable with the process. Now, I need to speak with Kyle alone."

The Protector rose and bowed. "It will be as you wish, my Zenith."

Jarod waited until the door closed softly behind Deion; his voice filled with concern. "How are you?"

"Me, I'm fine. What do you mean?"

"How has our discussion about my plans affected you?"

"I'm your Captain. I'm glad that I don't have to make the decisions you make. The burden of following those decisions is far less than that of making them. You became greatly concerned how your plans might change my relationship with Trina. She considered you sweet to be so concerned." Jarod half-choked on a swallow of juice, making Kyle grin. "We are truly fond of one another, but as close friends, and I doubt that it will develop further. We are content with things as they are."

Jarod nodded thoughtfully. His mind searched out more pressing needs. "There are many things to be learned from the High Desert People. I want you to go there to learn battle techniques that are different from those you already know. I want you to develop two courses of study: one to teach the techniques, and one to command the techniques. Battle officers will require both to use their men advantageously in the field. Special squads will be trained and attached to larger forces similar to those men trained by Gaz."

He went to the window and looked out over the City before continuing. "The Seven Realms fought the last war individually, and with the techniques of battle adopted separately by each realm. I want the one army of the Seven Realms to have the combined strengths of the realms. There will be priests attached to every force commanded by a Gal and those of higher rank to do much more than give solace. They will fight in special ways that I don't fully understand, but fight they will, as will anyone who takes power from the Stones."

He tapped the stone windowsill with his right hand, a sign of light irritation. "Our numbers have grown over the last two millennia. Disease after the war took its toll, especially in the first five hundred years afterward. We have fifteen times the population now, and only Light's Source knows how many of us there might have been otherwise. Our neighboring lands across the seas must be the same. The scope of this war will be far greater than the last one; it may well encompass some or all of those lands. The power of the Stones is also far greater than that used in the first war, and if our power is increased, than the evil that hunts us has certainly grown, too. Neither Light's Source nor Dark's Source is ready for this war. It's my belief that I'm to prepare and fight until Marc is ready, then he will lead the final battles." Jarod took a deep breath, letting it go slowly.

Kyle spoke gently. "You are tired. I have watched you working eighteen hours a day since your return. You won't be able to fight an eighty-year old woman if you don't get some rest. I said earlier that it's easier to follow your decisions than to make those decisions. Everyone has seen the strain pounding at you, and we are all concerned. You must pace yourself, or you will do little good—and probably some harm—if you continue as you are." Kyle steeled himself for a burst of anger. He knew how true his words had been when Jarod opened his eyes and merely nodded his head.

The sounds of the familiar fanfare of Northmount left he and Kyle staring at one another for a few seconds. They hurried to the window and peered down into the inner circle, where six magnificent horses were pulling a resplendent coach. White and black wormcloth, denoting mourning, intertwined and attached along the top of the coach, and flowed behind it to just above the wheels. Jarod's face withdrew behind a mask. "They know!"

The Zenith Lord, Lord Kyle Byrne, The Holy One, and the Mother met High Lord and Lady Northmount at the lift. The Lady's face looked drawn, and her eyes were red. The High Lord of Northmount crossed his arms over his chest and bowed deeply as his Lady curtsied low.

Jarod held out his arms to his mother-in-law as she rose and rushed into his arms, sobbing. "Oh, hells to the Dark One, I said I wouldn't do this!" She patted her eyes with a handkerchief the Mother produced. "My Zenith," she looked into Jarod's eyes. What she saw there left her speechless.

Travis stepped forward, stopping their bow with his upraised hand. "I will be glad to talk with you, and tell you what I know about your daughter, if the Zenith will permit." They turned to Jarod. There could be no doubt of the sadness and grief they each saw.

He nodded to Travis. "I will accompany you." His countenance left no room for argument, and Lady Northmount's protest died on her lips.

43

MOUNTGLEN and Clarence stopped earlier than usual. The next inn might have been midnight or later in coming. The journey remained less than half over; they felt the strain of the trip, and apprehension over the tasks at its end. Clarence stayed true to form with his drinking, and it seemed to be working. Shadure had not taken his mind in or out of a dream. He cursed almost silently when he held his bandaged hand in front of his face.

Light caught the corner of Clarence's eye, and in the same instant Mountglen flew upward, crashing into the ceiling of their room.

Shadure glared at Clarence. *"You too, little man!"* The vehemence in the quietly spoken words sent fear through his body with the pain of a vesicant running through his veins. Clarence hit the ceiling next to his father with such force that he wondered if he might pass out.

Shadure's finger pointed at Mountglen. *"Had you planned well, none of this would be happening, you idiot!"*

Clarence looked down at the black figure below; his voice slurred. "What happened, oh great Dark Sage?"

Shadure's entire form vibrated with rage. *"Do you want to die?"*

"No, but you will probably kill us in the end anyway. You need us, at least for now. You take great satisfaction in hurting us when you are angered. We will be no good to you if we are maimed beyond usefulness." The drunken words took twice the time of normal speech, but the meaning was still clear.

They hit the floor at the same time. Mountglen cried out when his foot landed askew, spraining his ankle. *"You will serve Dark's Source, the Lord of Masters."*

Pain enveloped Mountglen and Clarence. Searing, burning, liquid fire coursed through their bodies as if their blood had turned to molten rock, pain so intense they could not cry out. They fell to the floor moaning and holding themselves without relief for several minutes. The pain left them as quickly as it had engulfed them.

"You will kill the brat, or feel agony that you never dreamed possible. Heed my words well." Shadure walked through a newly formed dark void that appeared parchment thin and disappeared, releasing the power that kept them conscious, and let them fall into dark oblivion.

* * *

GAZ, summoned at midmorning to the main gate of the inner circle, saw a coach carrying the insignia of the Guard and the signs of a long and fast journey standing inside the gates while guardsmen led tired horses away. Awestruck, a woman and small girl looked at their surroundings. Gaz took one look inside the coach and uttered profanity, a rarity for him. He ordered a pikeman to notify the Mother and Tobias that he needed them. The pikeman did not know Gaz, and hesitated until his commander—who did know Gaz—sent him off at a run.

Zack smiled as Gaz stuck his head through the coach's open window, and winced at what he saw. "Now is that any way to treat a long-lost friend?"

Gaz could not help his own smile forming. "You had me a little worried. I trust you have a report?"

Zack handed him a roll of parchment as thick as his arm. "Ozlid does not have paper. This is Currat, he saved my life. And, the big fellow here is Ursel, he saved Currat's life."

The last comment elicited a weak smile from Currat. "He returned the favor twice."

Zack's voice became somber, "Gaz, these people gave up everything they had to help us. We need to make them as comfortable as possible until you have read my report. I urge you to show it to the Zenith. The report deserves his attention, and our friends deserve his thanks."

Gaz's eyes narrowed. "I will see about the eleventh level for you. I assume the lady and child will be in separate rooms from you or Currat?"

"Yes, oh master, the fidelity of the Seven Realms has been maintained."

"Zack, this is not the time for your curious form of humor. There is much happening of a most serious nature. Now, introduce me to the lady and child, and I will make the arrangements for your care and I will read your report before midmeal."

"I'm sorry, Michael. We are exhausted, and I'm not thinking right."

Gaz waved off the apology and his face softened. "No matter, my friend, can you walk?"

"I can do better than Currat. He will need help." Zack quickly introduced the others.

Gaz motioned for the Officer of the Gate and started giving orders. Doris and Rachel stood beside the coach with Ursel by the time he finished.

Gaz heard a comment, and fell into fluent Hamptorian dialect. "My Lady, we will try and make you and your daughter comfortable and look after your needs. You are safe here, and need not worry."

Doris looked past Gaz at the huge environment of the Spires. Her voice brought forth the awe she felt. "Oh, Master Gaz, I can see we are safe." Even Rachel laughed within a few seconds.

The Mother and Tobias arrived, and a new round of introductions followed shortly. Four heavily muscled pikeman brought a sedan chair for Currat, and two more tried to get past a glaring Ursel to help Zack from the coach. He waved them off, and Ursel half-carried a protesting Zack toward the main entrance to the Spires.

Gaz took the Zenith's lift at the rear of the Great Hall, glancing through Zack's report while it rose. He stepped from the lift when his eye fell on a name, one that he'd heard Kyle mention. He read on for a minute, and sent urgent messages to Jarod and Kyle for a meeting after midmeal.

* * *

JAROD and Kyle finished the last of their midmeal when Rolo announced Gaz. It was the first time Jarod had ever seen Gaz in any state that approached excitement. He carried a roll of true parchment, and several sheets of paper that some people of Stonefire still called parchment.

"My Zenith, I have urgent news."

"So your message read." Jarod motioned him to a chair across from him and to the right of Kyle.

"Kyle, you mentioned names of the minions of the Dark One that our Zenith encountered. Is one of those names Wathdure?" Gaz asked.

Jarod's voice reflected his sudden interest. "That is the name. What have you heard?"

"My Zenith, he has been the ruler of Ozlid for more than two hundred years. He caused the drought in Hamptor and Arestead. He controls the water to those lands, and charges a tax through a voucher system to secure his needs for Ozlid." The words had all spilled out in one breath. He held the parchment in one hand and the paper toward the Zenith. "This is the report from my agent who returned this morning, the papers are a summary of the report."

Jarod took the summary and began reading. He passed each page to Kyle when he had finished it. They became more intense as they read. Jarod leaned back in his chair after passing the last page to Kyle. The set of his face and the burning intensity of his eyes precluded any remark from the other two men.

Jarod sat staring into space for several minutes. His eyes became alert, and he concentrated his sending to Deion, *"Come!"* He looked at Kyle, "How quickly can the High Lords travel here with full support from the Guard?" His command voice carried urgency and directness in quite, precise words.

Kyle considered for only an instant. "Lords Wells, Mountglen, Lockley, and Northmount are already here or on the way, and they have the most distance to travel. Trueridge could make it by Naming Day; I'm not sure about Eastfall. Lord Romar reports ill. His oldest son will certainly make it by that time."

Gaz cleared his throat. "I regret to report that the younger Romar will be coming no matter what the timing. His father is senile, according to my last report."

Kyle shook his head. "I hope he taught his son well. He knew every hill, tree, and stream in Eastfall."

One rap sounded at the door. Deion entered, and went to the chair to the left of Jarod. Neither Kyle nor Gaz had ever seen his eyes so cold. "My Zenith, the matter is urgent?" Jarod handed over Gaz's notes.

Kyle continued, "High Lord Carlton knows Trueridge almost as well as Romar knew Eastfall."

The room remained quiet as Jarod's face again took on a trance-like countenance. He suddenly set up straighter in his chair. "Kyle, bring in ten thousand troops. They are to encamp south of the City. Send word that they are required to be here in two weeks. Notify the Master of the Horse to have an equal number of mounts rounded up and corralled. Get your men working on the logistics and supplies. You will be here for a State lastmeal tonight at the seventh hour. All Apex officers in the Spires will attend. Escort any person not housed within the Chambers by two guardsmen. Arrange for the High Lords or their sons acting in their stead to be here by

Naming Day. The Guard will provide assistance to facilitate their trip in that time."

He turned his attention to Gaz, who nearly jerked at the intensity focused on him. "Gaz, provide clothing and whatever else is needed for our guests from across the sea in order that they may attend tonight. I will receive them in the Zenith's study at the sixth hour. Forrest Workman is also to attend. Notify Rolo that the lastmeal will be in the State dining room on this level. He's to take care of the messages to the Circle of Villas, and he may help you in obtaining what the woman and girl will need. The ambassadors are not to bring any guests, including wives. Notify your agents at every port to report any unusual occurrences in the fastest way possible. Obtain a report from your agents inside the keeps of any unusual orders issued by the Lords. Arrange the protection for tonight. Guard the Darkslayer, no matter where he is. Neither Trina nor Marc will attend tonight. Send an invite to Lord Long in my name. I want him protected as well." He nodded once.

* * *

GAZ did jerk when Jarod swung his gaze to Kyle; he had never felt such strength from mere eyes and voice. He rose and bowed. "My Zenith." and hurried from the room.

* * *

JAROD continued, "Kyle, you are to keep a discreet guard assigned to yourself, however, this task you must do yourself and alone. You will activate the Angels and Lords of Death and bring them to me. They are on guard, always."

He went to his desk and handed Kyle a slim book from the top of the desk. Kyle's confusion was evident; he had never heard of what Jarod referred to. "This duty is best completed by my Captain of the Guard. The instructions are in the book. I will be here with Deion if I'm needed within the next few hours."

Kyle saluted smartly. Neither man found it unusual.

Jarod sat across from his and Marc's Protector. "And so, my friend, it has started."

The men conversed and planned for more than two hours. During that time, Deion felt the power within the Zenith rising to levels he had previously believed impossible.

Jarod's last command asked him to notify the Mother and His Holiness to attend the lastmeal that night with the prelates. They left together; Deion went toward His Holiness' rooms and Jarod to his suite of rooms.

44

KYLE read the book twice. He understood the plain instructions. Still, he had a hard time believing them. The last several pages, cut to provide a hiding place, held a brass key. It felt cold in his hand.

He descended beneath the Spires, through a hidden passage that he must have passed by several times without knowing it existed. He followed a circular ramp down by the light of the torch he carried. It became hard to keep track of the distance; he knew he was going farther beneath the Spires than he ever believed possible.

The ramp ended, and he entered a corridor through stone arches several levels high. The long corridor ended at a door of finely carved oak, highly polished with brass fittings that gleamed as if newly installed. According to the book, the door had not been touched since shortly after the last war. *Well, you certainly don't look two millennia old,* he determined.

The brass key held a small ruby. He placed the key in the lock. Light flared around the keyhole, and the key turned on its own. The door opened inward. Small gullies of oil ignited and traveled around the room at the level of Kyle's waist. The room was thirty yards wide and a hundred yards long. Life-sized statues made from a polished white stone that glowed iridescent lined the walls, with barely an inch between them. Kyle could not tell if the glow came from the flames or from within the stone. He suspected the latter.

Two statues stood on a raised dais at the end of the hall. The feeling of watching eyes made his skin crawl. He turned twice to see if anyone was behind him. The room seemed to return his stare as if to say, *"Yes, we are here."*

Kyle opened the book and read aloud: "Stones of the Light, I, Kyle Byrne, Captain of the Zenith's Guard, Lord of the Seven Realms, bid you come forth to fight for and protect the Darkslayer and the Zenith Lord in war with Dark's Source. The war is upon us. I call upon Light's Source to infuse you with the power of righteousness, and the Zenith Lord to infuse you with power from the Box of Stones."

Disembodied voices rang around the room in crystal clarity. *"Draw your sword. Draw your blood. Draw your Sign."*

Kyle's sword flared with tiny arcs of bright light as he drew it. They continued as he slit his right index finger along the razor sharp blade. Approaching the statue on the left side of the raised dais, he drew three vertical lines in a niche at the base of the dais. The lines formed a perfect triangle if the tips or bases joined together proportionate to the three spires above. He stood before the statue on the right and repeated the process.

Bells chimed, and then chimed again. The loudness of the third chime took him to his knees. Kyle gaped while the statues on the dais glowed brighter, until he had to cover his eyes. He sensed the lights diminish, and cautiously lifted his hands away, still looking down at the floor. He sucked in a deep breath at the sight of two pair of bright white boots less than a yard away. Kyle slowly raised his gaze to the incredible beauty of the man and woman before him.

They were dressed in the same bright whiteness as their boots. The cowl of a heel-length cloak covered their heads. Kyle had never seen such beauty in a man that remained completely masculine at the same time. The woman's beauty on his left, an identical twin, held the softness of her sex.

The man's voice possessed the clarity of the bell; thankfully, it sounded at a normal level. "Lord Byrne, I'm Darth, Captain of the Lords of Death."

The woman's voice sounded equal to Darth's voice. "I'm Sarth, Captain of the Angels of Death."

Kyle rose to his feet, hoping his voice would not break, and wondering if they could tell his anxiety. "My Captains, I'm bid to escort you to the Zenith Lord." The two nodded in response. Kyle retrieved the still burning torch from the white marble floor and became unsettled when the black marks and soot disappeared in the time it took him to stand upright. He turned and the Captains joined him on his right. His boots sounded as sharply against the marble as before. Theirs made no sound.

* * *

JAROD sat on the floor with his legs crossed, performing the breathing exercises that now formed an unconscious part of his daily life. His mind journeyed to the Gray Plane, and instantly shielded his presence there. Sensing the shields of the High Desert People, he entered their circle a second later. He reached out and shielded them. One by one, the individual shields came down. "I need Segquo."

The representations of the High Desert People knelt, and then rose as one. The simulacrum of the eldest spoke, "At once, Highest One." Their individual shields went up, and Jarod pulled his shield around himself in a circle five feet across and slipped to the edge of the group. Segquo appeared in less than a minute.

He bowed, "Highest One, how may I serve you?"

They spoke for a short time, and then disappeared at the same instant.

Jarod stretched out on his bed and fell asleep in less than a minute after his consciousness returned to his body.

*   *   *

ROLO entered much later to wake the Zenith for his bath. He approached Jarod with great tribulation; the Zenith floated a few inches above the bedclothes. "My...my...Zenith." Jarod sighed, and settled onto the bed as he woke.

He sat up to find Rolo drained of color. "Rolo, what is wrong? Is it Marc?" Jarod came instantly awake and moved to sit on the side of the bed.

"No, no, my Zenith. Marc is fine, as far as I know. My Zenith, you...you... were sleeping in...in...the air!"

"Oh?"

"Yes, my Zenith, you did!"

"Well, Rolo, you are likely to see many strange things in the years to come."

His servant adopted a look of resignation. "Yes, my Zenith. Your bath is ready, and the Captains of the Lords and Angels of Death await your pleasure." Shivers ran up Rolo's spine at the mention of the Captains. He had never seen one of their numbers, nor heard of them until today. They had completely unnerved him. "Will you wear the State Regalia tonight, my Zenith?"

It came Jarod's time to voice resignation. "Yes Rolo, unfortunately, I will."

*   *   *

JAROD bathed quickly and dressed in white boots, pants, shirt, and padded baldric. He fastened his battle sword to the belt and called, "Guard!"

A Gal opened the door. "My Zenith?"

"I will receive the Captains."

"At once, my Zenith. The Chambers are sealed, and Lord Kyle bid me tell you it's as you commanded." Jarod nodded as the Gal opened the door completely; he could see several Guards at focus position. The two Captains stood opposite his door; the guardsmen had shifted away from them on each side. The Captains entered into the room as one.

The light of the room darkened. The sweating Gal closed the door behind them.

"I am the Stone!" Jarod pulled his shirt open to bare his chest. The emerald light fell on the two Captains, and they glowed, filling the room with the same light from within.

Jarod drew the battle sword as the two Captains fell to their knees. He held the sword within inches of their faces. His disembodied voice filled the room. "The Darkslayer has been born and the Dark One is aware, the Protector named. I give you the life of the Stone." He focused his power through the sword. Emerald green arcs flashed along its edge. Each Captain placed an index finger on a side of the sword and drew a drop of blood. The small wound healed instantly, and each Captain's body pulsated with emerald green light.

The Captains lowered their heads to the floor, and then rose to their feet. Their voices came from every part of the room and from nowhere. "We guard the Darkslayer and the Zenith Lord!" They brought their right fists up over their hearts and bowed. Each movement was formed in perfect unison and otherworldly fluidity. Reaching up with their right hands, they pulled a veil from the inside of their cowl down and over their faces; then both faded into nothingness, and the light of the room returned to a normal level.

Jarod replaced the sword in its scabbard and opened the door. A nervous Gal saluted smartly and became visibly distracted when he saw beyond Jarod into a room empty of the Captains.

"Gal Overn, is it not?"

He recovered before Jarod could return his salute. "Yes, my Zenith. I'm pleased you remembered."

"Have the Darkslayer and his nurse brought here."

"At once, my Zenith."

Rolo appeared with the guardsmen protecting the State Regalia. Jarod motioned them inside. The guardsmen placed the crown's box and robe where Rolo directed and left, closing the door behind them. Rolo carried the ceremonial sword and laid it across the desk. He fastened Jarod's sash and reached for the sword.

"Rolo, the war has begun."

Rolo's expression became grim. "My Zenith, it could be nothing else with what I have seen in the past weeks. I'm sorry that the burden has fallen to you."

Jarod squeezed Rolo's shoulder, one of the few times he had overtly touched the man. "I won't be wearing the ceremonial sword until the war is over, perhaps never again. Marc is the Darkslayer and His Grace Lord Deion is his Protector. I will tell you many things from time to time, but now I cannot. I trust you as much as I trust Lord Kyle, and I have known you longer. You raised me as much as the Holy One and the Mother. You are near me whenever I'm in the Spires, and see and hear much. I know you never talk among the stewards and workers that service the Chambers or anyone else. You must be especially careful of what you say from now forward, and I wish to know if anyone requests information from you. Dark's Source has brought evil into the Spires before, and won't hesitate to do so again."

He withdrew his hand, but his eyes held Rolo in a tighter grip. "There is one thing more that I should have sensed to ask you sooner. Have you had any troubling or strange dreams?"

"No, my Zenith, none."

"Good. You must let me know at once if you do. You have protection on several levels, however, that does not mean that you might not become a target. Do you understand?" He looked over Rolo's shoulder, and saw a slight flicker of greenish light.

"My Zenith, my life is yours, and I will obey you completely." Rolo sounded as sad as he had ever heard him.

Gal Overn knocked and announced Trina and Marc. "Leave me for a few minutes, Rolo. Come back in when Trina leaves." Rolo bowed his way out. Jarod noticed he seemed a little unsteady.

Trina came in a most comely, flowing gown of the palest blue gathered at her waist with a white belt. Her hair, pulled up and fashioned on top of her head, changed her appearance dramatically. Jarod thought of Kyle. He began to pick up the slight empathic feelings of those around him, and realized it might have been more between them, but something had restrained them. She handed Marc to him and curtsied low, her eyes never leaving her charge.

Marc, awake and grinning, giggled. He wrapped his tiny fingers around Jarod's finger while gurgling in a deeper tone. Jarod smiled. Leading Trina to a plush chair, he sat across from her with Marc.

He eased into the chair and Marc promptly closed his eyes and slept. He spoke softly. "Trina, the Dark One sent his minions among us in the last war. Light's Source seeks balance in all things. The Angels and Lords of Death were created by Light's Source and placed under the first Zenith's command to counter some of the Dark One's threat. Their sole purpose is a last line of defense from a direct assault on Marc or me by the Dark One's minions and any others that might wish him harm."

Trina's eyes had become wide. She said nothing.

"The Angels and Lords of Death are with us now, in this room. You cannot see them, but they are here, and I will call them to appear in a moment. There is nothing to be afraid of, and they won't harm you." He shifted Marc to a more comfortable position in his arms. The babe slept on.

"The ones that are with us are their Captains, Lord Darth, who will guard me, and Angel Sarth, who will guard Marc, at least for now.

"Captains, I give into your care the Darkslayer, Marc Greatstone, the second of that name."

Pale greenish light flickered next to his chair for a half a second. The Captain's forms materialized quickly. They fell to their knees, placed their right fist over their heart, and touched their head to the floor. They rose to a stand in one fluid motion and dropped their fist to their sides. They said nothing.

Trina's mouth fell agape. She gurgled a little like Marc, but she too, said nothing. He nodded to the Captains. They pulled their veils down and disappeared.

"Sarth will be with Marc always for protection, and she may or may not appear or speak when you call her name. She will not converse with you unless it aids in Marc's protection." Jarod handed Marc to Trina with a slight smile. The babe hardly noticed, heaving a small sigh and continuing to breathe the soft rhythm of sleep. "You have nothing to worry about; you might never have known if I hadn't told you. But I thought you should know."

Trina released the tight hold from the arm of the chair and breathed a sigh before he continued.

"I have not invited you to the ceremony tonight for Marc's safety. I don't know some of the people attending."

"I understand, my Zenith. I'm glad you told me about the Captains. I will feel better knowing I'm not alone." Trina's genuine half-smile held as steady as her voice. He walked her and Marc to the door, and watched for a moment while they walked toward the nursery surrounded by guardsmen. He wondered if the guardsmen sensed Sarth in their mist. Rolo followed him into the room and closed the door.

He removed the battle sword, and Rolo helped him with the long white coat. He started on the long row of button orbs as Rolo slid the clasp through the coat eyelet and fastened the battle sword in place. Rolo felt the battle sword's full weight. Jarod noticed and said, "Now you know why Kyle and I work with exercise stones." Rolo attached the ruby dagger, stood away a few steps to make an appraisal, and nodded his approval.

Jarod looked at his image reflected in the tall mirror beside the wardrobe. *The battle sword looks right at my side.*

Jarod glanced at the clock. "Rolo, our time grows short. I will receive our guests without the robe and crown. I will be roasting tonight as it is."

He opened the door, and Rolo motioned for the guardsmen to carry the crown box and the wormcloth bag containing the robe. He listened absentmindedly as the guardsmen whispered behind him. "Hells to the Dark One, this is heavy!"

"The robe? You should feel the weight of the crown..."

* * *

ROLO stopped listening as his mind tried to digest what the Zenith had told him earlier. *Is he wrong? No, he has seldom been wrong, and never about anything this important.* Rolo swerved into the Zenith study's door that he'd nearly passed. He motioned the guardsmen to stand at the rear of the room.

* * *

KYLE followed Jarod when Rolo entered. Guards closed the door and remained on duty in the corridor. A guardsman entered from the door at the opposite end of the room, snapped to position and saluted. Jarod looked up and nodded once in the direction of the guardsman.

"My Zenith, Master Gaz awaits your pleasure."

Jarod nodded once more. Gaz entered followed by Zack, Currat, Ursel, Doris, Rachel, and Forrest, all of who lined up across the end of the room.

* * *

DORIS' mouth gaped for an instant before she realized her error. She had never seen two men so handsome and opposite in so many ways. The tall blond man in a splendid uniform, demanded attention by his presence. The one in white took her breath away. Sunlight reflected against the jewels and gold worked into their swords. She imagined nothing could have been more spectacular than the entrance to the Chambers and the many pieces of art she saw on her way to the study. Now, she wondered if she had been premature.

* * *

RACHEL looked at Jarod and then Kyle. *I think mother should marry the blond one,* she thought and spent the next several moments vacillating between the two.

* * *

ZACK had never seen Jarod in the State Regalia, and had only a glimpse of him a few years ago. His pleasure with his Zenith's bearing clearly showed. He and the Apex beside him, looked as if they could take on quite a few men at once. He decided he should come to the Spires more often.

* * *

CURRAT took the measure of the men at the end of the room, and reaffirmed his decision in coming with Zack.

* * *

FORREST looked lovingly at Jarod's battle sword.

* * *

JAROD stood at the end of the table and nodded to Gaz.

Gaz presented everyone but Forrest, and gave a short summary of the events that had importance to Stonefire. He finished with a comment, "—and my Zenith, our friend Forrest, awaits your pleasure for assignment."

Jarod's deduction abated his smile, as he sat at the end of the table. *Forrest must be pressuring Gaz a great deal to entreat that remark.* "Master Gaz, please seat our guests." Two guardsmen supported Currat's weight, and eased him into the first chair to the right of the end of the table. Currat's pain became evident. Doris sat across from Currat, with Rachel on her left. Zack sat on Currat's right, and Gaz at the end.

"We have reviewed the report presented to Us." Jarod spoke fluently in the Hamptorian dialect. Gaz suppressed a look of surprise. "Master Stand, We commend you on your efforts. The High Healer Tobias Sternwood and the Mother Mavis Grant will continue to treat you and the Master of the Blue Currat's injuries until you are both well. We unfortunately, can do nothing to ease the memories of your ordeals. Master Gaz will inform you of your next assignment when you are healed. It's one We believe you will enjoy."

Zack bowed his head toward Jarod. "I await your pleasure, my Zenith."

Jarod's eyes fell on Currat. "Master of the Blue Currat, We don't look upon your acts as treasonous to Ozlid. We believe that you acted in your country's best interest, and against an evil that we will face again. Your injuries have been grievous and dire. We regret the death of your father, Master of the Black Duval. We invite you to rest and heal here. Our pleasure is to provide you with choices for your future, and we will discuss those choices with you after you have had time to reflect on your own needs and desires. We order the sum of ten golds paid to you. We realize that this, will in no way, repay the debt freely given by your father and friends." Currat bowed his head and—not too successfully—smiled.

"Doris and Rachel Raven of Hamptor. Our pleasure is to provide you with a home and income for life." Doris' mouth opened and then closed with a snap. Her face colored while Rachel beamed a smile. "We will leave the location for you to choose once you are acquainted with our geography and the land available. You have our deep appreciation, and should you ever wish to return to your homeland we will facilitate your travel and resettlement there as well."

"Thank you...thank you, Zenith Lord." A look of disbelief played across her face.

Jarod had a perplexed look when he turned his attention on Ursel. "We have read your desire to raise an army from Arestead and Hamptor with interest. We also know of the valor and determination you exhibited in your actions for the well-being of Master Stand and Master of the Blue Currat. However, what you wish will require the consent of the kings of Hamptor and Arestead. We are glad you are here, and will make certain opportunities are available to you in the near future. We also order a sum of ten golds paid to you for the risks you have taken on the Seven Realms behalf."

Ursel's eyes seemed to nearly glaze over.

Jarod continued with a smile. "We hope that you will enjoy your visit, and we will shortly begin work on your varied interests."

"Zack Stand, We read of your desire to stay in our service. It is so ordered. Your pay will increase to that of an Apex and your retirement will be based on that rank."

Zack looked shocked, recovered quickly and bowed to Jarod.

Jarod again had to repress a smile when he set his attention on Forrest. "Master Workman, We are in need of your services, and command you to the direction of Master Gaz. You will have the pay and privileges of a Gal of the Guard, and have command of the same number of men, but not of the Guard. The statement, 'I wish adventure and challenge.' attributed to you in the past is fulfilled in your assignments. How say you?"

"My Zenith, you have given me the opportunity to satiate my desires. My life is yours."

"Unfortunately, Master Workman, that expression has deep meaning. Take care that We don't mourn you." No mirth rang in Jarod's voice. His voice softened as he looked again at Doris. "Mistress Raven, the guardsmen will escort you and Rachel to the feasting room."

She and Rachel rose and curtsied. Doris held Rachel's hand to steady her. Two guardsmen from the rear of the room politely ushered them out as Travis and Deion entered the study from the door at Jarod's end of the room.

They were both resplendent in the formal robes of the priesthood. Light gray wormcloth with a blue cast, cut in the same style as Jarod's regalia. The Tower radiated light from silver and black traceries over their heart. The deathcat lay at its base: silver and black on Travis, gold and black on Deion. Chairs were pushed backward, and all of the men rose when they entered. Currat tried to join them until the Zenith took note, and motioned for him to rest.

Travis' big hands took the Zenith Lord by the shoulders before he could kneel, and Jarod waved the men to their seats. "Gentlemen, please take your seats." Travis sat on Jarod's left, across from Kyle.

Deion stood, watching first Currat and then Zack. He bent to Jarod's ear and whispered, "My Zenith, may I ease their suffering?" Jarod's nod came immediately.

* * *

DEION concentrated on Currat first. His mind felt pain erupting with every breath the other man made. His eyes closed as he sent healing power through Currat's bones, muscles, and nerves.

* * *

CURRAT felt relief coursing throughout his body, and took his first breath without pain in four weeks. His eyes widened as he searched for the source and his benefactor. Moments later, Zack responded with much the same emotions.

* * *

DEION opened his eyes and wiped the sheen of perspiration from his brow with a startlingly white handkerchief. He sat next to Travis, saying nothing.

* * *

JAROD'S voice cut through the silence of the room. "Gentlemen, we are at war! You will hear that statement reaffirmed and proven tonight." The men looked at him with a new interest and concern plainly evident. "Forrest, you will journey to the High Desert People tomorrow. They expect you and your party. You are to select eight men from a group Lord Kyle will muster. You all will train with the High Desert People in several disciplines of combat you have never experienced before. Ursel may travel with you as the tenth member of your party, if he so desires." From the look on Ursel's face, there was no doubt that the number in the party would be ten.

"Zack will join you as soon as he's able." He shifted his attention across the table. "Zack, you and a like group will be trained in the fundamentals of those disciplines, and then you and your men will embark in another direction. Several of the High Desert People will do the training of you and your groups; they have command over your schedule and actions. Keep in mind that the men you choose will become the trainers of many more to follow, and will need the skills that requires. Zack, you will leave as soon as you are able to travel without detriment to your health and at a pace for a long journey. The High Desert People will take over the treatment of your injury until you are able to participate in the training.

"Holy One, We request you to send messengers to every assembly of priests, and request those that have the talents we discussed come to the Tower at once. Their training will commence as soon as they, you, and Lord Russell return to the Tower." Travis and Deion nodded as one.

The fanfare of the ambassador of Trueridge sounded faintly in the distance. "Master Currat, We would like to meet with you and a few others tonight after the lastmeal and formalities are over. We will discuss your involvement—or lack thereof—at that time."

Currat bowed his head toward the Zenith.

Jarod sat up with a sigh of resignation. "Guards, assist Master Zack Stand and Master of the Blue Currat to the feasting room, and see to their comfort until they retire for the night. Gaz, please remain a moment."

Zack walked behind as Currat settled into the sedan chair. Gaz took a chair beside Kyle. Silence reigned until the door closed behind the guardsmen and their charges.

Jarod nodded to the guardsman by the door. High Lord Lockley and the Pinnacle entered, followed by Hinston carrying Lord Long in his huge arms.

He waved them to seats at the table. Hinston gently seated Lord Long and then knelt before his Zenith. Jarod's voice became soft to the gentle giant before him. "Thank you, Hinston. We won't be long." Hinston hurried from the room.

Jarod motioned the guardsmen from the room. His voice took on a cold edge; he dropped the royal commands. "Gentlemen, I have received disturbing reports from agents returning from Ozlid and Hamptor. The sole ruler of Ozlid for the past two and a half centuries is a minion of Dark's Source. He has been there for three centuries!"

The newly arrived men at the table stared at Jarod with emotions playing across their faces from horror to despair to concern and finally, to determination. "I will inform the ambassadors that the war has begun."

* * *

DORIS had never imagined a dress as fine as the one she wore. Ladies-in-waiting had lavished Rachel and her with pampered care. The result allowed a woman of beauty and natural grace to emerge, with Rachel holding the promise of beauty to surpass her mother and most women.

They stopped walking when they stepped through the entrance to the State feasting room. Tables, laden with flowers, golden plates, and service ware that reflected gold tones from the many candles around the room, formed a horseshoe pattern, with the connecting table raised a few inches. The light from crystal goblets joined the symphony of color cascading in every direction, and armless chairs were set at each place, with ample room between them. The brightness of the candles washed the room with seeming daylight. An even plusher chair, inlaid with gold and gems, sat at the center of the connecting table. It had arms.

Heavily armed guardsmen in dress uniforms stationed three feet apart snapped to position. Large doors paned with glass stood open to balcony terraces. Cool breezes carried the fragrant scent of flowers throughout the room. Shadows of more guardsmen were barely discernible in the dimness of the balconies. The guardsmen, numbering one hundred, comprised from those sworn to secrecy on the night of Maress' death, stood alert and determined that no incident mar that night's festivities.

Doris and Rachel came out of their reverie at the major domo's slight cough. Ushering them to their seats, he whispered to them to stand until the Zenith came and sat. Rachel's built up chair would put her at the perfect height when seated. Doris marveled at the small cards in front of their plates with their names written in a beautiful script.

Zack resisted help to his chair, and remained standing. Two heavily muscled guardsmen carried Currat in, and set him between where Zack and Ursel stood across from Doris, halfway down the long tables. The guardsmen went to the rear of the room and stood with their eyes constantly scanning about the room. Forrest followed, and if he tried not to look awed. He failed.

The major domo's voice cut across the room as he announced the Apex officers who stood by their chairs at the end of the long tables. The ambassadors came next, accompanied by their fanfares, and stood next to the chairs closest to the connecting table. The Prelates entered and stood at the outside chairs of the connecting table. The Mother and Tobias took the next inside chairs. Hinston carried Lord Long in, and sat him next to the Mother, then stepped away to the closest balcony.

Gaz, announced simply as "Master Michael Gaz," stood at the place next to Tobias. Several of the ambassadors eyed him with curiosity.

Deion entered and stood at the chair next to Lord Long. The ambassador from Deepwells' mouth fell open when he saw his size and the Tower emblem with a gold deathcat. The Protector looked serenely—or deadly—calm. The ambassador evidently felt the latter.

The fanfares played with harps and strings added a muted drum when Travis' fanfare sounded. He entered in the full formal regalia of the priesthood. Those present bowed toward him.

The Pinnacle arrived in his State robes that few had ever seen. The sounds of full kettledrums shook the room, followed by harps playing the Zenith's fanfare creating a lush counterpoint.

Jarod entered through his private entrance as the last notes of his fanfare fell. Doris nearly fell from her curtsey when she looked up at him in the robes and crown of State. The power emanating from him froze those who had not seen it before.

The Zenith Lord bowed his head to His Holiness. Rolo, dressed in formal livery, came up behind him as he removed the robe and took it over his arm. Jarod removed the heavy crown and handed to Rolo, who departed with an armed escort, and then sat.

The room quieted after chairs stilled and the guests settled into their seats. Jarod's voice was animated and cool at the same time and his demeanor took on the subtle calmness that Deion exuded. "Lords, Ladies and Officers of the Guard, We are here to honor the men and women who have given great service to the Seven Realms and to whom We are indebted." He nodded to Gaz, who stood and introduced those people from Hamptor with no description of their deeds.

He continued. "We bid you enjoy our lastmeal and the company gathered here. The business of the Seven Realms will be discussed afterwards." Several people saw Jarod position his battle sword athwart his lap for easy access, and the action caused concern to register on their faces.

* * *

RACHEL had two desserts, and looked as if she had found paradise. Jarod ate little, and spent much of the time in quiet conversation with Kyle.

* * *

CURRAT remained impressed with Jarod and the Spires in general. He ate more than he had at one time since his torture. He did not know if this was due to the excellent food—that surpassed the palace in Ozlid—or his normal appetite had returned, after the curious healing he had received earlier. He suspected it was due to Deion's work. He felt relief from the majority of pain for the first time since sailing for the Seven Realms. The barbed needles used on him, racked across his bones gouging abrasive ridges that produced pain with the movement of adjoining muscles seemed healed.

* * *

ZACK, too, felt much improved, and had the itching sensations that accompany healing for the first time. He ate like a woodsman after a day of felling trees.

* * *

THE ambassadors remained edgy, and none of them enjoyed the food. This meeting, unusual in its hurried calling and in the way the Zenith made it a State affair, upset them. None of them had previously seen the coldness and determination he exhibited, and that alone gave them pause.

* * *

DEION felt the undercurrent weaving through the room and became surprised at the increase in the various emotions he felt. The Apex officers said little. They commented amongst themselves on the Zenith's battle sword and the number of guardsmen present. They ate little and drank less.

Jarod raised his right hand level with his breast. Quiet fell over the room while all eyes focused on him. "Lady Doris, We bid Rachel and you a peaceful night. Master of the Blue Currat and Master Ursel, We bid you wait upon our call."

* * *

DORIS and Rachel rose as their chairs were slowly pulled away by guardsmen, allowing them room to curtsy, and they left under escort. Doris felt she had the right of the curtsey. Rachel too, considered it great fun from her wide smile.

* * *

CURRAT bowed his head, and the two muscular guardsmen lifted and carried him from the room. The two entrance doors quietly closed and the locking beams fell in place with a *thud*, both inside and outside the doors. The Apex officers and the ambassadors noticed the unusual action of sealing the room from without and within, but made no comment.

* * *

THE mealkeepers refreshed wine goblets, left carafes of wine in chilled cooling stones and withdrew, rapidly followed by the musicians and the major domo. The doors they used bolted in the same fashion as the others caused additional concern.

Kyle stood and looked at various strategic points about the room. Guards saluted, signifying the room remained secure. Kyle returned their salute, left his right fist over his heart, turned to Jarod and bowed at the waist. He stood tall again, and his strong, clear voice sounded throughout the room. "My Zenith, the room is secure."

Jarod motioned Kyle to his seat. The ambassadors and Guard would soon understand the coldness in his eyes and the command in his rich full voice. "I have called the High Lords to the Spires. We are at war with Dark's Source!"

45

SHADURE turned when Wathdure approached at lighting speed and stopped three feet from him. Wathdure looked at Shadure's bare head approvingly. "I see you can tolerate the grayness."

"For short times. Nothing has the comfort of the dark."

"And...nothing ever will. Why did you call me?"

The blackness that comprised Shadure hesitated for the briefest second. "Do you still feel a Dark Stone separate from the one worn by that fool Mountglen?"

"It is still there. I don't know if it's another Dark Stone. It feels the same as the one your fool wears, but how can that be if you don't feel its power? I offered a reward that no one in Arestead or Hamptor could resist. The one person that came forward referred to your fool's Stone. I don't understand why you cannot feel it, too."

Shadure ignored the last remark. "You still cannot feel a direction from it?"

"No...it feels as if it comes from everywhere and nowhere at the same time. It's strange."

"I don't like it. You feel a Stone that I cannot discern, and I know shields are used below. Will you be ready for the brat by the Naming Day?"

Wathdure started at the change of query. "I will have ten thousand ready."

Shadure bent his head with his eyes closed in deep concentration. Moments later, a cloud sped toward them and a third figure formed. Her nude body held no flaw; her voice spilled out in pure musical tones. "Shadure, Wathdure, what is your request?"

"Plans are in place to destroy the brat. He hides away in the Spires. We may have a chance, even then. We will have ten thousand that are ready to fight. Can you transport that many?"

Gangedure's body shimmered and pulsed with lust, producing a smile from Shadure. "You like this new form?"

Shadure's voice deepened. "All of your forms have pleasured me." His right hand reached forward and traced Gangedure's right breast with his thumb and index fingers. He paused at the nipple and clamped his fingers together with enough force to break a small bone. He twisted it sharply to the right. The action brought a soft moan of pleasure from Gangedure. "Can you do it?"

"It will take much of my power, and I will be long in regaining it. I won't be able to protect the gray plane at the level it's now guarded."

"Wathdure and I will give you support if it's needed."

"Very well, but remember this: You will be vulnerable on this plane if I'm weakened too much."

"That won't happen!" Shadure's smile carried his promise when he released Gangedure's nipple.

The three nodded as one and disappeared.

The smallest beginning of a ripple formed a moment later, and then it too, disappeared.

46

ROLO'S knock brought Jarod's head up. "My Zenith, Master Gaz and a gentleman to see you." The servant held the door while Gaz and his companion entered, followed by four guardsmen, who fanned out to the corners of the room, then turned to face the men.

Jarod smiled warmly as Darius Openhand rose from his bow. "It has been two years, Darius. Your presence is welcome."

"Thank you, my Zenith, I never expected to be called to service again. I'm most pleased to offer my humble efforts in any way."

"I couldn't think of anyone more able when Gaz mentioned your name. Your special skills in diplomacy will serve us well with the kings of Hamptor and Arestead. Do you have any questions concerning the information Gaz supplied, or the need for secrecy?"

"No, my Zenith, I fully understand. It's my fervent hope that I complete this service before hostilities erupt throughout our land. I'm afraid that my years would be nothing but a hindrance in such a time." The twinkle in the old man's eye belied his spoken concern.

"You are well, are you not? You have no trouble sleeping?" Jarod asked. Gaz cut his eyes to Darius.

"I'm honored at your concern, my Zenith. I'm well and sleep like a babe on most nights." Mirth danced in the old man's eyes. "I will be well—that is—if the ship stays afloat."

"Send word from the garrison at Elizabethville on your return, and I'm told Captain Briggs has a new ship. Now, friend of Zeniths, I release you to your charge."

Darius enjoyed the old formalities. His bow always correctly timed and executed, he strode from the room with a natural dignity many a man in high position had envied. Two honor guards escorted him from the Chambers to his waiting coach.

* * *

THE next several days passed in a blur of activities for Jarod. He worked with Deion as often as possible to hone his skills with the power within him, and with Segquo and Carille to learn the ways of the Gray Plane. He exercised when he could find the time, usually alone. He spent afternoons in planning sessions that went far into the night as often as not.

High Lord Northmount sent messages to his keep ordering his men to start training his horses for battle. Lady Northmount took on the challenge of picking up where Lady Deanna's efforts had ceased. Kyle selected locations bordering each of the six realms, a few miles inside Stonefire, for new smithies, each one manned by an experienced arms master of the Guard with at least one apprentice and helper. Jarod and Kyle reviewed supply lines and planned for discreet enterprises easily changed over to the making of war materials.

With his councilors, he set in motion the planning and review of efforts needed in the coming war. He knew he could not think of everything the Seven Realms would need, and precious time might be saved when they needed it most, if they could begin by identifying the major tasks. Knowing he could not be present at the Spires for all of the decisions, he worked tirelessly to list his goals and assign a responsible person to make a decision in his absence. Often he worked alone in his small study, and was deep in concentration when Kyle interrupted.

* * *

KYLE had no trouble seeing Jarod's irritation, but his manner and voice left no doubt of the necessity. "My Zenith, Lord Mountglen arrived at the Circle of Villas. His ambassador heard the fanfare, and requests to attend his High Lord." Kyle softened his voice. "I think he follows form, as he didn't insist strongly, and still seems relieved to be out of it.

"Also, our two young heirs have arrived, and request an immediate audience to present their credentials to act for their realms."

* * *

JAROD'S face masked the rage and sadness he felt in equal portions; the idea of Mountglen being so near tore at fresh wounds. His reply, however, was calm and flat. "Provide the young lords suites in the Chambers and escorts. Ask Lord Long to review their credentials and return them to me with any comments.

He frowned. "Kyle, we have discussed these actions before. What is the real reason you are here?"

"Is it that obvious?"

Jarod said nothing, and settled in his favorite plush chair. Kyle sat opposite and watched him unconsciously rub the top of the right arm of the chair with two fingers, an action his father had also made under stress. The chair frame, decorated with carvings of acanthus leaves inlaid with thin gold trim, supported down cushions of deep burgundy. The four chairs surrounding the matching table, identical in every detail, formed a pleasant area for serious discussions or levity. Jarod and his father preferred the same chair in the group, and now, his same unconscious habit, which had dulled the finish on the chair arm away, made Kyle smile slightly. Jarod focused weary eyes on his Apex guardian and waited.

"Timmons, the guardsman that has won the archery

competitions every year for the last several years, requested to see me this morning. He refused to state the reason for the request to his commander, Lieutenant Branson, and he appeared agitated, with his uniform unkempt. Branson regards Timmons as a model guardsman, and his behavior was out of character. He brought Timmons to me, and I agreed to see him alone," Kyle said.

Jarod crossed his legs out in front of him and continued to stroke the chair arm.

"Timmons broke down in sobs," Kyle continued. "He confessed to killing Lawrence Burcock!"

"What did you say?" Jarod's gaze narrowed, and he pulled himself upright and leaned forward. "Did he give a reason?"

"Do you remember that he had a twin brother?" Jarod shook his head. "He left the Guard fourteen years ago...disappeared. His name was Carver. The brother that remained is Davad. Their father had died, and left Carver nothing. He left Davad two golds and a prized bow. The brothers excelled in archery, as the father had. Carver became a devil with it, killing birds for no reason, and wounding animals just to see them suffer. Davad said his character flaw came early on, as youngsters. Carver tried to pass himself off as his brother to get the bow and gold coins. His father remained ahead of him in death. He made it know that the brother not to receive his estate had a small birthmark on his inner-thigh. Carver stormed off when a priest required a physical examination.

"The Guard's discipline had kept him in line, but he became known as a troublemaker, and often tried to put the blame for his misdeeds on Davad. It didn't take long for his superiors to figure him out and they ordered Carver to shave off his moustache to distinguish him from his brother." Jarod rose and went to the credenza and poured a glass of juice. He looked at Kyle questioningly, and when he nodded, brought him a glass too. He returned to his seat and nodded for Kyle to continue.

Kyle sipped the cool juice. "Carver met Burcock during a drinking bout. The two men became fast friends. Carver went to see his mother, and declared that he would leave with Burcock for service with a man that would appreciate his talents and demanded half the golds left to Davad. An arrow, shot through the open window, split her chest when she refused. Davad witnessed the whole thing, and rushed to the window to see Burcock running away. He didn't see his face, but had no doubt of his identity. He next felt a Guardsman spilling water on his face and a bad headache. Carver was gone, their home had been thoroughly searched and in disarray, and Davad had been hit on the head with a wooden chair. All of it done in vain; the golds and bow remained hidden." Kyle sipped his juice again and sighed.

"A man purporting to be sent by Carver contacted Davad a few days after the mother's cremation, demanding the golds. Davad admits to beating the man senseless. He hammered each punch with the declaration that he would kill Carver or Burcock if he ever saw them again. He also told the man that he would swear out warrants on the three of them the following morning.

"I had the records reviewed; the warrants are still standing. An attached note stated that High Lord Mountglen had been notified, and denied Burcock's presence in the realm." Kyle finished his juice in one gulp. He sat the glass down carefully and pulled a paper from his sleeve. The high-grade paper matched a finely written script. "This is a message Davad found last night when he arrived at his quarters from duty. It's a plea from Carver, asking for mercy and forgiveness. He asks Davad to meet him so that he can make amends. He states that he has become wealthy over the years, and he wants Davad to share his good fortune, then he plans to take his own life, as he claims he can no longer suffer the guilt of his actions."

Kyle snorted. "Davad didn't believe any of it, and expects his brother has ulterior motives that may mean his death. He wanted to deliver the message to the City's Guard, but the final statements stopped him. It says there is a plot against the Zenith, and he will tell that only to Davad. He claims he will kill himself if anyone but Davad answers the message." Kyle leaned into the chair's soft cushions after handing the message to Jarod.

Pathetic ramblings filled the first half. The second half, written in the same hand, was much more direct in its assertions. It didn't take much to see that the second half came from a different mind. Jarod raised his eyes to Kyle with a questioning look.

"You are right. Davad says the first part is like his brother's desultory ravings, but the rest is unlike him, and follows a concise line of directions. He feels it's a trap, and I tend to agree. Davad Timmons is opposite his brother in most ways, and has courage. He's willing to do anything we ask of him." Kyle sighed, "Any part played by Davad will probably lead to his death."

"What have you discussed of this with Gaz?"

"He knows the inn the message refers to. It has several well-lighted entrances and perhaps more unlighted ones. It will be difficult to watch them all, and there may be some he does not know."

Jarod stood and slowly walked to the narrow window, not aware of the City spread out below him. Kyle rose up, waiting. "Proceed as you and Gaz see fit, but our main goal is to get information from Carver." *I cannot do everything.* The idea engendered a moment of profound sadness within him. His training with Deion came to the fore, pushing the emotion away. Still, he felt more than a twinge when he turned and his eyes beheld Maress' portrait.

Jarod's nod to Kyle drew a salute as he started to the door; the Zenith's voice stopped him midway. "Send a command to Mountglen. I will receive him at nine tonight in the Great Hall. You and I will detain him past midnight. That may distract their plans. Ask Gaz to make the arrangements." Jarod correctly interpreted a look of concern on Kyle's face. "Lord Darth will be with me in addition to the Guard. Send a message to our young lords, I will see them now." Kyle acknowledged the instructions with another salute. Jarod's voice became soft. "Kyle, thank you." Kyle's heartfelt grin softened the worry in his face.

Jarod knew that the days of his relaxed protocol had ceased. He turned toward the view of the City through his window, not seeing the grandeur below.

47

GAL Jerome Kess ordered his men to camp within sight of Mountglen's estate, and proceeded forward with a contingent of thirty guardsmen and those men detailed by Gaz for the search. Mountglen kept few troops at his estate. Jerome's men took up position at the entry points to the keep while he approached the main doors, stretching upward two levels. The doors swung inward as he reached the top of the three wide steps forming a semicircle in the front of the keep.

A man of medium height stood before him; his features reminded Jerome of a scaled-down version of Mountglen, with raised eyebrows and pinched lips. His voice, sounded crisp like that of a mother running after an errant child, "I'm the seneschal for High Lord Mountglen." His eyes veered away from Jerome's face and settled on his left hand at the hilt of his sword. Further coolness edged his voice. "The High Lord is not here. What is your business?"

Jerome towered over the man. His deep voice rumbled with a quiet forcefulness and coldness that exceeded the seneschal's words ten-fold. "I come on the business of the Zenith Lord. You will accompany my men and me to the High Lord's chambers. You will then send the High Lord's steward to me and leave us." Jerome pulled the warrant from the inside of his cloak and thrust it toward the seneschal.

The seneschal started as if the paper before him concealed a blade. He took it and eyed it nervously; his faced paled as he saw the unbroken seal. Jerome believed the man afraid to break the wax for a moment. He opened it carefully and looked first at the signature at the bottom. His eyes widened as he read and then read again the complete document. He gathered his composure as best he could. "Follow me."

Jerome's shock by the opulent arrogance of the room matched that of his men. Gaz's men opened the draperies, flooding the room with light and then descended on the massive bookcases. The seneschal returned with an elderly man, well past the normal age of service, with white hair and a slight limp. Jerome's stern face turned on the seneschal. "Leave us!"

The old man's eyes danced when the seneschal turned on his heel and walked quickly to the door. His voice held a warm consideration. "I'm Crawford. How may I be of service, Gal...?"

"Jerome Kess. Does that man have a name?"

A slight smile pulled at his mouth. "He's Eggart. He believes his name known by anyone important enough to seek him out. Perhaps it his due to having a name like 'Eggart,' that fosters such an attitude?"

Jerome smiled and relaxed. "The Zenith sends his regards, and asks if the irises are in bloom?"

"Ah...the Zenith does me honor in remembering. Yes, I tend them as best I can. The High Lord decided against them years ago. It's just as well; I enjoy them in my room. Your men seem quite thorough. What is it they seek?"

Jerome turned toward the men ranging over the floor to ceiling bookcase. "Books. We seek old books written long ago, and a new one written in Lord Mountglen's hand."

"I see." He pitched his voice across the room. "Middle bookcase, top shelf, first three books on the left. Careful, they are fragile." He quieted his voice. "Gal Jerome, I'm sworn to my lord. I may not give out any information as to his personal writings or speech."

"I understand. The High Lord may want an accounting of our actions. Please, remain with us?" Crawford nodded and leaned against a high backed, dark, plush chair, observing the men searching the room. Jerome stared at the largest private room he had ever seen. The slight smile and the sparkle in the old man's eyes never left him.

Jerome authenticated the old books, and oversaw their careful packing. He stood next to Crawford while Gaz's men spread throughout the room, enlarging their search in a methodical pattern. The men swapped areas of scrutiny and searched anew three times. The light began to fade when they admitted defeat. Jerome nodded curtly and announced quietly, "We will look again in the morning light."

Eggart jumped from the door when the men thrust it open and began to file out past Jerome and Crawford. Straightening his robe, the seneschal led the men toward the stairway to the first level.

Crawford raised his hand when the last man came abreast to him. Jerome closed the door, glancing at Crawford and the man he stopped with his hand. Crawford's manner remained light and his remark given in an off-hand fashion. "My good Gal Jerome, have you ever noticed how difficult it is to obtain and keep good cleaning people? No...no, I daresay that is something your profession lacks in need. This room for instance—it's large, and several come to clean it. Not as well as when I did it in my youth, not nearly as well."

Jerome watched him questioningly, but said nothing. "Why, you might ask yourself, do they not dust properly? They never dust the under edge of things. Grime and dirt most assuredly collect from the oil left on the fingers by food and all manner of debris." Crawford's smile broadened as he watched the two men surge to the table.

Jerome pulled the head chair away for the guardsman, who lay on his back, candle in hand, searching the underside of the table. Jerome held his breath. The air in his lungs exploded outward when a secret drawer shot from the table and caught him in the stomach. The long, black tome fit inside in so tight he almost missed it in the failing light. It floated toward him as if by magic. Jerome grabbed it and chuckled when he saw the hand that had pushed it from beneath.

When both men looked toward the door again, Crawford had disappeared. Jerome decided it just as well as he set the tome on the table. He opened it from the back cover and thumbed through several blank pages until reaching a page filled with small precise lettering. Straining eyes read the last page written by Mountglen's hand. Their intake of breath came almost simultaneously. Jerome closed the book; its length, nearly as long as his arm, but less than a foot wide, would be cumbersome to hide. He considered his options; stealth or force. The tome fit under his left arm, and he pulled his full guardsman's cloak around him. No one would know he carried it unless he were touched or jostled. "Cover my back."

The two men joined the rest of their contingent at the main doors. Egger's droll voice muttering, "—and rest assured that the High Lord will know of your actions."

Jerome assumed the tone he had used when first he met Eggart when he approached the man from behind. "As will the Zenith."

Eggart said nothing as he passed through to the outside. Crawford tended a small garden to the right of the entrance, a smile of contentment on his face that brought a chuckle to Jerome's lips. *And the Zenith will know his friends, too,* he thought. Jerome signaled his men to form up around him: two in front, one on each side, and four behind him. The formation held as they mounted and sped toward their encampment.

Jerome's first action sent the priest to the detachment in Glen. Three birds would soon fly with the same message to the Spires. He watched the priest gallop toward his destination with an escort of twenty men, wondering at the arrogant mind of a man that put such things as he had read in a tome.

* * *

JAROD entered from the guardroom to the dark passage. The four guardsmen snapped to position and saluted. He met the two coming from the massive, carved door at mid-room. He did not see or hear them stop at the sound of the doors heavy locks sliding open. The door opened and closed again as he passed through without touching the door, bolts setting into their recesses. The guardsmen's' faces drained of color. Metallic clicks signaled as the traps disengaged; again, hardly noticed. The door midway down the dark hall swung outward to receive him. His mind reached out in a flick of desire, igniting two torcheres of candles. He sat at the table before his mind acknowledged what had happened while reaching his destination. A cold smile of appreciation lasted a few seconds.

He closed the book before him an hour later and sat staring at nothing, his mind wandering. *My life has changed beyond any imagining in three weeks.* He comprehended the need for the Zenith's protocol and the discipline that must surround him in the future. *Will I ever again be able to dispense with it? Will I ever again play pranks on Kyle? Will they live that long?* His mind screamed the answer. *YES!*

A singular presence touched his mind. He rose while the door's bolts slid open and the door swung toward him as he came close to it. He became acutely aware of its happening and watched it silently close behind him; the candles extinguished midway, plunging the hall into darkness. His mind reached out, disclosing the hall's every detail in an unseen light as bright as any day. The change within him shone as bright and clear as the hall.

His men's eyes widened when he entered the

anteroom while the door to the hall closed and locked behind him by itself. He felt neither effort nor loss of energy in the actions his mind took.

Jarod walked quickly up to the first under-level, not focusing on those he passed. The liftman started as he entered and went directly to the lift. He barely remembered the rest of his journey to the small open area inside the Chambers, where Maress' pyre had burned, where he practiced his skill with Deion, where the sun shined with warmth that did not ease the coldness within him. He looked down at a death carriage while it rolled toward the inner-circle gates. Black draperies hung at its windows, and those it passed stopped their efforts in respect for the dead. Joy filled him as he recognized the forcefulness of his determination, skill, and the sense of righteousness, equally raging in strength beside his power.

* * *

MEN in deep shadows stepped silently, keeping in sight of their prey. The man dismounted without releasing the coarse sack that only stirred occasionally now. Arrows notched and bows bent to their full power. Each man in the circle, positioned in a manner so that a missed arrow would not find his opposite number, stood ready. Missed arrows did not occupy their thoughts. Thord reached for the lever to open the cages in the pit below. He spun around at the sound of Jerome's sword clearing its scabbard.

His head twisted about while the men surrounding him stepped into the light of the moon, his furious gaze coming to rest on Jerome again. "WHAT IS THIS?"

Jerome's voice matched the fury of Thord's. "Put the sack down and step clear. NOW!"

Thord held the sack out at arm's length. "This? This is food for my dogs." His voice eased into a gruff slyness. "I have done nothing to warrant your actions."

He stood still as his mind fought for an escape. *The pit! They could never get through the dogs before I could break out. The dogs will never attack me—I'm their Master. The brat will occupy them. Now, before they become sure of themselves.* Crouching as if to set the sack on the ground, he rolled with the surprising alacrity that had saved him many times before. His leg shoved the lever, and he disappeared into the pit while arrows flew above him, missing their target and the sack.

His dogs sprang into the open pit. The dog that missed his throat closed its jaws over the lower half of his face, muffling Thord's commands and the following scream. Pain erupted and devoured his senses while fangs pierced his right arm, buttocks, and crotch. The weight and momentum of the animal clinging to his face forced him backward, and he fell to the ground on his left side. The dog that had bitten his buttock bore down, then ripped his flesh away, followed a second later by the dog that had clamped onto his manhood. Pain doubled and redoubled while the dogs feasted on his flesh in a manner he had seen many times.

Suddenly, he floated beyond pain as blackness swirled above him. He longed for a pain as small and easy as that of burning. A black form stood before him, hardly distinguishable from the darkness surrounding him. The Dark One's voice exploded in his mind. *Welcome to the void. You are mine.* Thord's pain redoubled, and he became aware of its every nuance.

* * *

JEROME yelled for his men to hold his legs as he squirmed over the edge of the pit. For a heart stopping moment, he thought he fell among the snarling, snapping hounds, then strong hands grasped his lower legs and feet and the plunge into the pit stopped short of the floor by mere inches. He grabbed the sack and held it tightly, flailing his free arm about. His men pulled, and he felt himself rise. The pack continued ravaging the body of the man they hated.

Jerome gasped when a nearby upside down dog's snarling jaws snapped, dripping blood into his nares. His horror held the sneeze. Muscle spasms jerked Thord's free leg into the dog's hindquarters. It lunged on his dead master, and Jerome watched the destruction continue while his men hauled him free of the pit.

The gagged and dazed girl that tumbled from the sack looked about the age of Jerome's youngest girl. Sighing in relief, he assured his men that the blood covering his face belonged to Thord.

* * *

MOUNTGLEN paced in a wide circle at the entrance to the Great Hall, eying the throne at the opposite end of the large room with avarice. His rage screamed in his mind. *How dare he keep me waiting? He will pay, oh yes, he will pay!*

He had already tried to leave twice in the last two hours. The guardsmen had been surly in their denial of his wishes. His mind raced over types of tortures: slow, painful, killing. No chair or any other furniture in the Great Hall, except the throne, existed for his comfort. He had tried once to approach the dais to sit on the steps—or perhaps the throne—and the guardsmen stopped him thirty feet from his goal. His mind raged anew. *How dare they stop me—they actually touched me!*

He approached the Gal at the barred doors for the third time in the last hour. The shout rung through the room as his lips parted to speak. "FOCUS ON THE ZENITH!"

Mountglen spun around to face the dais and his nerve nearly shattered when he saw Jarod already sitting on the throne. His mind recoiled. *He's not even properly dressed to receive a High Lord!* Mountglen sped halfway to the dais before he realized the guardsmen had not kneeled. He heard their footfalls closely behind him. He approached a line of guardsmen facing him at the thirty-foot mark before the throne. They did not part as he neared. *This is an outrage!*

The Gal's voice behind him sounded rough and definitely not a whisper. "Kneel before your Zenith Lord!" The men in front of him parted. They held their position within sword's reach around him. Mountglen's body stiffened when he realized the order meant him and not the guardsmen. Fighting to control his rage, he knelt before the dais. *I kneel to the position, not the person.* The thought made the act barely permissible.

Mountglen's voice quavered. "My Zenith." His eyes met Jarod's, and the cold force they held shocked him. "I...I...trust you are well... and that your son is well, too." Mountglen waited for the command to rise. Instead, Jarod motioned with the index and middle fingers of his right hand. Mountglen rose to his full height. Jarod's eyes pierced Mountglen's bravado; and the High Lord shivered, once.

If Jarod's stare surprised Mountglen, his voice further unnerved him. "You are commanded to wait on me at the lastmeal before Naming Day. Until then, I command you to remain within the confines of your embassy on the Circle of Villas. You are dismissed."

The words slammed into Mountglen like physical blows. He staggered, and turned to go, dazed. He saw hands slap to sword hilts. The Gal's command came as a whisper this time, ominous in its quietness. "Kneel!"

Mountglen sunk to his knee; a gleam of gold caught his eye from Jarod's hand. The rage-fed high color in his face dissipated into pallor as he realized what he was looking at.

Burcock's ring!

* * *

DAVAD Timmons rapped at the door. It seemed his

own voice answered. "Enter." He stepped into the room, closing the door behind him.

Carver emerged from behind a screen, nude. Davad stood in shock: Not from his brother's nudity, not that he had grown his moustache exactly as his own, not the smirk on his face, his eyes told him his death loomed before him. Pain jarred him, and the brightness his eyes held reached beyond reality. The light lasted a part of a second, and became the last stimulus he felt, one he would never respond to, or any other. He had not seen or heard the man that hit him.

Five men hurried into the room from a rear door without a sound from their bare feet. They helped steady Davad and set about stripping the limp body as Carver knelt and applied a brownish dye to the inside of his unconscious brother's thigh. Carver dressed in his brother's clothes as the men dressed the limp Davad in the uniform of the Mountglen Guard. The uniform, old, dirty, and with the insignia removed, fit like a glove. Davad, placed carefully on the bed without sound, looked at peace. Five of the six men hurried from the room the way they had entered.

Carver stepped from place to place in the room reciting both parts of a carefully rehearsed dialogue. He walked to Davad's body, smiling; leaned down, cut his throat and dropped the knife on the bed. He went to the room's rear door where the man waited and turned to face Davad. The blow that rendered Carver unconscious would leave a lump unlike the one that fell Davad, but then, experts usually did a good job in their field of endeavor. His arranged attacker eased the stunned Carver, to the floor. He quietly left through the connecting door to the adjacent room and barred the door behind him. He crossed the room and disappeared through an open trapdoor in the floor. A rug attached to the trap door and flush with the flooring when sealed from below covered his escape. Gaz's men breaking into the room he had left became the last sound he heard from above, as he lowered and fastened the escape hatch. He smiled and hurried down the latter into the coolness of the tunnel.

48

KYLE knocked lightly at Jarod's door. Deion opened it, ushering him inside with a finger to his lips. Kyle's mouth gaped open. Jarod sat with his legs crossed and eyes closed, floating a few inches above his bed. He settled onto it within a few minutes and opened his eyes.

"Kyle." No surprise showed on Jarod's face. "I'm glad you are here. Wathdure is marshaling ten thousand of the creatures Zack described. We don't know how they plan to transport them to Stonefire, but Gangedure, the third being of the Old Ones, will facilitate their journey to Stonefire from the Gray Plane. Segquo heard their plans as he spied on them. Shadure will lead the fight from the Gray Plane with Gangedure. I don't know where Wathdure will be. The attack or attacks will take place during the Naming Day ceremony does not seem to involve them; I suspect Mountglen in that. I have commanded him to remain within his villa as we planned." Jarod's rush of words slowed as he took in Kyle's countenance, sensing trouble. "What went wrong?"

"Carver was murdered, and Davad found unconscious." Kyle repressed the desire to ask how Jarod knew it had not gone as planned. "They are still investigating how it happened."

"You are sure that it's Carver?"

"The messenger reported that the dead brother had a birthmark on his thigh."

* * *

JAROD rose from the bed, and walked slowly to the seating area between the bed and a desk. Two candles produced the only light in the room. He realized he saw his friends with preternatural light. Torcheres of candles ignited throughout the room. Kyle looked around with amazement, and a tinge of fear. Deion seemed not to notice.

Jarod motioned them to plush chairs. His voice became modulated and distant at the same time. "Something is not right with this. We didn't kill him, and Mountglen had no motive if he laid the trap. Keep Timmons confined to quarters and guarded when his injury is treated. Deion, do you feel anything amiss?"

"No, my Zenith," his voiced trailed off for a few seconds, and then continued with new strength. "I have felt a new presence, a priest. He's strong, but confused now. I sent him messages of assurance by bird and sending. His journey to the Tower will bring him to the Spires in a normal course. He will be escorted from here. His Holiness has received word that they have found others, and they escorted them on the way to the Tower in small groups. Their destination has not been divulged to them."

Jarod nodded, more to himself than Deion or Kyle, his fingers lightly rubbing the edge of the plush chair's arm. He pushed himself straighter. "Is everything ready for tomorrow night?"

Two voices sounded in unison, "Yes, my Zenith."

* * *

MOUNTGLEN paced his study; the rage from Jarod's audience the night before grew until he believed he would explode. Clarence entered and closed the door behind him. He glared at the opened draperies, and quickly turned his face away as he sat in a plush chair, his unsteadiness causing Mountglen to scowl.

"You won't be drunk tonight!" Mountglen's rage exuded from him in a near physical manner.

Clarence knew better; he and had not been drunk to the point of being flippant for some time. "I will do as you wish, Father."

Mountglen started at the gentleness in his son's voice. Looking closely at his son, he saw that softness had replaced the etched hardness of cruelty in his countenance. He saw something he had not seen in over two years that cut into his rage with the penetration and pain of the sharpest knife. He reached out to steady himself on a chair to his right while his rage and hate built again.

*　*　*

JAROD ate slowly at the small table in his room, with Rolo his only attendant. He had said nothing, and Rolo became so unobtrusive in his duties that Jarod forgot that he attended him. Several times, he paused in eating the lastmeal he neither enjoyed nor wanted to stare at the golden circlet resting beside his cloak and battle sword. He sipped a glass of cool white wine and reached out with his mind to the State feasting room across from the Great Hall.

*　*　*

MOUNTGLEN entered the receiving hall separating the Great Hall and the State Feasting Hall. Matched sets of double doors soared, three levels in height, one set opposite the other, carved with scenes of valor. The magnificent chandeliers blazed with brightness that belied their distance one and a half levels above him. He had purposefully delayed his departure from his villa to arrive last at the Spires. His deluded ramblings told him he had the right, since he would soon be the new Zenith. He had been startled at the size of the armed escort the Guard provided, and now he found the remaining High Lords waiting in the entrance hall. His mind quickly told him that too was a proper and correct action for his rank.

Something bothered him, something not quite right. He recognized it as his eyes became accustomed to the light. Two of the men paced wearing High Lord's cloaks, too young for their role, talking quietly between themselves. Mountglen identified them by the colors of their cloaks. His dismay at not knowing their temperament and politics was replaced immediately by the idea that they would be mutable to his desires, which eased his mind.

High Lord Wells washed his face and hands from a basin held before him by a steward. His spotlessly clean cloak hung in sharp contrast to the road-dirtied uniform beneath it. An officer in an equally dirty Deepwells uniform sat in a chair against the wall near his High Lord. Mountglen headed toward the center of the room. Clarence followed behind and to his right, his path varied only slightly from its true course.

The doors swung open to the High Lords. The Zenith's fanfare cut through the room as an honor guard of six Apex officers emerged from within the feasting room. They snapped to position and presented their swords in salute.

The High Lords entered, followed by the lords of Eastfall and Trueridge, with Clarence at the end. Officers escorted them to their seats at two tables, placed at the ends of the raised head table while guardsmen pulled the heavy doors closed and barred them with metal. Mountglen masked his surprise, unlike some of his peers. The chandeliers above and the torcheres along the walls produced nearly the light of day. The opposite end of the room remained shadowed; its end lay in complete darkness. The doors at each side of the room, some twenty feet distance behind the head table, opened.

His Holiness, followed by the Protector and Mother Mavis, entered and walked to the head table. High Lord Lockley left off chatting with High Lord Northmount and went to his seat at the head table in his capacity of High Councilor. Lord Kyle entered and walked briskly to join High Lord Lockley. The Pinnacle's fanfare sounded.

The Pinnacle entered, and took his place at the head table to the left of the Zenith's chair. He nodded in return to the obeisance of those before him, and surprised everyone when he placed his hand on the high back of the chair: the signal for the guests to be seated. "The Zenith Lord bids you enjoy the lastmeal and your company. The Zenith Lord will join us in time, and bids you not to wait upon him until then."

Officers of the Guard seated those at the table and replaced the guardsmen along the sides of the wall, relieving them to step as one body in precise cadence toward the dark end of the room to form in ranks behind the seated Apex officers.

Mountglen surveyed the room. The small tables formed a squat U-shape with the head table. The whole setting for the lastmeal became lost in the huge room, no matter the sumptuousness or the excellence of the meal.

Northmount sat at the table across from him, with Wells to his left and Clarence at the end. The two young pups sat to his right, looking around in awe at their surroundings. They spoke only between themselves. Perhaps they did not know the soundings in this room traveled as well as they did in the Great Hall and a word spoken in normal voice, heard halfway across the room. Then, *Perhaps they do,* he wondered. *Surely, they are not that astute.*

Musicians sat in near darkness playing string, horn and percussion at the far end of the room. The tables were set in lavish splendor, and he knew the lastmeal would be the best found in the Seven Realms: seafood soup, salad with fresh herbs, fried cheese, roaster venison, root vegetables, berries with sweet cream and nuts. *As is due me!*

Mountglen fidgeted with his food, eating small bites now and again, drinking only water. The visage of his son startled him from the corner of his eye. He glowed. Mountglen stared at him intently. He soon saw what caused the effect. His features retained their softness while he saw a fine halo of shimmering blackness surrounded him without touching his skin. *Obviously, the Dark Stone permits this discovery, as no one else has noticed,* he concluded. He relaxed his gaze, and the effect softened. Clarence ate heartily and drank wine sparingly. Mountglen found pleasure in that, if nothing else.

The servitors brought vessels of chilled wine and bottles of brandy after the last plate vanished. Glass liners formed inside chilled, porous stones kept the fine wines at the correct temperature, chilled in the gelid waters deep below along with the bottles. Air coming off the stone kept the wine chilled for hours.

Mountglen accepted the glass poured for him. He realized the servitors would not be returning when the officers moved to stand two paces behind and slightly to the right of each guest. He glanced at the dark end of the room. It still made him uneasy.

* * *

ARCHERS dressed in black behind grilled panels of dark wood, or if he could see the men in position on the balconies shielded by heavy draperies. The formation of the guardsmen and the Apex's chairs gave a clear shot to the entire room from the archer's positions. The guardsmen kneeled and sat on their haunches with their pikes laid beside them. Gaz watched Mountglen's every motion from behind his panel beside the archers.

The musicians followed the path of the servitors, reforming at the door to play the Zenith's fanfare before they, too, continued from the room. The guests stood, and the officers behind the chairs retreated five paces, drawing their swords to salute position in unison. Mountglen looked beyond the head table to watch Jarod's entrance, and started when those at the head table deeply bowed in the opposite direction. He spun around and staggered at the force Jarod generated at him. The motion of the assembled Lords kneeling brought him to his senses, and he joined them.

"Rise." Jarod's voice sent a shiver up Mountglen's spine. He stood ten feet in front of his Apex officers. The hafts of fifty pikes striking the floor in unison generated a deafening sound. It informed the Zenith that armed men at his back had sworn their lives to him, a custom from the time of the first Zenith.

Jarod wore a floor-length white cape, his hair pulled into a warrior's knot. Deeply tan skin made his sapphire blue gaze more striking; everyone that looked into his eyes saw power that had nothing to do with their color. The golden circlet atop his head glistened in the candlelight. The cape hung in preternatural stillness that Mountglen did not immediately perceive.

He saw blackness swirling from and around Mountglen, shifting his gaze to Clarence, and saw the same swirling motion, to a lesser degree, attempting to flow into him without success. Jarod's slight smile to his cousin warmed Clarence, and he returned it. The color drained from the faces of the young lords when the Zenith's attention fell to them.

Jarod's voice reverberated throughout the room, as clear as a bell's richest tone. "You are called here to be informed that the Seven Realms is at war with Dark's Source." His eyes went from Clarence to the young lords, and finally rested on Mountglen. "A call to arms will be issued after the Naming ceremony tomorrow."

* * *

MOUNTGLEN squirmed in his skin. He could not feel Shadure, and dared not call him. His voice shook slightly. "My Zenith—" Just speaking the title galled him. "—surely, you are mistaken. What proof have you?" He braced himself for Jarod's anger, hoping that might help discredit him, and perhaps buy more time for his master.

Jarod's voice remained calm. "The Zenith Lady's murder, attempts made on my son's life and the Lady Deanna's murder by Dark's Source should be proof enough." His voice softened further. "And, there is my word."

The two young lords stepped away two paces distancing themselves from him. Mountglen became aware of their actions. *Fools*, he thought, *I will deal with you soon enough.* He glimpsed his son's small smile and hooded eyes watching him.

"Jarod, you are grieving." Mountglen heard the intake of breath from several sources when he used the familiar name. He hurried on. "We grieve with you. You are the Protector of the Stones, but this seems irrational and ill-timed. I, and surely the rest of our company will help you examine these things in a better light."

Jarod's voice carried with it the edge of the sharpest knife. "Some things can be seen even in dull light." He nodded, once. Every second candle in the room instantly snuffed out. "I protect the Stones, for I am part of them now." His arms parted the cape and shrugged it over his shoulders, exposing his bare chest. Light streamed from the emerald, Sire's Stone, imbedded there, returning the room to its former brilliance.

The Pinnacle led the group from the head table to stand before Jarod. Mountglen wondered if perhaps he had found allies for the briefest moment before they kneeled, arms crossed in the ancient sign that pledged them to the Zenith unto their death. His Holiness had risen and stood behind and to Jarod's right side.

Mountglen stood in shock. Light caught his eye. Three officers glared at him, their swords pointed downward, their fists gripped tightly at the hilts. He suddenly realized he remained the last of the guests standing. He bent his knee, and brought his arms upward to cross before his chest. Pain seared through him, until he let his arms fall limply to his side. The pain lessened as he raised his head.

* * *

CLARENCE, not troubled with his father's problems, knelt before Jarod.

* * *

"RISE." Jarod held Mountglen's eyes locked to him when their gazes met. "High Lord Mountglen, we feel that protection is required for your person. We command you to remain within your villa under guard."

"You…you are arresting *me*?" The officer closest to Mountglen twirled his sword once and his hand clamped down again. The movement belonged to a master swordsman: The sword spun one rotation and had not changed position, pointing to the floor at a slight angle. Mountglen stared at the sword. "My Zenith."

"You will be guarded by your own troops within the villa, and ours on the outside. Unfortunately, this precludes your attendance at the Naming ceremony tomorrow. However, perhaps our actions will prevent the spilling of blood, and we hope to see Clarence in your stead."

Clarence's smile had a haunting quality. "I'm honored, my Zenith."

Jarod walked slowly to him, letting his cape fall forward in a preternatural, steady drape. Clarence knelt before him, and Jarod looked into eyes showing sickness in spirit. He rested his hand on Clarence's left shoulder. Mountglen watched his son's eyes widen. The shimmering, black shell around him turned to a dull gray, then dissipated into nothingness as a brightness returned to Clarence's eyes.

Jarod turned his back to Mountglen and whispered, "Will you be safe?"

"You have given me strength," Clarence replied. "I will do what I can, my Zenith and cousin. I thank you for your trust. I have only recently come to understand many things." Filled with sadness, the response was quiet and as hidden from Mountglen as the question had been.

Jarod again whispered, "Pray to the Source of Light for forgiveness."

He returned to where he stood before. The sounds of the door's bars jarred the quietness of the room when they withdrew. No voices sounded as the Pinnacle led the guests from the room in single file, each bowing to Jarod on their way.

Mountglen was last to leave, with an escort surrounding him. His cursory bow caused another twirl of a sword, one that he did not see.

49

JAROD awoke early the next morning, and headed to the room of stones. He was soaking under the rainmaker when Kyle entered, recovering before his body felt the renewed energy of exercise. "My Zenith, Lord Wells awaits your pleasure with the captain of his guard."

"Kyle, you and Deion are the only persons that may call me 'Jarod' and then only when we are alone. It's not a command, but I wish it so. I finally understand the reasons for certain protocols. Names make the sending of one into harm's way more onerous. I don't know why I feel that, death is death, after all. Where are they?"

Understanding caused pain that Kyle tried to mask. "They…they are outside."

"Give me time to dry off and dress before you bring them in. There is much to do, and I think time will be precious."

Jarod had dressed except for his shirt when Kyle entered again. He motioned for them to enter. High Lord Wells started to kneel. Jarod motioned, and he bowed instead. He turned toward the Deepwells captain. The man's face drained of color. He immediately dropped to his knees, and bent his head to touch the floor. He uttered a mantra in a soft chant and remained prostrate before Jarod.

Jarod looked as startled as Lord Wells by the captain's actions. He ordered him to rise, and the man obeyed. His voice shook when he spoke. "Visage of Visions, I pledge you my life."

Lord Wells looked puzzled. "My Zenith Lord, may I present Ta-Cern, Captain of my Guard."

Ta-Cern trembled and his voice remained unsteady. "Visage of Visions, He Who Fulfills Prophecy, in the name of my Empress, Va-A'cil, I pledge the might, power, and wealth of the Aviaries of Heaven to you and your line in your fight against evil. I stand ready to follow your command!"

* * *

CLARENCE heaved the big guard's body deep into the shadows with great effort and care. Blood-soaked cloaks might raise his father's interest, or perhaps not.

He went up the dark stairs to retrieve the tray of food he had left there before killing the guard. He savored the memory of the man's surprise while he cut his throat from behind. He had held his father's favor, and the bodyguard of his choice when Thord became unavailable, and the one that nearly matched Thord's cruelty. Clarence had jumped away when the knife cleared the man's neck, watching hate spill from the man as well as his blood. The violent spurts spattered the wall, merely gushing by the time he turned to face his attacker and slid down the slippery wall. The hate, gone now, replaced with a blank stare as Clarence continued down the dark stairway toward the hidden room.

He rapped on the door. The thick door muffled his father's startled voice. "Who is there?"

"Your son." Clarence counted sounds from two bars and two locks before his father cracked the door. Mountglen's eyes, still wide with surprise as he let his son pass, resetting the bars, ignoring the locks, saw only what Clarence wished him to. "I brought you a tray."

Mountglen's surprise turned to anger. "How did you know about this room?"

Clarence chuckled at the confirmation of his ignorance. "Mother may have delighted in telling you the secret passages and rooms she found with Richard as they grew up, but she delighted in telling me yours. Come father, put away your anger for now, and enjoy some hot food."

* * *

MOUNTGLEN, shaken by the calmness his son bore, relented. His walk remained steady, and he could not smell any wine on his son's breath; the first time he recalled his son being sober since early in their trip to Stonefire. The sheen of wormcloth and rich brocade showed under his heavy cloak. "You are going to the Naming ceremony?" His voice filled with disgust.

"Of course, father. I wish to see firsthand the results of your handiwork." He gave his father a sly smile.

Mountglen relaxed. "Oh, I wish I could be there. I have covered my tracks. I even had Lawrence Burcock kill those idiots Thord hired. Jarod has no right to keep me away, damn him! You mark the day well."

"I will, and perhaps you will be there, in sprit." Clarence placed the tray on a small table and let his hands fall within the cloak's protection. With a sneer, Mountglen ignored his son to sit at the table. Clarence backed away to give his father room. Coarse threads of the cloak contrasted with the smoothness of his fine clothes as he clinched his hands behind his back. He reached upward and loosed the bare sword that hung down his back.

Mountglen's long fingers lifted the cloth covering his food, and he leaned forward to enjoy the mouthwatering scents of his favorite foods, lamb with spices and garden vegetables in a thick broth. He saw the shadow of the raised sword on the wall opposite him, far too late to react. His head fell into the bowl of stew, and his body tumbled to the floor. Gold chain links glistened as they slid in gore across the floor.

The cloak did not fare as well this time; blood splattered down its front. Clarence folded it in on itself, carefully loosed the strings at his throat that had held the sword in place and let them fall to the floor, an oilskin pouch slid from its inner-pocket. The cape he pulled from it matched his clothes in style and color. He took a thick cloth—the only thing remaining in the pouch—and carefully folded the Dark Stone and chain within it, placing it within his tunic. He never touched the Dark Stone. He expanded the oilskin pouch to its fullest to receive the head. Mountglen's expression in death was one of surprise and horror. His father's oily hair caused Clarence to frown as he seated the head in the center of the oilskin pouch. He found a cloth and fresh water to cleanse his hands. He unrolled the flaps of the pouch fully, enough to wrap the head twice and secure it within.

Counting the stones in the wall, Clarence knelt on the floor below the fifth stone in the right hand corner of the room. His dagger chipped away wax that matched the coloring of the mortar, and he pulled the metal ring his efforts revealed. Smells of mold and dampness seeped into the room while a door swung away from him. He took a torch and lit it from a bank of candles, praying the tunnel remained clear to its opposite end, nearly two miles away. He placed the pouch inside the tunnel, closed the door, and disengaged the ring mechanism before entering the passageway.

Well father, this is one trip where any comments you make will disturb me greatly. Chuckling at the idea, Clarence started his journey.

* * *

JAROD stood at the window in his small study. The sky, clear and bright, did not improve his anxious mood. He watched below while his subjects arrived for the ceremony. Large, interconnecting benches formed seating for three thousand. He had seen the benches stored deep under the Spires since his naming Day ceremony. They soared forty feet at the rear and stepped down to floor level. It would be the grandest gathering in the Great Hall in his lifetime.

He turned toward the center of the room and reached out with his mind. *"Come in, Deion."* The big man entered dressed in the high robes of his order. His hair, styled in the manner Jarod wore his, sleeked tight into a warrior's knot. His ruby Stone hung by a gold chain in the middle of his chest, next to the badge of the Protector over his heart. A bright crimson wormcloth sash circled his waist, and hung on his right side to the bottom of his robes, an inch above the floor.

He looked pleased. "You are becoming good at sensing me, my Zenith."

"You and Marc are not difficult. His Holiness, sometimes and sometimes not."

"I heard that the crowds required the Guard to stop a fight or two over the winners of the drawing for admittance."

"The names have been collected since the announcement of Marc's birth. Still, three thousand is not many in a city of over a four million people."

The two friends sat and chatted. Jarod knew he had come to help break the tension, and found himself surprised at what a difference it made.

* * *

CARVER meticulously dressed in his dead brother's uniform, smiling at the neatness of the room, given to the annual winner of the Guard-wide archery contest, representing part of the prize. Davad had enjoyed the room for the last four years. *Another win and it would be yours for as long as you remained in the Guard, if you had lived. Well, you should have shared the golds.* Carver smiled at the too late proposition. *No, it made no difference. I would have killed your slimy ass anyway—maybe not this soon, but before too much longer. You ate at me every day, and that is not good for me.*

He checked his overall appearance in the small mirror

at various angles. Satisfied, he crouched in the middle of the small room and moaned loudly. His guard entered and knelt beside him, looking perplexed.

Carver sprang with well-practiced alacrity. His arm passed in front of the guardsman's face as he jerked to his feet, placing his knee in the man's back and pulling the garrote tight. The ball in the middle of the cord crushed his windpipe.

Carver stepped away quickly and closed the door. He watched the guardsman gurgling blood and trying to rise. Davad's polished boot shoved him to the floor as his life expired. He loosed the garrote and slid it inside his tunic. Grunting with the exertion, Carter dragged what he considered nothing more than a dead animal to the darkest corner of the room, in the shadows to the right of the door that were made even darker when it opened. He strapped the strong, short cavalry bow on his shoulder to hang under his left arm, and a small quiver of five arrows under his right. The crimson cloak covered both well. He looked around the room one last time and listened at the door before slipping into the corridor.

*   *   *

RIDING through the Spire's gate, Carver stabled his horse and went to the inner gate. Keeping his head down, he strode to the secret passage two levels below the Spires. He found the lower levels as quiet as Mountglen had surmised, and Carver had no trouble finding his way. He wondered briefly if he played a fool in trusting Mountglen's knowledge. How did he know where these passages lay, how to open them, and where they led?

He sweated from fear of discovery when he located the secret door and searched for its release stone. Heavy footfalls increased his anxiety while his hands searched over the tenuous shaping of the stones. Round indentations felt cool under his fingers. He pushed with all the strength he could muster and fell rather than walked through the door that immediately opened. His last glimpse of the corridor's light came from a torch encroaching on the gloomy darkness when the stone swung silently in place, plunging him into total darkness.

Panic seized him for a moment, and he searched wildly for the small alcove holding a lamp. His hand nearly smashed it when, at last, he found it. Lighting it became more difficult than he had imagined by touch alone in complete blackness. His flint made surprisingly bright sparks in the darkness. He found success after several frustrating tries, and looked up along the spiral stairway. Spider webs, the pervasive smell of mold, and a long journey greeted him. Cursing under his breath, he started to climb.

* * *

CLARENCE wondered about the time remaining him. *Carver should be in place an hour before the ceremony begins. How long have I been in this accursed tunnel? I must not come across him in the stairway.*

The three parameters plagued him repeatedly. He finally resigned himself to put his fears aside as he turned into one of the few changes of direction the tunnel made and stopped short. The tunnel ended scarcely two feet in front of him.

Clarence pulled the ring set into the carved stone before him, the workmanship much finer than the rest of the tunnel. Panic filled him when the stone did not give way. He recalled the stories his mother had told him; release mechanisms, the Mountglens loved them.

He raised the torch to peer closely at the stone. The light dimmed; it would not be long before the torch guttered. Panic traced with fear loomed in his mind. Despair gripped him, and he felt bile rise in his throat as he started his search over for the third time.

Closing his eyes, he softly touched the uneven surface of the stone. His eyes flew open at the feel of an unnaturally straight edge. The illusion formed from the carved stone hiding the actual release approached perfection. He pushed with his thumb as hard as he could and the reward of a small, grating sound from within let him breathe again. Keeping pressure on the indentation, he pulled the ring at the same time. The dual action threw him off balance when the stone door flew opened. Dirt fell into the tunnel, and the sudden brightness of daylight blinded him.

Clarence pulled the stone-gray cloak around him and brought the cowl up to hide his auburn hair and face. He kicked dirt over the torch and then tossed it aside. Shadows closed around him when he stepped from the tunnel at the junction of the southernmost Spire and the inner walls. Jarod had told him of the bolthole years ago, but his mother told him how to open it from the outside. *I wonder if even Jarod knows this way in. Perhaps his father never told him before his death.*

Clarence jumped at the sound of the stone closing behind him; he did not know the way into Mountglen's tunnel from the outside, but then he needed that knowledge as much as the dead torch. He went to the wall before him and melted into the stone itself, the colors of his clothes blending with the stonework.

It took him longer than he would have liked to find his way through the bolthole to the main sublevels, though he found the entrance to the spiral staircase easily. He took the nearest torch and disappeared into the upward passage. His thoughts worried him. *What if Carver is still in the staircase? Will he see the torch? Hells, just go, I probably will be dead before the day is out anyhow.*

The circle of light flowed up close to the wall. Clarence gripped the ropes containing the pouch tighter. *Well father, it looks like you will be present for the ceremony after all—part of you, at least.*

* * *

THE Spires radiated power that Shadure could not yet penetrate. His mind railed at not knowing every detail. He tried to calm himself with the knowledge that he would know instantly when the brat died. Perhaps then, he could kill his fool of a father.

He watched the arrivals to the Spires from the image that formed and reformed before him from the seamless hues of the Gray Plane. "Fools!" He wondered if Mountglen realized that the Spires harbored his only refuge. His awareness of Mountglen faded as a coach entered the Spires. Shadure assumed he knew the occupant.

* * *

CARVER watched from above. Mirrored light filled the lower half of the Great Hall, fading to darkness at the highest of the seven levels, one hundred and forty feet above the dais. The stacked benches at the opposite end had filled quickly with three thousand people from every station of life. A rich merchant sat next to a stable boy, an innkeeper next to a priest, producing a mixture of the peoples of Stonefire and the Seven Realms. The last row of seats towered a hundred feet from the floor.

The space in front of them began to fill with one thousand officers of the Guard. Guests and servitors of the Zenith filed in to seat themselves on low chairs before the officers. Musicians began to play from the alcoves high above.

Archers took their positions three levels above the crowd, their bows strung and arrows notched with a full quiver in easy reach. Carver settled himself one level above them while Clarence continued to follow the single set of dusty footprints past the third level.

The trumpeters sounded the fanfare of Stonefire, immediately followed by the sound of the major domo's staff striking the floor three times. His voice rang almost as loud. "The High Lords."

Five men in their cloaks of office filed in and took seats in plush chairs thirty feet in front of the dais. Archers tested the pull of their bows as the Guard fanfare sounded. The staff struck its three beats. The Great Hall became as quiet as if it contained five instead of nearly five thousand.

"Lord Kyle Byrne, Captain of the Zenith's Guard." Deafening roars of approval met Kyle's entrance, punctuated by the fists of his men hitting their breasts in salute. Kyle mounted the dais to the sixth level, and stood to the right of the throne. The Pinnacle's fanfare and announcement followed. Everyone in the room—except the Guard—knelt until the Pinnacle climbed the dais steps and stood opposite Kyle on the left side of the throne. Harpists sent the soft chords of the Order's Call out over the crowd. Knees bent again and heads bowed as His Holiness appeared to stand in front of the throne on the seventh and highest level of the dais. The members of the Guard saluted.

His Holiness motioned with his hands for the assemblage to rise. Forceful eloquence carried through the Great Hall. "May the blessings of Light's Source shine over you for all time."

Carver smirked at the pomp and circumstance until a question twisted it from his face. *Where is the brat?* Sweat beaded across his forehead as the voice below continued.

"I acknowledge that a new part of the Zenith has been born." The crowd cheered and only quit with the trumpeter's blast. "I swear by Light's Source that the forms have been maintained, and that I have received the oaths of witnesses at the babe's birth." His Holiness' hands quieted the crowd before their voices could erupt again and nodded imperceptibly—except to the one waiting for that sign—the major domo closed his right, gloved fist.

The Zenith's fanfare sounded three times as the crowd cheered once and knelt with their heads bowed. As one, the officers of the Guard turned to face the throne. Swords sang as they cleared their scabbards and swept up to salute position. The bright light of mirrored sunlight sprang four levels up, behind the throne. Many layers of stone gray wormcloth shimmered, pulled aside, one layer at a time, until the Zenith slowly appeared, standing in the alcove. Many people sneaked a glimpse as the process began, and their startled sighs awakened the curiosity of their fellows. The crowd marveled while the shimmering form of their Zenith in State regalia took shape.

Carver marveled too, for a different reason: He crouched no more than thirty yards away from the Zenith and on the same level. He immediately pulled tension on the bow, but his orders stopped him. *No! The brat first, you fool.* Carver slowly lowered his aim to the dais and released the tension on the bow. *Hells to the Dark One, where is it?* Mountglen told him he would appear with the Zenith Lord. The sweat on his brow increased.

* * *

CLARENCE eased the door open, heard the cheering crowd and saw the faint glow of a shielded light across from him at the side of a dark and deep alcove. Light filtered through the thin material from the Great Hall, outlining a kneeling figure.

Jarod's voice startled both of them. Clarence smiled to himself, and Carver cringed from the power and authority in the Zenith Lord's voice. "We, Jarod Greatstone, Zenith Lord of the Seven Realms, name a new part of the Zenith, Marc, the second of his name, THE DARKSLAYER!"

Power surged through the Great Hall in every direction. Shadure lay in a crumpled heap on the Gray Plane a split second later. Miles away, Wathdure moaned in pain,.

The crowd—for the most part—did not know the significance of Jarod's words. They cheered all the same.

Carver lost his patience, brought his aim back onto Jarod, and loosed the arrow. Greenish tinges of color filled the air around the Zenith Lord. The arrow stopped six inches before Jarod's chest and snapped, falling to the floor of the Great Hall. A hand wielding a whitestone sword appeared at the split second of impact, and disappeared as quickly.

Carver never saw what happened, automatically reaching for another arrow when the first one split through the thin material in front of him. He registered amazement when he looked up and saw the Zenith still standing and unharmed. He nocked the arrow and leveled it for another shot. Sudden pain gripped him when his head was jerked backward by his hair, and a knife blade cut deeply across his throat. He barely felt the boot that propelled him through the material. His pain grew rapidly as arrows scored his body in mid-air. He died before his head split open on the stone floor, with bits of grayish gore oozing out.

Jarod reached out with his mind, projecting calmness over the crowd. Guardsmen began escorting the shocked crowd down and away from the benches toward the main entrance of the Great Hall. Jarod stayed in plain sight while his subjects left.

* * *

A black, death coach stopped many miles away at the same instant Marc acquired the name Darkslayer. Prelate Thurston stepped out. He offered his aid to Trina; she descended with Marc held close. Four male deathcats formed around them, leading the way toward the entrance to the Tower's crater.

Marc smiled and gurgled once.

* * *

JAROD and Deion heard it, and knew when Trina carried him onto the gentle slope of the crater with the Tower in the distance.

* * *

TRAVIS and Deion entered the small study, followed by the Pinnacle and High Lords. Jarod spoke without turning away from the window, watching the golden glow of sunset. "Gentlemen, be seated."

Hinston placed Lord Long in a chair and departed, closing the door behind him. "High Lord Long, please report on your conversation with my cousin, Lord Clarence Mountglen."

"My Zenith." His voice rang clear and strong. "Both the Pinnacle and the High Lords of Stonefire questioned and examined your cousin, Lord Clarence Mountglen. I regret to inform you that he had his father's decapitated head with him." Jarod's shoulders tensed for a moment, and then relaxed in resignation. "A wrapped bundle in the oilskin pouch that held High Lord Eric Mountglen's head is of interest. Clarence screamed that no one except you should see what it held. It took some time, and my solemn promise to deliver it to you, before he became calm enough to speak further. He said, 'All I have done was in an effort to destroy the plans of Shadure and deliver the Dark Stone to you.'"

Jarod swung around to see a bloody rag on a silver tray. The High Lords wondered at his fierce countenance. His voice belied his visage; he spoke quietly. "Continue, please." He turned back to the window.

Lord Long succinctly covered the points of Clarence's involvement with the Black Stone, including its influence on him before his introduction to Shadure. "He confessed to many crimes of rape and assistance in the murders of children. His confessions reached such a magnitude that I doubt that he left anything out unless due to poor memory or the stress of the situation. He read his transcribed confession and signed three copies, witnessed and countersigned by the High Lords present.

"His Holiness spoke with Clarence at length. He may have other comments to give to you in private."

Soft knocks delayed Travis' answer. Deion answered it, and took a sealed note from Gaz. Jarod felt him approach and turned away from the window. He took the note, broke the seal, and read it through twice. "Gentlemen, I regret to inform you that Lord Clarence Mountglen has committed suicide in his cell. The guardsmen heard him praying and then wood breaking, and then the words, 'Great Source of Light, forgive me'". Lord Mountglen split apart a small board used to cover the sewage hole, and drove it through his chest before they could get the cell door open. He died within minutes." Jarod set the note on the table, and fell into his seat. He considered for a minute before continuing.

"High Lords of the Seven Realms, the realm of Mountglen is no more." Men shifted in their seats. "It is my right to take the realm under my protection and merge it with my own. I don't want to do that." Only the two young lords looked surprised. "We command that the realm formally known as Mountglen be ruled by a new dynasty. We elevate Lord Kyle Byrne to High Lord, and confer unto him the rights and privileges of that high office. We further give to him the realm formally known as Mountglen to rule as his own, with all the rights and privileges that entails. Lord Long will see to the documents of succession. We will inform High Lord Byrne of his new station as soon as is prudent." Various emotions crossed the faces of those present, settling into satisfaction. "Gentlemen, we have a war to plan." Jarod watched the men lean forward with interest, trying to ignore the bloody bundle in their midst.

* * *

THE Dark One rejoiced, feeling Clarence's spirit caress him. "You are mine!" The brightest of Light spread across the void for a split second. Clarence's spirit disappeared into the Light. The Dark One writhed in the greatest agony possible, a pain that he normally gave rather than receive.

* * *

ALONE at last, Jarod watched while the lights of the City finally began to wink out. News of the attempt on his life would travel fast, every detail exaggerated and distorted. A proclamation had been distributed in the early afternoon to ease his subject's minds.

He smiled, looked at the remaining documents lying face down on the low table near his favorite chair, ribbons streaming from under wax seals on the bottommost paper. Quiet mechanisms advanced the golden indicator on the clock over the fireplace to the two-mark when a soft knock sounded.

Kyle entered and closed the door behind him. Jarod motioned toward the plush chairs. Cheese, bread, and fruit with chilled wine set on the low table. "My Zenith, everything is ready for tomorrow. The Guard is formed for departure at your command. The description of Wathdure's creatures and their abilities disseminated."

"I'm sure you have made every preparation that can be done. I need something else; I wish you to advise me tomorrow."

Kyle asked cautiously, "Why would I not?"

Jarod smiled and slid the bottommost paper out from under the rest. "Because High Lords may not command the Guard." He turned the paper over, handed it Kyle, and watched while he read. He could not suppress a chuckle when the other man's eyes widened, and the color drained from his face. Lord Long had been as succinct as possible in writing the commands that elevated Kyle to his new rank. The lower third of the document was filled by the signatures and seals of the Pinnacle and the High Lords and acting High Lords of the Seven Realms that had born witness to Jarod's signature. "Tomorrow, you will wear the cloak of a High Lord." *I pray you live to return with it.* His mien turned as serious as his last statement. "Do you have any reservations about Dexter taking command?"

"I...I...no—Dexter has been in the planning meetings, and he's the most qualified. Jarod, I didn't believe it would ever really happen. Are...are you sure?"

"It is one of the few things I'm absolutely sure of. I'm afraid your formal installation as High Lord has to wait until we can get to Glen. Unfortunately, the pomp will have to wait. Messages have been sent to Glen with two full boulders of men to guard your estate until you arrive."

Rolo knocked and stuck his head around the door. "My Zenith, is this the proper time?" Jarod motioned him in.

"Kyle, I have chosen stone-gray and crimson for your colors. Your sigil will be a silver sword across a golden sun." He placed a suede pouch in Kyle's new colors before him, and gestured to Rolo.

Kyle had been too surprised to notice Rolo kneeling at his side with crimson fabric folded across his outstretched arms. Rolo's voice assumed an authority that seemed to deepen Kyle's surprise. "High Lord Kyle Byrne, I'm honored to present you with your cloak of office, signifying the stewardship of a realm of the Seven Realms, given in the traditional manner of steward to steward."

Rolo stood when Kyle did, and placed the heavy cloak over his shoulders. It fell about him; dark, stone gray wool of the highest quality and softness, with crimson trim and lined with the crimson fur of dyed fox.

* * *

KYLE stood before the full-length mirror, not quite believing the image he saw. He removed the cloak, folded it on itself, carefully placed it over one of the four plush chairs, and swept his hand over the soft fur before turning to Jarod. His mouth gaped open when he saw a gold ring in the Zenith's palm, held out to him.

Jarod stepped forward and placed the ring on Kyle's index finger of his right hand, pleased with the fit. The signet comprised a raised gold circle containing a flaming sun crossed by a sword. It matched the badge emblazoned on his cloak.

Jarod's voice was soft. "My brother, by this signet, you are invested with the authority of a High Lord." Kyle stood motionless; for the first time, Jarod had voiced their relationship with a name. Brother; it summarized how they felt and related to one another in the most positive of terms.

Rolo's knock made Kyle realized he had not been aware when the steward had left the room. "My Zenith, Apex Dexter Young, awaits your pleasure." Jarod motioned him in, and nodded in return of his salute. He handed Kyle the next paper from the low table, containing the appointment of Apex Dexter Young to Captain of the Zenith's Guard.

50

JAROD saw Kyle and was rather pleased with himself and how the events turned out at Kyle's elevation to High Lord, and it showed in his smile. He mounted Blackwind and nudged him gently with his knees. The magnificent steed nickered softly and stepped into the inner-circle of the Spires as Jarod's fanfare sounded and the gates to the outer-circle opened.

Kyle, dressed in new clothes of gray and crimson that matched his cloak of office, waited with Deion, Dexter, and the High Lords. The Protector, in lighter gray battle dress trimmed in gold and silver, sat a gray horse whose color formed a near-perfect match to his clothes. The sight of the battle sword at his side shocked Jarod. He had never visualized a priest carrying a sword, but then, no priest like the Protector had ever existed in the history of the Seven Realms, and he had given it to him through Travis.

Jarod's voice pitched softly to them alone. "We have never been in a real battle. Remember, the creatures we are likely to face have not been tried in battle either." He eyed the High Lords, mounted close together.

"The Dark's Source's main goal is to destroy the Darkslayer and me. The Dark has a way of spying on us, although it can't hear my words or know exactly where I'm located, and the same is true for my son. It will see the coach and escort and we hope it will assume we are transporting the Darkslayer and attack when and where we have set the trap.

"You have been advised of Wathdure's necromantic army. I strongly suspect he will take our bait and send his army against us today. I will do all I can to help. Remember, deathcats are our friends.

"My lords, you have your honor guards. Use them! Fight wisely and bravely, not foolishly. You must train your own troops on your return to your realms. It will be best if you lived to do that." Jarod watched the eagerness and the misplaced immortality of youth on the faces of the young lords slightly fade. "Lord Russell, fall to my right; Apex Young, fall to my left." Jarod raised his right arm high. Triple rounds of his fanfare blasted the quiet above the Spires as a full boulder of cavalry wheeled six abreast and proceeded through the gates of the outer-circle, followed by Jarod and his retinue. Six matched, white horses pulled a coach centered behind the High Lords: the bait. Instead of Marc, it carried four heavily armed guardsmen. Thin, black wormcloth covered its windows, allowing the men to see out, but the dark shapes inside would be hard to discern. A second full boulder wheeled in behind the coach.

They followed the road skirting the eastern side of the City to the staging area for ten thousand troops. His plan was simple: The plateau remained the one area that could contain the men and creatures in a battle that would not endanger his people. His men had the advantage of knowing the ground, and the cover of woods along the east and west sides, with artesian wells feeding several streams through the area, and preparations lay ready. An army of ten thousand mounted troops moved slowly, even if they did sit a horse.

* * *

SHADURE'S interest sharpened with the first formation of troops within the Spires. He summoned Wathdure and Gangedure to his side on the Gray Plane. He kept the images open while the morning progressed. Wathdure's caveats regarding his creatures meant nothing to him. This might be his only chance to kill the brat before he escaped and hid away, troubling possibilities, indeed. *This haste would not be necessary if I could only sense the brat or his fool father! No, the time is now. There are too many ways to slip him out on their march. It must be today, when they are tired and break for camp.*

The hours dragged by while he watched the army's movements. He tried to think of every possibility, but came to the same conclusions each time. Armies that size needed to encamp at least two hours before sunset, with certain resources at hand.

Shadure expanded his vision to include the countryside ahead of the army and projected their direction. The plateau covered many square miles, with trees edging the east and west and with cliffs falling several hundred feet at their outer perimeter. The south approach formed a gentle rise and open land; the north side gently sloped downward leading to the beginning of foothills with a road that skirted the mountain range to the flat lands in the east. Shadure's excitement mounted as he pointed to the vision of the plateau.

*   *   *

JAROD watched with growing apprehension. Supplies began to be unloaded, and stashes of weapons placed days ago were now uncovered and distributed. Men had dug shallow trenches diagonally across the south and north ends of the plateau, then covered them with straw. Picket lines for horses slowly filled as guardsmen brought their mounts from various watering spots. Fires sprung up while other guardsmen erected tents in straight lines and their pikes formed cones with crowns of death at measured intervals along the sides of the trees, leaving a wide expanse in the middle. His men did not venture more than a few feet into the woods, making do with whatever nearby deadwood they could find, and two dead trees pulled into the open with horses.

He expanded his senses into the trees. One hundred and three deathcats received his images as they fed on cattle driven there two days ago. They shared the kills among themselves without protest, and then quietly groomed their coats. They shared his thoughts with devotion and single-minded determination.

The shouts of men broke his connection with the animals. About a mile away, a black cloud hovered several hundred feet above the crest of the plateau. It rose high into the sky, its movement slow; it roiled in upon itself like a thick, foul, stew.

Quickly, whole picket lines of horses were moved into the woods, reestablished in safer surroundings. Barrels of viscous liquid dumped at the edge of funneling troughs seeped along the shallow trenches under the straw. Men grouped in clusters, easily deployed into killing fields. Archers formed protected ranks three deep and twenty men to a rank, oblique to the woods, the southern half facing south, the northern half facing north.

He sent word of the deathcats' presence and that they would aid them in the fight; it quickly spread through the ranks. One skeptical man fainted when he unexpectedly faced two large male deathcats totaling over two thousand pounds looking directly at him. He woke to a large, salty lick on his cheek.

Lady walked purposefully from the wood to Deion's side. He scratched her behind the ears, and earned a throaty purr in response. Two large males joined him and followed him wherever he went, always keeping him at their sides. He was continually amazed by their actions; they never ran into men, never in the way for more than a moment, reinforcing his calming thoughts back to him.

He made his way to an area three hundred yards from the crest of the plateau and at the side of the east tree line. Deion went to the south end and entered the west tree line. They linked their minds and waited while the coalescing cloud drew closer at a painfully slow rate. Jarod settled on a square blanket, ten feet to a side. Two of the deathcats lay at its edges, one in front and one behind. The others went just inside the tree line. Pikemen surrounded Jarod: standing shoulder to shoulder, three ranks deep, with high shields, facing outward and the deathcats at their backs. Archers hung in harnesses from high limbs with a foothold embedded in the trunk, keeping watch over their heads. Their Zenith stayed as protected as they could make him.

Deion's observations softly caressed Jarod's consciousness. *A projection is forming at the base of the cloud and arching toward the ground. It's about a hundred feet across, and looks much more solid than the cloud itself.* Jarod pointed at an archer to his left, and then to the arch. The arrow struck deep into the gentle, sloping arch and quivered there. Deion and the deathcats saw through his eyes. The ground shook when the arch touched down. Nothing happened.

Minutes passed as men waited, muscles cramping with tension. Wathdure's black-robed figure walked from the cloud at the apex of the arch a hundred yards away. Nearly a hundred arrows flew at him. Some penetrated the arch while others went wild, but at least twenty shafts passed through him as if he did not exist. Deion gave the signal to cease firing, and felt Jarod's instant approval. Several minutes passed before movement started within the cloud.

The first rank of forty necromantic creatures stepped from the swirling cloud onto the arch. Flesh had formed over their faces where nares and mouth had been. Their eyes stared unnaturally vacant, their black uniforms without padding or armor. Their right hands held swords hanging limply at their sides. The two in the center started down the arch at a run, followed by the next inside pair, then the next. Soon an arrow made of running creatures sped down the arch within seconds. The next rank stepped onto the arch when the last pair started their run.

Six ranks ran in full stride down the arch when the first pair touched the ground, their eyes searching for targets and their swords rising in death-giving fury. Arrows that had passed through them as easily as passing through the cloud while they ran on the arch now bit into flesh. Archers quickly focused their attention on the charging creatures when they landed on the sandy soil of the plateau. But still they ran forward, some with as many as twenty arrows in their dead flesh.

A pikeman swung in a wide arc. His slashing blade severed the creature's head. It dropped in mid-stride. The stench raised bile in many throats, and inhuman gore soaked the ground. Nearly three hundred of the creatures fought before the first lay still in the dirt. Word of the decapitation traveled quickly, and tactics changed. The first waves had taken terrible tolls on the Guard. The guardsmen learned quickly and creatures began to fall as often as men did. Deion reached out with his mind to the deathcats; flowing images of effective kills filled their receptive minds.

Two deathcats isolated a creature and knocked it to the ground. One deathcat pinned it with a huge paw while his partner closed its massive jaws around the creature's head, puncturing its neck with fangs. The deathcat jerked backward and the head tore free of the creature's body with a sickening sound. The deathcat snapped his head to the side, flinging the creature's head several feet in the air. The pair of beasts selected another victim while additional pairs of their brothers and sisters copied their kill techniques. No one had ever heard of deathcats working together; the guardsmen marveled at their efficiency and economy of movement, even in killing. Especially in killing.

The battlefield now reeked of the creatures' stench. Dexter gave a signal with his hand. The guardsman next to him raised his battle-horn and blew a piercing set of notes. The guardsmen regrouped into funnel formations of slashing swords and pikes, channeling the creatures into small groups on certain parts of the killing fields.

Flaming arrows struck the oil-soaked straw of the shallow trenches at the base of the arch. Flames leapt into the air. The depth of the gullies and oil kept the flames at below the knee level. Creature after creature exploded when the fire penetrated their skin. That information too, spread throughout the Guard's forces, and additional barrels of oil rolled to the front and archers prepared to switch to flamed arrows.

The creatures fought like fanatics run amuck with bloodlust. They fought on with missing arms or legs—or both—until the stinking fluids draining from them depleted their bodies to shells of bones. The guardsmen had soon adopted the tactic of severing the sword arms if the stroke missed the head; the creatures fought on, using their bodies as rams against the defenders. The Guard's casualties rose, but deaths remained low. The creatures fought in blind rage, at times killing their own. The few that ran into the wooded areas found deathcats waiting for them.

* * *

DEON watched as fresh troops from the north end of the plateau began to infiltrate to the south, taking the place of weary fighters. Teams of men pulled the wounded from the field of battle, protected by pikemen with high shields. Dexter sent new orders, calling for a butchering tactic used against wild herds. It worked well. Deion followed the progress of the deathcats. Few sustained injuries, and none were killed. He turned his attention to the arch, and his eyes widened.

His mind touched Jarod's with the fresh images before him. The waves of arrow formations had stopped. Masses of the creatures poured from the cloud in locked step as if they had one mind, which they must have, in a way. They ran in perfect unison, packed so tightly together that their bodies nearly touched. They kept the same pace when they set foot upon the ground.

Deion looked through the woods at his side. *Where are those barrels of oil?* he wondered. Unconsciously sending the question to Jarod, the reply came immediately: *"Soon."* He looked at the increasing sound of pounding feet landing like one huge monster bent on shaking the earth.

The massive column stopped forty yards out from the arch, in the space of a step; the whole formation on the ground and on the arch just stopped. Every creature, left open to a side, faced away from the center mass and raised their swords for attack. Pikemen set for the first wave's charge and did heavy damage. But the beheaded creatures seemed to grow anew, with each one that fell immediately replaced from behind. The constant replacements caused a rippling effect to flow back up into the arch. Suddenly, they took a pace to the north, again in locked step. Three times a minute they advanced, never stopping swinging at the defenders. The ground they covered amazed the Guard. Bodies and heads lay about their path to the point that details sent out with grappling hooks and rope to snag and pull away the heads and bodies quickly formed: Too many of Jarod's pikemen were falling over them, and being trampled by the advancing column. They almost immediately abandoned the practice. The ropes and hooks caused as much problem as the heads. They sent additional pikemen in to snag the heads with their pike hooks and draw it away. The stench caused some of Jarod's men to retch while they fought. The sight of the monstrous heads did not help. Deion felt the tug of Jarod's mind.

* * *

USING more information from Zack Stand's report, Dexter ordered bladders of saltwater slung from a small mangonel built for that purpose. Archers peppered the bladders as they arched over the unholy hoard. Creatures fell whenever touched by even a small amount of saltwater. Those behind them trampled the exploding bodies in mindless fury, hurrying forward. The overall toll of the saltwater slowed the creatures' ceaseless run, but did not stop the assault.

* * *

JAROD knelt down and guardsmen quickly surrounded him to provide his defense, and the deathcats nearly touched him His mind soared. Answering Segquo's call, he immediately found himself inside a shield. They flew across the Gray Plane before he could speak. A black vortex spun ahead of them. It rose into the air, and bent downward with more movement visible in the blackness. Part of a sword appeared for an instant, likewise, a head, arm, or foot would appear while the funnel cloud spun. They stopped near the base of the vortex.

The beauty of the reclining woman there astounded him. Her entire shape shone deep, inky black, yet clearly showed every detail of her body. The point of the vortex hovered over her head. Her body twitched with effort.

Segquo's voice startled him. "We found her moments ago. I feared you might not hear my call."

"Lower the shield. Warn me if you see danger approaching, then form the shield and get us away."

"Others are watching our backs, Highest One."

The shield came down at once. Jarod pointed his outstretched arms at Gangedure's head. Power flooded his mind, and green lightning bolts slammed into the black shape. Her body arched until she hardly touched the base she was lying on while she absorbed the force. Hideous shrieks rent the Gray Plane's silence. She flicked her hand, and he felt pain sear through his mind. He formed more power around him, and her subsequent attacks did not reach him. He felt himself losing strength, however.

Arcs of red power wove their way through his shield, searching for him. They joined with his green lightning, and renewed power slammed into Gangedure's writhing form. The vortex faltered, and then winked out. Gangedure's façade collapsed, leaving ugliness that defied Jarod's mind, one hideous form after another formed and melted into the next until a heap of ash lay smoldering in space. Jarod felt Segquo's shield close around him and they sped upward fifty feet. He felt lingering pain course through his mind. He formed a single command to Deion. *"Withdraw!"*

Shadure arrived below them, with Wathdure close behind. Wathdure's voice cracked with fatigue. "Gangedure burned!" Shadure cast his eyes about, his mind unable to grasp the concept. Gangedure could not be gone. The ashes before him dissipated into nothingness, as if in answer to his dismay.

Shadure sunk to his knees, and his presence shook. He raised his arms, shaking in rage. Great blots of black lighting shot from him in wide arcs. Segquo's shield quivered while wave after wave of power slammed against it. Jarod tried to feed power to Segquo, but immediately stopped as he felt Segquo reel from its force.

A soft voice settled on their consciousness, one that Jarod knew well. *"Don't fight the power. Use it to fling it back upon itself."* He bent his will, and Segquo soon joined his effort. They formed a path of power in a half circle, collected the power from Shadure, and flung it at the dark being's head. Shadure collapsed at the same instant the shield crumbled. The last evil bolt caught Jarod. Power drained from him, and his mind screamed in agony.

Segquo fled with Jarod's slight consciousness held securely with his mind. They stopped many miles away. "Highest One, are you aware?"

Jarod's simulacrum hung in the air before Segquo without stirring. Tentacle strands of red smoke the length of a hand appeared between them. Segquo quested gently with his mind. *"Take the Highest One to his body."* Segquo became instantly alone; a look of supreme sadness and worry overtook him when Jarod's image disappeared.

51

JAROD lay in his bed, stripped to his privatecloth. The Mother and Lady Northmount bathed him with chilled water. His ague caused small bursts of steam in the cloth's wake. The Mother stopped from time to time, dripping fresh water into his mouth. Angry, blood red stripes in the shape of a whiplash formed across Jarod's skin in an instant, and then slowly faded, replaced by other lashes. The Sire's Stone barely pulsed. His breaths were shallow and irregular.

*   *   *

DEION sat nearby; he would have stared at Jarod if his eyes had been in focus. When Jarod had returned to his body, the Protector had opened his mind to him once, but had been forced to retreat instantly. Mountains of pain and anguish encased Jarod. The heat of living fire blasted him. Since then, he had tried reaching out to Jarod's mind several more times, only to be repelled. Oddly, he believed it was Jarod's consciousness that was driving him away. Repulsion seared through his mind at Jarod's command in that split second before darkness closed around him, and left him unable to continue.

*   *   *

COOL drops like a summer rain pleasantly bathed Deion's face. He opened his mind to the freshness around him. His eyes blinked open to see forms near his face. Memory and awareness returned when the Mother's face came into focus above him. Guards helped him into his chair and he smiled weakly at her. "I will be fine. Mother Mavis, we must find the Dark Stone!"

* * *

THE Mother's countenance added consternation to her outward appearance. She considered Deion's words, and sat on the edge of Jarod's bed; her hand sunk into the soft, down mattress. She started when a hot vise grasped her wrist, and Lady Northmount gasped. Jarod's head rose, causing the sweat-covered muscles of his abdomen to harden in sharp relief. His face and eyes contained more pain then she had ever seen. He stared at her with a fierce intensity, nodded once, and then his body relaxed and his eyes closed as before. Mavis pulled her hand free from the limp hand, and then rose to walk slowly to the door, where she spoke briefly to a guardsman.

The Pinnacle paced at the foot of Jarod's bed. "Lord Deion, tell me again what you experienced."

Deion spoke the same words he had recounted twice before. "Tremendous pain. Jarod's projection contained the words, 'Bring the Dark Stone!' and I saw the bloody rag that we saw in the study. I passed out from the pain at that point."

He watched when Geoffrey stopped pacing and turned toward Mavis and Kyle. "If any of you know where the Dark Stone is hidden, please have it brought here at once."

Kyle's voice softened, and a trace of his relief became evident. "What prompted your decision?"

The Pinnacle answered wearily. "Deion saw the bloody rag, not the Dark Stone. You told me yourself that Jarod said he never opened the bundle. I trust Deion saw Jarod's true vision, based on that alone. I think that if the vision came from another, it would have shown the actual Dark Stone. Jarod never saw it, and therefore couldn't envision it. It's not much, but enough to sway me."

Mavis put her hand on Deion's shoulder. "Are the deathcats still near?"

The surprise on Deion's face reflected in his voice. "Yes, they are in the small wood near the hospice. The Guard has been herding game in their direction, and they have stayed close. Why?"

"Can you summon one?"

"Lady, perhaps, she's the one that is most attuned to me. But, I don't see the need."

Mavis smiled. "I have heard it said that the nose of a deathcat is more sensitive than our best dogs. The rag that Stone of Hell is wrapped in should be pretty ripe by now."

Kyle jumped to his feet and hurried to the door. "I will pass the word to let it through."

Traffic in and out of the Spires stopped; the gates were held open. Lady bound through the main entrance of the Spires and up the main staircase without hesitation. She emerged onto the top landing outside the Zenith's Chambers. The guardsman barely had time to open the golden doors for her to dash inside. She skidded past Jarod's bedchamber, trying to find purchase on the smooth floors. Seconds later, she walked gingerly into the room. She looked torn between Deion and Jarod, finally settling on the floor between the two. Deion brought her one of the buckets of fresh water used for bathing Jarod. Her tongue lapped slowly, but the water disappeared rapidly.

It took several moments for Deion to convey their need to Lady. They started in the Zenith's study where the bloody bundle had lay on the conference table. Lady entered without hesitation and proceeded slowly. Man's furniture folded in havoc, definitely not designed for thousand-pound deathcats. She flooded Deion's mind with images of blood and gore. She scampered from the room as quickly as the furnishings and people allowed. Deion led her down the corridor, with Kyle and the

Pinnacle in pursuit. She nearly caved in the first door she came to before Deion could get around her and open it. She poked her head in and then continued down the hall. She learned rapidly, waiting for Deion to arrive, open the door, give a brief sniff and scamper ahead to the next door. She skidded occasionally, and had the distinct look that it provided more fun than an annoyance. She suddenly ran past several doors and stopped in front of Jarod's small study. Statuettes flew across the room while her claws fought for a hold on the mantle above the fireplace. Deion reached up and scratched her behind the ears, sending reassurance and understanding. She settled on the floor with satisfaction.

Kyle took one look at where Deion and Geoffrey stood at the end of the fireplace. "Turn the gargoyle." Geoffrey's hand obeyed and the door of the small keep-safe swung open. The odor identified it without difficulty.

No one touched the Dark Stone. Mavis, Travis, Deion, Geoffrey, the High Lords and Dexter looked on while Kyle pulled the blood-caked chain loose from the cloth that held it. It fell into the basin of water with a *plop*. He drew the Dark Stone through the water, which turned reddish brown with blood. The chain felt cool to his touch; he did not want to know what the Dark Stone felt like. He let the water run off until the last drop fell into the basin. Deion carefully took the chain from Kyle.

The chain pulled toward Jarod's head when Deion let it swing over Jarod's body and he was relieved when it passed the dimly pulsing emerald. Cracks of thunder erupted in the room. It took Deion's massive strength—both mentally and physically—to hold onto the chain while arcs of black lightning flowed from Jarod to the Dark Stone. Wind swept his hair behind him, and he noticed Mavis holding tightly to her chair, as if she might fly away. The phenomenon lasted several minutes, while the force of the lightning attacking Jarod grew steadily weaker. Deion prayed the force was going into the Dark

Stone, and not Jarod. He noticed the emerald growing in color and brilliance near the end of the discharge, and breathed a sigh of relief.

When the last of the power drained into the Dark Stone, Jarod's eyes flickered open. His body fell in on itself with great fatigue. His voice sounded weak, and Deion leaned forward to hear his words. "What happened just before placing the Stone near me?"

Deion's answer conveyed his puzzlement. "Kyle cleaned it in water."

"Have Gaz select a room without any secret ways in. Place the Dark Stone, sealed in a metal container of water, in that room. Put a heavy guard on the door."

"Jarod, what was the pain I felt?"

Jarod squeezed his eyes tight with his remembrance, his words choked with emotion, "A portion of my pain." Deion shuttered and rose to convey the Zenith's commands.

52

JAROD remained standing while he motioned Gaz to a chair and turned to the window in his small study. A month had passed since the Dark Stone had taken the pain from him, but his body still felt weak. "Report."

"My Zenith, we lost four thousand, one hundred and twelve on the plateau. Only skulls remained of the creatures; we found close to five thousand. Some were trampled and many were burned to fragments. I fear we will never have an exact count." Gaz settled into the soft cushions of the plush chair and opened the leather pouch containing his notes when he continued.

"A steady flow of priests are traveling through Stonefire toward the Tower crater." Jarod snapped his head at Gaz. "No, my Zenith, I don't know where it is, exactly." Jarod had to smile and turned again to the window. "His Holiness sends word that Marc flourishes, and Trina is well. Prelate Thurston reports he would rather not leave the crater soon." Jarod chuckled at that. The sound pleased Gaz; he had not seen his Zenith Lord express much happiness of late.

"High Lord Kyle sent word that he has found several areas suitable for large-scale training, and has started construction on the most promising site. The administrators remained leery of him for a while, but have lately expressed their pleasure at his attention to the realm. It seems that little patriotism remained in the general populace for Mountglen. Little dissidence reported over the name change to Stonecrest from the people and lords alike. High Lord Kyle found some three thousand pounds of gold and over a hundred pounds of gems when the treasure room's defenses finally fell. He placed a third of it into commerce within the realm.

"We received a message late last night from the Pinnacle, stating that Ta-Cern left by ship four days ago. He expected to reach his homeland within two months.

"High Lord Northmount reports that the breeding and training of warhorses goes well. He's pleased to train his steeds again to their full potential. Both young High Lords have taken command of their realms with their family's support. They have expressed interest in the training by the High Desert People.

"That concludes my report, my Zenith." Jarod nodded without turning. Gaz was halfway to the door when he stopped. "My Zenith, might I inquire when you plan to visit the High Desert People?"

Jarod turned to face his spymaster. Gaz stood more erect at Jarod's direct attention. "Soon Michael, soon."

Gaz bowed and left the room. He wore a wide smile the guardsmen had seldom seen when he walked toward his quarters. Jarod had never called him by his first name. He found that he rather liked it.

* * *

SEGQUO did not jump when Jarod's faint simulacrum materialized before him inside his shield. "Is the time near, Highest One?"

"In a few moments."

Segquo nodded and they sped off. Jarod recognized the small signs of great speed while they traveled the Gray Plane. They stopped a few yards away from Shadure while he thrashed in pain. Wathdure crouched low a few feet away.

* * *

THREE days from land, Ta-Cern walked to the rail of the ship. Drawing a knife, he delicately sliced the wax from around the top of the metal container until it floated freely. He stuck the point of the knife in the floating wax and used the rail to steady the container. He pulled the plug of wax free and flipped it into the ocean. Muscles straining, he held the heavy, metal container out as far as he could, dropping it when the roll of the ship took him furthermost from the keel. It made a small splash when it hit the water and immediately sank beneath the waves.

Ta-Cern smiled at completing the first mission given him by the Visage of Visions.

* * *

ARCHING his back, Shadure cried out in mounting agony until he screamed.

"How did you know, Highest One?" Segquo asked.

"My sweat burned me."

"How did you know to trust Ta-Cern?"

"He thinks I'm his God. Thankfully, he's mistaken."

They disappeared at the same instant.

Back in his body, Jarod settled into his bed and drifted into sleep, a slight smile on his face.

GLOSSARY OF TERMS

MILITARY:

Pebble: Ten men led by a Skimmer
Rock: Thirty men led by a Rocker, first level officer
Tress: Ninety men led by a Lieutenant
Scree: Two hundred and seventy men led by a Thrower
Small Boulder: Six hundred men led by a Gal (iron bearing rock)
Boulder: Eight hundred men plus forty support personnel led by a Gal
Tor: Twenty-five hundred men plus fifty support personnel led by a Looker
Mount: Fifty-one hundred men plus one hundred support personnel led by an Apex

MAGIC:

Stones: Stones of power created by Light's Source and Dark's Source
Graystones: minor stone helps healers, allows a priest To send messages by controlling birds and aids in farseeing.
Compact Stones: more powerful and allows kinetic abilities
Major Stones: physically joins with the owner, provides great powers.
Dark Stone: evil stone of great power created by Dark's Source.
Grey Plane: A plane of existence where the minions of the Dark One can reside and where The High Desert People can visit.

CHARACTERS

Byrne, Kyle: Lord, Apex Captain of the Zenith's Guard
Carlton, Duncan: Acting High Lord of Trueridge
Darth: Captain of the Lords of Death
Dermouth, Suzan: Lady in waiting for the Zenith Lady
Gabbles, Trina: Marc Greatstone's wetnurse
Gangedure: Shadure's minion, Plane Master
Gaz, Michael: Spymaster of The Seven Realms
Grant, Mavis: Mother, Head of the Hospices for The
  Seven Realms
Grant, Travis: The Holy One, Head of the religion for
  The Seven Realm
Gray, Erwin: Lord, ambassador for Northmount
Greatstone, Jarod: The Zenith Lord
Greatstone, Marc: Jarod Greatstone's son,
  part of the Zenith
Greatstone, Maress: The Zenith Lady, part of the Zenith
Kess, Jerome: Gal in The Zenith's Guard
Lockley, Geoffrey: The Pinnacle Lord
Long, Matthew: High Lord of Justice
Matthews, Karl: Stable boy
Mountglen, Clarence: Eric Mountglen's son
Mountglen, Eric: High Lord of Mountglen
Raven, Doris: Hamptorian farmer
Raven, Rachel: Doris Raven's daughter
Romar, Davad: Acting High Lord of Eastfall
Russell, Deion: Lord, second to The Holy One, His
  Grace, the Protector
Sarth: Captain of the Angels of Death
Segquo: Leader of the High Desert People
Shadure: second only to the Dark One, Spirit Master
Sternwood, Tobias: Lord and High Healer

CHARACTERS

Strand, Deanna, Lady: Assistant to the Zenith Lord
    and Lady
Strand, Gayle: Lady in waiting for the Zenith Lady
Thord: Eric Mountglen's minion
Timmons, Carver: Davad's twin
Timmons, Davad: Carver's twin, champion archer
Wathdure: Shadure's minion, Flesh Master

ACKNOWLEDGEMENTS

I once wondered why an author acknowledged so many people. Now, I know! I'll start with my writer's group founded by Sam Barone who brought a talented group together, although to my dismay, the group is disbanded: Sharon Anderson, Deborah J. Ledford and Thelma Rea. These folks gave of their talent, friendship and time. Besides that, they are nice.

And then there are the editors. One thinks they have written a masterpiece until an editor gets their head wrapped around a manuscript. Nonetheless, they found the writing, character and plot flaws I never thought of while writing my first novel. Even with college training, this craft has a huge learning curve. I had a fine editor on this novel; John Helfers is a well-known editor and writer.

Fellow authors have given support, time and friendship. Chief among these is L. E. Modesitt, Jr. He has become a friend and good advisor of authorship over the years. Paul Genesse has been supportive and become another friend. Michael Stackpole gave me good advice and several tips about not only my novel but also the publishing industry.

Other friends in the industry have always been supportive and thoughtful in their counsel: Colleen Confit and Krista Wallace are but two of these. For several years I've attended the World Fantasy Conventions held in a different city each year. Nearly all of the authors, editors and other industry professionals are approachable and helpful.

I have been fortunate to know and learn from all these fine people. I wish them all the best in life and careers. Of course, the minute this manuscript goes to press, so to say, I'll remember someone who should have been included!

AUTHOR BIO

Dameon Cox grew up in Atlanta, Georgia, before joining the United States Air Force, and served in Texas, France, and Germany. He worked with large mainframe computers, and became a real estate broker before obtaining a nursing degree and practicing as a Registered Nurse. He then began to write, and found it more satisfying than his previous endeavors. He lives in Phoenix, Arizona, with a large Great Dane that thinks he's a lap dog.

www.ingramcontent.com/pod-product-compliance
Lightning Source LLC
Chambersburg PA
CBHW051548250626
47157CB00001B/226